Blacklight
Blue

Books by Peter May

The Enzo Files
Extraordinary People
The Critic
Blacklight Blue

The China Thrillers
The Firemaker
The Fourth Sacrifice
The Killing Room
Snakehead
The Runner
Chinese Whispers

Other Books
The Noble Path
Hidden Faces
Fallen Hero
The Reporter

Blacklight Blue

Peter May

Poisoned Pen Press

Copyright © 2008 by Peter May

First Edition 2008

10 9 8 7 6 5 4 3 2 1

Library of Congress Catalog Card Number: 2008923146

ISBN: 978-1-59058-552-8 Hardcover

Poisoned Pen Press
6962 E. First Ave., Ste. 103
Scottsdale, AZ 85251
www.poisonedpenpress.com
info@poisonedpenpress.com

Printed in the United States of America

For John, Iain and Suzanne

Ingram 11/18/08

Acknowledgments

As always, I received enthusiastic help and support during my researches for *Blacklight Blue* from the following people, to whom I would like to offer my grateful thanks: **Dr. Steven C. Campman**, Medical Examiner, San Diego, California; **Professor Joe Cummins**, Emeritus of Genetics, University of Western Ontario, Canada; **Alexander Tadevossian**, consultant interpreter, Geneva, Switzerland; **Philippe Boula de Mareüil**, researcher in linguistics, Paris, France; **Jean-Claude Morera**, writer, poet, and Secretary General of Paris Tech, for his advice on the Catalan language; and **Rufus and Jilly Dawson**, for allowing me to use their wonderful house in the Auvergne.

We are linked by blood,
and blood is memory without language.

—Joyce Carol Oates

Prologue

Spain, July 1970

She had caught the young woman's eye the day before. By the swimming pool. The little boy was in a foul mood, still unsteady on his feet and determined to defy his mother. But it didn't matter. She had already decided. He was the one.

His mother's smile was strained. 'He's hungry. He's always bad tempered when he's hungry. His brother's just the same.'

'We can all be a bit grumpy when we need to eat.' It was almost a defence, as if she was empathising with him already. His mother would remember the conversation for the rest of her life. And always wonder.

It was midday then, and across a sun-burnished bay the jumble of white, red-roofed buildings that clustered around the church was reflected in deepest turquoise.

Now, just two hours after sunset, it was moonlight that spilled across its mirrored surface, seen in a backward glance from where the dark hills folded one upon the other, before the Mediterranean disappeared from view. Yesterday's calm anticipation had been replaced by fear verging on panic. The blood, sticky and dark, was everywhere. On her hands, on the steering wheel. A careless moment, the razor-sharp edge of a freshly cut fingernail. A sleepy hand that grazed her cheek as it reached out to grasp her neck.

From the darkened terrace she had seen his parents in the light of the restaurant on the far side of the pool. Wine and laughter. Her whispered words of reassurance to the boy were superfluous. He was asleep already, his bloody panda left lying on the bedroom floor where it had fallen.

The road wound down in hairpin turns into the dark of the pine forest, gnarled roots searching among the stones of ancient terraces for a hold on the world, their parasol canopies like clouds shading them from a startling moon.

With the lights of Llança receding in her rearview mirror, the route north made its tortuous way around successive headlands, affording only occasional glimpses of the sea. Then, below, the floodlit railway junction at Portbou, massive lifting gear straddling a confluence of tracks. A change of gauge before crossing an invisible line beyond which everything would change. Language Culture. The future. The past.

The French frontier stood at the end of a long climb out of the town. It was the moment she had feared most. There was no one on the Spanish side. A light burned in the customs post, but there was no sign of life. The barrier was down at the French *douane*. A sleepy immigration officer looked up from his desk behind sliding glass as she drew to a halt. She fumbled for her passport with bloody fingers. What would she tell him? If she showed him her card then he would remember her for sure when the alarm was raised. But he didn't even look. He lifted the barrier and waved her through. He would never see the blood or her card or register her face or see the baby boy asleep in a cot on the back seat.

She was through. It was done. Only the future lay ahead.

Ninety minutes later she drove past the entrance to the commando training fort on the hill, a narrow road beneath twisting vines in brilliant flower, mired still in the shadow of night, and parked her car next to the little stone cottage that sat on the edge of the cliffs. She was home. And with child. And would spend the next sixteen years raising a killer.

PART ONE

Chapter One

Paris, February 1992

Yves watched the traffic in the boulevard below come to a standstill in the frigid Paris morning. The *bouchon* stretched as far as he could see, to the next traffic lights and beyond. He could almost feel the frustration of the drivers trapped in their cars rise to meet him like the pollution that spewed from smoky exhausts. The city air was not good for him. It was time for a change.

The long, repeating monotone in his ear was broken by a man's voice. 'Yes, hello?'

'*Salut*. It's me.'

'Oh, okay.' The voice seemed tense.

Yves was cool, relaxed. Each word delivered with the easy assurance of a soldier with an automatic weapon pumping bullets into an unarmed man. 'I'm sorry I didn't call yesterday. I was out of the country.' He wasn't quite sure why he felt the need to elaborate. It just seemed more casual. Conversational. 'Portsmouth. In England. A business trip.'

'Is that supposed to mean something to me?' Clear irritation in the other man's voice now.

'I just thought you'd wonder why I hadn't called.'

'Well, you're calling me now.'

'I was going to suggest tomorrow afternoon. Three o'clock. If that's okay with you.'

'Where?'

'Your place.'

He sensed the other's reticence in his hesitation. 'I prefer somewhere public, you know that.'

'Listen, friend, we need to talk.' If there was a threat in the forced intimacy of the word, 'friend,' it went unnoticed. He heard a sigh at the other end of the line.

'You know where to find me?'

'Of course.'

'Three o'clock, then.'

'Fine.' He retracted his cellphone aerial and saw that the traffic had not moved.

◇◇◇

Lambert's apartment was on the second floor of a recently renovated building in the thirteenth *arrondissement*. A newly installed electronic entry system was designed to cut costs by doing away with the need for a concierge. Which meant that no one but Lambert would witness his arrival. And no one, not even Lambert, would know when he left.

'Yeh?' The speaker in the wall issued a scratched rendition of Lambert's voice.

'It's me.' Yves never used his name if he didn't have to.

The buzzer sounded, and he pushed the door open.

Lambert was waiting on the landing. A gaping door opened into the apartment behind him. He was a strange young man, abnormally pale, sparse blond hair shaved to a cropped fuzz. Penumbrous shadows beneath darker eyes punctuated a skeletal face, and bony fingers clasped Yves' gloved hand in a perfunctory greeting. 'Come in.' He glanced towards the stairs as if concerned that someone might be watching.

The bay windows in the salon looked out towards the park, bearing out Yves' assumption that the room was not overlooked. A well-worn sofa and armchairs had seen better days, hiding their tawdriness beneath colourful, fringed throws. Yves smelled old garlic and stewed coffee coming from the open kitchen door. And the whole apartment was suffused with the stink of stale cigarette smoke. Yves felt it catching his throat, and as Lambert took out a fresh cigarette, he said, 'Don't do that.'

Lambert paused with the cigarette halfway to his mouth, and cast wary eyes towards his visitor. Then, reluctantly, he tapped the cigarette back into its packet. 'Coffee?'

'Why not?'

Lambert disappeared into the kitchen. Yves perched on the edge of the sofa and saw motes of dust hanging still in the slabs of weak winter sunlight that fell at angles through the window. He heard his own breath as he forced it in and out of contracting lungs. His blue eyes felt gritty at first, then watery. His tension was palpable.

Lambert reappeared with small cups of black coffee and placed them on the table. Yves leaned forward to drop in a sugar lump and poke it with a coffee spoon until it dissolved.

'Aren't you going to take off your coat?' Lambert sat opposite, in the armchair, keeping his eyes on his visitor as he raised his coffee cup to his lips.

'I'm not staying.'

Lambert's eyes dropped to his guest's hands. 'You can take off your gloves, surely?'

'I have a form of psoriasis,' Yves said. 'It affects my hands. When I have a flare-up I have to rub them with cream. I keep the gloves on to protect them.' He took a sip of his coffee. It was bitter and unpleasant, and he wished he had declined the offer. It was only putting off the moment.

'So what it is we need to talk about?' Lambert seemed anxious to get this over with.

But Yves wasn't listening. The tightness across his chest had become vice-like, and his lungs were reluctant to give up spent air. His throat was swelling, and he felt the rapid pulse of blood in his carotid arteries. Tears spilled from reddening eyes as did his coffee as he tried to replace the cup on the table. The sneezing and coughing began almost simultaneously. His mouth gaped, his eyes stared, and panic gripped him. His hand shot to his face, a politeness dinned into him during childhood years by a smothering mother. *Cover your mouth when you cough! Coughs and sneezes spread diseases!* For a moment, he thought that Lambert knew why he had come, and that there had been something in the coffee. But the symptoms were only too familiar.

It was nearly impossible to breathe now. In a world blurred by tears he saw Lambert get to his feet, and heard the alarm in his voice. 'Are you alright? What the hell's wrong with you?'

He sucked in a breath and forced it out again. 'Do you…do you keep pets?'

Lambert shook his head in consternation. 'Of course not. In God's name, man, what's wrong?'

As Yves struggled to his feet, Lambert rounded the table to stop him from falling. It was now or never. Yves clutched the outstretched bony arms and threw his weight forward. He heard Lambert's gasp of surprise, and then the air exploding from his lungs as both men toppled over the coffee table and crashed to the floor. Yves was on top of him, but could barely see, mucus and saliva exploding from his mouth and nose as his body fought against the toxins with which his own immune system was attacking his airways.

Lambert was screaming and flailing beneath him. Yves' gloved hands found the younger man's face, then his neck, and he squeezed. But his physical powers were failing, and he released his hold on the neck to seek out the head. He felt Lambert's barking breath in his face, before his hands found that familiar grip, one hand spread across the face, the other at the back of the head. And then it was easy, in spite of everything. A quick twist. He heard the pop of the disarticulated vertebrae, and almost felt the sharp edge of the bone, released from its cartilage, slice through the spinal cord. Lambert went limp. Yves rolled off him and lay fighting for breath. If he blacked out now, there was a good chance he would never wake up. This was as bad as he had ever known it.

It took a superhuman effort to force himself to his knees. He fumbled in his coat pocket to find the bottle of pills and closed desperate fingers around it.

He had no idea how he managed to reach the kitchen, or how it was even possible to force the pills over a throat that was swollen nearly closed. He heard the sound of breaking glass as the tumbler fell into the sink, and the rattle of pills as they spilled across the floor. But none of that mattered. If he didn't get out of here now, he would be as dead as the man he had come to kill.

Chapter Two

Sleet gently slapped the window like the soft touch of tapping fingertips, then turned instantly wet to run like tears spilled by the coming winter.

Kirsty watched anxiously from the top floor of the old house. She had been there six months now, the accumulated possessions of her gypsy existence finding more than enough space in the single room and kitchen. It was one of twelve studio apartments in this early twentieth century mansion, built reputedly by some wealthy German industrialist.

Strasbourg was a city unsure of itself. Neither French, nor German. Disputed for centuries by old enemies, it had opted finally to be European, a decidedly amorphous notion lacking any sense of common culture or identity. While its citizens spoke French, the German influence was pervasive, and the establishment of the European Parliament on its northern flank had brought a flood of politicians and civil servants speaking everything from Polish to Portuguese, Estonian to Italian.

Which, Kirsty reflected, was just as well. Since without them, she would be without a job. She glanced at her watch and felt a stab of apprehension. If her taxi did not arrive in the next few minutes, she would soon be looking for new employment.

She cursed the weather. And she cursed the fact that she had decided not to take her bike. Usually she cycled to the parliament, a twenty-minute daily ride through the Orangerie and the leafy suburban back streets that stretched along the river. But in the translation booths that overlooked the semicircular debating chamber, it didn't matter what she wore. Today it did. Today she would be in the full glare of the press corps, with their cameras and microphones and questions. She would be sitting at the right hand of a man whose financial muscle and political pull were almost unsurpassed in the European Union. She would be his ears, and his voice, and needed to look her best.

A horn sounding from below quickened her pulse. At last! She grabbed her coat and her bag and ran down the stairs. As she opened the door on to the Rue Bernegger she paused, raising her umbrella to protect expensively coiffed hair and carefully applied make-up. Then she slid into the rear seat of the taxi and shook the sleet back into the street.

'You're late.' She couldn't keep the annoyance out of her voice.

The driver shrugged. 'Traffic's a bitch. When do you have to be there?'

'Nine.' She heard him suck in his breath.

'Not much chance of that, *mademoiselle*. There's nothing moving over either bridge.'

She began to feel sick. This was turning into a nightmare. 'Well, can't you go downtown, and back out on the Avenue de la Paix?'

'The *centre ville* isn't any better. Only things still moving are the trams.'

She sighed her frustration. 'It's really important I get there by nine.' If she had been going to the parliament they could simply have driven down the Quai de l'Orangerie. But the press conference was in the Palais des Congrès, the huge convention centre on the north side of the Place de Bordeaux. And to get there, they needed to cross two of the myriad waterways that divided and subdivided the city.

She sat in the back, almost rigid with tension, and watched as the sleet-streaked windows smeared city streets thick with fallen leaves. They moved freely at first, and she began to relax. But as they approached the *pont* that bridged the river between the Boulevard de la Dordogne and the Boulevard Jacques Preiss, the traffic ground to a standstill. She saw that the sleet was turning to snow.

She took a deep breath and felt it tremble in her throat. There was no way they were going to make it. She had taken the one-week engagement in the hope that it might lead to better things. It had slotted in nicely between the end of her one-year probationary contract with the European Parliament and the start of a new two-year term on full pay. Very shortly she would sit The Test, and if she passed it she would become a career interpreter for the European Union. The prospect of which seemed to stretch ahead of her, like a prison sentence. If life was going to offer more, then she wanted to find out now what that might be.

Which was why she had jumped at the chance to work for the Italian. He was the chief executive officer of a major motor car manufacturer. But his company made most of its money from guided missile systems and air defence batteries, and the parliament was threatening to vote down approval given by the Council of Ministers for the production of antipersonnel mines and cluster bombs. However, unlike the Council of Ministers, whose majority vote had carried the approval, the Parliament required a unanimous vote to overturn it. A rare occurrence. But on the vexed and controversial question of landmines and cluster bombs, for once it looked like the MEPs might actually vote with one voice.

The Italian was in town to lobby against such a vote and to pressurise Italian members of the European Parliament whose constituents back home could lose jobs if the contract fell. He had employed Kirsty as his interpreter, and to be the attractive and acceptable face of his campaign. She had not fully appreciated that until the briefing at his hotel the day before, when no amount of oily charm had been able to disguise his naked intent. But she had already signed a contract and was committed to the job. After all, she told herself, she was just the messenger. She had no control over the message.

But neither had she any control over the traffic. Her eyes closed in despair. She had blown it. She should have ordered the taxi half-an-hour earlier. She fumbled in her purse for her cellphone and hit the speeddial key.

'Hi, Kirst. What's up?'

'Sylvie, I'm in trouble. I'm stuck in traffic in the Boulevard Tauler. There's no way I'm going to make it to the Palais des Congrès on time.'

'Is this the Italian job?'

'Yeh.'

'*Merde*! Is there anything I can do?'

'You can stand in for me.'

'Kirsty, I can't. I haven't been briefed.'

'Please Sylvie. You're five minutes away, and I know you're not on shift till this afternoon. Just hold down the fort for me. I'll get there as soon as I can.'

◇◇◇

It was after nine-thirty when her taxi swung in off the Avenue Herrenschmidt. The car park was filled with press vehicles and satellite vans. The flags of the European Union's twenty-seven member states hung limp in the grey morning light, and wet snow lay like a crust along the curves of an impenetrable bronze sculpture on the lawn beyond. She fumbled to find money in her purse as her driver pulled up below the *Strasbourg Evenements* sign. Then she flew across the paving stones towards the glass, her coat billowing behind her, concern for hair and make-up long forgotten.

Her voice echoed across the vast, shining concourse, and heads swung in her direction. 'The press conference! What room?'

A young woman looked up from behind a long reception counter, her face a mask of indifference. 'Tivoli One. First floor.'

Kirsty ran across pale marble set in dizzying patterns, the click of her heels echoing back from glass and concrete. Occasional standing groups of two and three broke from idle conversation to cast curious glances in her direction. Through open doors, beneath a strange ceiling like rows of silk pillows, she saw caterers laying out food, a young man setting up the bar. If you wanted the press to come, you had to feed and water them. At the foot of a flight of stairs, below a sign that read, *1er Etage*, she quickly scanned the list of names. *Salle Oberlin, Salle Schuman, Salle Schweitzer C-D*. Then there it was, *Salles Tivoli 1-2*.

She took the stairs two at a time, emerging onto a wide, carpeted concourse with floor-to-ceiling windows all along one side. The carpet absorbed the sound of her heels, and only her breath filled the huge space overhead, breath that came in short, gasping bursts. Away to her left hung a strange tapestry of warlocks and witches. A sign above a doorway read, *Salle Oberlin*. High above her, more silk cushions. She ran past a glass balustrade looking down on a sprawling maze of cloakrooms. A triangular overhead sign told her she was still on track for *Tivoli 1*. Up steps, through open glass doors, and she heard the voice of the Italian coming from the faraway room. Then Sylvie's clear, confident translation into English then French. The meeting room was full. Cameras ranged along the back wall, TV lights throwing everything into sharp focus. Sylvie sat a little to the Italian's right behind a desk on the podium, a sales chart projected on the screen behind them.

Kirsty pushed past bodies in the doorway and felt the heat of the explosion almost before the blast knocked her from her feet. Blinded by the flash of it, deafened by its noise, it seemed like an eternity before hearing and sight returned to reveal a smoke-filled world of jumbled confusion. Screaming, shouting, crying. As she struggled to get to her knees, a hand caught her arm, strong and gentle, pulling her back to her feet. She swept long, chestnut hair from her face and looked up into the eyes of the man who still held her. Blue eyes, filled with a strange serenity. He seemed untroubled by the chaos around him. Was he smiling? Someone was shouting from the podium. The man turned his head, and she saw that his right earlobe was missing.

'Signor Capaldi! Where's Signor Capaldi?' The voice was hysterical.

Another voice. 'He's alive! Jesus, he's still alive.'

A woman shouting, 'The interpreter…?'

'Man, she's gone. There's hardly anything left of her.'

The sound of someone vomiting.

Kirsty felt her knees buckling beneath her, and only the grip of the hand on her arm kept her on her feet. The man turned back towards her. 'You're a lucky girl.'

And Kirsty knew that but for the weather and a taxi that was late, it would have been her in pieces up there.

Chapter Three

The gardens below St. Etienne Cathedral were deserted behind grey railings in the cold November light. Dead flowers had been removed from their beds, and a layer of frost carpeted the lawns. Beyond the Place Champollion at the foot of the Rue Maréchal Foch, a chill mist still hung above the river. Enzo had heard it was snowing in the north. But here, in southwest France, it was just cold. A deep, penetrating cold.

Thursday was training day at the hairdresser's. Twenty percent off *sur la technique*. So it was natural that a Scot of parsimonious persuasion would choose a Thursday for his monthly trim. Xavier, his hairdresser, only ever took half an inch off the end of his long locks. Just enough to stop them from tangling when Enzo tied back his hair in its habitual ponytail.

The trainee had shampooed and conditioned his hair when he first arrived and now, under Xavier's supervision, was dragging a comb back through it before trapping it along the length of her index and middle fingers to snip off the ends. Enzo looked with mild concern at the hair that came away in the comb. Once black hair, now rapidly greying.

'Am I losing it?' he asked Xavier.

Xavier shrugged theatrically. He was exaggeratedly gay, somewhere in his middle forties, perhaps five or six years younger than Enzo. 'We're always shedding hair. It's natural. You've still got a good thick head on you.' He paused. 'I could give you a rinse, though. Something to take away the grey. Good practice for the trainee.'

But Enzo just shook his head. 'We are what we are.' He turned to gaze out towards the cathedral gardens across the street, a little knot of fear tightening in his gut.

Zavier cocked his head. 'You don't seem quite your usual self today, monsieur.'

'Then maybe I'm somebody else.'

The hairdresser chuckled. 'Oh, you are a comic, Monsieur Macleod.' But Enzo wasn't smiling.

Neither was he smiling when he emerged ten minutes later, his hair full and sleek after its blow-dry, and held at the nape of his neck by a ruffled grey band. His farewell was a distracted one as he turned away from the river towards the Place Clement Marot, past the internet café on the corner. Waiters in the *crêperie*, Le Baladin, and Le RendezVous next door, were already setting tables for lunch. In the Place de la Libération, there was the oddest sense of life as usual. Folks queuing at the *boulangerie* for bread, an old man outside the Maison de la Presse standing with a nicotine-stained cigarette in the corner of his mouth reading *La Dépêche*. But for Enzo, none of it seemed quite real.

He took the letter from his inside jacket pocket to check the address again. He had been trying not to think about it for days, but there was no longer any avoiding it. He had searched the map in the *annuaire* to find the Rue des Trois Baudus, and been surprised to discover that it was almost opposite the music shop in the Rue du Château du Rois. It was the shop where he habitually bought his guitar strings. The *rue* was little more than an alleyway, and he had never given it a second glance. A little further up the street was the old prison in the Château du Roi itself. The Tour des Pendus at the top of the hill was where they had once hanged prisoners in full public view. But the Rue des Trois Baudus had always escaped him.

His visit to the doctor had been routine. An annual check-up, which had never given him cause for concern. In fact, his doctor only ever got in touch to fix a date for the following year's rendezvous. So the letter had come like an arrow from the dark, a harbinger of what could only be bad news. An appointment made with a specialist to discuss his results.

Enzo breathed deeply as he walked up the hill past the pharmacy on the corner, past the comforting familiarity of Alain Pugnet's music shop, and turned into the Rue des Trois Baudus. He had searched his dictionary to find out what a *baudu* might be, but disconcertingly it was not to be found. Perhaps it was a name. Graffiti scarred the wall and the Toutounet dispenser which issued plastic bags for the disposal of dog shit. Not that anyone in the town of Cahors seemed to use them.

The alleyway was narrow and deserted. Windows were shuttered, and only a narrow slice of cold winter light from above pierced the damp and the dark below. Number 24 *bis* was on the right, beyond a brick-arched doorway. The door was pale, studded oak, and the window to its right was barred. A shiny plaque fixed to the wall made Enzo's stomach flip over.

Docteur Gilbert Dussuet
Oncologue

Below the bellpush was a small sign: *Ring and Enter.* Enzo did as requested and opened the door into a narrow waiting room with four plastic chairs and a tiny table littered with old magazines. It smelled of damp cellars in here, and there was no natural light. Just a single, naked lightbulb hanging from the ceiling. He sat down on the chair nearest the door, as if it might offer some hope of escape, and waited.

By the time the door to the doctor's surgery opened, Enzo knew every stain and scuff on the faded linoleum, had read and reread every poster on the wall. Exhortations to regularly self test for testicular cancer and cancer of the breast. Dire warnings about the melanomic consequences for the skin of failing to apply protection against the sun. None of it did anything to ameliorate Enzo's deepening sense of foreboding.

Doctor Dussuet was younger than he had expected. Late thirties or early forties. He was possessed of certain rugged good looks and had a charming smile. He held out his hand to shake Enzo's and ushered him into his inner sanctum. The office was sparsely furnished. A couple of filing cabinets, a desk, some chairs. There were a handful of posters on the walls, and the blinds were down, although there was hardly any daylight in the street outside. A desk lamp focused a dazzling circle of electric light on to the burnished surface of the desk, and the two men sat down on either side of it. There was a file open on the blotting paper, and Enzo could see his name at the top of it.

The doctor didn't look at it. Instead he clasped his hands in front of him and leaned his elbows on the desk. He looked at Enzo earnestly, a well-practised look of sympathy and sadness in his eyes.

'Do you know why you're here?'

Enzo shook his head. 'For bad news, I guess.'

The doctor allowed himself a moment of reflection, then refocused on his patient. 'You have a very rare form of leukemia, Monsieur Macleod.' He paused. 'You know what leukemia is?'

'Cancer of the blood.' Enzo heard his own voice, but it didn't seem to belong to him.

'Cancer of the blood. Or bone marrow. Characterised by an abnormal proliferation of white blood cells. These cells are involved in fighting pathogens and are usually suppressed, or dysfunctional. Leading to the patient's immune system attacking other body cells.'

Enzo stared at him. His face, in the intensity of the desk lamp, seemed to burn out before his eyes. 'Is it treatable?'

The doctor sat back suddenly and pressed his lips together. 'I'm afraid your disease is terminal, Monsieur Macleod. Of course, we'll put you on an immediate course of chemotherapy.'

But Enzo didn't want to hear any more. 'How long have I got?'

'With treatment…perhaps six months.'

'Without?'

Doctor Dussuet tipped his head apologetically. 'Three. At the most.'

Chapter Four

She was, perhaps, forty-five years old. Her hair was cut short into the back of her head, and was curled on top. She'd had it streaked blond, and she looked younger than her years. She had borne two children in her twenties, but still kept her figure. She was slim, attractive, and divorced, and her children were adults now. Which meant she was never short on male suitors. She worked afternoons at La Poste in the Rue du President Wilson, so was at home when her doorbell rang.

Her apartment was one of two in a converted suburban villa near the hospital in the southwest corner of Cahors. Her neighbour worked at an *agence immobilière* in the Boulevard Léon Gambetta, so she knew it wasn't her. It was gloomy on the landing when she opened her door, but she saw immediately that her caller wore a strange white mask over his nose and mouth. She barely had time to register surprise before he struck her with an iron fist. Light and pain exploded in her head and she fell backwards, unconscious even before she hit the floor. The man with the mask stepped over her, moving her with his foot so that he could close the door. He knelt over her prone form, pausing for a moment to consider that, really, she was quite a handsome woman. Which was a waste.

He cupped one hand behind her head, placed the other across her face, and felt an instant gratification with the *pop* that came as he pulled them in opposing directions. The hardest part of life was living. Death was easy.

With his gloved hands he carefully felt for the opening of her blouse, then ripped it apart. Buttons rattled across the floor. Her bra was black with small, frilly loops along the upper edges. He slipped two fingers between the flimsy half cups and tore it off. She had soft, round breasts with dark pink areolae. But that was not what he had come for.

He stood up and strode down the hall into the *séjour*. This was a woman who had enjoyed order in her life. Everything had a place and, apparently, was in it. His mother had been like that. Anally tidy. So it gave him some pleasure to introduce some chaos. Drawers emptied on to the floor, vases smashed, a display cabinet full of crockery and wine glasses overturned. In her bedroom he yanked clothes from the wardrobe and threw them across the bed. There was a drawer full of black lingerie, suspenders, a red garter. Either she enjoyed her sex, or was just an *allumeuse*. Whatever, she had no further use for these. He chucked them in handfuls out into the hall.

In the kitchen he swept everything from the worktops, opened the fridge and pulled meat and cheese and half-empty jars onto the floor. Then he spotted the clock on the face of the oven. A clock with revolving counters. He smashed the glass with the side of his hand then stooped to put his ear next to it. He could hear the electronic mechanism behind it trying to turn, but the counters were broken and locked in place. Eleven, twenty-nine.

He went back into the *séjour* where he had left her laptop computer untouched on the table. Now he opened the lid and booted it up, waiting patiently until its desktop filled the screen. He selected and opened its iCal software and watched as her agenda for the month displayed itself. As quickly as his gloved fingers would allow, he tapped in a new entry and saved it. Job done. Almost.

In the hall he bent over his victim and looked again at her pretty face. He removed a glove and felt her skin with the back of his hand. She was going cold already. He searched for and found a small, clear, ziplock bag in one of his inside pockets, and took it out.

Chapter Five

Kirsty sat motionless, hunched forward, her hands clasped between her thighs. Her eyes were burning, but incapable of spilling more tears. Her head was pounding, her throat swollen. They had questioned her for most of the night, until she had almost no voice left.

What was her relationship with Sylvie? How long had she known her? Why had she failed to turn up at the Palais des Congrès? How long had she been working for the Italian? They seemed not to believe her when she said she had only met him for the first time the day before the press conference.

The young detective had asked all the questions. The woman, who was older, sat in silence, just watching, never taking her eyes off her. She had made Kirsty feel like a criminal.

They had made her go over her daily schedule at the parliament. She had no idea why. She explained that they worked in teams of two during morning and afternoon, or morning and evening sessions. A typical session would be three hours, but each interpreter worked only one half hour at a time, then the other would take over. It was draining work that demanded extraordinary concentration. Between sessions you would eat, recharge your batteries, then take five or ten minutes to refocus and get the adrenaline going again. Just like an athlete. When you finished for the day, you were done. Spent. And it could take several hours to decompress.

Generally, you only socialised with other interpreters. People who understood the process and the toll it took. When you struck up a friendship with a fellow interpreter, it was a bond for life. Kirsty had only known Sylvie for a year, but in the hothouse that was the interpreter's booth, they had become the closest of friends. They did everything together, told each other their darkest secrets. They had been going to share an apartment when Kirsty began her second year contract on full pay. Which was why, after the initial shock of the explosion receded, Kirsty had found the empty space it left filled by a numbing grief. And then guilt. A dreadful, debilitating, invasive guilt. She had killed her friend, as surely as if she had triggered that explosion herself.

If she hadn't been late for the press conference, if she hadn't made that phone call, Sylvie would still be alive.

She had been alone in the room since first light had cast the feeble shadow of barred windows on the opposite wall, and she didn't know if she could ever contemplate life outside of it again.

She had no idea how long it was before the door opened and her young interrogator returned. The silent, older woman followed him into the room and sat down without a word. Kirsty raised glowering, sleep-starved eyes briefly to meet hers. She couldn't have said why, but every emotion she felt seemed concentrated in a powerful hatred of the woman. The young detective dropped a file on the desk between them and looked at Kirsty with an odd expression of puzzled curiosity.

'The *police scientifique* have made an initial assessment of the scene,' he said. 'Your employer was extremely fortunate to survive.' He looked up and seemed to be gazing at the grey light seeping in around the small windows high up on the wall. 'But that's probably because he wasn't the intended target.' He fixed Kirsty once more with quizzical eyes. 'It was a small explosive device, Madamoiselle Macleod. Limited. Targeted. It was placed under the podium, directly beneath the interpreter's seat. And since the seating arrangements had been fixed in advance, that can only mean one thing. The bomb wasn't meant for the Italian. It was meant for you.'

Chapter Six

Enzo walked through the town in a trance. A dead man walking. The streets and the buildings were painted with a sense of unreality, as if he were already one step removed from them. As if he had already embarked on the journey to that other place.

In his mind he had.

The streets were populated with ghosts. Some of them seemed familiar. Some even said *bonjour*, as if they knew him. But no one knew him any more. No one would know him ever again. He passed the Cathedral at the top of the square, and felt its cold air breathe out through the open door. He was not tempted to enter, to fall on his knees and offer prayers to someone else's God.

His mother had been a good Italian Catholic, but had raised him in a Protestant land, in a city where sectarian hatred had found focus in football. He had rejected it all, and wondered now if faith might have brought comfort. Somehow, he doubted it.

As he passed La Halle, and the Café Forum on the corner. He heard someone call out his name. A familiar voice. But he kept on walking.

He had no idea if Sophie would be at home or working out at the gym. But if she was still at the apartment, he couldn't face her. Not yet. He wasn't sure if he would ever be ready for that. How could he tell her that the life she had spent without a mother was soon to have the father taken, too? Her grief would be too painful. Greater even than his own self-pity. After all, she would have to live with it. In three short months his life would be over.

He retrieved his car from the lock-up, his beloved restored 2CV with its roll-back roof and soft suspension, and drove south out of town, over the Pont Louis Philippe, before turning left after the statue of the *vierge* and beginning the long ascent.

The Mont St. Cyr was ill-named. It wasn't really a mountain. Just a very high hill. But it had commanding views over the town below, contained in a long loop of the River Lot, and beyond the Pont Valentré to the viaduct that carried the RN20 over the deep gash of the river valley south towards Toulouse. Tourists were attracted here in the summer, to take in the spectacular aerial view, to gaze through the pay-binoculars, and take photographs. But it was deserted on this misty cold November day, as it had been when Enzo first came here more than twenty years ago, the night that Pascale died and left him to bring up their newborn daughter on his own.

He climbed the few steps down to the bench where he had sat that night wondering where he would find the courage to carry on living. Now he wondered how he would find the courage to die. It wasn't the dying itself. We were all going to die, and we knew it. We just didn't know when. And that was the hardest thing. He remembered when he was still a kid in Glasgow, just four or five years old. Someone had died. It might have been his grandfather. And he had come face to face for the first time with the realisation that he, too, would die some day. He had sat on the edge of his bed and thought about it for some time, before deciding that it was a long way in the future, and that he wouldn't worry about it until the day came. A convenient compartmentalisation of death that had served him well for most of his fifty-one years. Only now, someone had broken the seals and opened the compartment, and he found himself staring in the face the moment he had so conveniently dispatched to a far-off place. Dammit, his destiny might have been to die in a traffic accident tomorrow. But he wouldn't have known it until the last moment, if at all. To watch the last precious weeks and days slip through his fingers like sand, seemed like such cruel torture.

And then he thought about Kirsty, the fruit of a relationship back in Scotland that had withered and died when she was still a child. He thought about all the lost moments, the things they might have shared and didn't through all the years of estrangement. He had always thought that somehow there might still be time. To catch up. To make up. There had been a rapprochement of sorts, but she was still tender and touchy and kept him at arm's length. And now the time he thought they still had was being taken away, and all the regrets seemed to weigh so much more heavily.

He let his eyes wander over the jumble of roofs below until they came to rest on the twin roofs of the cathedral. They were perfectly round, like a woman's breasts, and topped by short, moulded lightning rods like two erect nipples. He thought of all the women he had known, those he had loved, those he had failed, those who had frustrated him to distraction. He shook his head and allowed himself a tiny smile of sad regret. It was all behind him now. The game was almost over. All that remained was to wait for the referee's whistle at the end of extra time.

◇◇◇

He weaved through the empty tables on the *terrasse* outside the Lampara restaurant and pushed open the door to the stairwell beyond. He climbed the steps with heavy legs and hoped that Sophie would not be there.

He called her name when he opened the door, and was relieved to be answered by silence. In the *séjour* he threw open the French windows and let in the cold air from the square below. The trees had shed most of their leaves, and lay thick and still brittle with frost among the cars in the car park. It wasn't until he turned back into the room than he noticed the red light winking on his DECT phone. Someone had called and left a message. He was tempted to ignore it. After all, whatever it was, it would no longer have any importance for him. But even as he shuffled idly through the papers on his desk, it kept on blinking in his peripheral vision, until he couldn't stand it any longer. He lifted the phone, pressed the replay button, and put the receiver to his ear. It was with something like shock that he heard Kirsty's voice.

'Dad…? Where are you? You're never there. Please, you've got to come to Strasbourg. I don't know what to do. Someone's trying to kill me.'

He replayed it twice before hanging up. If ever he needed a reason to live, he had just found one.

Chapter Seven

Commissaire Hélène Taillard enjoyed the distinction of being only the sixth woman in the history of the République to be appointed Director of Public Security to one of the country's one hundred *départements*. She had been promoted from the rank of *inspecteur* to the title of *commissaire* in the Département du Lot three years earlier, inheriting a large, comfortable office in the *caserne* of the Police Nationale in the Place Bessières at the north end of Cahors.

Following a call from the crime scene early that afternoon, her driver had taken her downtown to the west end of the long Rue Victor Hugo, which transected the town east to west at the southern end of the loop. Now, as she stepped out of the car, she tugged at her blue uniform jacket where it had ridden up over her ample bosom. She was an attractive woman, still in her forties, but if her male colleagues had thought that her female touch might be a soft one, they had quickly learned their mistake. Hélène Taillard was a good cop, as tough as any man who had filled her shoes, and maybe tougher. She was fiercely loyal to those who were loyal to her, but God help you if you crossed her. She had separated from her husband when it became clear to them both that her career was more important than her marriage.

There were several police vehicles in the street outside the house, lights flashing. Two white, unmarked vans belonging to the forensic *police scientifique* were drawn up on the sidewalk opposite. Blue-and-white striped crime scene tape fluttered in the icy breeze that blew in off the slate-grey waters of the river.

The house had been subdivided into two apartments, one on the ground floor, one on the upper floor. The victim had been found upstairs. Commissaire Taillard climbed the internal staircase to a poorly lit landing where a number of her officers were gathered outside the apartment. They spoke in hushed voices and watched keenly for the *commissaire's* reaction. Murder in Cahors was a rare event.

Inspecteur David Truquet shook her hand. 'She's just inside, *commissaire*. The other side of the door.' And he handed her a pair of latex gloves and a couple of plastic shoe covers.

The police photographer had erected lights in the hall, and the body was thrown into sharp relief. Forensics officers in white tyvek suits moved aside to let the *commissaire* through. She looked down at the dead woman. Her skin seemed pale and waxy, all animation long gone from a once pretty face. Her head lay at a peculiar angle, her blouse ripped open and bra torn away to reveal her breasts. There was deep purple bruising down one side of her face.

'A sexual attack?'

Inspecteur Truquet raised an uncertain eyebrow. 'You might think so at first glance, *commissaire*. But she was still wearing her panties, and the *médecin légiste* says she hasn't been interfered with…you know, down there.' He was uncomfortable at having to discuss a woman's private parts with his female boss. 'And the place has been turned over. It's possible he was looking for something.'

'He?' Commissaire Taillard disliked sexual stereotypes of either variety.

'Whoever hit her took her down with a single blow, then broke her neck. A quick, clean break. A real pro job, the pathologist says. I think it might be fair to assume it was a man.'

'So why did he rip open her blouse?'

Truquet shrugged and shook his head.

The *commissaire* looked along the hall towards the mess in the *séjour*. 'Did he take anything?'

'Impossible to say. She lived alone, so it's going to be difficult trying to establish if there's anything missing. He really trashed the place, though. Like maybe he was getting something out of his system.'

'A grudge killing?'

'Possible.'

'How about time of death?'

'Just before eleven-thirty this morning.'

She turned a look of surprise towards her investigating *inspecteur*. 'How can you know so precisely?'

He started towards the kitchen and indicated that she should follow. They picked their way carefully through the debris on the floor, and the stink of ripening goat's cheese, and he showed her the broken clock on the oven.

'Eleven twenty-nine. Assuming he broke it when he was trashing the kitchen, and that he'd already killed her, that would put time of death sometime shortly before then. Just over three hours ago, and rigor mortis is only just beginning to set in. So it all fits.'

'How convenient.' She looked around the kitchen. It was in the American style, with wall cupboards and worktops and a central island. 'Who discovered her?'

'The postman. He had a *colis* for her and needed a signature. The door wasn't properly shut, and when he pushed it open…'

'So who is she, or rather, who was she?'

'Audeline Pommereau. Forty-six. Divorced. Mother of two. Kids are grown up. She worked afternoons at La Poste in the Rue du Président Wilson.'

She detected his hesitation. 'What?'

He lifted Audeline Pommereau's purse from the worktop and took out a dog-eared business card from one of its inside pockets. He handed it to his boss. 'We found this.' And he watched for her reaction.

Commissaire Taillard held it carefully between latexed fingers and felt her professional detachment suddenly depart. But her face remained expressionless, concealing the confusion behind it. She was holding the business card of Enzo Macleod, Professor of Biology, Paul Sabatier University, Toulouse. She turned it over and saw, in a familiar scrawl, his home telephone number and the words *Call me*. She heard herself saying, 'So she knew Enzo Macleod. That doesn't mean anything.' But the colour was rising now on her cheeks, betraying a history of failed emotional involvement that seemed somehow to be common knowledge among her junior officers.

'That's not all, *commissaire*.'

She followed Truquet through the hall to the *séjour*. The officers of the *police scientifique* had returned to the task of examining the body of the victim in the minutest detail before removing it to the morgue. Amid the mess, a laptop computer sat open on the table, a slide selection of family photographs, installed as a screensaver, illuminating its monitor.

Truquet leaned over the keyboard and banished the screensaver, to reveal a monthly agenda. He stood up. 'This is what was showing on the screen when we got here.'

Commissaire Taillard peered at it, flicking her eyes across four weeks of entries until they settled on today's date. And her heart seemed to push up into her throat to try to stop her breathing. *Enzo—11am*, it said.

'*Commissaire*.' A voice from the hallway.

She looked up, but was distracted, and it took a second call before she reacted. She went out into the hall. The senior forensics officer was standing astride the body in his shower cap and white plastic suit. In one latexed hand he was holding a pair of tweezers, which he held out for her to see. 'Hair recovered from the victim's clothes, ma'am. Not hers. Definitely not hers.'

She took a step closer and saw several long, black hairs held between the legs of the tweezers.

'Long, like a woman's,' said the forensics officer.

'Or a man with a ponytail.' David Truquet's voice came from behind. She turned to see him watching her closely, and a sick feeling of dread descended, like a shroud on a murder victim.

Chapter Eight

Kirsty pushed through the crowds in the Place de la Gare towards the huge glass bubble they had built, unaccountably, to mask the station's historical façade. An architectural aberration to be endured by generations of Strasbourgers to come. Work to renovate the station and link it into the city's growing tram network had only recently been completed, along with this glass monstrosity.

Earlier sleet had turned to rain, blowing in on an east wind all the way from Siberia, and travellers hurried, heads bowed beneath battered umbrellas, on pathways that converged like the spokes of a wheel on the hub that was the Gare de Strasbourg.

The huge clock in the departure hall showed nearly four-thirty. Her father's train was due in very shortly. Kirsty glanced nervously at the faces of passengers who seemed to press around her on all sides. If someone was trying to kill her, she thought not unreasonably, it could be any one of them. How could she know?

Kirsty had been unable to sleep since Sylvie's death. She had lain, tossing and turning in a friend's apartment the previous night, torn between guilt and confusion. She had no idea why someone might want her dead. It was inexplicable to her. And yet there was, it seemed, no doubt that she had been the target. No doubt, too, that since her would-be killer had failed the first time, he might very well try again. She felt vulnerable, exposed, and powerless to do anything about it.

The call to her father had been a reflex response. A return to childhood. A little girl reaching out towards safe and comforting arms. Someone who would never let her down, no matter what. And, yet, hadn't he done just that for all those years?

A Jewish cleric with a long white beard and black hat was staring at her, and she turned away self-consciously, hurrying through a series of stone arches towards the arrivals hall.

Which was when she saw him.

Just a glimpse. An oddly familiar face beyond the dozens of people queuing at the Alsace grocery store. She stopped, catching her breath. Where was he? And then she saw him again. He was looking at her, a strange serenity in piercing blue eyes. And then he was gone, and no matter how hard she looked, she couldn't recatch sight of him. Who was he? She knew she knew him. Then it came to her. Like a moment replayed. A strong hand helping her to her feet. *You're a lucky girl*, he'd said. And a shiver of fear shook her rigid.

◇◇◇

She saw her father almost as soon as he stepped off the TGV. He was nearly a head higher than the other passengers, and although his hair was greying, the trademark white stripe that ran back through it from his left temple still stood out. Her resolve to remain strong immediately dissolved, and she pushed through the oncoming tide to throw herself into his arms. He dropped his overnight bag and held her as if there might be no tomorrow—which, for him, was only too close to being true.

He felt her sobs pulsing against his chest, and he held her until they began to subside. When, finally, she drew away, brushing the tears from her eyes, platform four was almost deserted. She ran a hand back through her long hair, clearing it away from a strong, handsome face. She had dark eyes, and full lips like her mother. But she was tall, with square set shoulders and long legs, like her father. When she spoke, her usually strong, confident, Scottish voice was hoarse, barely a whisper.

'I'm so scared.'

He held her by the shoulders. 'I won't let anything happen to you, Kirsty. Ever.' And it was with a jolt that he was reminded that, for him, 'ever' was just a few months. After that, she would be on her own.

He took her hand and they went down the steps to the long marbled corridor that led to the front of the station. Her grip on his hand tightened every time she saw a man approach, and he glanced at her to see the pale tension etched in her face. He put an arm around her shoulder and guided her through the shopping arcade towards the station buffet. It was packed here, and he thought she might feel safer in a crowd. A girl behind glass in the ticket office glanced at them as they passed, as if their insecurity were visible. They sank into tubular metal chairs at a table in the corner, from where they had a view of anyone approaching, and an impossibly thin oriental girl served them coffee. A huge wallposter of a *croque-monsieur* reminded him that he was hungry. He had not eaten since overnighting in Paris and killing time till the first available seat in a TGV. But there were more pressing things to deal with.

He had to raise his own voice above the echo of the others that rang among the pillars and vaults, and the constant announcements that blared from the speaker system. 'What happened?'

And she told him. About her one-week contract interpreting for the Italian. Her disappointment when she discovered why he was in town. How the weather had brought traffic to a standstill on the morning of the press conference, and how she had called Sylvie from her cab to ask her to stand in.

'It's hard to believe that you were the target and not the Italian. He must have plenty of enemies.'

'The police were certain. The bomb had been placed beneath the interpreter's seat. The one I should have been in. Not Sylvie.'

She choked on the words, and he put a reassuring hand over hers. 'It's not your fault, Kirsty.'

'That bomb was meant for me. It should have been me at that press conference.'

It was almost as if she wished herself dead. Death would have been easier than the guilt. Enzo thought about how he would be feeling right now if Kirsty had got there on time. And he knew that no matter what horrors he might face himself, his job right now was to protect his child. With his life if necessary.

He glanced at her. She was still distracted, eyes flickering nervously towards the passing crowds in the arcade. 'Are you still seeing Roger?'

The eyes darted quickly in his direction, and fixed him with a look of hurt and disappointment. 'Does it matter? I know you don't like him, but he's got nothing to do with this.'

He wanted to say that it didn't matter a damn whether he liked Raffin or not. The point was he didn't like him being with Kirsty. But he kept his own counsel. 'Does he know what's happened?'

She shook her head, and he felt some tiny crumb of comfort in the knowledge that the first person she had turned to was him.

He dropped some coins on the table and stood up. 'Come on. We'll go to your apartment and pack a bag, and you'll come back with me to Cahors. You'll be safe there, and we'll figure out what to do.'

But she made no move to get up. 'I haven't been to the apartment since…since it happened. I stayed with a friend last night.' She hesitated. 'I'm frightened to go back.'

He nodded and took her hand. 'We'll get the cab to wait for us. I've booked us a hotel, and we'll get the first train to Paris in the morning.'

But still she wouldn't stand. 'There's something else…'

He frowned. 'What?' He sat down again.

'When I got there, you know, just as the bomb exploded, the blast knocked me from my feet.' He could see the consternation in her eyes. 'This man picked me up. Just kind of lifted me to my feet. It almost seemed like he was smiling. You know, completely unaffected by what had just happened. There was panic, people were screaming. Smoke everywhere. And he just looked at me and said, "You're a lucky girl."'

Enzo had no idea where this was going. He searched her face for some understanding. 'You were.'

'But it was like he knew I should have been up there. How would he know that?'

'You ever heard of dog acting?'

Her face creased in puzzlement. 'What do you mean?'

'In TV and movies, when they cut away to a shot of the dog, the dog has no expression on its face. We, the viewer, read into it whatever expression is appropriate. Good actors know that. They can make a blank face say a thousand different things.'

'Dad, I don't understand.'

'You were right. How *would* he know that you should have been up there? You were the only one who knew that. So you were the one who transferred that interpretation to him.'

But she took no comfort in his words and simply shook her head. 'No.' She drew a deep breath. 'You see, the thing is, I just saw him again.'

'Where?'

'Here. In the station. Just before your train got in.'

And he felt the same shiver of fear that she had experienced just fifteen minutes before.

Chapter Nine

It was dark when they got there. The snow was wet, falling through the light of the streetlamps in drifts, like down, and thickly enough that it was starting to lie again. Enzo told their driver to wait for them and glanced around as Kirsty unlocked the front door. There was a *boulangerie* and an *agence immobilière* on the ground floor. Some of the windows on the upper floors had small balconies closed in by cast-iron railings. There was a modern apartment block next door, and a row of upmarket villas on the far side of the main road.

So this was where his little girl lived. The names on the doorplate all looked foreign. *Bozovic, Marinelli, Boukara*. He wondered if they were all interpreters like Kirsty. An electrician's van parked in the Rue Bernegger bore the name *Droeller-Scheer*. Nothing about this place seemed French. He might have been in another country.

He followed her up a dark stone staircase to a long landing with doors leading off to left and right. She hit the light switch and nothing happened. She said, 'It's an energy saver. Goes off by itself. Sometimes it just doesn't work.'

He held her arm to stop her going any further, and took out his keyring. There was a small pencil torch attached to it, about three inches long, that he used to find keyholes in the dark. 'I'll go first.' The thin beam of light pierced the darkness ahead of them.

'It's the one at the end. On the left.'

He stopped outside the door and shone his torch at the lock. He felt himself tense. 'Have you had a break-in recently? Forgotten your key, had to break in yourself?'

'No. Why?'

'This lock's been tampered with. See the scratches?'

She peered into the burned-out circle of light around the lock and saw tiny scratches shining in dull brass.

'Give me your key.'

She handed him her key and watched as he unlocked the door and pushed it gently inwards. If it were just himself, the knowledge of his impending death might have made him reckless. But responsibility for Kirsty made Enzo careful.

'Where's the light switch?'

'On the left.'

He felt for it with his left hand and found it. There was an audible click, but it brought no light to their world. 'Fuse box?' He spoke in little more than a whisper, although he was not sure why. If there was someone waiting for them inside, then he would know they were there by now.

'On the wall, on the right.'

He pushed the door wide and swung the pencil-thin rod of light up and right. He saw the square door of the box set into the wall. Then he flashed the light quickly around the room. It looked shambolic, and he heard Kirsty gasp. But there didn't seem to be anyone there. He stepped smartly inside, reached up to flip open the box and shone his torch into it. The *disjoncteur* switch was up. It should have been down. He flicked it down and the tiny studio apartment where his daughter lived was flooded with sudden harsh light.

'Oh, my God!' Kirsty gazed, horrified, around the studio. It was a mess. Furniture overturned, drawers emptied, clothes and papers strewn across the floor. She crossed quickly to her workdesk below the window. The drawers had all been pulled open. She checked the top one and saw that her passport, and a foldout wallet of credit and bank cards, were still there. 'He doesn't seem to have taken anything.'

Enzo swung open the door to the bathroom and turned on the light. There was no one there. But the contents of the wall cabinet had been thrown into the shower, and clean towels lay in untidy piles on the floor. He turned back towards Kirsty and saw that all the blood had drained from an already pale face. She looked shockingly white. He said, 'Looks like maybe he was just leaving a calling card. A message to say he'd been here.' He saw her bite her lower lip and crossed the room in three strides to take her in his arms. He rested his face on the top of her head and smelled the distant, familiar smell of her. 'Come on, pet. Throw some stuff in a bag and let's get out of here.'

He stood by the window waiting, watching the snow outside drift through the headlamps of the taxi. There were circular, dark, wet patches in the shadows cast by the trees across the street, and he saw a man emerge from one of them to leave a trail of black footprints as he crossed the road. He pulled up the collar of his long overcoat as he walked, then stooped at the open window where their driver was smoking a cigarette. They talked for half a minute before the man reached under his coat to bring out a wallet. Money changed hands, and he opened the taxi's rear passenger door and slipped inside.

'Hey!' Enzo shouted and banged on the window, then searched feverishly for the catch. Kirsty hurried through from the bathroom as he slid it up.

'What is it?'

'Some guy's taking our taxi.' He leaned out into the night and bellowed. 'Hey! Stop!'

If he heard him, the taxi driver took no notice. He swung the car across the street, then reversed into a three-point turn. Enzo and Kirsty watched helplessly as their taxi began to accelerate away in the opposite direction. And, as it did, they saw the upturned face of the man who had taken it, caught for just a moment in the streetlight.

Enzo heard his daughter catch her breath, and felt her fingers close around his arm. 'That's him!'

He turned towards her. 'Who?'

'The man at the press conference. The one I saw again at the station.'

Enzo turned to watch the taxi disappearing into the night. He felt himself succumbing to fear and confusion. This man was playing some kind of game. First he had tried to murder his daughter, and now he was toying with them. Almost laughing at them. Who in God's name was he? Why was he doing this? And for the first time, he had a strange sense of foreboding. Of something more than met the eye. Of something personal and pervasive. He turned back to Kirsty. 'Finish packing.' I'll phone for another cab.'

It was a further ten minutes, working his way through the Strasbourg *annuaire*, before Enzo finally got a taxi firm to answer his call. Only to be told that it would be up to an hour before a car would become available.

'I'm not waiting here.' Kirsty stood by her fold-down bed, like a child, clutching a sports bag stuffed with toiletries and underwear and a change of clothes. 'We can take a short-cut through the park, and maybe pick up a cab on the Avenue de l'Europe.'

◇◇◇

There was a traffic circle two hundred metres to the west of the apartment, and beyond that the brooding darkness of the Parc de l'Orangerie. They left foot-trails in the snow all along the sidewalk. There was precious little traffic on the roads. Temperatures were forecast to plummet, and all this wet snow would soon turn to ice. No one wanted to be out on a night like this. And those who were had taken every available cab.

They rounded the circle and crossed the street, and Enzo hesitated at the edge of the park. The path leading into it was half-obscured by leaves and snow, and vanished very quickly among the trees. 'I don't like this. Let's just walk around it.'

'It's okay, Dad. I've cycled and jogged through here a hundred times.'

'In the dark?'

She made a face. 'No one's going to be out in weather like this. And, anyway, it opens up once you get through the trees. Honestly, it'll take us twice as long to go around it.'

She took his arm with her free hand as they plunged off into the dark making virgin tracks in the snow. The path dipped a little before rising again through the trees. Across a stretch of open parkland to their right, Enzo could see the streelights along the Quai de l'Orangerie, and the headlamps of the occasional passing car. They had covered, perhaps, half a kilometre before he heard what sounded like footsteps following in their wake. He stopped and put a finger to his lips and listened. Nothing. Only the dead sound of the night, muffled by the snow.

'What?' Kirsty whispered. But he just shook his head and hurried them on. The park seemed to close in around them, suffocating and claustrophobic in the falling snow. He increased his pace, and Kirsty struggled to keep up.

And then there it was again. Only this time he didn't stop. He took his daughter's hand and started to run. At first she pulled back, but then she heard it too and glanced behind them to see shadows emerging from the dark. Now she needed no encouragement, and they ran as hard as they could towards the distant lights.

But suddenly the lights were not so distant. They were straight ahead of them, shining in their faces, blinding in their intensity, and they pulled up sharply, breathless and afraid. A flashlight came on behind them and, by its light, they could see four youths up ahead in hooded jackets. Two of them had flashlights, and Enzo saw a baseball bat hanging ominously from the hand of another. Two other youths approached from behind, their flashlight trained on Enzo, and he saw more bats. He put a protective arm across the front his daughter and steered her backwards to the side of the path.

'What do you want?' He let his bag drop to the ground.

'A bit fun. What do you say?' The face of the youth who spoke was hidden by the shadow of his hood. The young men had formed a half circle and were slowly closing in.

Enzo said, 'I've got a six inch blade on my hip, and I know how to use it.'

'I'm so scared.'

'You should be. There are five of you. And you'll take me down. I know that. But one of you, maybe two, are going with me. Count on it.' He paused to let the thought sink in. 'Who's going to be first?' There was an almost imperceptible hesitation in their forward movement.

'*Putain.*' It was one of the others. 'Just give us your wallet.'

'Why should I?'

The first one spoke up again. 'Just think what's going to happen to your daughter after we take you down.'

Enzo flinched. He reached beneath his coat and drew out his wallet, throwing it towards them so that it landed in the snow.

'You, too.' A flashlight swung into Kirsty's face and she threw her bag at their feet.

One of them stooped to open it up. He riffled quickly through the contents until he found her billfold with credit cards and notes. He removed the notes and stuffed them in his pocket and let the billfold drop back into the snow. He tossed her bag away and went through Enzo's wallet, removing the notes but leaving the plastic. He stood up, and flashlights that had been trained on the ground at his feet swung up again into the faces of their victims.

There was an odd hiatus, a momentary stand-off when it seemed that no one knew what would happen next. The one who had spoken first broke the silence.

'You really got a blade?'

Enzo stared boldly back at him. 'You want to find out?'

But the boy didn't take long to think about it. He turned to the others. 'Let's get out of here.'

Flashlights were extinguished, plunging them into sudden blindness, and the five hooded youths melted away into the falling snow.

Enzo and Kirsty stood for nearly a full minute before Enzo stooped to recover his wallet and Kirsty's billfold. She looked at him curiously as he went to retrieve her bag. 'Do you?' she said.

'Do I what?'

'Have a blade?'

He almost laughed. 'Of course not. But they didn't know that.' Then he shook his head and she saw the confusion in his eyes.

'What?'

He met her gaze. 'This wasn't just some chance mugging, Kirsty. They knew who we were.'

She frowned. 'How can you know that?'

'How else would they know you were my daughter?'

Chapter Ten

It took them forty minutes, once they left the park, to walk to the Place de Bordeaux. Every taxi was taken, and there were few other vehicles on the road. By the time they got to the shelter of the tram stop at Lycée Kléber they were both soaked through and frozen numb. At the north end of the square was the Holiday Inn, and beyond that the Palais des Congrès. Kirsty was unable to bring herself even to look in that direction.

She was unable, either, to stop shivering, and Enzo stood holding her in the dark, miserable and bewildered and depressed. The digital display overhead told them that the next tram would in three minutes. With fingers that had lost all feeling, he fumbled to use a credit card to buy them a ticket from the machine. After the third rejection he tried another card. And still the machine wouldn't accept it. Neither would it accept any of Kirsty's cards. He cursed, and felt like kicking the damned thing. They had no cash, and so they would have to ride the tram without tickets. Maybe they'd be arrested and thrown in jail. At least it might be warm there.

They waited alone, in silence, until the lights of the tram emerged from the darkness, its bell ringing as it rattled across the junction.

There were only a handful of other passengers on it. They cast disinterested glances at the cold, unhappy couple who got on board at the Lycée Kléber and sat side by side without speaking.

The tram creaked and strained and wound its way south along the Avenue de la Paix, around the Place de la République, and then east towards the Place de l'Homme-de-Fer—which translated, curiously, as Iron Man Square.

There they reluctantly stepped back into the icy blast, sheltering beneath a strange, circular construction of steel and glass. Then out into the snow again, huddled together, crossing the bridge on the Rue de Sebastopol to the Place des Halles where the Hôtel Ibis rose high into a snow-smudged sky, above the incongruously British C&A department store.

Enzo was already dreaming of a hot shower as they climbed the steps opposite the Lion d'Or Chinese restaurant, and glass doors slid aside to draw them into the warmth of the hotel reception.

'I have a reservation. Two rooms under the name of Macleod.'

The girl behind the desk tapped on her keyboard and scrutinised her screen. 'I'm sorry, monsieur, we've given those rooms away.'

Enzo stared at her in disbelief. 'What? Why?' His hot shower was suddenly fading into an uncertain future.

'I'm afraid your credit card was rejected.'

Enzo snorted his frustration. He had given them the number over the phone. 'That's not possible. There must be a mistake.' He fished in his wallet for his card. 'Here try it with the actual card.'

'I'm afraid it won't make any difference. The hotel is full.'

'Just try it, will you?' Enzo snapped at her and she winced, but decided not to argue. She slipped the card into the machine. He tapped in his code. They waited, and then she shook her head, with an undisguised pleasure. 'I'm sorry, monsieur. It's still rejected.'

He sighed heavily and gave her another card. 'Try with this one.' The girl set her jaw in sullen acquiescence and they went through the same procedure again. The second card was also rejected.

Kirsty pushed a card at the girl. 'Try one of mine.'

The same thing.

Enzo looked at his daughter. 'So it wasn't a faulty ticket machine at the tram stop. It was our cards.' He waved his hands in frustration. 'All of them. And that can't be a coincidence. Like the mugging in the park that left us without any cash. We're being shafted, Kirsty. Royally screwed.'

The girl behind the desk smiled at them with an infuriating smugness. 'I'm sorry. Like I said, the hotel *is* full. I'm going to have to ask you to leave.'

Outside, Kirsty fought to hold back the tears. She was very close to the end of her tether, and Enzo wasn't far behind. But crying about it wasn't going to help. She went into her purse in search of her cellphone. 'I'm going to call Roger.'

Enzo felt an irrational spear of anger jab at him through his misery. 'Why? What can Roger do? He's in Paris.'

'He can use his credit card to book us into a hotel by phone. And maybe he can come and get us in the morning.'

Enzo cast her a surly look. To involve Raffin would be like admitting that somehow he had failed. Good old Enzo charging to the rescue and falling flat on his face. But right now, he couldn't think of a viable alternative.

◇◇◇

They sat in a bar nursing coffees paid for with the handful of coins they had managed to scrape together from pockets and purses. Enzo stared morosely out into the street, watching each passer-by on the sidewalk, wondering if any one of them might be the stranger who was so efficiently deconstructing their lives. He tried not to listen as Kirsty explained their predicament to Raffin. He could just imagine how the young Parisian journalist would interpret their circumstance as somehow being Enzo's fault. He could picture the look of supercilious superiority on the face of his daughter's lover.

And then they waited, for nearly half-an-hour, before Raffin phoned back with the news that he had found them rooms at the Hôtel Regent in La Petite France.

◇◇◇

The River Ill divided in the centre of Strasbourg, sending a loop around the very heart of the old city, before it rejoined the main flow a couple of kilometres downstream. So the original mediaeval city centre, with its cathedral and six churches, was effectively an island. The east end of the island, with its wharves and waterways, and ancient narrow streets, was known as La Petite France. In the middle ages, it was home to the city's merchants and burgeoning middle class. It was now a main tourist attraction, filled with restaurants and hotels and souvenir shops.

Enzo and Kirsty turned down through a deserted square, the last customers sitting in the window of a vegetarian restaurant. A seventeenth century house on three floors, white-painted wattle and daub transected by ancient oak beams, was in the process of renovation. Staff were washing out the kitchens in the Maison des Tanneurs restaurant, with its Alsacienne specialities of *choucroute* and *tarte flambée*. It exhaled tantalisingly warm air at them as they passed. A revolving bridge led them across the river to where the Hôtel Regent had established itself in an old mill which had once served tanneries lining the riverbank.

As they trailed across the foyer to the reception desk, wretched and cold, Enzo noted with some satisfaction that a room cost nearly three hundred euros a night, and *petit-déjeuner* another twenty. Raffin would be less than happy with a bill on his credit card of more than six hundred euros.

Their rooms were high up in the roof, with windows overlooking the water below cutting deep into steeply sloping walls washed by subtly concealed lighting. The original supporting beamwork was painted white. Enzo carried Kirsty's bag into her room and they shed sodden coats. She went into the bathroom to fetch towels and threw him one to dry his hair.

He perched on the luggage rack at the end of her bed, weary and defeated, and loosened his hair from its band before rubbing it briskly with the towel. His skin was stinging in the warm air of the hotel room. He looked up and saw that Kirsty was flushed, and that her eyes were raw and puffy. He stood up. 'Come here.'

And she dropped her towel and let him fold his arms around her.

'We're going to be alright.' He wanted to say that they should make the most of their time together, because there was so very little of it left. But he didn't have the heart to tell her that he was dying. 'Have you finally forgiven me?' he whispered. And she immediately drew away.

She looked at him with a strange, distant hurt in her eyes, like a pet dog that has just been kicked by its trusted master. 'No,' she said simply. 'I'm not sure I can ever do that. You stole half my childhood, and that's not something I can ever get back.'

He wanted to tell her it wasn't like that, but there didn't seem any point. Linda had used her as a weapon against him and ended up poisoning her own child in the process. All he could think to say was, 'I'm sorry.' As he had said a thousand times before. 'If I could do it all again…'

'You'd what? You wouldn't leave us for your French lover?'

'I never left *you*. If I could have taken you with me I would.' But in his heart of hearts he knew that even if he could have done it all again, he would still have left for Pascale. And as he looked his daughter in the eye, he knew that she knew it too.

She said, 'When you came back into my life, you brought the pain back with you. And I had to confront the realisation then that the reason it hurt so much was because I loved you. And still do. Even if I can't forgive you.'

They were both startled by the shrill ring of his cellphone. The emotion between them dissipated like smoke in the wind. He glanced at the display and saw that it was Sophie, and he realised the irony in that. She was jealous of Kirsty and the place that her half-sister had in her father's heart. She might have taken some satisfaction from knowing that she had interrupted an intimate moment between them. But the thought quickly vanished when he heard the distress in her voice.

'Papa, there's been a disaster!'

'What is it, Sophie? What's happened?' He glanced up to see Kirsty watching him with her mother's dark eyes.

'There was a fire tonight. Bertrand's gym's been burned to the ground.'

Enzo closed his eyes and felt Bertrand's pain. At first, he had disapproved of his younger daughter's boyfriend. He was seven years older than her, wore studs and earrings and gelled his hair. But time had revised first impressions, and Bertrand had earned his grudging respect. He knew how much the gym meant to the boy. How he had held down two jobs to pay off the loan he had taken to convert the old *miroiterie* into a successful gymnasium, how he had worked to graduate from the CREPS centre in Toulouse with his degree in *musculation*, all the while supporting his widowed mother.

'Is he okay?'

'He closed up about an hour before it happened. We heard the fire engines before we saw the light in the sky. Someone phoned to say it was the gym.' He heard the catch in her voice. 'We stood on the Pont de Cabessut and watched it burn.'

'He's insured, though, yes?'

'Papa, you know how long that'll take to pay out. Bertrand doesn't know what he's going to do. He'll have to find the money to repay all the customers who've paid subscriptions.' He could tell that she was on the verge of tears. 'Papa, where are you?'

'I'm still in Strasbourg.'

There was a strange moment of silence, and then her voice fell away to barely a whisper. 'The police have been looking for you.'

'What? Why?'

'They wouldn't say. They've been at the door twice. Several of them. Papa, it wasn't a social call. I told them you'd gone to Strasbourg, but they didn't look like they believed me when I said I didn't have an address.'

Enzo was suddenly on full alert, his mind working over-time, slicing through the fatigue, making connections, drawing unpleasant conclusions. 'Sophie, I want you to leave the apart-ment immediately. You and Bertrand pack a bag each. Get him to take you to Nicole's father's farm in the Aveyron. You know where it is, don't you?'

'Papa why?'

'Just do it, Sophie. Trust me. It may be that the fire at the gym wasn't an accident. It's possible that there's a connection with what's been happening here in Strasbourg.'

'I don't understand…'

'You don't need to. Just believe me when I tell you that you could be in danger. I'll call Nicole's papa to let him know you're coming.'

When he hung up, Kirsty was looking at him perplexed. 'How can a fire in Cahors be connected with someone trying to kill me here?'

Enzo met her gaze with a steady intensity. 'I'm beginning to think that what's happened in Strasbourg isn't about you at all.'

'I think someone trying to kill me is very much about me.'

He shook his head. 'No. There's too much else going on. The mugging in the park. The credit cards—yours *and* mine. Bertrand's gym burning down, the police looking for me.'

'What do the police want you for?'

'I don't know. But I think there's a good chance that none of this has anything to do with you, or Bertrand, or Sophie. I think this might be about me.'

She looked at him long and hard, then picked up the towel she had dropped on the bed. She sighed wearily. 'It's always about you, Dad, isn't it? Always has been, always will be.' She turned towards the bathroom. 'I'm going to have a shower. You can let yourself out.'

Chapter Eleven

Yellow light reflected darkly off polished wooden floors. Rusted cogs and wheels and screws dipped down into dark waters behind glass walls, the machinery that once powered this old mill. There was only one other person at the bar, a woman nursing a champagne flute of pale, sparkling Dom Perignon.

Enzo hoisted himself onto a stool at the far end next to a large glass bowl filled with champagne bottles cooling in ice. The room was illuminated by the upward glow of backlit sheets of wafer thin marble that dressed the bar. He ran his eye along glass shelves lined with bottles. Although the hotel promoted this as a champagne bar, it had a decent selection of whiskies. He ordered a Glenlivet from a bored-looking young barman who poured him a large measure and then retreated to polish glasses at a discreet distance.

Enzo slumped over his drink for some time, simply looking at it, trying to find solace in its pale amber. But it wasn't the colour that would bring comfort, it was the alcohol. And if not comfort, then perhaps oblivion. A painful journey, on which he seemed reluctant to take the first step. And so he continued to stare at it, fighting to keep conflicting and unpleasant thoughts from his mind.

'It'll evaporate before you drink it.'

He looked up to see the only other customer regarding him with a quizzical smile. Until now he had paid her no attention.

But looking for the first time, he saw that she was attractive. Not in a pretty way, but with a strong jawline and well-defined cheekbones. Her eyes were dark, almost black, and she had an unusually small mouth with full lips. Until she smiled. It was a smile that split her face.

Long, silky brown hair was pulled back from her face and piled up loosely, untidily, behind her head. She was a woman well past the first flush of youth. Enzo thought she could be around forty, tall and lean. But she dressed younger. A short, black leather jacket, jeans and sneakers, and not a trace of make-up. Which was unusual for a woman of her age. She was either supremely self-confident or simply didn't care.

Her skin was tanned, as if she had just spent time somewhere in the sun, and examining her hands he saw that they were strong and elegant, with unpolished nails cut short.

'Maybe that's what I'm waiting for.'

'Why would you do that?'

'If I drink it, I'll only order another.'

He held her gaze for a moment, then returned it to his drink. He reached for the water jug, poured in a little water to release the flavour locked into it by the distiller, then filled his mouth to let it slip slowly over his throat. The aromatic flavour of it filled his nostrils, and its warmth burned all the way down into his chest. It felt good, but there was a long way to go before he would find the solace he sought.

'You know, it's funny...'

He looked up, surprised to find her still watching him. He had almost forgotten her already. 'What is?'

'It's not often that I find myself alone in a bar, and not being pestered by some man.'

'You should make the most of it, then. Some man might come in at any moment and try to pick you up.'

She gave a small shrug of resignation. It seemed that Enzo was not going to be the one to try. 'I guess maybe I'm getting to an age where men just stop noticing me.'

Enzo found a smile from somewhere. 'They'd have to be pretty blind.' He took another mouthful of whisky. 'Don't be offended. It's not you. It's me.'

She cocked an eyebrow. 'Gay?'

Which made him laugh unexpectedly. 'No. It's just...I have other things on my mind.'

'A problem shared is a problem halved.'

'Two swallows don't make a summer.'

For a moment, her forehead creased in a frown. And then she saw what the game was and a smiled snuck across her lips. 'Two minds are better than one.'

'An empty barrel makes the most noise.'

'Wise men agree, and fools seldom differ.'

But now his smile was strained. The game was already losing its power to distract, puerile and pointless. He had come here to get drunk. He drained his glass and ordered another.

She watched in silence as the barman refilled his glass, then she ordered another glass of champagne for herself. When the barman had poured it, bubbling to the rim of her glass, she lifted it and moved along the bar, slipping on to the stool next to Enzo. On another day, in other circumstances, he might have felt a tiny frisson of sexual excitement. Instead he felt that she was encroaching on his space, and he might have resented that. Except that she didn't give him the time.

'Why don't I buy you that one? I'll do the talking, and maybe that'll take your mind off whatever's worrying you.'

He was surprised for the second time by the smile that found his lips. 'Never fails.'

'What?'

'Every time I go into a bar on my own, I get pestered by some woman.'

It was her turn to laugh. 'Then I should introduce myself. That way I won't just be "some woman".' She held out her hand. 'Anna.'

He hesitated for just a moment before taking it. 'Enzo.' Her handshake was firm and warm. 'Women adore me.'

She grinned. 'Oh, do they?' She tilted her head and her look became appraising. 'Maybe I can see why.' She paused. 'Different coloured eyes. Very unusual.'

'Waardenburg Syndrome. Goes with the white stripe in the hair.'

'Is it fatal?'

He flicked her a look. But, of course, there was no way she could have known. 'Not the Waardenburg, no.' He drained his glass and felt the alcohol going straight to his head. He had still not eaten since breakfast. He waved the barman to refill the glass.

'Put them all on my room,' she told the barman. She sipped her champagne and looked at Enzo speculatively. 'Enzo. Short for Lorenzo, right? But you don't sound Italian.'

'Scottish.'

'And what brings you to Strasbourg?'

'I thought you were going to do the talking.'

'Well, I'd tell you what brings me to Strasbourg, but you probably wouldn't be interested.'

'Try me.'

'Parents,' she said, and she pursed her lips in a smile of regret. 'Elderly and failing, and full of recriminations about the daughter who doesn't come to see them often enough.'

'Why's that?'

'Because I'm never here.'

'In Strasbourg or in France?'

'Both. I'm a ski instructor. Based in Switzerland in the winter. I spend summers in the Caribbean teaching scuba diving. Which keeps me fit for the winter months.'

In spite of all the thoughts crowding an already overcrowded mind, Enzo finally found himself interested. Distracted. 'How does someone become a ski instructor?'

'There's not much else to do when you can't compete at the top level any more.'

'You were a professional?'

'Skied for France in two Olympics. Didn't win any medals, but I made the top ten. Trouble is, the body starts to decline just as the brain starts to develop. The intrinsic contradiction faced by every athlete. When you're young the flesh is willing, but you lack the experience. When you have the experience, the flesh is no longer willing. *Et voilà.* Those who can, do, and those can't, teach.'

'A bird in the hand's worth two in the bush.'

Her smile was a patient one. 'We're not going to start that again, are we?'

'Not if you don't want to.' He sucked down more whisky. 'So where to now? Switzerland?'

'Too early. The season's not properly underway yet. And my contract doesn't start for another month. I'm heading up into the Auvergne for a few weeks.'

'Pretty bleak up there at this time of year.'

'That's how I like it. English friends are lending me their holiday house. It's near a tiny village, lost in the hills somewhere to the east Aurillac. My sanity saver.'

'You're going up there all on your own?'

She shrugged. 'No one else to share it with.' She sipped at her champagne and stared into the endless stream of bubbles rising through her flute to break the surface. 'Funny, I never imagined I'd make forty and still be on my own.'

Enzo said, 'I've been on my own for twenty years. You get used to it.'

She looked at him curiously, then slipped her hand very gently over his. 'No one should have to be on their own. Ever. Life's too short for that.'

He turned towards her, to find a strange dark intensity in her eyes. Something almost sad. Compelling. And he felt a flutter in his stomach like startled butterflies. She had no idea just how short.

◇◇◇

The lights of La Petite France reflected off the water below, projecting flickering, amorphous images through the arched window and on to the far wall of Enzo's bedroom. By its monochrome light, he watched as Anna slipped off the tee-shirt she wore beneath her leather bomber, and shimmied out of her jeans. Until she stood in just black bra and panties, tall and elegant, with an almost boyish figure. Her skin was clear and tanned and smooth, and she moved with an innate grace towards the bed, the sure-footed balance of the skier in every step, dropping her bra on the floor to reveal the curve of small, firm breasts with dark, succulent areolae. She kicked off her pants and he saw the thin strip of her Brazilian-waxed pubis below the belly. Then she released the clasp behind her head to let her hair tumble freely across square shoulders.

In all his wildest imagination, he could never have foreseen this when he boarded the train in Cahors yesterday. And yet there was something about it that felt just right. To make love to a stranger on the eve of his death. No promises made, and none to keep. Perhaps the last time he would ever make love to a woman.

But it wasn't the sex, although she had succeeded in arousing powerful sexual instincts within him. It was the human contact. Skin on skin, the warmth of another person wrapped around him, comforting, consoling. A moment without past or future.

She straddled his chest, leaning over him, her breasts inches from his face, to release his hair and fan it out across the pillow. Then she dipped to kiss his forehead, his nose, his lips. Gentle, intimate kisses as if they had known each other all their lives. She ran fingertips through the hair on his chest, and slid down until her lips brushed his belly, and he felt the rush of blood to his loins. He ran his hands down her back, feeling smooth, firm muscles beneath his palms, and cupped full buttocks before turning her over, taking her by surprise, driven by sudden lust. She gasped as she felt his erection press hard against her belly, and he found her lips and tongue with his mouth to silence her. His fingers sought the soft, wet place between her legs, and grazed her repeatedly until she arched against him, and he slid down to bite her nipples and tease them with a darting tongue.

He felt her fingers digging into his back, and through palpitating breath heard her whisper, 'Now. Please, now.'

When it was over, he was spent in a way he had never known before. Fatigued beyond reason, in body and mind. He wanted to weep, to tell her everything. About Kirsty and Sophie and Pascale. And the sentence of death which had been passed on him just yesterday. But these were secrets best kept. Secrets that he would carry with him to the grave.

She lay beside him, curled into his hip, her breath on his shoulder, her hand on his belly, and he felt her take comfort in him. She too, had her secrets. Stories she would never share. A sadness behind dark eyes that she would never breach. He leaned over to kiss her forehead before closing his eyes to slip away into an unexpectedly deep sleep.

Chapter Twelve

It was raining, as it always seems to be. He was at a funeral. A Gaelic funeral, like they have in Scotland, the coffin resting on the backs of two chairs set out in the street. He was one of the bearers, dressed all in black. The women watched as the coffin was lifted, and the long walk to the cemetery began. They would not follow, for the women were not allowed at the graveside.

As they came over the top of the hill, the bells of the church ringing in their ears, they saw the gravestones like so many cropped stocks on the machair below, and he couldn't stop himself repeating the lines of the poem by John Donne,

And therefore send not to know for whom the bell tolls; it tolls for thee.

Over and over, like a mantra, penetrating his soul.

The bearers were soaked through by now, and his hands had become wet and slippery. He found that he could no longer keep his grip. Again and again he moved his hands to try to secure a firmer hold on his corner of the coffin. But it was slipping away from him, heavy and awkward. He called for help, but it was too late. It slid from his shoulder and pitched forward to the hard earth. There was a loud crack, and the polished wooden box split open, spewing the dead man from its silk interior to a grotesque final resting place on the metalled surface of the road.

Enzo watched in horror as the corpse rolled in slow-motion towards him, a face like death itself, eyes wide and staring, a purple bruised tongue protruding from pale lips. And he realised that he was looking at himself.

He woke up, still gasping from the shock of it, bedsheets damp and twisted around his body. His hair was in his eyes and his mouth. He sat up and swept it from his face, breathing hard, unable to shake off the knocking sound in his head, loud and insistent.

A grey morning light filtered from the semicircular window that overlooked the millpond below, and he realised, finally, that someone was knocking at the door. And suddenly he remembered Anna, and making love to her the night before, and he turned towards her. But the bed was empty. Cold. She was long gone. Like a dream. Perhaps, after all, she had really only been a figment of his imagination.

He slipped from the bed, a painful consciousness slowly returning, and pulled on a towelling bathrobe. The rich, red carpet felt soft under his feet as he walked to the door and opened it.

Raffin had his hand raised, ready to knock again. Kirsty was at his shoulder.

'For Heaven's sake, Dad, why didn't you answer? We thought something had happened to you.' She pushed past the journalist and into the room. Raffin followed and closed the door behind him.

Enzo was still sleep-confused. 'I…I was sleeping.' He looked at Raffin. 'When did you get here?'

'I got the six o'clock TGV from Paris.' He didn't look as if he had risen early. As usual, he was immaculately groomed. Cleanshaven, his hair a shining brown, swept back to the fashionably upturned collar of his linen jacket. His pale green eyes regarded Enzo speculatively. 'You sleep pretty soundly for a man whose daughter's life is under threat.'

Enzo looked for his watch, but his wrist was naked. 'What time is it?'

'Nearly nine.' Kirsty stooped to pick up Anna's meagre black bra. She looked at her father in disbelief. 'What's this?'

There was something like a smirk on Raffin's face. 'Well, it doesn't look like it would fit your father.'

Kirsty turned her consternation in Enzo's direction.

But before he could think of anything to say, the bathroom door opened, and a startled Anna stood in the doorway, a bathrobe hanging loosely on her angular frame, a towel wrapped around wet hair. 'Oh, I'm sorry, I didn't realise there was someone else here?'

Enzo glanced with embarrassment towards his daughter, and saw anger and humiliation blazing in her eyes. Raffin stepped in quickly. 'We were just leaving.' He took Kirsty's arm and led her firmly out into the corridor. He cast Enzo a parting glance that seemed to carry the conflicting attributes of both admonition and admiration.

When the door shut, Enzo turned sheepishly towards Anna. 'I thought you'd gone.'

'Who were they?'

'The girl's my daughter. Kirsty. Raffin's her boyfriend.'

Something in his tone made her cock an eyebrow. 'You sound as if you don't approve.' She began gathering her clothes together.

'I don't.'

'And does her mother share your view?'

'I wouldn't know. I divorced her more than twenty years ago. Kirsty's never forgiven me.'

'Ah.'

'What does that mean?'

'Just…ah.' She clutched her clothes to her chest. 'I think I preferred it when we didn't know too much about one another. And I certainly don't want to get between a father and his daughter.' She gave him one of her sad smiles. 'I think I'd better go.' She crossed the room to give him a tiny, soft kiss on the lips. 'I loved making love with you last night.' And then she hesitated. 'Although you should know…I'm not in the habit of sleeping with strangers.' She closed her eyes for a fleeting moment of introspection. 'I was feeling pretty low, too. Maybe fate brought us together, just to take the pain away for one night.'

He nodded. 'Maybe.'

She looked at him long and searchingly, and he thought that whatever pain it was that she was suffering, it brought a kind of tortured beauty to her face. She crossed to the dresser and laid her clothes in the chair and lifted a hotel pen from the desk. She turned a pad of letterheaded notepaper towards her and scribbled a quick address and phone number. She tore it off and held it out towards him. 'That's where I'm staying for the next few weeks. If you get lonely.'

He took it, almost absently, folding it and slipping it into the pocket of his robe. 'Sure,' he said, knowing that he would never see her again.

She lifted her clothes and headed for the door. A fleeting, backward glance and she was gone.

Chapter Thirteen

The dining room, behind long net drapes, doffed its cap to the colours and culture of the sixties. Red leather chairs and black steel tubing, faux woodgrain formica veneer, and shaggy grey carpet. Hotel guests dipped croissants in steaming black coffee and tried to give the impression that they couldn't hear Kirsty railing at her father.

Her voice was shrill, and filled with accusation, despite Raffin's best attempts to calm her down. He disliked scenes.

'Someone tried to kill me a couple of days ago. I'm being stalked by the man who was almost certainly responsible for that. The same man who probably broke into my apartment, and set a bunch of kids to steal our money in the park. The same man who somehow fixed it that all our credit cards are out of credit…' She drew a deep breath for the denouement. 'And all you can think to do is pick up some woman in a bar. To follow your dick, just like always?'

Raffin was shocked. 'For God's sake, Kirsty!' He glanced anxiously at the heads turning in their direction.

But she was past caring. This was betrayal. This was the man in whom she had put her trust. The man she had turned to for help when her world was crashing around her. And while she was crying herself to sleep in the room next door, her father was screwing some woman he'd just picked up in a bar. It was unforgivable.

Enzo saw the pain in his daughter's eyes, the absolute belief that somehow he had let her down. And maybe he had. Maybe he always had. But with the selfishness of a child, she never made any allowance for the feelings of others. He shook his head. 'You don't understand.'

'No, I don't. And I don't want to.'

'Well, maybe that's part of the problem. You don't know me. You've never wanted to know me.'

'Oh, and you know me, do you? You weren't around for most of my life, so how's that possible?' She was right on the edge, breath coming in short, sharp bursts.

Enzo stared at her, anger, frustration, guilt, all boiling together inside him. 'You've spent twenty years blaming me. For all those little things that didn't please you. For every unhappiness you ever felt. It was my fault. Never yours, never your mother's. Always mine. You've defined your entire life by blaming me for everything that's wrong with it. Well, you're going to have to find someone else to blame pretty damned soon. And maybe that's a good thing. Because when I'm not around any longer, you won't have some convenient scapegoat to blame for your own shortcomings. And maybe, finally, you'll start taking responsibility for yourself.'

He screwed up his napkin and threw it on the table. Almost on the verge of tears he stood up, turning abruptly through the net curtains and striding away across the marble foyer.

Kirsty was stunned to silence. She had never been on the receiving end of her father's ire. Never felt the full force of his hurt and frustration. And it took a moment before the implications of what he had said fully sank in. She turned to search Raffin's pale green eyes for reassurance, but found only embarrassed bewilderment. Colour had risen high on his cheeks. 'What did he mean?'

Raffin shook his head. 'I've no idea.'

Kirsty rose quickly, nearly upsetting the table, and went chasing through the columns after her father.

The elevator doors were closing by the time she reached them. She got a hand in just in time, and they slid open again to reveal Enzo standing alone under the harsh electric light. He looked tired, washed out, dark shadows beneath his eyes. Diminished somehow. And almost for the first time in her life she saw him as being old, failing, less than the image of tall, youthful strength she had carried with her since childhood. The doors slid shut and they rose slowly together through the old mill in an awkward silence that neither knew quite how to break.

Finally she said, 'What did you mean, you wouldn't be around any longer?'

He pursed his lips. 'Nothing.'

'It didn't sound like nothing to me.'

'A turn of phrase.'

'Bullshit.'

He looked at her and found himself speared by her dark, searching eyes. He might have resisted a little longer, kept his secret to himself, a little ball of poison screwed up inside of him. But there didn't seem any point any more. She would find out soon enough. They all would. 'I'm dying.'

Two simple words, dropped like toxic pearls into a young life that had never contemplated a world without him. He was right. She had used her anger at him to define everything about herself. When she had failed, it was his fault. When she had succeeded, it was to show him that she didn't need him. But she did. She heard her own voice like a whisper in the dark. 'How…?'

'Leukemia. They say I've got six months if I take the chemo. But I'm not going to do that.'

'Why?'

'It's been a checkered life, Kirsty. I've known pain and tragedy, sure. But I've loved some wonderful women. I have two beautiful daughters. And I've always had my health. I'm not going to spoil my last months by taking chemotherapy.'

The elevator jerked to a halt and the doors drew apart. He pushed past his daughter and strode down the hall towards his room, afraid that she might see his tears. He had almost reached his door when she caught up with him, grabbing his arm and forcing him to face her.

She was flushed, her face shining and wet. 'I'm sorry, Dad. I'm so sorry.' She drew a long, fibrillating breath. 'You're right. I was so obsessed with blaming you for everything, it never occurred to me there might be a time when you wouldn't be there. And who would I have to blame then?'

He put his arms around her and pulled her tightly to him, and she was just his little girl again, tiny and vulnerable and dependent.

Her voice was muffled against his chest. 'You asked me last night if I'd forgiven you. And I said no. Well, I was wrong. I just realised, for the first time in my life...there's nothing to forgive.' He felt her body racked by sobs. 'I don't want you to die.'

At the far end of the corridor, elevator doors opened and Raffin stood looking down the hallway at father and daughter in each other's arms.

Chapter Fourteen

They headed north and west out of the city in the BMW that Raffin had rented. The slip road from the D263 took them on to the A4 for Paris. There were signposts to places like Hagenau, Karlsruhe, Saarbrücken. Ghost names from a German past, punctuating an Alsatian landscape where men had fought and died for the right to fly a flag, and pay their taxes to another master.

Enzo lounged in the back watching the dull November landscape slide past, grey and misty and damp. He would never see another spring, or ever again feel the warmth of the summer sun. If he could have chosen a time to die it would not have been in winter. Kirsty sat in a brittle silence in the passenger seat, hands clasped tightly between her legs. There didn't seem anything left to say.

They were about two kilometres from the *gare de péage*, where tickets were dispensed for the toll portion of the *autoroute*, when they hit a tailback, vehicles backed up all the way from the rows of booths strung across the highway ahead. Raffin shifted down to second gear and they crawled slowly forward through the exhaust fumes.

It was Raffin, finally, who broke the silence. He half turned towards Enzo. 'So why do you think you're the target for all this *merde*?'

'Because there's too much going on with only one thing in common.'

'And that's you?'

Enzo nodded. 'What else connects an attempt to kill Kirsty with the burning down of Bertrand's gym? A robbery in a park, with the cutting-off of my credit?'

Kirsty turned in her seat, her face a mask of incomprehension. 'But why? What's the point?'

'I can only think of one reason.'

Raffin was watching him in the rearview mirror. 'Which is?'

'Your book.' He saw Raffin's eyes crinkle incredulously.

'What are you talking about?'

'You researched and wrote about seven unsolved murders, right?'

'I don't see the relevance.'

'Given the media coverage we've had, there can't be anyone in France who doesn't know that I'm engaged in trying to solve those murders. Including the killers.'

Kirsty said, 'You think it's one of the murderers who's done all this?'

'Of Roger's seven cases, I've cracked two in the last couple of years. If you were one of the remaining five, wouldn't you be starting to feel a little insecure?'

Raffin said, 'But why wouldn't he just kill you?'

'Someone already tried at Gaillac. But that was before I caught the killer there. If someone were to assassinate me now, it would seem pretty obvious that it was one of the remaining murderers. And someone else might start going after them. But if he just wrecks my life, takes it apart piece by piece, my investigations will simply stop. And it's highly unlikely that anyone else is going to step in to fill my shoes.'

They lapsed again into silence, absorbing Enzo's theory, picking at its flaws, unravelling its frayed edges to see if it would still hang together.

Then it was Enzo who broke the silence once more. 'If only he'd known I was going to die anyway, he wouldn't have had to bother.'

They were approaching the tollbooths now, and beyond the lines of traffic ahead, saw for the first time what was causing the tailback. There was a phalanx of blue *gendarmerie* vans parked off to one side, and twenty or more *gendarmes* checking papers before allowing anyone through the booths. They wore tall, kepi hats, and waterproof capes to protect them from the rain, nervous hands never far from holstered guns.

'Must be a terrorist alert,' Raffin said. It was unusual for every car to be stopped for a simple traffic check.

As they approached the head of their line it became clear that the *gendarmes* were carrying out identity checks on all the occupants of every car, driver and passengers alike. Raffin fumbled for his ID card, and Kirsty took out her passport. Enzo found his *carte de séjour* and flipped it absently between his fingers, brooding still on the man who had so nearly killed his daughter just to ruin his life. Whichever of the five remaining killers he might be, Enzo's investigations to find him would no longer revolve around a professional re-examination of the evidence. This was personal. And he didn't have much time.

Raffin drew up and three *gendarmes* peered in through wet glass. He rolled down the driver's window and held out his ID card. But the *gendarme* was looking beyond him, towards the back seat. He flicked a quick glance at his colleagues, and one of them opened the rear passenger door and drew his gun in one swift movement.

'Hey!' Raffin turned in alarm to see Enzo being pulled from the car. He turned back to find a pistol pointed at his face.

'Out of the car! Everyone out of the car!' Suddenly all the *gendarmes* were shouting at once. There came the sound of feet running through the wet, men in dark blue crowding around their car, Raffin and Kirsty dragged roughly out into the rain.

Kirsty saw her father face down on the tarmac, five *gendarmes* around him. His arms were pulled behind his back and she heard the snap of handcuffs locking in place. It all happened so fast, there was no time even to think about it. But now she screamed as loud as she could, before being spun around and banged up against the car. All the breath was knocked from her lungs, and she couldn't even find a voice to raise in protest. But she could hear Raffin's angry admonitions.

'What the hell do you think you're doing? I'm a journalist!'

And the voice that replied, tight with tension. 'So maybe you'd like to tell us why you have a killer in the back of your car?'

PART TWO

Chapter Fifteen

South of France, June 1986

Richard had mixed memories of the place. He had hated school. In those days it had been on the Rue de la Démocratie, opposite the *boulodrome* and the beach, with a view out across the bay to the red-roofed Eglise Notre Dame des Anges, with its distinctive Byzantine bell tower. There was something not quite right about being stuck in a classroom, with all that blue Mediterranean on the other side of the glass.

On fine days, when stormy seas allowed, he would follow the stone quay beneath the towering walls of the Château Royal to the Quai de l'Amirauté, where yellow and blue painted sail boats with their crooked crossed masts bumped and creaked and strained against the swell. A quayscape made famous by the paintings of André Derain.

He would lean on the railings and watch the commandos training, streaming out from the *château* and into the water in full kit to launch rubber dinghies into the bay. Sometimes they would be taken out beyond the harbour wall and tipped overboard, to make their own way back to shore.

With his home in the Rue Bellevue being almost directly below Fort Miradou, he had grown up with the sight of soldiers in the street. He had always admired the way they carried themselves and how their hair was cropped, and the green khaki of their uniforms above shiny black boots. It was here, perhaps, that the seeds of later ambition had been sewn.

The Rue Bellevue was aptly named, running along the clifftops above the old town, looking out to sea. He lived with his mother at the end of a row of stone cottages at the far end of the street. When it was stormy, the house took a battering. When it wasn't, he would spend hours perched on the rocks at the end of the garden watching the sea break against the cliffs below.

There was a time when he was bullied at school. Until he jabbed a pencil into the eye of the school bully and nearly blinded him. No one had come near him after that.

It had been the beginning of the end of the relationship with his mother. There had never been any love lost between them. She had been unbearably protective, smothering him with a love that had been suffocating and selfish. And as he grew into his teens, he had become rebellious, argumentative, disobedient. Their relationship, finally, had been fatally fractured when she'd had his dog put down. It had been done at her insistence after he'd suffered a severe allergic reaction which nearly killed him.

It had been inexplicable. Domi and Richard had been best friends for five years, ever since his mother had brought the dog home as a puppy. Richard had never once suffered a reaction in all that time. But the doctor had said that almost anything could trigger an allergy.

Richard had never believed it was Domi. Not then. Not till later. But that came after the discovery that would shake his life to its very foundations.

He was due to sit his *baccalauréat* the week he found out. Which is why he never took the exam. His mother had been out somewhere, and he was studying. Or, at least, trying to. But he'd been distracted by the sunshine, bright light coruscating like scattered diamonds across the deep blue waters of the bay. Looking back, he could never remember what had drawn him to the attic. Boredom, probably. It was years since he had been up there in the dust and the heat.

A bright slash of sunlight falling from the skylight lay across the forgotten junk of a lifetime in dazzling, jagged splinters. And it was amongst that junk that he found his mother's old trunk and its treasure of family memorabilia, the detritus of a life he knew nothing about.

His father was dead. She had told him that much. But she had never spoken of grandparents or siblings or cousins or aunts and uncles. And here were photographs of people he had never seen. Family albums filled with fuzzy black and white prints, faded names written in English in an old-fashioned hand. Grandfather Peglar, Granny Topps, Aunt Hylda, Selena and Frank. Richard looked at unfamiliar faces staring back at him from a long forgotten past.

Of course, he knew his mother was English. It was the language she had insisted they always speak in the house, but it had never occurred to him that there might still be family back in England. The pictures in the album, however, were from another era, and these folk, at least, were long dead.

He rummaged through the trunk and found a pack of coloured photographs that looked as if they might have been taken in his lifetime. He squinted at the top picture and saw the date burned red into the bottom corner of the photograph by the developer.

23/07/70

He shuffled through the photographs. Views across a bay to white Mediterranean houses clinging to a steep hillside leading to a large church, a jumble of rooftops, red terracotta Roman tiles. Shops along a seafront. Posters in Spanish promoting a local corrida. This was Spain.

Then a family on a beach. A mother and father and three children. They were posing for a photograph, smiling at the camera. But not the one that took this photograph. There was an unseen photographer somewhere off to camera right. There were two boys and a girl. The boys were little more than toddlers. The girl was about five. One of the boys had his head turned away, and the other was looking straight towards the lens that had captured his image. Straight towards Richard.

If it was possible that your heart could stop, and yet you could go on living, Richard would have said that his heart had stopped. Because there was absolutely no doubt in his mind. He was looking at himself. And in some very strange way, he was almost able to conjure a recollection of the moment.

But even stranger was that none of these other people was familiar.

He flipped quickly through the other photographs, but that was the only one of the group on the beach.

He was unsettled. Who were these people? His mother had never spoken of a holiday in Spain. He put the photographs aside and delved deeper into the trunk, finding a worn leather document holder. He opened it up to find a collection of yellowing family papers, extracts from the register of births, marriages, and deaths. There was his mother's birth certificate. Selina Anne Peglar, born 19th May, 1939. A certificate of marriage to his father, Reginald Archangel, on September 9th, 1964. Then his father's death certificate, dated just six months before the birth of his son in September, 1968. Beneath that was his own birth certificate. September 20th. He looked at the entry for his father, which described him simply as *Schoolmaster*, and wondered briefly what he had been like. But he quickly put away the thought. It made no difference now.

He slipped the final certificate out from its plastic sleeve, and everything he had ever thought he knew about himself fell headlong into a place of impenetrable darkness. In trembling hands he held the death certificate of an eighteen-month-old boy who had died from heart failure on March 18th, 1970. The boy's name was Richard Archangel.

It was his own death certificate.

Chapter Sixteen

Cahors, November 2008

The mist and cloud which had hung over Cahors for days had finally lifted. A winter sun hung low in the clearest of blue skies, banishing the dreary November damp, and replacing it with cold, crisp air.

Enzo could see cracks of sunlight around the edges of shutters closed firmly on the barred windows of his interrogation room somewhere in the bowels of the *caserne*. It was a small room, walls scarred by graffiti, witness to the hundreds of prisoners who had spent time here under the harsh glare of fluorescent light, claiming innocence, just like him.

The police had heard it all before.

Enzo was restless, like a caged animal. He couldn't stay in his seat for more than a few minutes at a time, prowling the room, angry and depressed, in desperate search of a way out of all this.

The *gendarmes* had told him nothing, treating him like a criminal already tried and convicted by the courts. He had remained handcuffed during the long, eleven hour journey back to Cahors in the back of a darkened van, cramped and uncomfortable, allowed out only twice to relieve himself at the side of the road, blinded by the sudden daylight.

Now, after a night in the cells of the Police Nationale in Cahors, he faced the woman he had once considered as a prospective lover.

Commissaire Taillard was still an attractive woman, silky brown hair tied in a bun at the back of her head to reveal a strong, faintly slavic face with high cheekbones and gently slanted almond eyes. Her dark cherry red lips were full, and set in an unaccustomed line of genuine gravitas as she gazed at him with dark, disappointed eyes across the interrogation desk.

He tried to remember why it was they had never quite hit it off. On the face of it they'd had a lot in common. The local chief of police, and a man who had once been the top forensic scientist in his native Scotland. They had dated on a number occasions. She had been his partner on invitations to several dinner parties. People had begun to talk about them as a couple, to speculate. Oddly, he had preferred her in uniform. Out of it, there was something strangely old-fashioned about her, and although she was a passionate woman, she had failed to arouse the same degree of passion in him. Perhaps, had they consummated their relationship, that might have changed. They had come close one night after dinner at his appartment. Things had advanced to a state of semi-undress when Sophie returned with Bertrand, catching them *in flagrante delicto*, an inconvenient and embarrassing *coitus interruptus* that they somehow never managed to complete on any future occasion.

He supposed it was he who had let the relationship wither. Not a conscious decision, just a gradual retreat. And he had the sense that she somehow blamed him.

Now he was being forced to deal with her on quite a different basis, and the presence of the armed officer guarding the door precluded the possibility of any communication between them on a personal one.

He wanted to say, *For God's sake, Hélène, it's me. You know I'm not capable of anything like this.* But all he said was, 'It's absurd, *commissaire*, completely insane.'

'Do you deny knowing her?'

'Of course not. I met Audeline at a party about six weeks ago. I've seen her a few times since.'

Commissaire Taillard consulted an open folder on the table in front of her. 'You had dinner together last week at the Fils des Douceurs floating restaurant.'

Enzo flicked her a look. It was where he and Hélène had first dined alone together. But she was impassive. 'Yes.'

'Were you having sex?'

Enzo felt himself flush with unaccustomed embarrassment. It seemed like such a bald question on such a personal matter, especially coming from a woman with whom he had failed to become intimate. He glanced at the officer guarding the door, but if he had thoughts on the subject, his face did not betray them. He decided on flippancy. 'Not during dinner.' It felt as if the temperature in the room had dropped ten degrees. He revised his approach. 'How is that relevant?'

'There may have been a sexual element to the attack, Monsieur Macleod. The victim's blouse had been ripped open and her bra torn off, so the question is pertinent.'

Enzo closed his eyes. It was easy to forget, as he drowned in a sea of his own troubles, that a woman who had aroused feelings in him had been murdered. Very probably because of him. He opened his eyes again to banish the unpleasant images that came to him in the dark.

Commissaire Taillard still held him in her gaze. 'Your e-mails were certainly of an intimate nature.'

So she had read their e-mail exchanges. Enzo blushed, in spite of himself. He should have known better than to commit his feelings to writing. But sometimes the Italian in him would overcome the natural reticence of the Scot.

'No,' he said.

'No what?'

'No, we weren't having sex.'

Still there was nothing in her expression to betray her emotions, but he noticed that her face, in contrast to the colour he felt rising on his own, had grown very pale. 'What was the purpose of your visit to her apartment on the morning she was murdered?'

'I wasn't at her apartment.'

'According to her computer diary you had a rendezvous at her apartment at 11am.'

'I can't help that. I wasn't there.'

'Where were you, then?'

He hesitated. 'I had an appointment with an oncologist.'

She frowned. 'An oncologist?'

'A cancer specialist.'

'I know what an oncologist is!' The unasked question got as far as her lips but not beyond them. 'Where?'

'Here in Cahors.'

'And presumably this…doctor, will be able to bear that out?'

'Of course.'

She seemed torn, as if somehow wanting to believe him, and not. Both at the same time. 'You should know that the sample of your hair that we took on your arrival yesterday has been sent to Toulouse for comparison with several long, black hairs recovered from the clothes of the deceased.'

Enzo shrugged. 'So they won't match.' He pulled up his chair suddenly and sat down opposite her, leaning forward with earnest intent. 'Look, Hélène, I've got a cast iron alibi. A paper trail that leads all the way from my GP to the oncologist, and then the doctor himself at the end of it. Why don't we just follow that trail and put an end to this nonsense?'

◇◇◇

It was good to have the blue sky overhead, and fresh, cool air in his lungs again, even if only for a few moments. The police car pulled up outside Enzo's apartment and a uniformed officer helped him out from the back seat. His hands were cuffed in front of him, and he caught a momentary glimpse of his reflection in the window of the Lampara restaurant. They had taken away his hairband, although the notion that he might have tried to hang himself with it seemed more than faintly absurd. So his hair was a straggling mess, tumbling over his shoulders. He hadn't shaved in two days. His jacket was stained and dirty from where they had pinned him down on the wet tarmac.

He saw the faces of people he knew, shopkeepers, neighbours, regulars at the restaurant, turning to watch with shocked curiosity as he was led by a uniformed officer to the door of the stairwell. Commissaire Taillard followed stiffly in their wake. A woman of authority on public display.

On the first landing, she rang the doorbell and waited. There was no reply. She looked at Enzo as if he could explain why there was no one at home. He just shrugged, and she took his keys and unlocked the door.

As they went into the hallway Enzo saw, through the open door of the spare bedroom, Kirsty's *valise* on the unmade bed, and Raffin's distinctive soft leather overnight bag on the chest of drawers. So, they were sharing a room.

In the *séjour* he crossed to his desk and began searching through his papers. He had tossed his letter of appointment into a wire tray where he placed documents awaiting filing. He'd had no idea where to file it, or if he ever would. But it wasn't there. It should have been on top of the heap. He lifted out the untidy pile of miscellaneous bills and letters and shuffled through them with an increasing sense of alarm.

'It's gone.'

'The letter from your GP?' Commissaire Taillard was looking at him sceptically.

'Yes.'

'The one with the date and time of your appointment with the oncologist?'

'Yes.'

'How very convenient.'

'It's not at all convenient. Maybe Sophie or Kirsty took it.' Enzo could feel the colour rising on his cheeks. 'Look, why don't we just cut straight to the chase. If you just take me to see the oncologist, that puts an end to it once and for all.'

She sighed, patience stretching to its limit. 'What was it you were seeing him for?'

Enzo's eyes dipped away towards the floor. Only Kirsty and Roger knew the truth, and each time he had been forced to say it out loud it just seemed to compound its inevitability. 'I've got terminal cancer,' he said. And looked up to see the shock in her face.

◇◇◇

The Rue des Trois Baudus looked different in the sunshine. In Enzo's memory it had been a very dark place. Now sunlight spilled down between the buildings, bringing colour to brick walls and painted shutters. They had walked up the Rue du Château du Roi from the Place de la Libération, where the police driver had parked. The assistant in the music store had waved as they passed, but his hand had frozen in mid air when he saw that Enzo was in handcuffs. Sunshine struck the building at the far end of the Rue des Trois Baudus where it took a right-angled turn to the left out into the Rue du Portail Alban. Even the graffiti, in black and purple, seemed more decorative than defacing.

They stopped outside the pale oak door of number 24 *bis*. The window to the left was still shuttered and barred, but the oncologist's plaque had been removed, leaving only four small screw holes in the wall to bear witness to its ever having been there. Enzo stared at the blank space in confusion. The *boîte postale* to the right of the door was stuffed to overflowing with *publicité*.

'Is this it?' Commissaire Taillard was beginning to lose patience.

Enzo tried to stay calm. 'Yes. There was a plaque on the wall right here. The doctor's name was Gilbert Dussuet. And there was a sign below the bellpush saying ring and enter.' But there was no sign there now. Commissaire Taillard pressed the bellpush and they were greeted by silence.

'Sounds like it might have been out of commission for some time,' she said.

Enzo lifted his chained hands and made fists to bang on the door. There was no response. 'I'm not lying.' He turned towards her troubled gaze. 'This is where I was the morning Audeline

was murdered. This is where Docteur Dussuet had his *cabinet*.'
He shrugged in frustration. 'He must have moved.'

'What's all the damned noise down there!' A voice rang out
from above, and they all swung their heads up to see an elderly
woman leaning from a window on the first floor opposite. She
had thrown her shutters wide, and was so pale you might have
thought she had not seen daylight in months.

'Police,' the Commissaire said. 'Who occupies this property
here at 24 *bis*?'

The woman looked down at them as if they were mad. 'No
one. Place has been empty for a couple of years.'

'There was a doctor's surgery here,' Enzo called up to her. 'A
Docteur Dussuet.'

'No.' The old woman shook her head. 'Never been a doctor
here in all my time. And I was born in this house.'

Enzo felt the world falling away beneath his feet. The certainty that had fuelled him was dissolving into bewilderment
and confusion. He turned to meet his nearly lover's cold stare.
Her cellphone rang, and she put it to her ear.

'Commissaire Taillard...' She listened in silence for a long
time. Then, 'Thank you,' she said, and hung up. Her eyes never
left Enzo's. 'Well, well, well. It seems that the sample of hair that
we took from you yesterday matches the hair found on the body.'
She pursed her lips, all sympathy and willingness to believe him
long since vanished. 'What do you suggest we do now?'

◇◇◇

Clémont Marot had been a fifteenth century French poet, a
protégé of Marguerite de Navarre, the sister of the then king,
François Premier. A famous son of Cahors, it seemed slightly
insulting to have named such a mean little square after him.
You might pass it without noticing. But it was through a large,
arched *portail* on its northeast corner, that Enzo's GP had his
practice, in a building shared by several *notaires*.

His receptionist said that Docteur Julliard was with a patient
and that they would have to wait. So the two police officers and

a dishevelled Enzo sat in the crowded waiting room for more than ten minutes, studiously avoiding the openly curious stares of patients awaiting their appointments.

When, finally, the receptionist showed them into his surgery, Docteur Julliard rose, startled, from his desk. He looked at Enzo in disbelief. 'Good God, man, what's happened to you?'

Commissaire Taillard said, 'Monsieur Macleod is being questioned in connection with a murder which took place in the town three days ago.'

'No!' Docteur Julliard could not conceal his disbelief.

'Monsieur Macleod insists that at the time of the murder he had a rendezvous with an oncologist which you made on his behalf.'

Now the doctor turned his disbelief towards Enzo. He shook his head. 'I don't understand, Enzo.'

'You sent me a letter, following my blood tests. An appointment with a Docteur Gilbert Dussuet.'

'I'm afraid I didn't. I would only have written to you if anything abnormal had shown up.'

'And it didn't?' the Commissaire asked.

'No. Everything was as it should be.'

'So you didn't refer Monsieur Macleod to an oncologist?'

'Certainly not.'

Enzo stood staring at his doctor, uncertain whether to laugh or cry. At a stroke his death sentence had been lifted, and he had become the prime suspect in a murder.

The Commissaire clearly shared the thought. She turned to him, a tiny sarcastic smile playing around the corners of her mouth. 'You see? Nothing wrong with you, Monsieur Macleod. You're not going to die after all. You're just going to spend the rest of your life in prison.'

Chapter Seventeen

Guildford, England, July 1986

Richard walked through the carpark towards the nineteenth century Artington House with its brick gables, and twisted wisteria. It stood behind manicured lawns shaded by tall trees in full summer leaf. The roar of traffic from Portsmouth Road retreated behind him as he climbed the steps to its main entrance.

At first she had denied it. Insisted he had made some kind of mistake. But when he threatened to go up to the attic to retrieve the certificate, she had forbidden him. He had never to go up there again. It was off limits. And then she simply refused to discuss it. He had exams to study for, and better things with which to fill his head.

And as far as she was concerned, that was an end to it.

But for Richard it was just the beginning.

He had retired to his room then, and looked around it for the last time without the least sense of emotion. These were the walls that had contained him for most of his seventeen years. Home to the accumulated junk of childhood. His collection of toy soldiers, posters and paintings and albums, his old rugby strip hanging over the back of a chair. His Spanish guitar. So many things he knew he would never miss.

He packed a sports bag with some underwear, a couple of tee-shirts, a pair of jeans, tennis shoes, and a pair of open-toed sandals. He took all his savings from the envelope he had taped beneath his desk drawer and stuffed it in his wallet. He lifted his favourite denim jacket from the back of the door, slipped his passport into an inside pocket, and released the catch that held his bedroom window.

He dropped through the dark into the little square of garden behind the arched gate that led to the lane beyond, and crouched there for a moment listening to the sound of the cicadas. The warm evening air was filled with the scent of bougainvillea and pine and the smell of the sea. As his eyes adjusted, he glanced down to where phosphorescent waves broke over glistening black rock fifty feet below. The sea felt alive. His sea. He could hear it breathing. It was the only thing he would miss.

◇◇◇

The woman behind the desk in the office smiled at him. He said he had phoned earlier about acquiring a copy of his brother's death certificate. She remembered him, and he was struck by how readily she took him at face value. He might have been born in this country, but he had spent all his conscious life in France. He spoke French with a southern accent. He listened to Francis Cabrel and Serge Gainsborough. He had a crush on France Gall. And yet his English was so convincing this woman took him for a native. Perhaps he even looked English. One more chip out of his sense of self.

She produced the freshly printed extract and signed it, and he paid for it with the strange notes and coins for which he had exchanged his francs at the bureau de change in London, before catching the train down to Surrey. He glanced at the certificate, and felt again the touch of icy fingers on his neck when he saw his name on it. 'Can I see the original?'

'I'm afraid not. The originals are all kept in our vaults, and are not available for public scrutiny.' She had a sense of something lost in his demeanour and glanced again at the extract she had given him. 'He died very young. Still a baby, really.'

'Yes. He never had the chance to grow up.'

She looked at him and smiled again. 'Maybe he'd have turned out a bit like you.'

Richard flashed her a look, and felt his skin darkening. 'No!' His contradiction was unnecessarily abrupt. 'He wouldn't have been anything like me!'

◇◇◇

The traffic on The Mount was a distant whisper behind the walls of the cemetery. Somehow everything seemed quieter here. Richard sat in the grass next to a small headstone, discoloured by time and moss, and traced the outline of his own name with tentative fingers. How many people, he wondered, got to visit their own graves? It was a hollowing experience. He felt tears burn his cheeks, and the emptiness inside him ached.

If Richard really was dead, then who was he?

Chapter Eighteen

Cahors, November 2008

Enzo felt foolish. Almost embarrassed. He wasn't going to die after all. At least, not in the next three months. Not if he could help it. And all that depression and self-pity in which he had been wallowing since his appointment with the phony oncologist, seemed horribly indulgent. But he had learned something very valuable. Life was for living. To the full. Every last, precious second of it.

He held both his daughters in an embrace that he wanted to go on forever. Sophie's tears were staining his shirt. She'd only had a single day to live with the knowledge of her father's impending death. A day that had seemed like an eternity, eyes burned red raw by endless tears, spilled now in happiness rather than grief.

And Kirsty. He drew back to look at her. The proximity of death had taught them something about themselves, forced both a confrontation and a reconciliation. There was no past, no history. Today was the first day of the rest of their lives. Lives to be lived in the moment.

Unfortunately, at this particular moment, Enzo still stood accused of murder. And whoever it was that was trying to ruin his life was still out there, capable of God only knew what else.

His tiny cell seemed full of people. He hardly knew who they all were. Nicole insinuated herself between the half-sisters, to thrust large breasts at her mentor and crush him with a bear-hugging ferocity.

'Shouldn't you be at university?' he said.

She cocked her head at him. 'Classes have been cancelled, Monsieur Macleod. Apparently our professor's been arrested on some trumped up murder charge. And he'll probably need my help to solve it, like he usually does.'

He smiled at her fondly. She was his brightest student and had already proved an invaluable assistant in helping him solve two of the murders in Raffin's book. A big girl of farming stock, what she lacked in the social graces she made up for in intelligence. Long, straight hair that reached down almost as far as her ample hips, was pulled back severely from a round, pretty face, and tied in a ponytail. She frowned at him.

'I can't let you out of my sight for a minute, can I?'

He looked beyond her and saw Bertrand at the open door, uniformed officers at his back, and he felt the desolation in the young man's eyes. There was something different about him, odd. Then Enzo realised that the nose stud and eyebrow piercings had gone. His face seemed strangely naked without them. Gone, too, were the spikes gelled into hair which was now swept simply back from a pale forehead. He looked older, as if suddenly, in the face of tragedy, he had been forced finally to discard his youth.

Enzo held out his hand, and the boy shook it firmly. 'What's the situation with the gym?'

Bertrand made a face. 'It's history. The fire chief says it was arson. There was an accelerant used.' Years of study and work lost in a single night of flames.

'I'm so sorry, Bertrand.'

'Why? It's not your fault.'

'I feel responsible.'

But Bertrand wouldn't have it. 'Don't. Whatever I've lost I can rebuild.' He glanced at Kirsty. 'You nearly lost a daughter.' Kirsty reached out to touch his arm. The bond between them was evident. When someone saves your life, you owe him forever. When you are the one who saved the life you become, in some way, responsible for it. Bertrand and Sophie were lovers, and while that might some day come to an end, his relationship with Kirsty was for life.

Sophie said, 'The Maison de la Jeunesse has offered him temporary space, and the bank have said they'll give him a bridging loan to re-equip until the insurance money comes through.'

Bertrand shrugged bravely. 'All I've got to do is figure out how to make the payments.'

Out in the hallway, they heard a metal door slam shut, and voices, and a man appeared behind Bertrand. He was wearing a suit, thinning dark hair dragged back from a bearded face. It was so rarely that Enzo saw Simon in a suit that he almost didn't recognise him.

'Uncle Sy!' Sophie threw herself at him with the unrestrained pleasure of a child greeting a favourite uncle. Except that he wasn't really her uncle. Kirsty took his hand and kissed him on both cheeks, strangely formal, before Simon turned towards his oldest friend. He wasn't smiling.

'How come they let everyone in here?'

'I've got influence with the boss.'

'Not enough to get you out, though.'

'No. Not quite that much.'

Simon glanced at Kirsty. 'Well, we'd better see what *we* can do to get your dad out, then.' He stepped forward, and the two men stood looking at each other. They had started school together on the same day, aged five. They had played in a band together through all their teen years. And now here they were in their fifties, facing one another across a police cell, one of them suspected of murder, the other his lawyer. The only call allowed to Enzo had been made to Simon in London. He couldn't practice law in France, but he had some influential connections in the French legal world.

Enzo's first instinct was to hug him. But Simon pre-empted the embrace by holding out his hand for a formal handshake. 'We'll get you the best *avocat* in the Southwest. I've already spoken to some people in Toulouse.' He seemed unusually detached, coldly professional. 'They're allowing me a half-hour interview. You brief me, I'll brief the *avocat*. We'll need to clear the cell first.'

'Not before we figure out what we can do in the meantime.' They all turned towards Nicole who became suddenly self-conscious. And then defiant. 'Well, I'm not hanging about twiddling my thumbs while Monsieur Macleod rots in here. There must be something we can do.'

'She's right, Dad,' Kirsty said. 'You must have some thoughts. You're an expert on crime scenes, after all.'

'Oh, I've given it a lot of thought, believe me,' Enzo said with some feeling. 'And if I was investigating this thing myself, I'd start with the phony surgery in the Rue des Trois Baudus. Someone had access to that place. Someone with a key.' He paused for just a moment. 'And the hair they found on the victim's body? I've got a pretty damned good idea where that came from.'

◇◇◇

The cathedral of St. Etienne stands at the cultural and religious heart of the old Roman city of Cahors, a stunning example of the transition from late Romanesque architecture to Gothic. Resembling a fort, more than a church, it was built in the eleventh century by bishops who were also powerful feudal lords defending their roles as counts and barons of the town. Now it stood in the repose of more tranquil times, a perch for pigeons, a repository for their guano, and the magnificent stained glass of the arched window in the apse looked out on to the barren winter gardens opposite the salon of Coiffure Xavier.

Xavier was performing a red henna rinse on the head of a bird-like-middle-aged lady whose hair had gone prematurely grey and begun thinning alarmingly. She wanted her scalp to be the same colour as her hair to disguise the fact that she was balding. Xavier was trying to persuade her that the disguise was unlikely to work. The door opened, and the bell above it vibrated shrilly in the hot, ammoniac air of the salon.

Xavier immediately sensed hostility. One of the two young women seemed faintly familiar. And he had certainly seen the young man before. A body like his, sculpted during hours of patient exercise, was one you wouldn't forget in a hurry. Attractive though he was, however, there was something distinctly aggressive in his manner. Xavier took a step back from the henna'd head. '*Bonjour messieurs dames.*' He regarded them cautiously. 'Can I help?'

Kirsty looked around the cramped little salon with undisguised contempt. Why on earth would her father come here to get his hair trimmed? And almost as if she had read her sister's mind, Sophie said, 'He comes once a month on Thursdays. Thursday's training day.'

Kirsty raised her eyes to the heavens and sighed. It was typical of her father to live out the world's stereotypical view of the mean Scot. She said, 'You cut our father's hair.'

Xavier looked at her blankly. 'Who's your father?'

'Enzo Macleod,' Sophie said. 'And he's in prison on a murder charge because of you.'

Xavier blanched. 'Me? I've never murdered anyone in my life.'

'It's running down my neck.' The bird-like lady squirmed in her seat, and Xavier glanced at the trails of red on white skin that disappeared beneath her plastic shoulder cover. But he was distracted.

Kirsty said, 'Hair found on the body of a woman murdered in Cahors three days ago matches my father's.'

Sophie pressed the point home. 'But that's not possible, since he wasn't there.'

Kirsty finished the tirade. 'And he didn't kill that woman.'

Xavier's pallor quickly turned pink as blood rushed to the surface of his skin. 'I don't see what that has to do with me.'

'Xavier, I can feel it running down my back.'

Bertrand took a threatening step towards the hairdresser who instinctively flinched, oblivious to the distress emanating from the red head at his fingertips. 'There's an easy way of doing this, Xavier, and there's a hard way. Your choice.'

'Okay, okay.' Xavier raised his hands in self defence. Red for stop. 'I admit it. I did give him some of Monsieur Macleod's hair.'

'Who?' Sophie looked as if she were about to physically attack him.

'He said it was for a joke.'

'Who!'

'I don't know who he was. He came in here about a month ago, just after Monsieur Macleod had left, and said he wanted to buy some of his hair.'

'You mean you took money for it?' Sophie was incredulous, and her vehemence caused Xavier to take a further step back.

'I refused at first. But he was very persuasive. And in the end, I didn't really see the harm.'

'Well, you see it now.' Bertrand glared at him. 'How much did he pay you?'

'Honestly, I'd stick needles in my eyes before I'd do anything to hurt Monsieur Macleod.'

Bertrand said, 'That might still be an option. How much?'

'A hundred euros.'

They stared at him, their disbelief reflected in Kirsty's astonishment. 'A hundred euros! For some strands of hair?'

'Xavier…!' the woman in the chair wailed.

Xavier ignored her. 'He didn't want clippings. He wanted the hair that had come away in the comb. I hadn't even had a chance to clean it out. Monsieur Macleod's chair was still warm.'

'So this guy paid you a hundred euros for a few lengths of my father's hair, and you didn't think that was odd?' Kirsty's belligerence seemed almost as threatening now to Xavier as Bertrand's.

'Like I told you, he said it was for a joke.'

'Some joke!'

Xavier looked at Sophie and noticed for the first time, quite incongruously, the faint strip of white running back through her dark hair. 'You've got the same badger stripe as your father,' he said, as if he thought they might be distracted by this and forget about his transgressions

'Magpie,' she said.

'What?'

'It's Magpie they call him, not Badger.'

Bertrand said, 'I think you need to shut up your salon, Xavier, and come up to the *caserne* with us. The police are going to have to take a statement.'

'I don't want to get into any trouble.'

'Maybe you should have thought of that before you went selling your customers' hair.'

Xavier sighed theatrically, then took in the stripes of red on the neck of the client wriggling below him in her chair. 'Oh. My. God! What a mess!' He immediately began dabbing it with a wet sponge, but it had already begun to dry. 'It'll take me a few minutes to sort this out.'

'We'll wait,' Bertrand told him.

And Kirsty said, 'What did he look like? This guy that bought Enzo's hair?'

Xavier waved a distracted hand in the air. 'Oh, I don't know. I hardly remember him.'

'Try.'

Another theatrical sigh. 'I suppose he must have been about fortyish. Quite good looking, really. His hair was short. I do remember that. Sort of fair. And, oh…' His eyes lit up. 'Ears. Hairdressers always look at ears. You have to in this business. Too easy to cut one off.'

'What about his ears?' Kirsty was staring at him intently.

'Well, it looked like he'd had a nasty accident in a barber's shop. His right earlobe was completely gone.'

Chapter Nineteen

Commissaire Taillard viewed the pink-faced hairdresser and the three young people sitting on the opposite side of her desk. The sombre figure of the Scottish lawyer, Simon Gold, stood behind them, leaning his hands on the back of a chair. Whatever his faults, Enzo Macleod certainly inspired loyalty among his family and friends. And she felt a tiny pang of regret with the thought that she, too, might have been one of that inner circle, that *sérail*, had things turned out differently between them.

'It doesn't prove that he wasn't there,' she said.

Simon straightened himself, and tugged at his beard with long, bony fingers. 'And the fact that you found his hair at the scene doesn't prove that he was. He was having a relationship with the woman, for God's sake. People shed hair. You might expect to find some of his hair on her clothes.'

Kirsty cut in. 'The point is, why would someone pay a hundred euros for some of my father's hair if it wasn't to incriminate him?'

Sophie added, 'And why would somebody set him up with a phony doctor's appointment if it wasn't to blow his alibi out of the water?'

Commissaire Taillard shook her head. 'This is all just speculation.'

Simon said, 'In the same way, *commissaire*, that the only evidence you have is circumstantial.'

But the police chief was conceding nothing. 'We have a computer diary entry that places him at the scene at the time of the murder. We have hair that ties him to the body of the victim. And his alibi is laughable. People have been convicted on less.'

Simon said, 'Just stop and think for a moment, *commissaire*. If you were going to commit a murder, wouldn't you come up with a better alibi? You know that Enzo is not a stupid man. Why would he invent such a ridiculous story in the full knowledge that it wouldn't stand up to a moment's scrutiny?'

There was a knock at the door, and it was opened by a uniformed officer. But Commissaire Taillard's thoughts were focused elsewhere. 'No one is suggesting that the murder was premeditated. It might well have been a crime of passion, a moment of anger. And Enzo Macleod left town almost straight afterwards. He probably never imagined that we might tie him to the scene. He never had time to concoct a credible alibi. And the fact is that the building in the Rue des Trois Baudus had been empty for two years.'

'No it hadn't.'

Everyone turned towards the door. Nicole stood clutching a beige folder and looking very pleased with herself. She was breathless and slightly flushed.

'I've been round every *agence immobilière* in Cahors trying to find out who had 24*bis* Rue des Trois Baudus on their books. Turned out to be an estate agent at the foot of the Boulevard Léon Gambetta.' She waved her beige folder in the air. 'And guess what? They rented the building to a Paris-based company three weeks ago. A one-year lease.'

Hélène Taillard gave a tiny gallic shrug of dismissal. 'I don't see how that helps Monsieur Macleod.'

Nicole said, 'Well, if you check with the registrar of the Commercial Court in Paris, as I just did, I think you'll find that the company which took the lease doesn't exist.'

Everyone took a moment to digest this.

Then Sophie leaned forward on the desk and looked earnestly at the police chief. 'Madame Taillard, you *know* my dad didn't do this. You guys were…' She stopped suddenly, halted by an image of the semi-undressed Hélène Taillard on the *canapé* with her father, a shared memory which brought a flush to the older woman's cheeks. 'Well…you were pretty close. You know there's not a bad bone in his body. He'd be incapable of killing anyone.'

The *commissaire* sat back in her seat and sighed deeply. 'I wouldn't disagree with you, Sophie. But it's not my call to make. I am the chief of police. I am bound by rules and procedures. There is a limit to how much I can intervene. The *juge d'instruction* already thinks I am compromised because I know your father socially.'

Simon took the folder from Nicole. 'But surely, *commissaire*, the testimony of the hairdresser, and the fact that the building in the Rue des Trois Baudus was leased by a company which doesn't exist, throws further doubt on an already weak case.' He smiled. A persuasive smile of reassurance, normally reserved for a jury during summing up. 'Perhaps, in the light of developments, you might consider discussing with the *juge d'instruction*, the possibility of letting Enzo out on police bail.'

◇◇◇

Enzo stepped out from the glass-fronted Hôtel de Police and drew his first breath as a free man in nearly forty-eight hours. Brittle leaves from the plane trees in the car park lay in drifts among the cars, and rattled across the tarmac in the icy breeze that blew down from the old city walls.

Inside him welled a great, burning sense of anger. Greater even than his sense of injustice, or his relief at being released unexpectedly on bail. Someone had murdered an innocent woman, just to set him up as a suspect. In order to create a false alibi, he had been duped into a consultation with a phony doctor, and suffered through two days of believing he was dying from an incurable disease. That same someone had tried to murder his daughter, and burned down Bertrand's gym.

It had all been one-way traffic. All designed to ruin his life, to distract him from an investigation that someone feared would uncover a murderer. A murderer who, until now, had escaped justice. Of that Enzo was certain.

But he was certain, too, that he had reached a turning point. A moment in this whole sad and sordid tale, when his adversary had done his worst, and in doing so revealed enough of himself to give Enzo a starting point to fight back. He clung to that thought with a grim tenacity.

'You don't look very happy to be out.'

Enzo turned to look at Commissaire Taillard. She had walked him up to the front door from the cells. 'I'm sorry,' he said. 'I don't mean to be ungrateful. I ought to thank you for everything you've done.'

She took his arm and led him through the trees towards the Musée de la Résistance on the corner. 'Don't thank me yet, Enzo. This isn't over. There is still a killer out there. And a few of my officers still think it's you.'

'But you don't?'

Her concession was reluctant. 'I never really did, Enzo. In fact, I might even have put money on you being innocent.'

His smile was rueful. 'You bet on me once before and lost.'

'You got lucky on the Jacques Gaillard case. I don't hold that against you.'

They stopped and she turned to face him, her breast lightly brushing his arm. There was a moment between them, a tiny frisson suggesting that perhaps the flame hadn't been entirely extinguished.

He said, 'The only way I'm going to clear my name here is by catching the killer myself.'

She shook her head. 'That's our job.'

He gave her a look, but refrained from comment. 'There must be something you can tell me, Hélène. About the murder or the crime scene. Something that would give me a starting point.'

'Absolutely not. You're just out on bail, Enzo. I can't go divulging information like that to a suspect.'

'If I really did it, you wouldn't be telling me anything I didn't already know. At least tell me how she was murdered.'

Commissaire Taillard held him in a long, hard stare before blowing through pursed lips in exasperation. 'She was struck on the face. Sufficiently hard probably to render her unconscious. But that's not what killed her. The pathologist's preliminary autopsy report says her neck was broken.'

Enzo stiffened. 'Deliberately? I mean, she didn't break it accidentally when she fell?'

'Oh, no. The *médecin légiste* was quite clear. The neck was broken by a clean, twisting movement that severed the spinal cord between the third and fourth disarticulated vertebrae. A real pro job was how he described it.'

Enzo whistled softly. 'Then I know who did it.'

'What?' the Commissaire looked at him in disbelief.

'At least, I know who else he's killed. In a Paris apartment, nearly seventeen years ago.' His eyes shone with the cold, hard steel of revenge. 'Which also means I know where to start looking for him.'

Chapter Twenty

He had been surprised at how easy it was. The newspaper's archives were open for anyone to see, transferred now to microfiche, viewable on any one of a number of machines in the reading room.

Richard had found the offices of the Daily Mail easily enough. It was before the Associated Press had moved its headquarters to Kensington, and its suite of newspapers was still to be found in the old Northcliffe House in Whitefriars Street, not far from Fleet Street.

He was not quite sure why he had chosen the Daily Mail, except that it seemed a little classier than the other tabloids, but still certain to carry stories of popular interest. He had no idea what he was looking for. But he had a starting date. One imprinted in his memory, just as it had been burned in red into the bottom corner of the photograph. July 23rd, 1970. Almost exactly sixteen years ago.

Outside, the City of London baked under the hot July sun, bankers and journalists finally abandoning coats and jackets for open-necked shirts and summer frocks. But in here it was dark and cool, and Richard's focus was on the screen in front of him as he wound the spool through the reader. He found July 23rd quickly enough, but if anything newsworthy had happened, it would surely have come after that date. Nothing up until then, at least, had disturbed the happiness of a family on a Spanish beach. He spooled quickly through that day's news stories before moving on to the 24th. But it wasn't until the 25th that he found what he was looking for. And it shook him to the core.

Snatched, was the headline. And the sub-head read, *Toddler Taken From Spanish Holiday Hotel.* Richard ran hungry eyes over the text of the story:

> The Bright family from Essex were still in shock today after the abduction of their 20-month-old son, Richard, from their Spanish hotel room.
>
> The only traces left by his abductors were the child's blood-stained panda, and a smeared trail of blood leading into the hall. The kidnappers appear to have made their escape down an emergency staircase at the back of the building.
>
> Police in the tiny Spanish coastal resort of Cadaqués, near the home of artist Salvador Dali, have sent blood samples for testing. They hope to be able to determine whether the blood belonged to the kidnapped toddler or one of his abductors.
>
> Local police chief, Manuel Sanchez, said: "We have no idea yet why the child was taken. There has been no demand for ransom. If it turns out that the blood was that of the little boy, then I think we have to fear the worst."
>
> The alarm was raised late on the evening of Thursday the 23rd when Richard's parents returned to their room from a meal in the hotel dining room. They had left baby Richard, brother William, and older sister Lucy, asleep in the room, confident that the children would be safe while they ate.
>
> A hotel babysitting service had been employed to check on the children every fifteen minutes, but in fact no one had looked in on the room for more than an hour.

It was after midnight before the local police informed the area headquarters in Gerona, and it was another eight hours before police forces throughout Spain were put on alert. Pictures of the kidnapped Richard were flashed on nationwide Spanish television yesterday, along with a public appeal for information. Investigating officers are now sifting through dozens of reported sightings, from Cadiz to San Sebastian.

Distraught parents, Rod and Angela, were yesterday being comforted by friends and family. A family spokesman told reporters, "We are still hopeful of having little Richard returned to us. And we would appeal to whoever might have taken him not to harm him. Leave him somewhere safe and inform the police."

The one-time fishing port of Cadaqués is situated on a remote peninsula north of Barcelona, on the Costa Brava. A haven for writers and artists, it is regarded as an upmarket resort, unspoiled and largely underdeveloped.

There were photographs of the whitewashed Mediterranean houses of the old port with an inset picture of the bizarrely moustachioed surrealist, Salvador Dali. A snapshot of the missing boy grinning at the camera. Richard stared for a long time at the picture, a shock of blond curls above a chubby round face. He had seen enough photographs of himself at this young age to be in no doubt that he was the abducted child.

He wondered if the strange fragmented images that now flooded his thoughts were real memories or imagined ones provoked by the shock of reading about his own abduction. He thought he could remember a darkened room, a woman bending over his cot, lifting him into safe arms, his fingernail catching her cheek, sticky blood on his fingers. His panda falling to the floor. And, then, out of the darkness, being carried from a car.

The sound of the sea somewhere far below, exhaling into the night, filling cool air with its salted perfume.

So his mother was not really his mother. And all that suffocating love, her soft warm bosom and rose-scented cologne crowding his senses, throttling his childhood, had in the end driven a wedge between them. He realised now it had really been some desperate attempt to win him over. As if, somehow, he had known the truth.

Was it possible that he really did remember something? That it was those memories that in some way prevented the two of them from ever having a normal relationship? How disappointed by him she must have been.

He spooled through the ensuing days. The story was never off the front pages, with background pieces and feature articles inside. Experts speculated on the reasons for the abduction. Everything from the white slave trade and sexual abuse to a secret sale on the underground adoption market. Kidnapping for financial reasons had been ruled out when no ransom demand was made. And in any case, Rod Bright, while a successful businessman in Ilford, could hardly have been described as wealthy.

There was an in-depth article about the Bright family themselves, Rod and Angela and their three children, but Richard couldn't bring himself to read it. Not yet, anyway. Days and weeks passed before his eyes as gradually the story slipped from the front pages, a tale of frustrating police failure confining itself to smaller and smaller paragraphs on the inside, until finally it simply disappeared. Upheavals in Northern Ireland were now grabbing the headlines. The Social Democratic and Labour Party had been formed to fight for Catholic civil rights in the troubled province.

And then suddenly, six weeks later, a young female journalist from the newspaper's features staff had flown out to Spain to interview Angela Bright. She was still in Cadaqués and refusing to leave until either her child was returned to her, or he was proven to be dead. The blood, it had turned out, was not his. To leave, she told the journalist, would be a betrayal of her son.

It would be to abandon him, to admit that he was gone forever. And she simply couldn't do it. And so this picturesque resort, where discerning people took their holidays, had become a prison, a gilded cage that would hold her until either she found her Richard, or she died. She had already rented a house and was discussing with the local authority the possibility of putting her children into the state school.

Her husband, meantime, had returned to England, where his business interests demanded his presence.

There was a photograph of her sitting in a wicker chair staring forlornly at the camera. Richard stared back at her for a very long time. He had evidently inherited his colouring from his mother. Fair hair, and even from the black and white photograph, he could see that she had the palest of eyes, almost certainly blue like his. But she looked substantially older than her thirty-three years. Drawn, haunted.

He looked away, unable to maintain eye-contact with this ghost from his past, blinking hard to disperse the tears that filled his eyes.

He stood up and went in search of the index. Now that he knew what story he was following, he would be able to find all future references and go straight to them. As it turned out, there were very few. How quickly the world forgot the suffering it shared over breakfast for a few brief days or weeks.

The last reference he could find was in September, 1976, on the occasion of his eighth birthday. Some news editor had figured it was an anniversary on which to hang a story. Perhaps it had been a poor month for news. And so a reporter had been dispatched to do a follow-up interview with Angela Bright, who was still in Cadaqués. A free holiday for a journalist from the features desk.

Señora Bright, as she was now known locally, had purchased a large house just below the church which sat up at the top of the town overlooking the bay. The elder of her remaining children, Lucy, had just started secondary school. Richard's brother, William, was still in primary school. Angela and Rod had separated eighteen months previously. A good Catholic, Angela was refusing to give him a divorce. But their marriage was over. He had wanted to move on. And she was unable to do so. Still locked up in her gilded cage, resigned to spending the rest of her days there, believing that her son might be dead, but never quite able to release her grip on that last shred of hope that he might somehow, somewhere, still be alive.

She prayed for him each morning in the church, just a few paces from her door, and spent her days in quiet solitude behind shuttered windows or in the cool shade of her tiny, walled garden. In the photograph she seemed to have aged twenty years.

There were photographs, too, of his brother and sister, and short interviews with each. And Richard realised for the first time what he had missed by skimming through all those previous pieces, what would certainly have become clear to him had he read the article on his family background.

He stared at the screen with an extraordinary sense of déjà vu and felt himself freefalling once more into the unknown.

Chapter Twenty-One

Cahors, November 2008

As they crossed the square, Enzo looked up beyond the red brick of the old town to the tree-covered hills rising all around the far side of the river, cutting a high, dark line against the deep blue of the winter sky. 'I'm going to get the bastard.'

As if he hadn't spoken, Simon said, 'I have a flight from Toulouse at four.'

They had walked together without speaking down through Cahors, past the imposing Palais de Justice, where Enzo might yet stand trial, across the busy Boulevard Gambetta and into the Rue Marechal Foch, leading into the Place Jean Jacques Chapou.

The cathedral stood in chilly silence, casting its shadow of Christian disapproval on the thoughts of revenge that filled Enzo's head. He had been so wrapped up in them as they passed through the town that he had failed to register Simon's unusually sombre mood.

Simon had always been mercurial. At one moment the manic extrovert, saved only by his charm from the consequences of a destructive impulsiveness. At another, the manic depressive who, in the blink of an eye, might descend into a black funk from which it could be almost impossible to rouse him.

His mood this cold November morning, as a pale sun sent long shadows sprawling north across the square, was neither manic nor depressive. He was subdued, and his breath clouded in frigid air as he spoke.

'I'm in the middle of a court case in Oxford. I only got the judge to agree to a two-day suspension of proceedings by pleading a family emergency.'

A woman with big, yellow rubber gloves was packing ice around freshly displayed fish in the L'Océan fishmonger on the corner.

'Well, at least come up to the apartment and have a glass of wine with me. I could do with a drink.'

'No, I need to talk to you.'

'We can talk in the apartment.'

'In private.'

For the first time, Enzo detected something ominous in his friend's tone. He glanced at him, and saw the shadows beneath his orange-flecked green eyes. 'I'll buy you a drink in Le Forum, then.'

He steered him past a blue and white 2CV with a crumpled fender and into the café on the south side of the square, opposite the indoor market of La Halle. A butcher's van was unloading fresh meat in the street under the watchful gaze of an alsation dog whose dreadlocked owner squatted in a doorway, begging cup on the sidewalk in front of him.

Inside, steam issued from a coffeemaker behind the redbrick bar. Enzo ordered a couple of brandies, and several customers shook his hand as Simon followed him in back. A rerun of a rugby game was being shown on a television screen high up above the door. They slipped into leather bench seats to face each other across the booth by the *cheminée*. They both felt the warmth of smouldering oak embers that filled the place with a sweet scent of winter woodsmoke.

They sat in silence until the brandies came, and Enzo could feel Simon's tension. '*Santé.*' He lifted his glass to his lips and the liquor burned its way down into his chest.

Simon just stared at his glass before looking up and meeting his friend's eye with a curiously loaded stare. 'You're a fucking idiot, Magpie, you know that?'

'What?' Enzo was startled. This was no idle jibe made half in jest. This was a heartfelt criticism made whole in earnest.

'She was better off before.'

'Who?'

'Kirsty. When she wasn't talking to you. When you had no contact. Nobody was trying to kill her then.'

Enzo sighed and let himself slip back in his seat. So that's what this was all about. After Enzo and Linda had broken up, Simon had stayed in touch with Enzo's ex, playing the role of surrogate father to the surly Kirsty. It was Simon who had been there on school sports day. It was Simon who had taken Kirsty and her mother out for a celebration meal when Kirsty graduated. It was Simon, during all the years that Enzo wasn't around, who had kept a mindful eye on his absent friend's daughter.

'She almost died in the catacombs in Paris. Someone's just tried to murder her in Strasbourg. And why? Because of you. Because of your stupid bets and your stupid pride, and this crazy crusade to solve every cold case in France.' He paused. 'Or, at least, all the ones in Raffin's book.' He was on a roll. 'Just to show the world how fucking clever you are. Enzo Macleod. Great mind, great scientist. Smarter than all the rest. Look at me, mammy, I'm dancing.'

Enzo's face stung as shock brought colour to cold cheeks. He felt as if he had been struck. There was vitriol in Simon's accusation, searing words smeared with Scottish sarcasm. And he wasn't finished.

'Do you care at all that you're putting at risk the very people you profess to love?'

Enzo remembered how Simon had been the leading light in the school debating society. And while he could at times be vulgar and foul-mouthed along with the rest of them, he'd had a talent for being able to articulate his opinions with cutting clarity. Making him, of course, an ideal lawyer. And if he meant to pour petrol on the coals of Enzo's anger, then he succeeded.

'Don't lecture me on fatherhood, Sy. You've never stayed in a relationship long enough to be one. You're more likely to be having sex with a girl Kirsty's age than worrying about her well-being.'

Simon glared back at him, stung by the rebuke. Perhaps because there was more than just a grain of truth in it. 'You just walked away from her.'

'Not my choice.'

'Of course it was. You were the one who left. Not Kirsty. She didn't ask for that. Now she's suffering the consequences of reconciliation. And what are you going to do? You're going to go after this guy. You're going to put her in even more danger. You just don't care, do you?'

'Of course I care! Jesus Christ, man! If I don't stop this guy, no one else will. And now that I know it's not just me he's after, do you not think I'm going to do everything I can to protect the people I love?'

'How? How are you going to do that, Magpie? Send them to Mars? Get real. You don't know who this guy is. You don't know the first thing about him. But he knows everything about you. He could be sitting in this café and you wouldn't even know it.'

Involuntarily, Enzo's eyes strayed beyond the booth to the customers smoking and drinking at other tables. It was true. Apart from the regulars whom he recognised, he could not have said who any of the others were. A young man, *La Dépêche* open on the table in front of him, was sipping a steaming *noisette*. He glanced up and caught Enzo watching him, before his eyes dipped self-consciously back to his newspaper A middle-aged man at the bar was engaged in an animated conversation with the proprietor. He was dark, muscular, a fading tattoo on his right forearm. Enzo had never seen him before. He forced himself to meet Simon's critical gaze. 'Nothing's going to happen to Kirsty or Sophie or anyone else. I'll die before I'd let that happen.' Even as he spoke the words, he realised how hollow they were. And he could see in Simon's eyes that he knew it, too. How could he possibly keep his children safe from an enemy he couldn't even see?

Simon leaned slightly towards him and lowered his voice. 'Just so you know, Enzo…Anything happens to that girl…'

'And what?'

But whatever response might have reached the tip of Simon's tongue remained behind pursed lips. He simply got up, his brandy untouched, and weaved his way between the tables to where cold sunlight slanted across the cobbles outside.

◇◇◇

Enzo had forgotten that Raffin was there. The journalist had not visited him at the *caserne*, but Enzo remembered seeing his bag in Kirsty's room when Commissaire Taillard brought him to the apartment to look for the doctor's letter. He was not particularly pleased to see him. And barely had time to consider why Simon's disapproval did not extend to Kirsty's relationship with Raffin, before he was mobbed by the girls. They took it in turns to hug and kiss him and fretted and fussed collectively. Enzo caught Raffin watching him with a slight, sardonic smile. The old sage surrounded by his adoring acolytes.

He had been surprised, too, to see Nicole. 'Where are you staying?' he asked her.

'She's sharing with me.' Something in Sophie's tone communicated a certain discontent. 'Where's Uncle Sy?'

Enzo turned away towards the *séjour*. 'He's had to go back to England.'

Bertrand rose from the table, where he was poring over papers and catalogues. He gave Enzo a strong handshake. 'Good to see you back in the land of the living, Monsieur Macleod.'

Enzo nodded towards the papers strewn across the table. 'What's all this about?'

'Just trying to work out how much I need to borrow from the bank to cover the cost of new equipment.'

'How much?'

'A lot. I don't think I can afford my wish list, so I'm trying to cut it down.'

Enzo crossed to his bureau and returned to the table with his cheque book. He sat down opposite Bertrand and held out his hand for the two estimates. 'Let me see.' He scanned the sheets that Bertrand had handed him, then opened his cheque book and started writing.

Bertrand watched him, perplexed. 'What are you doing, Monsieur Macleod?'

Enzo tore out the cheque he had written and held it for Bertrand to take. 'Get your wish list, Bertrand. Tell the bank you don't need their loan. You can pay me back when the insurance money comes through.'

Bertrand looked at the cheque and shook his head. 'You can't afford this, Monsieur Macleod.'

'With all due respect, Bertrand, how would you know what I can afford?' He snapped his cheque book shut. 'I've been to the bank and transferred money from my savings account to my checking account.'

'Papa, that's all the money you've got in the world.' Sophie was staring at him in disbelief.

Enzo smiled. 'You know, one thing that occurred to me, Sophie, when I thought I only had a few months left? What a crime it would be to die with money in the bank.'

'But you're not going to die now.'

'We're all going to die sometime, Soph. And, anyway, I expect Bertrand to pay me back before then. So don't worry, your inheritance is safe. Or, at least, what'll be left of it after the French government have taken their pound of flesh.'

'Oh, Papa!' she scowled at him.

Bertrand stood, still frozen, with the cheque in his hand. 'I can't take this, Monsieur Macleod.'

'Of course you can. And anyway, I need a favour in return, Bertrand. There's no such thing as a free loan.'

'Anything.'

'I need you to come with us. Someone to look after my girls.'

Nicole pre-empted both daughters, including herself without a second thought as one of Enzo's *girls*. 'Where are we going?'

'There's someone out there trying to destroy me, Nicole. Someone who burned down Bertrand's gym, who tried to kill Kirsty. Someone who murdered a woman the same way he murdered a young man in a Paris apartment nearly seventeen years ago.' He lifted his eyes to meet Raffin's, and he saw the journalist frown.

'The Pierre Lambert case?' And when Enzo nodded, 'How do you know that?'

'M.O. A trademark killing. Spinal cord severed between the third and fourth vertebrae. A mistake, because it gives us a starting point. But this guy is still a ruthless, cold-blooded killer who's prepared to do anything to stop me finding out who he is. So no one's safe. None of us. Not until we get him.' He let his gaze wander around the five sets of eyes fixed upon him. 'We need somewhere that's not known to him. Somewhere safe. A base from where we can start to track him down.'

Sophie said, 'What about Charlotte's cottage in the Corrèze?'

Enzo shook his head. 'He knows everything about me, Soph. Charlotte's in the States right now, so she's safe. But he's bound to know about her. So he'll know about the cottage. We need to make a complete break with everyone and everywhere we know.'

Kirsty said, 'Do you have someplace in mind?'

Enzo reached into his pocket and pulled out a folded sheet of hotel notepaper. 'Actually, I do.'

Chapter Twenty-Two

Bertrand drew his van into the curb beneath the stark, leafless skeletons of the plane trees in front of the station. Enzo held the door open for Nicole to step down and glanced anxiously across the street.

There were a couple of men in the Hertz car rental office, bent over the counter, intent on signing paperwork. The Maison du Vin de Cahors appeared deserted. A man sat reading a newspaper in the weak winter sunshine outside the bar of the Melchior *brasserie*. He didn't look anything like either Kirsty or Xavier's description of the man with the missing earlobe. But that made no difference. The man whom Kirsty had seen in Strasbourg was not necessarily the killer. And the murderer had already employed someone to play the role of Enzo's oncologist. They had no way of knowing who else might be in his employ.

Sophie leaned out to kiss her father and squeeze his hand. 'Take care,' she whispered. Only by dividing and subdividing themselves, could they hope to shake off anyone with a watching brief. Raffin had already set off in a hire car with Kirsty.

Enzo slammed the door, and Bertrand revved his engine, peeping on his horn before pulling away, and accelerating up the steep incline of the tree-lined Avenue Charles de Freycinet.

Nicole clutched her suitcase nervously. It was, as always, huge, and packed to capacity. Enzo had no idea what she took with her on her travels, but her *valise* was invariably too heavy for

her to lift. He was pleased to see that she had invested for the
first time in a case with wheels and offered to take it from her
without fear of slipping a disc. 'Do you think he's watching?'
she said in a low voice, trying not to move her mouth.

'Probably not, Nicole. But even if he is, I doubt if he can
lip-read.'

He trundled her case across the tarmac, and doors slid open
to admit them to the main concourse. It was crowded with
passengers awaiting the imminent arrival of the train to Paris.
Others were gathered to greet friends and family travelling up
from Toulouse. Through yet more sliding doors, they stood in
a queue at the *billetterie*, until waved forward to a *guichet*. The
girl behind the glass said a weary *bonjour*. Enzo slipped her a
sheet of paper containing the code and details of the booking
they had made on the internet just an hour before.

The girl glanced at the two faces watching her through the
window. 'Just the one ticket?'

Enzo nodded. 'Just the one.'

A dot-matrix printer chattered and spat it out. The girl slid
it under the glass. *'Bonne journée.'*

They passed back through to the concourse, and Enzo made
an extravagant show of validating the single ticket in the *borne*
by the door to the platform, and then handing it ostentatiously
to Nicole. The message would be clear to anyone watching.
Only Nicole was travelling. Enzo bumped her case downstairs
to the underpass, and then up again to the platform, where they
stood shivering in the cold wind that blew down the railway
lines from the north.

'I'm scared, Monsieur Macleod,' Nicole whispered. Her eyes
were darting back and forth along the length of the *quai*, flickering
from face to face, assessing each as a potential killer, ruling some
out and some in. 'Do you really think he might be here?'

'Impossible to know, Nicole. Which is why we're not going
to take any chances.'

The SNCF jingle echoed high among the steel girders of
the steeply pitched glass roof, and a voice warned passengers to

stand back from the edge of the platform. The Paris train from Toulouse would be arriving in just a few moments. Enzo peered south and saw the train rounding the bend in the distance.

When finally it groaned and creaked to a halt, doors flew open up and down its length and passengers streamed out to fight for space with those queuing up to get on, a confluence of conflicting interests. Enzo waited until others ahead of them had climbed into the train before he hoisted Nicole's case up to chest level to push it through the door. The effort left him perspiring, tiny beads of sweat turning immediately cold as they formed around his eyes. Nicole threw her arms around him and kissed him on both cheeks. 'Goodbye, Monsieur Macleod.' Enzo could almost believe she had tears in her eyes.

He stood back as she climbed aboard and swung the door shut, and then he walked along the platform, following her progress through the coach until she found her seat. She sat by the window and pressed her forehead against it, looking down at him with concern. She gave a tiny wave. Enzo waved back, and as the crowds thinned, swallowed by the stairway that led down to the underpass, the guard raised his hand and gave a sharp blow on his whistle.

Several more doors slammed, and the train jerked and sighed, and began its slow progress out of the station. Enzo walked with it, waving at Nicole as it gathered speed, until he could only have kept up with it by running. He glanced down the platform. There were just a handful of people left on it now, and he grabbed a door handle as it passed, running with it and swinging the door wide. He heard the shouts of the guard somewhere behind him. If he mistimed his leap he would be in serious trouble.

He took off, and felt himself flying through the air, hovering for what seemed like an eternity on the swing of the door, before his feet found the steps, and he scrambled up into the train. As he leaned out to pull the door closed, he glanced once more back along the platform. No one else had attempted to jump aboard the moving train, and he felt confident that if anyone had been following him, then they had just lost him. The door slammed shut and he stood breathing hard, back pressed against the wall. He was too damned old for this.

Nicole was watching for him as the carriage door slid open, and he staggered unsteadily along the central aisle. She gave him another hug. 'I was so worried you were going to break your neck, Monsieur Macleod.'

'Yeh, well that's exactly what'll happen to me if we let this guy get too close.' He slumped into the seat beside her and glanced at his watch. They would be at Souillac in an hour and meet up again with Bertrand and Sophie. He looked up and saw the conductor approaching from the far end of the carriage. He sighed. The more immediate problem was going to be trying to explain why he didn't have a ticket.

Chapter Twenty-Three

Late afternoon sunlight slanted yellow across a landscape that lay somewhere between fall and winter. Trees clinging to the hillsides that rose up around them had retained much of their foliage, late autumn colours of russet and ochre smeared on green.

As the sun sank lower, the valleys fell into deep shadow, while the rocky volcanic outcrops that broke a reddening skyline glowed orange in the last of the sun. The streams and rivers that cut and wound their way through them lay like silvered pink ribbons. Everything magnified into pin-sharp focus by the cold, clear mountain air.

The motor of Bertrand's van strained as they continued to climb, leaving below them the lush pastures of southwest France for the rocky wastes of the country's central plateau. Enzo could almost feel Raffin's impatience in the car behind. The road was climbing more steeply now, and their progress had slowed since leaving Aurillac. As night approached, the temperature was dropping fast. Even in the blast of hot air from the van's heating system, they could feel the cold creeping into their feet.

Nicole sat in the front, between Sophie and Bertrand, the map on her knee. Enzo and Kirsty sat in the back watching the changing landscape unfold, lit from behind them by a dramatic sunset. Nicole peered through an increasing gloom, into which their headlights now barely penetrated. 'There should be a left turn just up ahead. I guess it'll be signposted.' Conifers scaled the slopes around them, and night seemed to fall suddenly, like a cloak of darkness settling on the land. 'There it is!'

The signpost caught their lights. *Miramont 4.* Bertrand dropped to second gear and swung them into the narrow, single-track road. There would be a problem if they met another vehicle in the next four kilometres.

They continued to climb through the trees for several minutes, before suddenly the road took a sharp turn and they emerged on to a high plateau bathed in unexpected moonlight. Away to the west, the sky still glowed the deepest red. Above them it was already crusted with stars sparkling like frost. The road followed a straight line then, for two kilometres or more before beginning a slow descent through folds of rock and stubbled pasture into a shallow, tree-filled valley, and they saw the lights of Miramont twinkling their welcome in the gathering night.

Although the school and the church were floodlit, there was no sign of life in the village. Granite cottages huddled together under steeply pitched Auvergnat roofs of hand-chiselled stone *lauzes*, shutters closed already against the cold and the night. The water in the fountain in front of the church would be frozen by morning.

'She said it was a right turn at the head of the village.' Enzo leaned forward from the back, then pointed. 'There, I think that's it.' And across a barren winter field, surrounded by tall trees, stood a big, square house, lights blazing into the night from its tall, arched windows. They passed a swimming pool covered over for the winter, and a *pigeonnier* with a double-tiered roof, before drawing up in front of stone steps climbing to the front door from either side of it. Raffin pulled in behind them, and they all got out stiffly on to the pebbled drive. Gardens dipped away below to a wall, and the field beyond. And the lights of the distant village spilled towards them across its fallow, fur-rowed rows.

The front door opened, throwing light on to a slabbed terrace, and Anna stepped out to lean her hands on the wrought iron rail. She smiled down at the upturned faces and found Enzo's.

'Glad you could make it,' she said. She cocked an eyebrow. 'I hope I have enough rooms.'

◇◇◇

Her breath billowed in the chill night air. 'I have to confess, I didn't really expect to see you again.' She glanced at him by the yellow of the streetlights in the deserted main street of this ghost village. The only sign of life came from behind the steamed up windows of the Bar Tabac Restaurant, *Chez Milou*. They could hear voices raised in laughter inside.

Enzo had known that they needed to talk and suggested they take a walk somewhere away from the house. She had wrapped up in a winter coat and scarf, and slipped her arm through his for added warmth. He glanced at her now and saw the lights in her coal dark eyes, and remembered how attractive she was. He remembered, too, the touch of her skin, the firm, fit body of an athlete. He had made love to her, a dying man in desperate need of comfort. Now that his death sentence was lifted, he found himself wanting to make love to her again. This time slow and sure and gentle, in the knowledge that tomorrow could always wait. He smiled. 'I was convinced of it.'

She tipped her head and looked at him quizzically. 'There's something different about you, Enzo. Hard to define. When we met in Strasbourg you seemed like a man with the weight of the world on his shoulders. But now you seem…I don't know…less burdened.'

'When we met in Strasbourg, I had three months to live, Anna. Now, I've got as long as the next man. However long that might be.'

She frowned, and he laughed.

'Some day, maybe, I'll tell you about it. But right now, I owe you an explanation about why we're here. It wasn't something I could tell you on the phone. And if you want us to go, then we'll leave first thing in the morning.'

She tightened her grip on his arm. 'Why would I want you to go? Even if I don't have you to myself, I'm not going to turn you away. It was starting to get pretty lonely up here. This is almost like having a family again.'

They passed the *mairie* with its French and European flags and tattered notice board, and he told her everything. About his history in forensic science in Scotland before coming to France to teach biology in Toulouse. About cracking the cold cases in Raffin's book of unsolved murders. About how one of the murderers was out to stop him any way he could. The attempt on his daughter's life, the burning of Bertrand's gym, the killing of an innocent woman to set up Enzo as the prime suspect.

She listened in thoughtful silence, and as he glanced at her it seemed to him that she had paled just a little. They needed a place, he said, where they would be safe from the killer. From where they could figure out who he was and how they could catch him.

When he had finished, they walked on for some way in silence. Past the three storeys of the floodlit school to the end of the village, where finally she stopped and gazed across the ploughed field to the lights of the house. They could see Bertrand heaving Nicole's case up the steps to the door. She turned suddenly towards Enzo. 'That's pretty scary stuff.'

'If you want us to go, I'll understand. But if we stay, we'll pay for our keep. And the kids'll do what needs to be done around the house.'

She pursed her lips, lost in momentary thought. 'And if you didn't have here, where else would you go?'

He shrugged. 'I don't know. We'd find a hotel somewhere, I guess.'

She looked very directly into his eyes. 'I don't know anything about you, Enzo. Not really.'

He smiled ruefully. 'But you'll let us stay tonight, at least?'

She hesitated for a long moment. 'You can stay as long as you like. That night in Strasbourg, I knew nothing about you then. We were complete strangers. But you made me feel…I don't know…safe somehow. You still do. And if I can offer you safety in return…' She reached out and took his face in her hands, and he put his on her waist and leaned forward to kiss her. A soft, gentle kiss on cool lips. Then he took her in his arms and held her there. 'Thank you, Anna.'

He felt her soft breath at his ear. 'Are you sure your daughter won't be jealous of me? She didn't seem very pleased to find me in your room in Strasbourg.'

'Daughters, plural,' Enzo said. 'And since I have no say in their love lives, I don't see why they should have any in mine.'

◇◇◇

'A one-night stand?' Sophie looked at Kirsty incredulously.

'Well, that's just typical,' Nicole said, and the sisters turned to look at her. She flushed with embarrassment and back-tracked. 'Well, I mean, when your father's around, there never seems to be a woman very far away.'

Sophie turned back to Kirsty. 'Someone had just tried to kill you, and he was picking up a woman in a bar?'

They were in a wood-panelled sitting room with double doors opening off a long stone-flagged hallway. Immediately opposite, the doors of an enormous kitchen stood wide, and good smells issued from a Raeburn stove set in the original *cheminée*. In the *séjour* a log fire burned in a marble hearth laden with ornaments and candlesticks. The room was filled with big, comfortable sofas and armchairs, its walls hung with myriad paintings of washed-out, watercolour countryscapes of an alien land.

Kirsty slouched in an armchair, relaxing for the first time in days, and felt guilty for having betrayed her father's secret. 'I guess he had other things on his mind. He thought he was dying, after all.'

But Sophie wasn't about to be so forgiving. 'So his answer was to go off and spend the night with someone he doesn't know.'

'Leave him alone.' Bertrand perched on the sofa beside Sophie. 'The only reason we've got somewhere to stay is because he met this woman in Strasbourg.'

'And we don't know any more about her than he does!' Sophie was incensed. 'What do you think, Monsieur Raffin?'

They all turned towards Raffin, who was sitting at a small table by the window with his laptop running and a book open beside him. He looked up when he heard his name. 'What?'

'Never mind, Roger, it's not important.' Kirsty waved a dismissive hand and turned towards her sister. 'Let it go, Sophie, please. We're here now. Like her or not, she's given us a roof over our heads when we had nowhere else to go.'

'How much to do you think she knows?' Bertrand said.

'As much as Dad's telling her right now, I imagine.' Kirsty ran long fingers back through silky hair. 'Though how much that is, who knows? It's a lot to dump on someone out of the blue. Particularly someone you've only known for one night.'

They heard the sound of the front door opening and turned expectantly towards the hall. Enzo and Anna brought the cold in with them, chilled faces flushing pink in the warm air. Anna smiled uneasily. The awkward silence made it clear that she and Enzo had almost certainly been the topic of conversation.

She said, 'I've got a stew keeping warm on the stove. Should be enough to feed us all. But we'd better sort out the sleeping arrangements first. There are only five bedrooms.'

A further few moments of awkward silence were broken by Sophie. 'Bertrand and I will share,' she said boldly, daring her father to contradict her. Enzo held his tongue. 'And Kirsty and Roger.'

Roger looked up from his computer and caught the glare that Enzo turned in his direction.

'Good,' Anna said. 'That solves any problems, then. Enzo and...' she turned towards Nicole, '...the young lady, can have a room each.'

Enzo was stung. He had imagined that he and Anna would be sharing, as had everyone else in the room. No one wanted to meet his eye. To cover his embarrassment, he said, 'We'd better get settled in then, and have something to eat. I'd like Roger to brief everyone on the Pierre Lambert case tonight.'

Chapter Twenty-Four

'The point is this,' Enzo said. 'If he is so keen to stop me investigating this crime, he must believe there is something in all the old evidence that could lead to him. And he thinks I'll find it.'

The debris of the meal lay scattered across the long dining table. The *civet de sanglier*, wild boar stew, had been rich and delicious, served with steaming new potatoes, and *haricots verts* with garlic. They had got through three bottles of wine, and Enzo and Roger were sipping cognacs with their coffee.

Oak doors opened on to the kitchen, and French windows led onto what, in summer, would be a shaded terrace that looked out across the fields. An oil painting of an English hunt scene hung on the end wall. A retractable lamp had been drawn down from the ceiling so that the table was brightly illuminated, but the faces around it were half in shadow.

Anna had sat at the opposite end from Enzo, and he had watched from a distance as Raffin chatted easily to her, exerting the full force of his charm. He had noticed, too, how Raffin's attentions had put Kirsty's nose out of joint. He wondered what she had ever seen in him. He was a man obsessed by his own image, convinced of his own intelligence. And while he had a certain charisma, there was a sense that his charm was something he could turn off and on at will. That it was phony, a façade that failed to reflect the real Raffin. Whoever that might be. Enzo certainly had no idea, and wondered if his daughter had somehow managed to find something more substantial beneath the veneer. But he doubted it, and remembered someone once saying of a shallow acquaintance, *Scratch away that surface veneer and what do you find? More veneer.* Enzo suspected that something a little more sinister lay behind the image the journalist presented to the world. Something dark, as Charlotte had once said to him. Something you might find lurking under a stone. For all her twenty-eight years, Enzo feared that Kirsty's experience of life was limited, and her interpretation of it naïve. He was afraid that her relationship with Raffin would only end in tears. Hers.

Raffin had brought his laptop to the table. The book he had been examining earlier was his own. *Assassins Cachés.* Hidden Killers. He had reread the chapter on Lambert, and consulted his computer notes for further detail. He eyed Enzo down the length of the table. 'You're absolutely convinced it's the Lambert case?'

Enzo folded his hands on the table in front of him. 'It was sealed for me by what the pathologist who autopsied Audeline Pommereau said. Hélène Taillard told me he'd described the occipital disarticulation of the third and fourth vertebrae as a real pro job.'

Raffin nodded. 'The same words used by the pathologist on the Lambert case.'

'It's too big a coincidence, Roger. And too specific a skill to be a copycat killing designed to put us off the scent. So let us assume that we *are* dealing with whoever killed Lambert.' He unfolded his hands and waved one towards Raffin. 'Maybe you should start by telling everyone the facts of the case?'

Raffin glanced around the curious faces all turned in his direction, and Enzo sensed how he enjoyed the limelight. The journalist took a sip of his brandy. 'Pierre Lambert was a homosexual. A rent boy, operating out of an apartment in Paris. But he wasn't someone you would pick up on the street. He made his appointments by telephone. According to his friends, he kept a diary of his engagements and an address book full of phone numbers. Neither of those was ever found.'

He paused as he scrolled through a document on his computer.

'Lambert was rumoured to have had an affair with someone high up in government. But that rumour was *courant* only among his friends and derived from his own boasting. Boasting that never included a name, or any other details. He had been known to embroider his life with fanciful exaggerations. So no one really knows how much truth there was in it. If any. The police wasted a lot of time pursuing that line of enquiry to no avail.'

An extraordinary silence had settled over the table, curiosity morphing into fascination.

'He advertised his services in the classified columns of various Parisian newspapers and magazines, and while by all accounts he was never out of work, his income could never have been enough to explain the very large amounts of money being paid on a regular basis into one of his bank accounts.'

Nicole leaned into the light. 'What kind of sums?'

Raffin consulted his notes. 'Various. Ranging from one hundred thousand to five hundred thousand francs.' It was amazing how, in only eight years, the value of the franc had retreated into the mists of history. Everyone around the table did the calculation, turning francs into euros. But Raffin voiced it for them. 'That's around fifteen thousand to seventy-five thousand euros. Payments were made, on average, every two months, amounting over a period of eighteen months to nearly half a million.'

'Blackmail?' Kirsty said.

Raffin gave a tiny shrug. 'Perhaps. But there is no evidence of that. If it was blackmail, we don't know who or why. The money was always paid in cash, into an offshore account on the Isle of Jersey in the Channel Isles. And it was never declared for tax purposes.'

He opened his book at a place he had marked earlier with a slip of paper, and ran the heel of his hand between the pages, breaking the spine to keep it open. 'We really don't know that much more about him. I did some research into his family background, which was entirely unremarkable. He came from a working class family in a Paris *banlieue*. His father died when he was very young and he grew up in a household that consisted of his mother, his sister, and an aunt. So his role models were all women. He played with dolls, and indulged in girls' games with his older sister. Make-believe games like hospital. He was a low achiever at school and left early to train as a waiter. He worked for a couple of years at a restaurant on the Left Bank, which is where he met his first pimp, and discovered that there was more money to be made by exploiting his sexuality. He knew a lot of people, but didn't have many friends. From all accounts he was not a very likeable young man. He was twenty-three when he was murdered.'

He flipped through a few pages to his next marker.

'Now this is where it gets interesting.' He looked up, a slight smile widening the corners of his mouth. He had his audience in the palm of his hand. 'He had just taken on the rental of a pretty expensive furnished apartment south of Chinatown, in the thirteenth *arrondissement*. The apartment building was in the Rue Max Jacob. It had been recently renovated, and his apartment was one up, overlooking the Parc Kellerman. He was found murdered in his *séjour* by his cleaner on the morning of Thursday, February 20th, 1992. As best the pathologist could tell, he'd been dead for around fifteen to sixteen hours. Which puts his time of death at sometime the previous afternoon.'

Enzo said, 'I haven't studied the case in any great detail yet, but as I recall from my original reading of it, it was a very curious crime scene.'

Raffin inclined his head in acknowledgement. 'It was. In various respects. The murder itself, for a start. Lambert appears to have been half-strangled, before his killer finally decided to break his neck. A manoeuvre performed, apparently, with well-practised precision. A real pro job, as the *médecin légiste* said.'

'Which,' Enzo interjected, 'makes you wonder why his killer was trying to strangle him in the first place. It seems very untidy.'

'It wasn't the only untidy aspect of the crime scene. A coffee table had been shattered, apparently by the combined weight of the two men falling on it. So it seems there was a struggle. Bruises on Lambert's back and skull led the pathologist to conclude that the killer had been on top of him when they fell. There were coffee stains on the carpet, a broken cup and two broken saucers. A second was still intact. There was a smashed sugar bowl, and lumps of sugar were scattered across the floor. It appeared that the men had been drinking coffee together before the attack, leading to an assumption by the police that the victim had known his killer.'

'That's quite an assumption to make on the basis of two broken coffee cups.' It was Bertrand's observation that broke the flow of Raffin's narrative.'

Raffin raised a finger and waggled it. 'No, there was more. But I'll come to that in a moment. The next interesting piece, or should I say pieces, of evidence were in the kitchen. On the kitchen counter, next to the sink, investigators found a small, empty bottle. A brown medicine bottle which had contained pills, most of which were scattered across the kitchen floor, along with its plastic cap. The pills were short-acting prescription antihistamines known as terfenadine, sold under the brand name of Seldane. Although these were prescription drugs, this was not the bottle they had come in, so there was no label. And more curiously, no fingerprints. None at all.

'In the sink there was a broken glass tumbler. One of a set of six. The remaining five were found in a kitchen cupboard. The only prints recovered from it were Lambert's. Now here's the thing…' He looked around the rapt faces fixed upon his. 'Antihistamines like terfenadine were taken to counteract the effects of severe allergic reactions, like hay fever or animal allergies. But Lambert had no history of allergy. None. His GP had never prescribed him an antihistamine.'

'So they belonged to the killer,' Sophie said. 'He was having an allergic reaction.'

Raffin inclined his head in such a way as to cast doubt on her theory. 'Maybe. Maybe not. The murder took place in February, so he couldn't have been suffering from hayfever. Lambert didn't keep cats or dogs, so it wasn't an animal allergy. There was nothing obvious in the apartment that he would have reacted to.'

'So why would he have spilled pills all over the place and left the bottle on the counter?'

'If we knew that, Sophie, we probably wouldn't be sitting here tonight.'

Bertrand said, 'You said there was some other reason the police thought that Lambert knew his killer.'

Raffin nodded. 'Yes. Probably the most enigmatic, and tantalising piece of evidence in the whole case. Sixteen years ago, people still used telephone answering machines that recorded messages on cassettes. On the cassette on Lambert's answering machine, police found what appears to have been an accidentally recorded conversation. The machine was set to answer after four rings. Lambert must have picked up the receiver at the same moment the machine kicked in, unaware that it had done so. The whole conversation was recorded.' He sighed. 'Unfortunately, it was a very short conversation. No names were used. The caller was male, and made a rendezvous to meet Lambert at his apartment at three o'clock the following afternoon. The day of the murder. Coinciding pretty closely with the time of death estimated by the pathologist.'

'In other words, whoever made that phone call was the killer,' Bertrand said.

'That's what the police figured. The trouble is, it didn't lead them anywhere. There was nothing in the conversation that gave the least clue as to the identity of the caller. The entire conversation only lasted about forty seconds. Very frustrating. They could listen to the killer's voice, but they had no idea who he was.'

'Or why they were meeting?' Enzo had read the text of the call several months previously but couldn't remember the precise nature of it.

'No. Just that they needed to talk.'

Enzo's brain was working overtime. 'Remind me. There were no fingerprints recovered, were there?'

'None. At least none that were of any use. Lambert's of course. His cleaner. Some partial prints that matched the previous renters. A few others of unknown origin, that didn't match anything in the police database. It was pretty much assumed that the killer was wearing gloves. The lack of prints on the medicine bottle. Or on the broken glass in the sink. Only Lambert's prints were recovered from the coffee cups, the saucers, the sugar bowl. And the pathologist, in his report, said that the shape of the finger bruising around Lambert's neck was consistent with his attacker being gloved.

'Very odd,' Enzo said, 'that you would sit drinking coffee in someone's house with your gloves on. And then the medicine bottle, if it *was* his, no label, no prints.'

'He was being very careful,' Nicole said.

'So careful, in fact, that he could only have come to Lambert's apartment with one intention. To kill him. So careful that he would carry his medicine in an unmarked bottle. Then careless enough to leave it lying on the kitchen counter. Which makes me think that Sophie might have been right. That he was having an allergic reaction to something and losing control. Spilling the pills, breaking a glass.'

'A reaction to what?' Raffin said.

'I don't know. We're going to have to go back over all the old evidence. Is there any way we can access that?'

'Maybe. The original investigating officer is retired now. But when I spoke to him, I got the impression that it still niggled. Unfinished business. You know, one of those unresolved cases that mars an otherwise outstanding career. I think we could count on his help.'

Enzo thought about it. '1992. It's a long time ago. The trail will be pretty cold by now. But there must be something there. Something the killer's scared of. And we shouldn't forget that he's left a more recent trail. Kirsty's description of the man at the press conference in Strasbourg and at the station two days later. We both saw him, if just for a moment, in the taxi outside Kirsty's apartment. The same man who purchased strands of my hair in Cahors. He may or may not be the killer. But at least we have a face.'

'Two,' Nicole said, and Enzo smiled.

'You're quite right. We also have the phony doctor who told me I was dying of cancer. That man's face will live in my memory for a very long time. And he was good. You know, convincing. Like a professional.'

'Like a real doctor, you mean?'

'No, Nicole. Like an actor. And if there's one thing we know about actors, they put their faces out there. For hire. Someone found him to hire him, so maybe we can find him, too. But first of all, I think we have to go to Paris.'

Kirsty seemed surprised. 'All of us?'

'No, just me and Roger. The minute we step into the frame again, we become targets.' He glanced at Raffin who looked less than pleased at the prospect of making himself a target. 'Because I'm already pretty much convinced about one thing now.'

Raffin frowned. 'What's that?'

'Lambert's murder wasn't some random act of revenge, or a *crime passionnel*. The man who killed him really was a professional.'

◇◇◇

He stood outside on the *terrasse*, leaning on the wrought iron at the top of the steps for a long time, warmed still by his anger. That this man should so cold-bloodedly have murdered a woman whose only crime was that she knew Enzo, that he had tried and only just failed to kill Kirsty, was fuelling a sense of outrage and revenge—the like of which Enzo had never felt before.

He became aware of how tightly he was gripping the rail, and forced himself to relax. The nearly full November moon had risen high over the village, and a frost was settling like dust across the fields. It seemed wrong that such a beautiful night should be spoiled by such base feelings.

He took a deep breath and turned away, opening the door and stepping into the darkened hall. A night light at the far end cast a faint illumination on the spiral staircase the led up to the floor above. Everyone else had gone to bed. Anna had said nothing more to him than a cursory *bonne nuit*. Perhaps she was regretting allowing them to stay. And then he remembered how animated she had been with Raffin during dinner, and a seed of jealousy stirred deep inside of him.

As he approached the stairs, he saw a line of light beneath doors leading to a study at the back of the house. Someone was still up. He nudged open the door, and Nicole turned from a desk pushed against the far wall, a bank of computer monitors flickering in the muted light of a desk lamp.

'Oh, hi, Monsieur Macleod. I thought everyone had gone to bed.'

'What are you doing, Nicole?' He shoved his hands in his pockets and walked over to the desk.

'It's great, isn't it? All this computer stuff. High speed internet, colour laser printer, fax, flatbed scanner. There're four computers here, and about five hundred gigs worth of external hard drive.'

'Yes, but what are you doing with it?'

'Anna said it would be okay. I've plugged in my laptop, connected up to a thirty-inch cinema screen. I can drag files backwards and forwards between screens, backing up on to a firewire hard drive.' She paused, eyes shining. An only child, a lonely girl raised on a remote farm in the Aveyron, Nicole had found her focus and her talent in an alternative, virtual world. 'What did he look like?'

'Who?'

'The oncologist. The actor.'

Enzo closed his eyes and saw him as clearly as if he was right there in front of him. And he wondered if the man had the least idea of the hell he had put Enzo through. 'He had short, dark hair. But it was flecked through with grey, receding from the temples. I remember thinking he was a good-looking man. He had blue eyes, dark blue, like deep ocean reflecting blue sky. A square sort of face. Tanned. Fleshy lips. I'd say he was early forties. Quite tall. Not as tall as me, but well-built. When I think

about it now, he didn't seem quite comfortable in his suit and tie. I guess I probably thought his uneasiness was because of me. Because of what he had to tell me. But looking back, the suit was probably not his natural habitat. If you were to cast him in a movie, he might well play a military man, or an action hero.'
He opened his eyes again and found Nicole staring at him.

'If he can be found, Monsieur Macleod, I'll find him.'

'How?'

'I'll start with the internet. I already Googled *acteurs* and *France*. There are a lot of actors' agencies and directories online, and most of them carry photographs. With a description like the one you gave me, I should be able to narrow them down pretty quickly.'

Chapter Twenty-Five

He wasn't sure how long he'd been asleep. In fact, he wasn't certain he had slept at all. He was in a large room at the front of the house, with views towards the village. He'd left the shutters open, and tall windows laid elongated arches of moonlight across polished wooden floors scattered with Chinese rugs. The light kept his demons at bay but his mind in an unsettled state that hovered indeterminately somewhere between sleep and consciousness.

He had been aware of the noises of the night. The house, like all old houses, had its own characteristic sounds. Sounds, that with time, you would stop hearing. The cracking of the central heating pipes as they cooled. A deep creaking in the roof as the stone tiles contracted, applying pressure to the oak they were nailed to. The scurrying of field mice finding shelter from freezing temperatures among the rubble between thick stone walls. Outside, an owl in the trees was exchanging hoots with another somewhere across the valley.

He lay on his back trying not to think, eyes half-shut, semi-focused on a crack in the ceiling, when a floorboard creaked outside his door. Like the sound of a footstep in wet snow. He pulled himself up onto one elbow, wide awake now and stared towards the door as it opened to let in a sliver of light from the hall. The shadow of a figure slipped into his room and drifted through the moonlight like a ghost, until he saw the curtain of dark hair tumbling across her shoulders as she let her dressing gown slip to the floor. A swish of silk on smooth skin.

Black eyes found his in the dark. He said, 'I thought…'

'Shhhh.' She put a finger over his lips. 'This way no one has to be embarrassed about our sleeping arrangements. Especially your girls.'

Something about her discretion, her concern for his daughters, touched him, and he felt a wave of affection for her. As she bent over him, he took her head in his hands and kissed her.

◇◇◇

He had meant to make love to her slowly, surely. A slow hand, a steady beat. But in the end he had consumed her quickly, devouring her almost in a single bite. Now they lay breathless from the exertion, side by side, damp sheets twisted around spent bodies, cold air on burning skin.

He had no idea how long they stayed like that, limbs cooling in the falling temperature of the bedroom. He was already drifting in some netherworld, when he felt her lips on his face, a soft, fond kiss, and then she reached over to cover them both with the quilt. He thought he heard her whisper, 'I love making love with you.' An echo of Strasbourg. But he couldn't be sure.

◇◇◇

It felt as if he had been asleep for hours. But when he woke, it was still pitch dark. The moon had dipped in the sky and was casting its light now on the wall above the bed. As he came to, in the silence he heard her breathing. Not the slow, steady rhythm of sleep. The shallower, more rapid beat of impatient consciousness. He was lying face down, and rolled on to his side to see her lying on her back, staring wide-eyed at the ceiling. He reached out a hand to touch her face and she turned towards him.

He said, 'What's wrong?'

'Nothing. I can't sleep, that's all.'

'Why?'

'Just…everything. You calling out of the blue like that. Arriving with your family and friends in tow. The whole, incredible story. I can't stop thinking about it.'

'I'm sorry.'

'Don't be. It's not just you. There're other things in my head, too.'

'What sort of things?'

'Oh, you know, the sort of things that keep me awake on other nights.'

'We all have our demons.'

'Yes, we do.' She smiled. Then turned away again to gaze at the ceiling.

'I have no idea what yours are.'

'That's because I haven't told you.'

He looked at her profile caught in the moonlight, and thought how its cold, colourless light aged her, sinking her eyes into shadow. 'You haven't told me much of anything.'

Her mouth widened slightly. A small smile. 'I'm more enigmatic that way. Keeps the mystery alive.'

'You ski in the winter and scuba dive in the summer. You once represented your country at the Olympics. Your parents live in Strasbourg. That's about the sum total of my knowledge.'

'So what else do you want me to tell you?'

'I don't know. Is it where you grew up? Strasbourg?'

She shook her head. 'No. My mother comes from Strasbourg. But they only moved there when my father retired. I was brought up in Lyons.' She inclined her head to find him watching her. 'Is that really what you wanted to know?'

'You told me, that night we met, that you never expected to be forty and alone.'

'Does anyone?'

'Why are you alone, Anna? You're an attractive woman. You have a lot of life still ahead of you.'

She turned her gaze back to the ceiling and pressed her lips together, as if afraid of the words that might spill out if she opened them. She held her silence for a long time. When, finally, she spoke, it was in a very small voice. Little more than a whisper. 'You look back on your life sometimes, and wish you'd made different decisions. You know, the big decisions. Career over personal life. One man over another. And then the little things that sometimes have even bigger consequences. Like deciding you don't have time to go to the shops. There's a laundry needing done, and you say, go on, don't wait for me. The shops'll be shut by the time I'm done here. And if you hadn't, they might still be alive. Or you might be dead with them and it wouldn't matter.'

Enzo saw a tear trickle from the corner of her eye and catch the light of the moon. 'Who?'

'My husband. My little boy.'

His voice was hushed. 'What happened?'

She brushed the silver tear from her face. 'Road accident. You know, the sort of thing you read about all the time and never think about the pain of the ones left behind. And how it never really goes away. You can replace almost anything but people.'

Enzo closed his eyes and shared her pain. 'I know.'

But she was lost in her memories and missed his empathy. 'I was so determined not to have children until my career was over, it was too late to start again. I only married André because he got me pregnant. But I kind of loved him, in a way. Because I knew he loved me.' She drew a deep breath and he heard the tremble in it. 'But none of that matters now. Can't go back. Can't undo it. Any of it.'

'You're not too old to still have children.'

'Physically, maybe. But in my head, that time came and went.' She turned her head towards him and forced a smile. 'Anyway, I bet you're wishing you'd never asked. Enigma's more interesting than tragedy.'

He laid his hand on her cheek. 'I'm sorry, Anna.'

'Oh, God, can we change the subject? Or neither of us'll get any sleep tonight.'

'Sure. What do you want to talk about?'

'I don't know.' She rolled her eyes in an extravagant show of thinking about it. 'How'd you get in tow with that creep, Raffin?'

Which took Enzo by surprise. 'You don't like him?'

'No, I don't.'

'You seemed to be getting on very well with him over dinner.'

'I was being polite. He's such a phony, and I'm way too long in the tooth to fall for that crap. What on earth does Kirsty see in him?'

Her words echoed almost exactly his own earlier thought. 'I wish I knew.'

'At least you're taking him away with you to Paris.' She thought for a moment. 'When do you plan to go?'

'First thing tomorrow.'

She raised herself on one elbow and looked at him, half of her face caught in full moonshine, the other in deep shadow. 'You're kidding. You only just got here.'

'My life's on hold, Anna, until I deal with this. When someone is trying to destroy everything that is dear to you, the only way to stop him is by getting him before he gets you.'

She looked at him pensively. 'I thought I'd have more time with you. When will you be back?'

'I don't know.'

She slipped a cool hand beneath the quilt to find the soft warmth between his legs, and he felt himself respond immediately to her touch. 'Then maybe we'd better just do this again. Give ourselves something to remember, until the next time.'

And this time, he knew, he would make love to her the way he had meant to before. With a long, slow burn to warm the cold night.

PART THREE

Chapter Twenty-Six

You wouldn't normally expect to find customers sitting out at pavement tables on a cold November day in Paris, even under the protective cover of an awning. But since the smoking ban had come into force earlier in the year, die-hard tobacco addicts had taken to sitting out on the sidewalks, nursing their *noisettes* and puffing on their Gaulloises huddled over tables in coats and hats. France was changing. The stereotypical chain-smoking Frenchman was a dying breed. Literally.

Enzo and Raffin found the retired *commissaire*, Jean-Marie Martinot, at his habitual pavement seat outside the Café Maury in the Rue La Fayette, not far from the Gare de l'Est. A hand-rolled cigarette smouldered in the corner of his mouth. A glass of red wine stood on the table beside him, and his face was buried in an early edition of *France Soir*. This stereotypical old Frenchman, at least, was still alive and kicking.

He drew his nose out of the newspaper as they pulled up chairs to join him. 'Ah, Monsieur Raffin.' He held out his hand. '*Comment allez-vous?*'

'I'm well, Monsieur Martinot. This is the gentleman I spoke to you about on the phone. Monsieur Macleod.'

Martinot extended his hand to Enzo. 'Delighted, monsieur. Your reputation goes before you.'

'Would that be the good one or the bad one?'

The retired policeman chuckled. Then his smile faded. 'So you think you're going to crack the Lambert case?'

'Only with your help.'

'I spent ten years sweating it before I finally gave up. Hate to admit defeat, monsieur. But *la retraite* was beckoning. And it was time for me to call it a day.' He took a final puff on his cigarette and stubbed it out in the *cendrier*. 'Still niggles, though.' And as the smoke leaked from the corners of his mouth, he drained his glass. 'You can buy me another, if you like.'

He had a full head of white hair dragged back from a high forehead and unusually blue eyes. He was a big man shrunken by age. A hard man in his day, Enzo guessed. Tough, physical. And yet there was a gentle quality about him, a reflection perhaps of something more cerebral, a sense of humanity that had, against all the odds, survived a lifetime as a cop. He wore a heavy, dark blue overcoat buttoned up almost to the neck, and there was a wide-brimmed felt hat on the seat beside him. Enzo noticed that he wore different patterned socks, and that his shoes had long since lost their shine. There were food stains on the front of his coat, and it occurred to Enzo that Jean-Marie Martinot was either a widower or a confirmed bachelor. Either way, he was certain that the old policeman lived on his own.

Enzo settled in his seat and glanced a little anxiously along the sidewalk. He knew there was no way the killer could know where he was. But he felt exposed here on the streets of Paris. Vulnerable. Raffin ordered three glasses of wine and raised his voice above the roar of the traffic. 'So do you think you can help?'

'Of course. What else have I got to do with my time? I've got so much of the damned stuff I can't give it away. People say it passes more quickly when you get older. But since Paulette died, every day feels like a year. And the nights even longer, especially when you can't sleep. *Santé.*' He raised his glass and took a sip of wine. 'Besides, I'd like to see you get the bastard. He still haunts me, you know. Poor little Pierre Lambert. It's funny, I spent twenty years working homicide, and I always felt a kind of responsibility for the victims. Like I was the only one who could represent their interests in the world they had just departed. They had no voice in it, no way of seeking justice. That was my job, and if I failed, I felt I'd let them down.'

He took out a plastic tobacco pouch and a pack of Rizla cigarette papers and began rolling a fresh smoke. 'He'd have been forty this year. Maybe that's why time drags. I've got all his lost years to live out, too. Along with all the others.' He shook his head, pulling pinches of tobacco from each end of his cigarette. 'There were a few, sadly.'

Enzo lifted his glass and took a sip. The wine was cold and bitter on the tongue. Cheap red wine. *La piquette*, as the French called it. 'So why does Lambert haunt you more than the others?'

'I suppose it wasn't him so much as his mother.' Martinot looked from one to the other. 'It's always the hardest bit. Talking to the loved ones. Breaking the news. She was a poor soul. Widowed when she was just a young woman, left to bring up two children with only her sister-in-law to help. Worked her whole life, with nothing to show for it in the end. Her sister-in-law found herself a man finally and left. Her daughter got MS and ended up in a wheelchair. And then I arrive. A messenger from hell to tell her that her son's been murdered. Her boy. The only one in the whole world who cared. And since she'd had to give up her job to look after her daughter, he was her only means of support.

'Lambert was keeping them both, his mother and his sister. He'd told them he was going to move them into a nice apartment in town. It's a pity he didn't do it before he died. Because the authorities couldn't have taken it away from them. As it was, his family didn't get a penny from his offshore account. That was sequestered for the case. Money of dubious origin.'

Enzo said, 'Did she know where his money came from?'

Martinot smiled sadly and shook his head. 'Didn't have a clue. She thought her precious boy had a part share in a successful restaurant. She had no idea that he was gay, never mind a male prostitute. In a way, perhaps, it was better for her that the case never did come to court. She would have learned things about her boy she would never have wanted to hear. And I certainly wasn't going to tell her.'

'Did you come to any conclusions at all about who might have murdered him or why?'

The old man shook his head. 'No. There was precious little evidence, and what there was proved frustratingly contradictory. I've thought about it a lot since, though. And I suppose if I was to make a guess, I'd probably say that Lambert had been blackmailing someone and pushed them too far. But whoever he was blackmailing, I don't think that was who killed him.'

'Why not?'

'It was a messy crime scene, monsieur. And for that I have no explanation. But Lambert's killer came prepared, left no prints, and killed him in a way you or I wouldn't know how. My best guess would be that he was killed by a professional. Someone paid to do it.'

Enzo and Raffin exchanged glances.

'But the best laid schemes of mice and men gang aft agley, as your countryman once wrote, and something went wrong that afternoon. None of it went quite as planned.' He looked at Enzo. 'I checked you out, monsieur, after Raffin called. You know your stuff.'

Enzo inclined his head in acknowledgement. 'Crime scene analysis used to be my speciality.'

'Then maybe you can throw some light on what it was that went wrong for our killer. And if you can, then maybe we'll have a key to unlock the case.'

Enzo said, 'Obviously the crime scene is long gone. But I take it the police still have the evidence?'

'Locked up safe and sound in the *greffe*.' Martinot looked at his watch and realised he hadn't lit his cigarette. He leaned over a burning match and smoke rose in wreaths around his head. He looked up. 'I still have some influence at the Quai des Orfevres. In half an hour, you'll get to see everything we had.' He finished his wine. 'Which gives us just enough time for another glass.'

Chapter Twenty-Seven

The Palais de Justice lay at the west end of the Île de la Cité, between the Quai des Orfèvres and the Quai de l'Horloge. *Le greffe,* the evidence depository, was situated deep in its bowels. Enzo had been here once before, when he found clues that led him to the missing Jacques Gaillard in a trunkful of apparently unrelated items recovered from the Paris catacombs.

In a vast, high-ceilinged room, row upon row of cardboard boxes were squeezed onto metal shelves that ranged from floor to ceiling. Every box told a story. Of murder, rape, theft, assault. The detritus of decades of crime. Evidence that either cleared or condemned, quashed or convicted. Or sometimes, simply baffled.

Martinot pushed open the door of a small room at the end of the main hall, and Enzo placed the box marked *Production No. 73982/M* on a plain metal table against the far wall. The retired *commissaire* looked at the label and recognised his own signature. He chuckled. 'It's been a while since I signed one of these.'

He took off his overcoat and hat and hung them on a coat-stand by the door. His shirt was buttoned up to the collar, but he wore no tie. His jacket was held closed by a single button. The other two were missing. He opened the box. '*Et voilà!*'

Enzo looked into it and felt a strange, breathless sense of anticipation. This was what the killer had been trying so very hard to stop him from ever doing. People had died and lives been ruined in the process. There was something in here, Enzo knew, that would shine a light into a place which had languished in darkness for nearly seventeen years. It was up to him to find the switch.

One by one he lifted out all the bagged evidence from the crime scene that had been Lambert's apartment. The antihistamines, now back in their bottle. Shards of glass from the tumbler smashed in the sink. The broken coffee cup and saucers. The shattered sugar bowl and lumps of sugar. The victim's clothes and underwear, wrapped in brown paper. His shirt, a woollen sweater, jeans, sneakers. From all of which it was apparent that Lambert had been a slight-built man of less than average height.

Enzo examined the cassette from the telephone answering machine in its ziplock bag. 'Could I have a copy made of this?'

Martinot shrugged. 'I don't see why not.'

Enzo turned back to the treasure trove of evidence. There was a box of paperwork. The original police reports. Martinot's tattered black notebook. The old cop picked it up and flipped through it with nostalgic fingers. A scrawling script written by another man in another time. Observations on life and death.

Pictures of the crime scene taken by the police photographer were slipped into plastic sleeves in a clip folder. Enzo glanced through them. Coarse colour under bright lights. A dead man lying among the debris of the struggle, his head turned at an impossible angle, a look of surprise frozen on his face.

Enzo was shocked by how slight he was. There was something fragile about him. An attractive young man whose life, and death, had been defined by his sexuality. He had a fine-featured face with full, almost sensuous lips. Dark, slightly curly hair fell untidily across his forehead. The bruises and scratching around his neck were plainly visible.

His appearance was dated already. Although less than seventeen years had passed, it seemed as if he had come from a different era. In seventeen years, Enzo had not changed so very much. He'd had his ponytail back then. Wore baggy, loose-fitting shirts, cargo pants. Sneakers. Timeless, unfashionable. But Lambert reflected the fashion of his time. Today, even at the same age, he would have looked quite different.

Enzo examined the chaos around the boy. The shattered coffee table, an upturned chair, an occasional table that had been sent flying, ornaments strewn across a luridly patterned carpet. That there had been quite a struggle was evident. He looked up to find Martinot smiling at him.

'I know what you're thinking. If the killer was a professional, like we figure he might have been, how on earth was Lambert able to put up such a fight? Look at him. You could have blown him over.'

Enzo nodded and reached for the autopsy report. He flipped through it until he found the pathologist's description of the neck injuries, and saw why the *légiste* had concluded that the attacker was wearing gloves. Seam stitching along the fingertips had left a pattern on the skin. The bruising itself was messy. In a classic case of strangulation, the killer might have left three or four marks on one side of the neck from his fingers, and a single mark on the opposite side from his thumb. A good patterned injury in the shape of a hand was rare, but recently cyanocrylate fumes had been used successfully to bring out the shape of a finger or hand print, sometimes even with enough detail to collect a fingerprint from the skin. Such a technique, even had it been available, would not have helped in this case.

The abrasions on the neck, Enzo figured, had been made by Lambert himself, trying to prise free his attacker's grasp. He flipped through a few more pages to confirm his suspicions, and found what he was looking for. The pathologist had recovered skin from beneath the victim's fingernails. His own skin, gouged from his neck in the heat of the struggle.

He had, it seemed, been at least partially successful in preventing his attacker from strangling him. As Martinot had observed, that seemed odd given Lambert's slight build. In the end, however, he had been no match for a technique that had severed his spinal cord in a single, deft twist of the head.

'So what do you think?' Raffin's impatience was palpable. But Enzo raised a hand to quiet him. He was not going to be rushed. He lifted the plastic bag containing the pills and looked at the label on it. *Twenty-one* comprimés, *terfenadine, brand name Seldane.* He turned to Martinot. 'You're certain that Lambert did not suffer from allergies?'

'As certain as I can be. His mother knew nothing about it if he did. He had never been prescribed antihistamines, and there were no others in the house.'

'But terfenadine was a prescription drug?'

'Yes. We always figured they belonged to the killer.'

'Although you found nothing in the apartment that might have triggered an allergic reaction?'

'Our best advice at the time was that almost anything can trigger a reaction in sufferers. Even someone's aftershave. But Lambert wasn't wearing any, and there was nothing else that suggested itself to us.'

'So why was there a broken glass in the sink and pills spilled all over the kitchen floor?'

Martinot shrugged. 'We can only guess at that, monsieur.'

Enzo picked up the crime scene photographs again, this time examining as much of the room as he could see beyond the immediate area of struggle. A large settee and two armchairs that looked as if they had seen better days, half-hidden beneath colourful woven throws. The lurid, thick-piled carpet, plush velvet curtains hanging in oriel windows. 'This was a furnished rental, right?'

'Right.'

'He hadn't been there very long.'

'A couple of months.'

'Did you talk to the previous *locataires*?'

Martinot picked up and riffled through the reports. 'Yeah, here we are. Two days after the murder. A middle aged couple. They'd moved across town. Fourteenth *arrondissement*. It was just routine stuff. They couldn't help.'

'Would we be able to find them again?'

'Who knows? Sixteen years. They could have moved again. They might be dead. Why?'

'We need to know if they kept pets.'

'Pets?' Martinot frowned and scratched his head. 'You know, now that you mention it, I can actually remember going to their place. Sticks in my mind only because they had these two thundering great Irish setters that just about knocked me over. Huge beasts. Made a big apartment seem small.'

Enzo let his eyes wander over the crime scene photographs once more. 'Then that's probably what did it.'

'Did what?' Raffin said.

'Sparked the reaction.'

Martinot said, 'But there hadn't been dogs in Lambert's apartment for over two months.'

Enzo shook his head. 'Doesn't matter. Both cats and dogs shed something called dander. The word has the same origin as dandruff. It's a natural phenomenon in hairy animals. The outer layer of skin, the epidermis, is quite thin in dogs. It's constantly renewing itself as layers of new cells push up to replace the old ones above. The process takes place every twenty-one days or so. The outer cells flake off into the environment as dander. People think it's the animal's hair that causes allergy. It's not. It's the dander.'

Raffin said, 'Are you saying the killer had an allergic reaction to dogs that weren't even there?'

'Well, consider this. Epidermal turnover is more rapid in breeds that are prone to various forms of dry and oily seborrhea. Breeds like Cocker or Springer spaniels.' He paused. 'Or Irish setters. These dogs shed old skin every three or four days. So the previous occupants of Lambert's apartment had dogs that were producing up to seven times the amount of dander most dogs produce. And there were two of them. That dander would have permeated the entire place, sparking possible allergic reaction in a sufferer even months after the dogs had gone.'

He handed the folder of photographs to Martinot. 'Look at the place. Soft furniture, plush curtains. Thick-piled carpet, the worst repository of all for dander. It would be my guess, monsieur, that the killer had a severe allergy to dog dander. He maybe knew that his victim didn't keep pets, so he went unsuspecting to an apartment that was just laden with the stuff. Symptoms would have started within minutes. Judging by the struggle, the ineffectual attempt to strangle his victim, the killer was probably under serious stress. Semi-incapacitated. Severe allergic reaction develops very fast. If it reaches anything like anaphylaxis, whole body reaction, it can be disabling, sometimes even fatal.'

He picked up the plastic bag with the pills. 'The terfenadine wouldn't have been particularly effective. He must have tried to get as many into himself as he could. But the best way of dealing with a reaction like that is getting away from the source of the allergen as quickly as possible. Which would explain his panic in getting out of the place, and why he left a trail of evidence in his wake. It's even possible he might have required hospital treatment.'

'Jesus!' Martinot's oath slipped out in a breath. He had a very vivid picture now of a scene he had been trying to piece together for almost two decades.

Raffin said, 'So he had an allergic reaction, how does that help us?'

Enzo turned to him. 'If Monsieur Martinot can get us a Wood's Lamp, I'll show you.'

Martinot cocked an eyebrow. 'With all due respect, monsieur, what the hell's a Wood's Lamp?'

'It's a lamp that gives off an ultraviolet light. Standard kit for a forensic scientist. But any ultraviolet lamp will do.'

◇◇◇

It took Martinot more than an hour to procure an ultraviolet lamp and return to meet up with Enzo and Raffin once more at the *greffe*.

'I don't know if it's a Wood's Lamp,' he said, 'but it gives off ultraviolet light.' It was around nine inches long and three inches wide in a black casing, most of which was to contain a battery to power the tubular bulb.

'It'll do perfectly.' Enzo handed it back to Martinot and removed Lambert's patterned blue and red woollen crewneck sweater from its paper parcel, spreading it carefully on the table top. 'Ultra violet,' he said, 'otherwise known as blacklight. Or blacklight blue, in the trade, to distinguish it from those bug zapping lamps. It was delivered as a light source in a lamp more than a century ago by a man called Robert W. Wood. First used in the diagnosis of infective and pigmentary dermatoses. But more recently as a diagnostic tool for certain skin cancers.'

He took back the lamp from Martinot. 'Most often employed in forensic science to detect the presence of semen on the skin and clothing of rape victims.' He turned to Raffin. 'Would you turn out the light, please, Roger?'

The windowless room was plunged into absolute darkness. Enzo took a deep breath. He was about to shine a light into the past. A blacklight to illuminate a brutal killer. He pressed a switch, and the lamp flickered several times before casting its eerie light around the room. He held it six inches above the fabric of Lambert's sweater and made a slow pass over it. All three men could see quite clearly the glow of fluorescent silver across the chest and neck, woven into the yarn, it seemed, in random patches and trails.

Enzo said, 'You can turn on the light now.'

They all blinked in the sudden glare of harsh electric light, and Enzo turned off the ultraviolet.

'What the hell is that silver stuff?' Raffin said.

'Dried mucus. Saliva. Phlegm. Invisible to the naked eye. And the pathologist would never have thought to pass a Wood's Lamp over the victim's clothes.' Enzo turned to Martinot. 'This man came to Lambert's apartment to murder him. But as you surmised, his plan went well agley. He succumbed to a severe allergic reaction brought on by dog dander from the apartment's previous renters. His immune system went haywire, responding to the dander by producing vast quantities of Immunoglobin E, known as IgE. The IgE would have gathered very quickly on the mast cells lining his nose, throat, lungs, and gastrointestinal tract. The union of the IgE and the allergen would have been explosive, releasing a torrent of irritating chemicals, primarily histamine. The man would have been coughing and sneezing and choking as his throat closed up, his body using nose, mouth, and eyes to try to expel the histamine like an aerosol. Even as he fought to see and murder his victim through streaming eyes, he must have been spraying him with mucus and saliva. Clear, wet liquid that would have dried to invisibility in minutes.'

Enzo turned back to the sweater. 'It couldn't be seen, but it was there, expelled at great velocity, and almost certainly rich in white blood cells. Particularly the eosinophils involved in allergic reactions. Even better, there may be a stray sloughed nose hair or two, along with respiratory epithelial cells. Which means there's a better than even chance we'll be able to recover DNA.'

'Even after all this time?' Raffin said.

'It would have been more certain had the clothes been refrigerated. But it's relatively cool down here in the *greffe*. A steady temperature. I think the chances are good.'

Martinot whistled softly in admiration. 'Man, I wish you'd been around sixteen years ago.'

But Enzo shook his head. 'Wouldn't have made any difference, monsieur. Back then, we might have found the cells on his clothing, but we'd never have been able to extract the DNA.'

He turned to Raffin. 'I think our man knew that. I think he knew that if we revisited this crime we were almost certain to find those cells and recover his DNA. And he could only be afraid of that for one reason. His DNA is in a database somewhere.'

Even as he spoke the words, Enzo felt their effect. He shivered, as if someone had stepped on his grave. He had taken a huge stride towards the possible identification of his nemesis. It could only be a matter of time before the killer would know that, and try to stop him from going any further. Any way he could. The stakes had just been ratcheted up to breaking point, and it seemed there was no way Enzo could avoid going head to head with him.

Chapter Twenty-Eight

Cadaqués, Spain, September 1986

Outside the church, on the slate-paved terrace, two Mediterranean conifers offered a pool of shade, a momentary escape from the dusty blast of the sun. Below, across the Roman tiled roofs, boats bobbed gently at moorings in a bay like glass. The reflection of sunlight on whitewash was blinding.

Richard hesitated in the shadow of the trees. He felt strangely choked. He had watched her leave the house just minutes earlier. A woman of fifty, whom the years had not treated kindly. Once lustrous blond hair now gone grey, pulled back severely from a thin face, pinched and turned mean by time and disappointment. A woman who passed him on the steps without a second glance.

His mother.

He was not quite sure why he had come. Curiosity, he supposed. A need to connect with his past. A tiny Spanish fishing port from where he had been snatched sixteen years and two months ago. A place which had become a prison for the woman who had loved him then. And if she still did, it wasn't really him she loved. It was the memory of the child she had lost all those years before.

There was something shocking in seeing her. In knowing that she was going to church to pray for him. He had stood on the steps, caught by surprise. And if she had met his eye he might have said, 'Hello, mother,' and released her from her misery. Instead, he had frozen, unable to move, unable to speak, and she had passed, preoccupied, within a few inches of her missing boy.

Now that he was here, he didn't know quite what to do. But the cool of the Església de Santa Maria drew him, like an inhalation of breath. An escape from the furnace. And he walked in through an opening in the tall, studded door, only to see a reflection of himself in glass behind wrought iron gates. Dark glasses and baseball cap, shorts and a tee-shirt. Not exactly the respectful attire expected of those who came to worship.

He turned into the church and removed his cap and shades, blinking in the dark as his eyes adjusted to the change of light. And then suddenly the apse at the far end of the nave was bathed in soft yellow, as a tourist dropped a coin in a metre, and an altar of extraordinary extravagance, fashioned from pure gold, rose up into the vaulted dome. Angels and cherubs adorning columns and arches rising in tiers to a winged figure in flight almost at the confluence of the dome's ribs.

For a moment Richard gazed at it in awe. He had never seen anything quite like it. At least, not on this scale. Then his eyes drifted among the rows of pews searching for his mother. But she wasn't to be seen. He walked carefully through the echoing vastness, almost afraid to breathe, until he saw a red, net curtain hung in the entrance to the transversal chapel. A sign in the doorway read, *A Place of Prayer*. And through the curtain he could see a more modest altar presided over by a figure of Christ washed in sunlight from windows high up in the walls. A solitary soul knelt before it in silhouette.

Angela Bright was quite still, head bowed, her hands clasped in front of her. Richard stood watching her for some minutes, safe in the knowledge that even if she rose unexpectedly he would not be immediately visible to her. If she was praying for his return, then her prayers had been answered. But he had already decided that she would never know it.

He retreated to the back of the church to sit beneath the huge circle of stained glass and stare at the altar, until the time purchased by the coin expired, and it retreated suddenly into its habitual obscurity. He was backlit through the glass at the door, a silhouette like his mother, cut in sharp contrast against the rectangular halo of sunlight beyond. When she emerged, finally, from her chapel, she walked past him without even looking. She had an odd, shuffling gait, like an old woman.

He rose and followed her out, slipping on his dark glasses and pulling the peak of his cap down to shadow his face. She turned into the narrow, slate-cobbled street below the church that led to her house, a white-washed, three-storey building with rust-red shutters and arched brick lintels. He wondered what she did all day in this rambling old house with its walled garden, bougainvillea climbing the whitewash and weeping its purple tears. Did his brother and sister still live here, too? He looked up and saw patterned ceramic tiles beneath the eaves. Who paid for it all? His father?

His mother pushed open a mahogany red door and was swallowed by darkness. Richard stood staring after her for some minutes. The street descended at an acute angle below him into the old town, narrow and shaded by tall houses and more bougainvillea. A few paces down, on the other side of the street, was a small restaurant, a chalkboard sign outside with the menu of the day. Just a handful of *pesetas* would get him lunch and a carafe of wine.

He was served by an attractive young waitress who clearly found him interesting. She hovered attentively at his table, happy to talk. She had just left school to work in the family business, and after a busy season things were quieter now, she said. Her French was good. And her English passable. He ordered gaspacho, which came with soft chunks of rough, Spanish bread, and then catch of the day, which was dorado, or sea bream, soft white flesh moist and delicious, reminding him of home. Although now that he knew who he was, it no longer felt like a place he could call home. It was where he had grown up, with a stranger pretending to be his mother.

He asked if there were a lot of foreigners buying property in the town these days, and she told him there were more and more. There was an old English lady living across the street. But she'd been there for years. Señora Bright. And she was no holidaymaker. Hers was a sad story.

'Oh?' Richard gave her his most charming smile. 'Tell me?'

She glanced back towards the kitchen before running an eye over the other tables, and decided she had time. She told him about the abduction of Señora Bright's child, although she was too young to remember it herself. The old lady had lived opposite ever since she could remember. She'd had two children with her. But she hardly knew them. Her parents had sent her to a convent school, so she didn't know a lot of the other kids in town. But she'd seen them occasionally in the street. She looked at Richard. 'The boy looked a little like you.' She tried to picture him without the baseball cap and sunglasses. 'But he had much longer hair.'

Richard said, 'You speak about them as if they weren't around any more.'

'They're not. They went back to England a couple of years ago. To live with their father, my mother said. And good riddance. She doesn't like the English.'

Richard lingered over his meal, smoking several cigarettes, thinking about what he was going to do with the rest of his life. Who he was going to be. After all, he was free now to be whoever he wanted. But his money wasn't going to last forever, and that was a problem.

Through the open door of the restaurant, he saw his mother passing. Dressed all in black, like a widow in mourning. He paid up quickly and said a hurried farewell to the disappointed waitress. Emboldened by a half-litre of rough, red Rioja, he set off after the old lady.

She was carrying a woven shopping basket and had a black headscarf tied loosely around her hair. He followed her, recklessly close, all the way down through the town, past the Carretera del Dr. Callis and a tiny art gallery on the corner to the Casa de la Vila at the bottom of the hill. He leaned on the rail and looked down into the clear, green water of the bay below and watched his mother climb stiffly down the steps to the curve of the harbour road.

He wondered again what point there was in this. Perhaps he was simply delaying the moment when he would have to decide what to do next, but still he felt strangely compelled to go after her.

Past the café-bar in the Casino, she turned off the Place Frederic Rahola into the main street opposite the town's long, shingle beach and climbed steps into a small supermarket. Richard lingered for several minutes out on the sidewalk before following her in. He hovered, pretending to look at the wine, as she chose a selection of fresh vegetables from tiered racks, then felt his heart seize suddenly solid as she turned in his direction. She, too, wore dark glasses, so he couldn't see her eyes. But she stopped, for all the world as if time had simply decided to stand still. She was looking right at him. Right through him. What were maybe only a few seconds seemed to stretch into eternity, but he felt naked, bathed in the spotlight of her confusion and uncertainty. And he turned and hurried from the shop without looking back. His heart was hammering against his ribs so hard he felt sure that people in the street could hear it above the noise of the traffic. He daren't stop. He kept on walking until he knew there was no way she could still see him, then he pressed himself against a wall and tried to control his breathing.

He had been foolish, careless, and wondered if she had realised. If there was any way she could have recognised him. And, of course, he knew that there was.

It was time to go. Time to get on with the rest of his life. And it had occurred to him now exactly where to start.

Chapter Twenty-Nine

Miramont, November 2008

Returning to Miramont, tucked away in its mountain valley high up in the Cantal, was an anticlimax after Paris. Enzo was not quite certain why Raffin had opted to come with him, but suspected that the journalist was being drawn back by an interest in Anna. There was no doubt that she was an attractive woman, and Raffin had so clearly been fascinated by her that first night. Enzo was uncomfortable with the thought but had no evidence with which to back it up. And so he held his peace.

When they got there, it seemed colder than before, although the sky, if anything, was a clearer, deeper blue. The winter sun cut the sharpest of shadows among the folds of the hills that rose up around the house, and the frost stayed white all day in those shaded places that the sunlight never reached.

Enzo had spent a restless few days at Raffin's apartment in the Rue Tournon, just a stone's throw away from the *Sénat*, and the wide-open spaces of the Luxembourg Gardens. The weather had been grey, and misty, and cold, and he had passed the time walking in the park, wading through the drifts of leaves, drinking coffee and reading the papers behind the steamed-up windows of the crowded café-restaurant near the north gate.

It was not until the fourth day that he received word from the laboratory of the *police scientifique*. Cells had been recovered from the dried mucus on Lambert's *pull*, and a DNA profile successfully obtained. Enzo felt a sense of triumph. They had the killer's code. All they needed now was to find a match. But that was likely to take time and to be a complex and labyrinthine process.

'Why?' Nicole demanded to know on his return.

And Enzo explained that it was because they had no idea what databases to search. There were twenty-seven countries in the European Union, each with its own DNA database. And while they had all signed up the previous year to the Prum Agreement, allowing national law enforcement agencies automatic access to the DNA and fingerprint databases of other member states, Enzo did not constitute a national law enforcement agency.

'So how are you going to get access to them?' Nicole said.

'I'm not. Jean-Marie Martinot, the cop who handled the original investigation, has to persuade his former colleagues to re-open the case. Even then, they'll still have to sell the idea to the Police Nationale. And you know how quickly French bureaucracy moves, Nicole. It could be a while.'

'Well, if he's on anyone's database, it'll probably be ours.'

Enzo shrugged. 'Maybe, maybe not. The French database it pretty limited. The British have got the biggest in Europe. In fact, the biggest in the world. But there's nothing to say he's on any of the European computers. There are dozens of databases around the world now. And then, of course, there are the Americans, who have the second biggest. Getting access to that will generate a blizzard of paperwork all on its own.'

They were in the computer room at the back of the house. Nicole had several screens up and running. Enzo ran his eyes across them. 'So how's the search for the good doctor going?'

She made a face. 'It's not. There are loads of agencies and directories. It's hard to believe, but a lot of them don't even have photographs. Then there are all these sites with so-called actors advertising their services.' She blushed. 'Mostly it's about sex. You know, exotic dancers, escorts. That sort of thing. But I think you might find it easier to identify your doctor with his clothes on.'

Enzo smiled. 'I think I'd know the face, no matter what.'

'Well, I've got a few for you to look at. I'm not too confident, though.'

In fact, she had fifteen jpegs collected in a folder. Enzo leaned over the desk as she opened them one by one. These were photographs taken by professionals, always against a neutral backdrop, faces lit to show them off to best advantage. Those with few advantages had their deficiencies masked by soft focus. A catalogue of men in their forties showing teeth that were too white, pulling in paunches, smiling eyes trying hard to hide an optimism long lost to failure. None of them was his doctor.

Nicole grimaced an apology. 'I'll keep looking.'

Enzo had been disappointed by the coolness with which he had been greeted by Anna. He had hoped for the same warmth with which she had sent him off. The taste and scent of her remained vivid in his recollection. But she was still being discreet in front of his daughters.

Now, as he left the study, she was waiting for him at the foot of the spiral staircase and gave him a quick kiss and squeezed his hand. 'I missed you,' she whispered.

He ran his hand up through her hair to cup the back of her head in his hand and draw her to him to kiss her back. A much longer kiss, filled with the passion aroused by her very proximity. She drew away, smiling, and wagged a finger at him.

'Not in front of the children.'

He grinned.

She took his hand. 'I've got a surprise for you.' And she led him into the *séjour*, where she had removed all the paintings from one wall to mount a large whiteboard at eye-level. He had told her at some point how he liked to think visually. How at home he always worked on a whiteboard, jotting down thoughts and observations, trying to find links between them and connecting them with arrows.

He looked at it in astonishment. 'Where on earth did you manage to find that?'

She shrugged dismissively. 'A few phone calls, and a *monsieur* from the village to install it.'

'But won't your friends object to you defacing their house like this?'

'Oh, they won't mind.'

Enzo thought, if it was his house, he would have minded. But all he said was, 'Thank you.' And kissed her again to demonstrate his gratitude. 'How have things been?'

She tilted her head a little to one side. 'Okay.' But she didn't sound convincing. 'Sophie's pretty restless. And Bertrand, too. I think he wants to get back and sort out his gym.'

Enzo sighed. 'I feel bad about that. But it's not safe yet. It really isn't.'

'Anyway, they go for long walks, and they lunch sometimes in the village. They're out right now.'

'What about Kirsty?'

Anna made a face. 'I think she's still in shock, Enzo. Someone tried to murder her, after all. And her best friend was killed. Roger didn't call once, and she's spent most of her time in her room. He's up there with her now.'

Enzo didn't even want to think about what they might be doing. He said, 'I've got something I want everyone to listen to. But I'll leave it until after we've eaten tonight.' He took her face in his hands. 'Is anyone helping you with the cooking?'

She let him kiss her and laughed and said, 'I'm enjoying it, Enzo. It's such a long time since I had anyone to cook for but myself.'

◇◇◇

He slipped the cassette into the stereo system and hit the play button.

All through the meal he had watched Raffin monopolising the conversation with Anna, flirting with her, exuding charm like oil. And he had seen Kirsty become more and more subdued. At one moment, he had caught Anna's eye, and felt her embarrassment, her silent plea for rescue. And he had broken up the *tête à tête* by calling her into the kitchen on some pretext. He was itching to break his silence on the subject, but didn't want to create a scene in front of Kirsty and the others. And so all his attention was focused on the tape.

Intent faces around the room strained to listen. Two voices distorted by time and telephone. A murderer speaking to his victim the day before he killed him:

'Yes, hello?'
'Salut, it's me.'
'Oh, okay.'
'I'm sorry I didn't call yesterday. I was out of the country. Portsmouth. In England. A business trip.'
'Is that supposed to mean something to me?'
'I just thought you'd wonder why I hadn't called.'
'Well, you're calling me now.'
'I was going to suggest tomorrow afternoon. Three o'clock. If that's okay with you.'
'Where?'
'Your place.'
'I prefer somewhere public. You know that.'
'Listen, we need to talk.'
An audible sigh. 'You know where to find me?'
'Of course.'
'Three o'clock, then.'
'Fine.'

The conversation ended abruptly. Enzo had listened to it over and over again. He had his own thoughts, but he wanted fresh input. 'What do you think?'

'I think they didn't like one another very much,' Sophie said.

'Why do you say that?'

'Well, because the killer's being very polite, and the other guy can hardly conceal his irritation.'

Bertrand said, 'I'm not sure he's irritated so much as just tense. Wary.'

Nicole asked if they could listen to it again, and Enzo rewound the tape to replay it. When they finished listening for a second time Nicole said, 'They don't know one another very well, do they? I think maybe they've met only a handful of times before.'

'Why do you say that?'

'Because he had to ask if the other guy knew his address.'

Kirsty said, 'They'd obviously met often enough for Lambert to have established that he only wanted them to meet in public.'

'So why did he agree to let him come to his home?' It was Raffin this time.

Enzo said, 'Because the killer was threatening him. Very subtly, but unmistakeably. He was in complete command of the conversation. He was using the familiar *tu*, while Lambert was using the formal *vous*. Lambert was being spoken to like a child. His caller had failed to make some pre-arranged call the day before, but his apology was perfunctory. When Lambert expressed his preference for meeting in public, he was slapped right back down. *Ecoute-moi*. Listen, we need to talk. There's more than a hint of a threat in that. We hear Lambert sigh. He doesn't want the caller to come to his house. But he gives in straight away, because he's lacking in confidence. He's scared, intimidated.' Enzo looked around at all the faces focused in his direction. 'But there's something else. A single word in that whole conversation that sticks out like a sore thumb.'

When the faces looking back at him remained blank, he turned to his elder daughter. 'Come on, Kirsty. English is your native tongue. You must have heard it, surely?'

Kirsty stiffened, feeling the weight of her father's expectation. She had never been quite sure that it was something she could live up to. She desperately wanted to please him, but she couldn't think of anything.

'He said he'd been out of the country. In England. The town of Portsmouth.' He swung his attention towards Bertrand. 'Say Portsmouth, Bertrand.' Bertrand looked at him blankly. 'Just as you would normally.'

'Portsmouth,' he said.

Enzo swivelled back towards Kirsty. 'See? Hear how he said it? The way the French always say it.' And he pronounced it

phonetically, just the way that Bertrand had said it. '*Porsmoose.*
The French just cannot get their brains around the concept of
four consecutive consonants. RTSM. How do you pronounce
that? They can't. They say, *Porsmoose.* But his caller pronounced
it just the way an Englishman would. *Portsmouth.*'

Kirsty nodded, understanding now what her father had
meant. 'Are you saying he was English?'

'That's just it. I don't know. He doesn't sound English to me.'
He turned to Anna. 'Did he sound like a foreigner to you?'

She shook her head. 'He sounded like a Frenchman to me.'

'He had a southern accent,' Sophie said. 'He's French. I'd
put money on it.'

Enzo smiled and shook his head. He reached for a book he
had placed on the shelf beside the stereo. He opened it at a page
marked by a Post-it. 'The Murders in the Rue Morgue,' he said.
'By Edgar Allen Poe. Let me read you this paragraph.'

He slipped a pair of half-moon reading glasses on to the end of
his nose and perched himself on the arm of Sophie's *fauteuil*:

> The Frenchman supposes it the voice of a Spaniard,
> and might have distinguished some words had he been
> acquainted with the Spanish. The Dutchman maintains
> it to have been that of a Frenchman; but we find it
> stated that not understanding French this witness was
> examined through an interpreter. The Englishman
> thinks it the voice of a German, and does not understand
> German. The Spaniard is sure that it was that of an
> Englishman, but judges by the intonation altogether, as
> he has no knowledge of the English. The Italian believes
> it the voice of a Russian, but has never conversed with a
> native of Russia. A second Frenchman differs, moreover,
> with the first, and is positive that the voice was that of
> an Italian; but not being cognizant of that tongue is, like
> the Spaniard, convinced by the intonation.

He looked up at the array of rueful smiles around him. 'Not
easy, is it? We all have our own perceptions, very often based on

preconceptions which are false.' He paused. 'You know what a *shibboleth* is?'

Raffin said, 'It's a password.'

'We use it in that sense, yes. But it's the origin of the word that's interesting in this context. It's an old Hebrew word. And its present usage derives from a story told in the old Hebrew bible. A story of civil war between two Hebrew tribes, the Ephraimites who have settled on one side of the River Jordan, and the Gileadites who have settled on the other. If an Ephraimite who crossed the river tried to pass himself off as a friend, the Gileadites would make him pronounce the word *shibboleth*. It actually meant flooding stream. But in the Ephraimite dialect, initial *sh* sounds were always pronounced *s*. So the Ephraimite would say, *sibboleth*, and give himself away.'

Kirsty said, 'So *Porsmoose* is like a *shibboleth*.'

'Exactly. It tells us something very important about our killer. The trouble is, I don't know what.' He closed his book and took the cassette from the stereo. He held it up between thumb and forefinger. 'But I know a man who might. I need to get this in the post first thing tomorrow.'

Chapter Thirty

When Kirsty awoke, there were long slivers of gold slanting through half-open shutters, and she heard the church bell strike nine. She had lain awake for much of the night, and was surprised now to find that she had slept at all. The bed beside her was empty.

She got up, brushing tangled hair from her face, and slipped on her dressing gown, padding then in bare feet across polished boards to open the French windows and throw the shutters wide. The sun, still low in the sky, blinded her, and the rush of ice-cold air shocked her from her drowse. Frost lay thick across the field, sparkling in the sunlight. Long shadows cut sharp lines across the white-roofed houses of the village.

In normal circumstances, a morning like this would have raised her spirits, keening her anticipation of the day ahead. But nothing, it seemed, could lift her out of her depression. The tumultuous events of the last few days, and the death of Sylvie, had settled on her like a fog, laden with guilt and regret. Compounded now by the mercurial behaviour of her lover.

In the days that he had been away, Roger had neither called nor e-mailed once. And then on his return, he had been caring and attentive, making love to her in the afternoon, easing her depression with a balm of soothing words. Only to ignore her all through dinner, turning his attentions exclusively towards their hostess. Kirsty knew that everyone else around the table had been aware of it. Nicole had prattled away to Sophie and Bertrand, and they had prattled back, a way of covering their embarrassment. And Kirsty had been conscious of her father's smouldering anger at the far end of the table. But his expected explosion had never come.

Kirsty was intimidated by Anna. She felt dowdy and naïve by comparison. And she was sure that for the erudite and experienced Roger, Anna's more worldly sophistication cast Kirsty in the shade.

She had tried to speak to him about it last night when they went to bed. But he had said that he was tired. It had been a long day. She was just depressed and not seeing things clearly. They would talk about it in the morning.

But now that morning was here, he had risen before her, and she wondered if that was a harbinger for a day that would be spent avoiding the issue.

She showered and dressed and slipped out into the hallway, filled with trepidation. Light from the windows in the stairwell reflected off dark, polished floorboards, and the spiral wooden staircase curled up and down from the landing, supported by nothing that Kirsty could see. It was attached to the wall on one side, and its bannister spiralled around fresh air on the other. A fairytale staircase in Kirsty's personal nightmare. It creaked ominously at each step, as she made her way down to the hall below.

Even as she reached the foot of the stairs, she could hear raised voices in the kitchen. Roger and her father. Curtains half-drawn across the hall obscured the kitchen doorway, and she stood listening, transfixed.

'Oh, piss off, Enzo. You're just jealous.'

Enzo's voice was steady, controlled, but Kirsty could hear the tension in it, and was shocked by his words. 'Even if I didn't know that Anna thought you were a prick, Raffin, I'd have no cause to be jealous.'

'True enough. Why would you go getting jealous over some whore you picked up in a bar.'

There was a very long, dangerous silence, in which the imminent threat of violence had time to recede. Enzo's voice was stretched to breaking point. 'Anna and I owe each other nothing. Neither loyalty, nor fidelity. We're enjoying each other in the moment. No history, no future. And none of that has any relevance here.'

'Oh, and what has?'

'Kirsty.'

'I think she's made it more than abundantly clear to you that she and I are none of your business. Alright?'

'Yes, she has. And that's her choice. Her right. Like it or not, I've got to respect that. But I'll not stand by and see her hurt.'

Raffin said, 'You're full of shit, you know that?'

'Just stay away from Anna.'

There was the sound of something banging onto a worktop, and then a heavy footfall. Kirsty quickly ran down the first few steps of the stairway leading to the cellar, the curve of it hiding her from view as Raffin emerged from the kitchen, pale-faced with anger. He headed upstairs two at a time. Kirsty remained hidden, listening for her father, in case he might follow. But after a long silence she heard him moving through to the dining room, and the sound of the French windows opening on to the *terrasse*.

She took several tentative steps back up to the hall and stood in the semigloom nursing mixed feelings. Not so long ago she would have been furious with Enzo. She would have stormed into the kitchen and told him he had no business and no right interfering in her life. But somehow in these last days, her perception of him had changed.

'You're up late this morning.'

The voice startled her, and she turned to find Anna standing in the half-open door of the computer room. 'Oh, hi. I guess I slept in.'

Anna tilted her head, giving her a curious look, a tiny empathetic smile curling the corners of her mouth. 'Have you had breakfast?'

'I'm not hungry.'

'Why don't we go for a walk, then? It's a beautiful morning. Who knows, you might work up an appetite.'

'I don't think so.'

But Anna wasn't taking no for an answer. 'What else are you going to do?' And when Kirsty couldn't think of a quick reply Anna took her arm and led her towards the door, stopping only to lift their jackets from the coat stand.

The frost was beginning to melt now on roofs and across the fields where the sunlight lay. The garden was spread out before them, sparkling and wet, a tiny fountain set in a circular flowerbed gurgling through the ice. They walked across the grass, leaving trails through the frost, past the swimming pool and down on to the path that led to the road.

'Where is everyone?' Kirsty said.

'Sophie and Bertrand have driven down to Aurillac for the day. Nicole's got her face stuck in a computer screen, as usual.' She glanced back towards the house and saw Raffin watching them from the balcony outside his bedroom. On the *terrasse* at the side of the house, Enzo was leaning on the rail following their progress. Neither man could see the other. Anna slipped her arm through Kirsty's. 'You don't like me very much, do you?'

Kirsty drew away. 'What do you mean?'

'Some woman your father picked up in a bar. A one-night stand. What sort of woman could that be? Certainly not good enough for him.'

Kirsty said, 'It takes two to make a one-night stand. And from all accounts, it wouldn't be atypical of my father.' No sooner were the words out of her mouth, than she immediately regretted them. That was the old Kirsty talking. Her father had believed he was dying. She had no right to judge him.

But Anna just grinned. 'The young are such prudes. One set of values for themselves, another for their parents. But actually, it was me that did the picking up. If I hadn't, I doubt your father would even have noticed me. He was pretty preoccupied. I was in Strasbourg for the funeral of a friend and feeling a bit low. It was more about comfort than sex. For both of us.'

'And now?'

Anna twinkled. 'Oh, now, it's definitely the sex.'

Which made Kirsty laugh for the first time in days.

They walked on in silence, until they reached the road that ran through the village. A monument in front of the church listed the dead of the Great War. Even in a tiny village like this, the death toll had reached nearly forty, wiping out a whole generation of its young men. Brousse, Chanut, Claviere. Taurand, Vaurs, Verdier.

'So what's the story, Kirsty?'

'What story?'

'Between you and your father.'

'He hasn't told you?'

'We're still strangers in the night, Kirsty. We make love, not conversation.'

And Kirsty felt overshadowed again by the older woman's easy wit and sophistication. It made her behaviour through all the years of rejecting her father seem childish and inconsequential, and she glossed over it. 'Oh, he left my mother for another woman when I was just a kid. He set up home here in France with his French lover. And then she went and died in childbirth, leaving him to bring up Sophie on his own.'

'And you resented him for it?'

'I didn't understand why he'd gone. It was like it wasn't my mother he was leaving, it was me. At first I thought it was my fault. Me and mum used to row all the time. I thought I'd driven him away. Then my mum made me see it wasn't my fault, or hers. It was just my dad. That's how he was. He didn't care about anything or anyone but himself.'

There were tables and chairs on the *terrasse* outside Chez Milou, and they sat down to soak up what little warmth there was in the sun. An old man came out and took their order for coffee.

Kirsty examined the backs of her hands, avoiding Anna's eye. 'It took me nearly twenty years to understand that it wasn't that simple. That dads suffer, too. And that you can't choose who you love and who you don't.' Which made her wonder about Roger, the feelings she had for him, and why, in spite of everything, she still had. She lifted her eyes to meet Anna's. 'Anyway, we've had a kind of father-daughter *rapprochement* of late. I think I understand him better now. Which makes it easier to forgive. And I suppose I never really realised how much I loved him until I first met Sophie and saw how she doted on him.' She smiled. 'He's difficult, and cranky, and brilliant, and after all the years I had to do without him, I don't know how I'd survive without him now.'

Anna gazed off towards some distant, unseen horizon, then snapped back to the moment as their coffees arrived. 'We never can imagine how we'll survive without the ones we love,' she said. 'Until we have to.' She turned her gaze directly on the younger woman. 'And then we just do.' And there was something cold in her tone, like the touch of icy fingers.

◇◇◇

When they finished their coffees, they walked on to the far end of the village before turning back. It took nearly fifteen minutes to get back to the house. They heard the phone as they were passing the swimming pool, and when the ringing stopped, they heard Nicole calling for Enzo. They had reached the foot of the steps by the time they heard him return her call. He was coming down the stairs when they came through the front door. Nicole was waiting for him in the hall, and handed him the phone. 'It's Monsieur Martinot.'

Enzo took the phone as Raffin appeared on the curve of the staircase above him.

'*Allo? Oui, bonjour, monsieur.* I didn't expect to hear from you so soon.' He listened intently for a few moments, and Kirsty saw his expression change. 'Well, that's wonderful. When do you think we can expect some kind of feedback?' His expression changed again, and she saw his skin flush dark. 'The British? Well, who is he?' As he listened his expression altered once more, this time to one of incredulity. 'Monsieur, that is simply not possible....Well, do we have a name and address...?' He waved his hand at Nicole who grabbed a pen and notepad from the hall table. He cradled the phone between neck and shoulder and scribbled on the top leaf. 'There has to be some mistake. Will you check it out?' His face lapsed into resignation. 'Okay, well thank you, Monsieur Martinot. I'll see what I can find out myself.'

He pressed the *End Call* button but still held on to the phone, lost in thought. Raffin came down the rest of the stairs. 'Well?'

Enzo came out of his trance. 'It seems that the system put in place by the Prum Convention works better that I had hoped. Once it was cleared by the brass at the Quai des Orfèvres, they were able to run our man's DNA through all twenty-seven European databases.'

'And?' Nicole could barely contain her excitement.

'They found a match. In the NDNAD. That's the UK national database.'

Raffin looked at him. 'But?'

'The man whose DNA profile matches our killer's was serving a prison sentence in England at the time of Lambert's murder.'

Nicole said, 'That's not possible,' echoing Enzo's own words of just a few moments earlier. 'There must have been a mistake.'

'Apparently not. They were an exact match. And here's the thing. A DNA profile consists of twenty numbers and a gender indicator. The probability of the DNA profiles of two unrelated individuals matching is, on average, less than one in one billion.'

Chapter Thirty-One

London, October 1986

The apartment building was at the south end of Clapham High Street, not far from the green open spaces of the common. It was a six-storey block, with a pebbledash facing, built in the nineteen-thirties. During a recent renovation, rusted art deco windows had been replaced by double-glazed units that kept the heat in and the noise out. Unwelcome visitors were kept out, too, by a door-entry system that required a six-digit code. The nearest station was Clapham Common, and you could be in central London within thirty minutes.

Richard sat in a café across the street wondering what it must feel like to live in a place like that. To have a flat you could call your own, money in your pocket, parents you could telephone when you were in trouble.

He wondered what Christmases must have been like in his family. Very different, he imagined, from those he had spent alone with his mother in the house on the cliffs. She had done her best, with decorations and a Christmas stocking. She had showered him with presents he didn't want, a vain attempt to win his affections. But it was always just them, and he got bored. If she had friends or relatives, they never came, never called. She never watched TV, preferring to sit and read, driving him to his bedroom where he spent solitary hours nursing his resentment of the good time he knew his friends from school would be having.

He couldn't finish his coffee. It was weak and milky, and no amount of sugar would give it flavour. He liked his coffee strong and black. Real coffee. He couldn't get used to the way the English served it, powder from a jar drowned in milk.

In the street outside, he was assaulted by the roar of the traffic and waited at the lights until he could cross. There was a red pillar box on the corner where people posted letters, and he lit a cigarette and leaned against it, pretending to read the copy of the Evening Standard that he had bought in the newsagent's. From here, he had a clear view of the entrance to the apartments, and could make it in thirty seconds if he chose.

He watched a middle-aged couple emerge and head north along the High Street, and then a young man in a great hurry who took the steps to the door two at a time before Richard had time to intercept him.

It was nearly an hour before the perfect opportunity presented itself. A young woman, who could have been no more than twenty-five or twenty-six, hesitated at the foot of the steps, juggling several bags of shopping. She retrieved a slip of paper from her purse, and by the time she reached the door, Richard was right behind her. He could see the code written in a neat hand, as she fumbled to try to punch it in. She must have been new, the number not yet committed to memory. She dropped a bag, and onions spilled down the steps. Richard stooped quickly to retrieve them and pop them back in the bag. She flushed with embarrassment.

'Thanks.'

He handed her the bag. 'Hi, how are you doing?' he said, as if he knew her. 'Why don't you let me do that?' And he punched in the number he had just read over her shoulder.

'I'm so clumsy,' she said, and pushed the door open with her foot as the buzzer sounded. He held it open for her, so that she could go through into the lobby. There were post boxes all along one wall, and an elevator at the far end of the hall. 'You're on the fourth floor, aren't you? I've seen you before, in the lift.'

'That's right,' Richard said. 'And I never forget a pretty face.'

She blushed, this time with pleasure, as they squeezed together into the intimate space of the elevator.

'You haven't been here long,' he said.

'No. Just a couple of weeks.'

'You're really going to have to work at remembering that number.'

'Oh, I know. I've just never made the effort. Stupid, isn't it? I can never remember it when friends are coming round and they ask for the code.'

The elevator jerked to a halt on the fourth floor and Richard stepped out into the hallway. 'See you around, I hope.'

'Yeh, I hope so, too.'

The doors slid shut and Richard looked along the length of the corridor. He had no idea which door it was, and walked quickly along, checking each nameplate.

Bright was second from the end. He stopped outside the door and listened for a moment, although he was certain the apartment was empty. He drew out a long, stout screwdriver from inside his jacket, inserting it between the door and the architrave and levering it several times until the wood splintered and the lock gave way. He stood perfectly still, holding his breath, listening for any sign that he had been heard, before opening the door and slipping quickly inside.

He closed it behind him and leaned against it, taking deep, steady breaths to calm himself. He was standing in a short hallway. Two doors opened to the left. One to a bedroom, the other to a kitchen. There was a toilet at the far end. To the right, a door opened into a living-dining room with windows overlooking the High Street.

Richard had the oddest sense of familiarity. He had never been here, and yet felt strangely at home. A calm descended on him, and he went into the bedroom. The bed had not been made. The shape of a head was still pressed into the pillow. The stale smell of sleep, of spent air and sweat, made him think of the bedroom in which he had slept and dreamed and masturbated his whole life. He opened the wardrobe. Men's shirts and jackets, overcoats and trousers, hung untidily from the rail. There were tee-shirts and sweats and hoodies folded on the shelves, shoes on the rack along the bottom. Leather shoes, and sports shoes, a pair of Doc Martens.

He dropped his bag on the bed and stripped to his underwear and tried on several shirts. They fit, as if he had bought them himself. A pair of jeans were slightly loose on him, but he found belts in a drawer, and tried on a couple of suits. Perfect.

There was a suitcase on top of the wardrobe. He took it down and opened it on the bed, then turned to the wardrobe and began systematically lifting out clothes to pack. He wouldn't need to buy any for quite some time.

In the kitchen he found cans of beer in the refrigerator, and opened one, taking large mouthfuls as he wandered through to the living room. The remains of a carry-out pizza were still in its box on the table, along with two empty cans of beer. The tabletop was stained with the countless rings left by cans and glasses and mugs. There was a huge TV set in one corner, a futon drawn up in front of it. There were more empty beer cans lined along the windowsills and on top of the television. The shag-pile carpet was littered with the debris of life, crumbs and clothes, and cigarette ash, and Richard wondered, fastidiously, if anyone had ever passed a vacuum cleaner over it.

A brand new Amstrad computer with green phosphor screen stood on a cluttered desk pushed against the far wall. Richard slid open the top drawer and smiled as his eyes fell on the gold-crested blue cover of a British passport. He hesitated, almost savouring the moment. It was who he would be from now on. He picked it up and felt its texture between his fingers, before opening it to look at himself smiling up from a photograph stamped with the official seal of the United Kingdom Passport Agency.

Chapter Thirty-Two

London, November 2008

Clapham High Street hadn't changed much in the twenty-two years since Richard Bright had been there, although Enzo remembered it from earlier than that. He had stayed in a bedsit off Clapham Common for four months in 1978 during his four-month training attachment to the Metropolitan Police Forensic Science Lab.

It felt strange being back, revisiting what had been little more than a fleeting moment in his life. He had been someone else then, and he found it hard to remember the gauche young Enzo, fresh from his one-year Masters in Forensic Science, a Scottish fish out of water in the great big London pond.

The café hadn't changed much either, since the half hour Bright had spent in it in 1986, sipping at a milky coffee he would never finish. But Enzo wasn't to know that. If the café had been there in Enzo's day, he had no recollection of it. What remained true was that it still provided a perfect view of the apartment block across the street.

He sat at a table in the window, a bitter, black, watery coffee in front of him. He had known to ask for his coffee black, but had forgotten how bad it would be and wished he had ordered tea instead. Kirsty sat opposite, sipping a diet Coke. She was more freshly acquainted with British bad taste.

He still heard Sophie whining in his ear, begging him to take her with him. That she was becoming more jealous of her half-sister was clear, and she didn't want to hear it when Enzo explained that the only reason he would risk taking Kirsty was because she could identify the man from Strasbourg. If, indeed, the man whose London address Martinot had given him was the same one. Which was a long way from certain.

They had lunched in the café and spent much of the afternoon there, watching the comings and goings across the street. There had been quite a few. But no one remotely resembling the man who had picked Kirsty off the floor in the Palais des Congrès. Enzo was finding it hard to contain his impatience. He had checked the nameplates when they first got there. And now he wanted simply to cross the road and press the buzzer marked *Bright*. But if this really was their man, then he would be putting Kirsty, as well as himself, at risk.

He looked up to find Kirsty watching him. 'Whatever happened with you and Charlotte?' she said out of the blue.

He had met Charlotte when he first began his investigations into the murders in Raffin's book. She had been in the throes of breaking up with Raffin at the time, and Raffin had never forgiven him for getting into a relationship with her. 'Charlotte's a free spirit, Kirsty. She's happy to sleep with me, but doesn't want a relationship. I was happy to sleep with her. But I wanted more.'

'It's over then?'

'With Charlotte, I never know.'

'Roger says she's real bitch.'

'She speaks well of Roger, too.' In fact she'd told Enzo that there was something dark about Raffin. Something beyond touching. Something you wouldn't want to touch, even if you could. He wanted to tell her that, but didn't, and Kirsty didn't pursue it.

Instead, she said, 'And Anna?'

'I like her a lot, Kirsty. I know you don't approve...' He raised a hand to pre-empt her objections. 'But that night, in

Strasbourg, we were both, you know, pretty low. It was good for each of us.'

'She told me. You thought you were dying. She'd just come from a funeral.'

Enzo shook his head. 'No, she'd been visiting her parents, and they'd given her a hard time.'

Kirsty looked at him. 'That's not what she told me. She said she'd just been at the funeral of a friend.'

Enzo shrugged and contemplated another sip of coffee, but decided against it. 'Maybe she'd been at a funeral, too. Doesn't really matter. The fact is that our paths crossed, and I'm not sorry that they did.' He looked up to see Kirsty staring out of the window, her face pale, fear frozen in her eyes. 'What is it?'

He turned to see a man standing on the other side of the glass, cupping his hands around a cigarette to light it. He had close-cropped fair hair, and wore a dark, Crombie overcoat. 'It's him.' Her voice was barely a whisper. 'He just got off the bus.' If there had not been a window between them she could have reached out and touched him.

'Are you sure?'

'Absolutely certain. I'd know him anywhere.' The bus moved away, and he turned towards them, blowing smoke at the window. He was looking straight at them. Enzo heard the panic in Kirsty's voice. 'Dad, he's seen us!'

But a hand went up to smooth back his ruffled hairline, and he inclined his head slightly to one side, lifting his jaw. And Enzo realised that he didn't see them at all. He was looking at his own reflection in the glass. And then, as he turned away, Enzo heard Kirsty gasp.

'Oh, my God!

He looked at her concerned. 'What?' The man was starting to cross the road.

'I don't think it is him. I mean, it can't be.'

'How's that possible, you were absolutely certain just a moment ago?'

'The man in Strasbourg was missing his right earlobe. I told you that. The same as the man in the hairdresser's in Cahors. But that man's ear is intact. Just as he turned away from the window I could see it quite clearly. Earlobe and all.'

'Jesus!' Enzo said suddenly. 'That explains everything. Come on.' And he grabbed her hand and they ran from the café. They could see the man in the Crombie overcoat climbing the steps to the door of the apartment block, but the traffic lights were at green and they couldn't get across. Then there was a break, and Enzo dragged Kirsty between the cars, to a chorus of horns, and they reached the far sidewalk just as the man was punching numbers into the door-entry system. By the time they were running up the steps, the door was swinging shut and nearly closed. Enzo caught it before the lock engaged, and pushed it wide. The man was entering the elevator at the far end of the hall. 'William Bright!'

The man put his hand between the doors to stop them closing and took a half-step out as Enzo and Kirsty ran up the hall. 'Who the hell are you?' Kirsty felt a chill of fear run through her. But he looked at them both without recognition.

Enzo tried to catch his breath. 'My name's Enzo Macleod. I need to talk to you, Mister Bright. About your family. Just a few minutes of your time.'

◇◇◇

Bright's apartment, on the fourth floor, was small. A typical bachelor pad, cluttered and untidy. ''Scuse the mess. Cleaner doesn't come till tomorrow.' He held the door open for them. 'Go on through to the living room. I'll be with you in a minute.'

The living room floor was piled high with books. A small gate-leg dining table was stacked with cardboard boxes. There was a huge plasma TV mounted on the wall and a couple of recliners positioned for watching it. They heard the toilet flush, and the faucet running, then Bright came into the room and looked around it with sad resignation. He seemed to feel the need to explain. 'Half this stuff isn't mine. Been letting it for years. Had to give the last tenant notice when my bloody wife kicked me out. I've only just moved back in.' He found Kirsty staring at him with an odd intensity and turned to Enzo. 'So what can I do for you people?'

'You spent nine months in prison in 1992 after a brawl in a night-club.'

'Jesus Christ! What are you, cops?'

'I'm a forensic scientist, Mister Bright, investigating a murder.'

Bright shook his head. 'I never killed the guy.'

'I know that. Just beat him unconscious.'

'It was self-defence. A bloody miscarriage of justice!'

'Then you were re-arrested twelve years later on suspicion of dealing drugs.'

'And never charged. What the fuck is it you want, mister?'

'Maybe you weren't charged. But they held you for question-ing for twelve hours, during which time they took a DNA swab from the inside of your mouth. I don't know if you're aware of it, but from that time on, your DNA has been held in the UK national DNA database.'

'So what?'

'That's how we found you. A sample of DNA recovered from a crime scene in France was a perfect match with the sample you provided the British police. '

Bright frowned. 'That's not possible. I've never even been to France.' Then he paused. 'What crime scene?'

'The murder I'm investigating.'

Bright laughed in their faces. 'Got fuck all to do with me! I never murdered anyone.'

'I know that, Mister Bright. You were in prison here in the UK when the murder was committed.'

'Then you couldn't have found my DNA.'

'But we did.'

Bright was shaking his head. 'Not possible.'

Enzo drew a deep breath. 'Do you have a twin, Mister Bright?'

'No.'

Enzo was momentarily discomposed. 'Are you sure?'

'Of course I'm fucking sure. I'd know if I had a twin, wouldn't I?' Then he paused, and pulled a face, and waved a dismissive hand towards no one in particular. 'Well, okay, technically maybe I did. Once. I mean, I *did* have a twin brother. But he's dead. Has been for nearly forty years.'

Enzo stared at him wondering how that was possible. 'Explain.'

Bright pushed his hands in his pockets and wandered away towards the window. 'Jesus, I don't even know that I want to talk to you people about it.' He pressed his forehead against the glass and looked down into the street below. 'It's something I never think about. Christ, I can't even remember him.' His breath exploded in little patches of condensation.

He closed his eyes, and it seemed as if he had been somehow transported to another place. That his spirit had left the room, and only the body remained. Then his eyes snapped open and he turned to face them. 'We were on holiday in Spain. July, 1972. A place called Cadaqués, on the Costa Brava. My parents, my sister, my twin brother and me. They used to put us to bed in our hotel room before they went down to eat every night. The hotel had a babysitting service that was supposed to keep an eye on us.' A small explosion of air escaped his lips. 'Fat lot of fucking good they were. My folks came back up one night to find blood all over the place, and Rickie was gone.'

'Your brother?'

'Yeh. We were about twenty months old at the time. Me and Lucy, that's my older sister, never heard a thing. Turned out the blood wasn't Rickie's. But he was never found. No one ever knew who took him, or why.'

'So what made you think he was dead?'

'The cops. After about three months, they gave up. Told my folks he was almost certainly a goner. 'Course, my mother never believed it.' He looked at them and shook his head. 'She's still there, you know. Couldn't bring herself to leave, as long as there was a chance Rickie was still alive and might come back. Kept

us there, too, Luce and me. It's where I grew up. Speak Spanish
like a native. For all the fucking good it does me.'

Enzo stared at the strangely sad face of the twin who'd been
deprived of his brother, and felt all the hairs stand up on the
back of his neck. 'I don't know whether this is good news, or
bad, Mister Bright. But your brother's not dead.'

William Bright said nothing. Simply stared back at Enzo, as
if he had just seen a ghost.

Enzo said, 'Only identical twins share identical DNA. Which
means that when you were in prison here in England in 1992,
your twin brother was murdering a male prostitute in a Paris
apartment. And he's still very much alive today.'

All colour had drained from Bright's face. He opened a pack
of cigarettes with trembling fingers and lit one. 'I need a drink,'
he said, and he went through to the kitchen to get a can of beer
from the refrigerator. They heard the fizz of the can opening,
and Bright came back clutching it in an unsteady hand. He
took a long pull at the beer, then dragged on his cigarette. His
mouth curled into an expression of something like anger. 'So it
was fucking Rickie that nicked my passport.'

Enzo frowned. 'What do you mean?'

'It was years ago. Sometime in the mid eighties. Not that
long after I came back from Spain. It was a real fucking mystery.
Never forgotten it.'

'What happened?'

'I stayed with my old man for a while when we first got back.
Then he set me up with this place. Couldn't believe my luck.
Eighteen years old, and I had my own private knocking shop.
He said it was a good investment. Bloody right. It's worth a
fortune now.' He blew cigarette smoke at the ceiling. 'So I came
in one night to find the place had been broken into. Bastard
nicked half my clothes, credit cards, passport. But this is the
weird bit. When the cops talked to the other residents, this girl
two floors up said I came in with her that day, and that we'd
shared the lift on the way up.' He looked at Enzo. 'But that was
impossible. I was in Ilford. A party at my dad's place. I think

the cops thought I was trying to pull some kind of insurance scam. But it wasn't me. I had a dozen witnesses to place me on the other side of town.' He paused. 'Must have been Rickie.' He shrugged his consternation. 'What the hell would he want with my passport?'

Enzo said, 'Your identity.' And he knew that if he was to solve Lambert's murder, he was going to have to go back another twenty-two years, to find out who abducted a little boy from a coastal resort in northern Spain.

Chapter Thirty-Three

The light was fading fast when they emerged from the apartment block on to the steps. There was a fine, cold mist in the air, making haloes around the streetlights. The traffic, like cholesterol, was clogging the artery that was Clapham High Street, belching carbon monoxide into air fibrillating with the sound of petrol and diesel engines.

Kirsty said, 'So now you know who he is.'

But Enzo shook his head. 'We know who he was, thirty-eight years ago. A little boy abducted from a holiday hotel in Spain. We've no idea who he became, or who he is now.'

'You said he'd stolen his brother's identity.'

'Sometime in the eighties, yes. For however long it suited him then. But it would be no long term solution to take on the identity of another living person. Too risky.'

'So we're not really any further on at all?'

'Yes, we know what he looks like, Kirsty. We know that the man you encountered at the Palais des Congrès in Strasbourg is the man who killed Lambert, the man who tried to kill you and who murdered Audeline Pommereau in Cahors. From the tape in Lambert's answering machine we know that he speaks French with a southern accent. Speaks it like a native. Which means he probably grew up there. What we don't know is who, or exactly where he was all those years.'

'So how do we find out?'

'By going back thirty-eight years to a hotel room in Spain. To find out who took him. And where they went.'

Enzo felt Kirsty's fingers tighten around his arm. 'Dad…' He barely heard her above the roar of the traffic.

He turned. 'What?'

But her gaze was transfixed. She was staring straight ahead of her, almost as if trapped in some demonic trance. Enzo followed her eyeline, and as a truck cleared his line of sight he saw, standing on the sidewalk on the far side of the street, the man they had just left in the apartment four floors up. But it couldn't be him. Enzo felt a chill run down his back, like a trail of cold fingers. He shivered. He was looking straight at Lambert's killer. The man who had murdered Audeline Pommereau and tried to kill his daughter. And the man was looking straight back at him.

For a moment Enzo lost all reason, an irresistible surge of anger robbing him of both fear and rationale. He tore his arm free of Kirsty's grasp and leapt down the steps to the sidewalk. He heard her calling after him. A taxi driver leaned on his horn as it seemed that he would plunge out into the flow of traffic. And he was forced to stop on the curb as a bus thundered past, the air it displaced nearly knocking him from his feet.

When it cleared his vision, Rickie Bright, or whatever he might call himself now, was gone. People in coats and scarves stood in a line at the bus stop. Others, with collars turned up, huddled against the cold and moved in rush hour streams in either direction, silhouettes against the brightly lit shopfronts opposite. Now Kirsty was at his side, clutching his arm again, her voice insistent. 'For God's sake, Dad, what are you doing?'

And as his first flush of anger subsided, fear rushed in to fill the void. 'Jesus, Kirsty, I don't know. I must be off my head.' He turned to look at her. 'He knows we know. We're in more danger now than ever.'

◇◇◇

The platform of the underground station at Clapham Common was jammed with rush hour commuters. They were heading back into the city on the Northern Line. Their train, preceded by a blast of warm air, screeched to a halt with a penetrating squeal of brakes. Doors slid open spewing people on to the already overcrowded strip of concrete. War broke out as passengers fought to get on and claim their place. Enzo and Kirsty were carried along by the flow, squeezing into an impossibly small space between the doors and those who had got in ahead of them. A buzzer sounded, and the doors slid shut. The train jerked, throwing everyone off-balance, before accelerating into the dark of the tunnel.

On the way to the station, Enzo had looked for another glimpse of Bright, turning constantly to check behind them, eyes flickering among the myriad faces that flowed past them like a river in spate. Now he craned to check up and down the carriage. Those who had already claimed seats had faces buried in newspapers and books. Those forced to stand, studiously avoided eye contact. Above the roar and rattle of the train, he could hear people sneezing and coughing germs into the fetid air of this winter incubator of flus and colds.

And then he saw him. In the next carriage, face pressed against the window of the separating door, making no attempt to conceal himself. He wanted them to know he was there. He wanted them to be afraid. Enzo tugged at Kirsty's arm and nodded towards the following carriage. Her eyes tracked his to meet Bright's, and she turned ghostly white. 'What are we going to do?'

'We need to lose him.'

'How?'

'I don't know. As long as we're in a crowd we should be safe.' But he was thinking of the dark, quiet backstreets of Shad Thames behind Butler's Wharf, where they were going to spend the night at Simon's apartment. Simon was still tied up by his court case in Oxford but had e-mailed them to say they could pick up the keys from a neighbour and use the place in his absence. Enzo knew they would have to try to lose Bright before they changed at Cannon Street to board the train for Tower Bridge.

He watched the names of the stations glide past as they pulled up, one by one, breathing out passengers, sucking in others, and then moving on to the next. Kennington, Elephant and Castle, Borough. London Bridge was the last stop before Cannon Street, where they would have to negotiate a labyrinth of foot tunnels to get to the Monument tube station on the Circle and District line. He checked to see that Bright was still there, then whispered to Kirsty. 'We'll get off here. Wait till we see him on the platform, and then jump back on just before the doors close.'

'That won't work.'

'Of course it will. I saw it in a film once. And it worked in Cahors.'

'There probably wasn't anyone following you in Cahors. And anyway, there are far too many people. There won't be any room to get back on before the doors close.'

The train jerked and rumbled and swayed into the brightly lit London Bridge station, its platform choked with yet more commuters pressed up against the hoardings, girding themselves for the battle to get aboard. The doors slid apart.

Kirsty pushed the hesitating Enzo. 'Come on, get off.' And they tumbled out with dozens of others to fight against the oncoming torrent. Enzo strained for a glimpse of Bright above a sea of heads. And there he was, elbowing his way down on to the plaform. Enzo turned to grab his daughter, but she was gone. For a moment he panicked, then saw her pushing through the crowds to where two uniformed police officers on terrorist alert stood cradling short, black, Heckler and Koch MP5 machine guns. They listened intently as she stopped in front of them, talking fast, before turning and pointing back towards Bright. Enzo saw their expressions harden, and they immediately started towards him. One of them shouted, "Hey, you!' The buzzer sounded, warning that the doors were about to close. Bright turned, shouldering his way back into the carriage as the doors shut. Enzo could see the fear in his face. If just one door along the length of the train had been impeded, they would all open again, and he would be caught.

But the train juddered and strained, picking up speed out of the station, and Bright allowed himself a tiny, frustrated smile through the glass as it carried him off into the night.

The policemen were talking to Kirsty again, and Enzo heard one of them say, 'Sorry miss. All you can do is report it, but I don't suppose it'll do much good.'

She thanked them, and turned away towards the exit. Enzo caught up with her on the escalator. 'What did you say to them?'

She looked at her father and grinned. 'I told them he'd had his willie out on the train, flashing it at me all the way from Elephant and Castle.'

◇◇◇

They came down the steps from the south end of Tower Bridge, and passed beneath a brick archway into the narrow Shad Thames. Streetlights barely punctured the dark of this ancient walkway between towering warehouses, where once the spoils of empire had been unloaded from the boats docked at Butler's Wharf. Girdered metal bridges ran at peculiar angles overhead. A huge gateway gave on to the Thames itself. In the nineteenth century, workers had queued here each day in the hope of a few hours' work. Now these vast brick edifices had been converted into luxury apartments, homes for the wealthy, serviced by wine bars and gourmet restaurants whose windows lit up the cobbled lanes.

The lights of Pizza Express blazed out in the dark, and they turned past Java Wharf, a freezing fog rolling up from the river, turning people into wraiths, and buildings into shadows. It seemed impenetrably dark. A barge sounded its foghorn somewhere out on the water, and the noise of the pubs and restaurants they had left behind receded into the night. Only their own footsteps, echoing back from unseen walls, accompanied them.

Enzo put his arm around Kirsty's shoulder, and drew her to him for comfort and warmth. She yielded gratefully, letting her head rest on his shoulder. They were both weary and cold, exhausted by fear and apprehension. At the gated entrance to Butler's and Colonial, Enzo tapped in the entry code that Simon had e-mailed, and they crossed the cobblestones to the entrance of what had once served as a warehouse for storing spices. He remembered Simon telling him that he had toured the building in a hardhat before work began, and that the whole place smelled of cloves. But if the scent of the past still lingered there, then neither Enzo nor Kirsty had been aware of it when they had collected the keys to drop off their bags that morning.

Enzo stopped at the gate and made Kirsty turn to face him. She looked wan and tired. He said, 'You probably don't remember, but when you were very young, I used to carry you up to bed every night. There was a Crosby and Nash album I was listening to then and a song on it called *Carry Me*. I used to sing it to you when I carried you up the stairs.'

Tears sprung instantly to her eyes. *Carry me, carry me 'cross the world.* Of course she remembered. She just hadn't thought that *he* would. But all she did was nod.

'If I could I still would. Carry you up the stairs, I mean. But you're too big, and I'm too old.'

She laughed, and laid her head on his chest and put her arms around him. 'Oh, shut up, Dad.'

He grinned and she took his hand, and they hurried through the gate to the door. Enzo unlocked it, and they stepped gratefully into the warmth of the tiny hall at the foot of a flight of steep, narrow stairs. The ground floor was for parking, accessible from the street. Simon's apartment was one up. Kirsty laughed and said, 'You'd have had trouble carrying me up these stairs, even twenty years ago.'

But Enzo stood stock still and raised a quick finger to his lips.

Her smile vanished. 'What is it?'

'I turned all the lights off when we went out this morning.' His voice was low and brittle with anxiety.

She looked up to see the cold light issuing from the naked yellow bulb hanging in the stairwell, and her eyes drifted upwards to the top landing. 'The door's open.'

Enzo saw that the door to the apartment at the top of the stairs was fractionally ajar. There was a seam of light around two of its edges. He looked about him for a weapon of some kind. A golf umbrella in a coat stand at the foot of the stairs was the only thing to suggest itself. Not much protection against a professional killer. He reached for it, all the same, and held it in both hands. 'Stay here.'

'No.' Her voice was insistent. 'This is crazy. We can still get out of here and call the police.'

He shook his head. 'I'm not going to spend the rest of my life looking over my shoulder. There comes a time when you have to confront your fears. If I get into trouble, go for help.'

'Da-ad…!' But he wasn't listening. He pulled himself free of her grasp and started slowly up the stairs, trying to make as little noise as possible. By the time he reached the landing, he could hear someone moving around inside the apartment. But only just. The sound of blood pulsing through his head was drowning out almost everything else. Very gingerly, he pushed the door open. The long hallway that led to the vast, open-plan space at the far end, was in darkness. The light came from an open door leading to one of the bedrooms. A shadow crossed the oblong of light that fell out into the hall, then loomed large as a figure emerged from the doorway. Enzo grasped the umbrella so that he could use its stout wooden handle as a club, and raised it level with his head.

The figure turned towards him, startled by the movement caught in his peripheral vision. A switch was flicked, and the hall flooded with light. Simon stood staring in astonishment at Enzo clutching his golf umbrella. He said, 'Is it raining out?'

Chapter Thirty-Four

It was apparent very quickly that Simon had been drinking. There was a slight glaze about his eyes, and he enunciated all his words too carefully to avoid slurring them.

There was a lack of warmth in his greeting for Enzo, a cursory handshake, before giving Kirsty an extravagant hug, almost lifting her from her feet. She was both pleased and relieved to see him.

'What are you doing here? I thought you had a court case in Oxford.'

'Prosecution dropped the charges. Right out of the blue. Seems they had misplaced a piece of vital evidence and were unable to produce it in court. So my client walked free, and I was able to come home to see my favourite girl.'

One side of the huge open floor of the warehouse had been closed off to build bedrooms and a bathroom. The rest of the space was divided only by furniture, creating defined areas for eating, relaxing, cooking. It was punctuated by enormous potted plants with fleshy leaves and fronds and flowers that breathed out oxygen to the keep the air sweet. Concealed lighting picked out the redbrick walls and steel beams. Tall windows on one side looked out onto the street below, with patio doors leading on to a wrought iron balcony at the back. Simon had lived here on his own for most of the fifteen years since his divorce, entertaining a succession of younger women, none of the relationships lasting beyond the initial flush of sex and enthusiasm.

There was a twelve-string acoustic guitar hanging on the wall. Enzo nodded towards it. 'Do you still play?'

'Only to entertain my lady friends.'

'Ah. That explains why you go through so many of them.'

Usually Simon would have laughed. It was the kind of friendly insult jousting they had indulged in all their lives. But he turned away to conceal his irritation. 'I don't know what I'm going to feed you.'

'We could go out somewhere,' Kirsty said.

But Simon was quick to spike the idea. 'No, I've got cheese in the fridge and wine in the rack. That should be French enough to keep your father happy.'

He opened a bottle of Wolf Blass Australian cabernet sauvignon. 'Sorry, got none of the French stuff. I prefer Australian or Californian. Even Chilean. You've got to pay through the nose for a decent French wine these days.'

They sat around the table in the kitchen area, a lamp drawn down from the girders above to contain them within its bright circle of light, and Simon put out several different cheeses on a board, and some bread reheated in tinfoil in the oven. He filled their glasses and took a long pull at his, before sitting back to look at them both. 'So you never told me what brings you to London.'

Kirsty said, 'Dad recovered DNA from an old crime scene and tracked the killer to an address in Clapham.'

Simon flashed Enzo a dark look. 'And you brought Kirsty with you why?'

But Kirsty answered for him. 'I was the only one who'd really seen him. He was the same guy who tried to kill me in Strasbourg. Only it turned out not to be him at all. He has a twin brother who thought he was dead. The brother was pretty shaken up to find out he wasn't. And then we saw the real killer outside his twin's apartment.'

'What?' Simon turned his concern towards her.

'He was waiting for us in the street, and followed us into the underground. But we lost him at London Bridge.' She laughed

and reached for Enzo's hand, giving it a squeeze. 'Dad was so
funny. He wanted us to jump back on the train. But I told these
cops with machine guns that the guy had been flashing at me,
and it was him who had to jump back on the train. You should
have seen his face as the train left the station with him in it, and
us still on the platform.'

But Simon didn't share her amusement. He leaned across
the table towards Enzo. 'You fucking idiot! I thought I told you
to give up all this shit. You're putting people's lives at risk, you
know that?'

Kirsty was shocked by Simon's sudden outburst. Enzo met
his old friend's eye. 'This guy's trying to destroy me, Sy. And
everyone close to me. You know that. The only way I can stop
him is by tracking him down and exposing him for the killer
that he is.'

Simon stared at him hard for several long seconds, before
sitting back in his seat and draining his glass. He refilled it.

'It's not Dad's fault, Uncle Sy. He's got all of us in a safe house in
the Auvergne. And he didn't make me come to London. I wanted
to. That guy tried to kill me. I want to see him caught.'

Simon took a mouthful of wine and pursed his lips. Thoughts
that flashed through his mind behind sullen eyes remained
unspoken. He seemed to relax a little. 'Yeh, well, it might be an
idea if you went back to that safe house and stayed there until
all of this is over.'

'That's exactly what she's going to do,' Enzo said.

'Am I?' Kirsty seemed surprised.

'I'm putting you on the first flight to Clermont Ferrand in
the morning. I'll call Roger to pick you up at the airport.'

'And where are you going?'

'Spain.'

Simon looked from one to the other. 'I'm not even going
to ask.'

An intangible tension hung over the rest of the meal. Kirsty
tried her best to ignore it, to be bright and chatty, as if nothing
had been said. But Simon remained sullen, drinking more wine

than was good for him, and opening another bottle when the first one was empty. Both Kirsty and Enzo refused refills, and Simon made a start on it by himself. Enzo asked if he could log on to Simon's wi-fi, and Simon flicked his head towards his own laptop and told him to use that. It took Enzo less than ten minutes to track down a flight for Kirsty, leaving from Stansted the following morning. And a cheap Czech Airlines flight to Barcelona from the same airport. He bought e-tickets and printed them off, and when he returned to the table said, 'We were lucky to get you one for tomorrow. There are only three flights a week to Clermont Ferrand.'

Kirsty stood up. 'I'd better go to bed then. Try and get some sleep.' Both men rose and she gave Simon a perfunctory kiss, and her father a big hug. 'See you in the morning.'

Enzo and Simon sat for a long time in silence. They heard Kirsty getting ready for bed, and then it all went quiet. Finally, Enzo said, 'What's wrong, Sy? What's all this about?'

Simon just stared into his wine glass. 'You seem to be getting on pretty well these days, you and Kirsty.'

'Yeh, we are.'

Simon grunted. 'Funny how fast she just dropped her surrogate dad for the one who deserted her.' He sucked in more wine. 'You know, before all this shit in Strasbourg, I hadn't heard from her in months. And then someone tries to kill her and it's you she calls, not me.' He looked up, and Enzo was shocked to see tears in his eyes. 'All those years, I was the one she turned to. Always. And you were off fucking some woman in France. But the minute she's in trouble it's you she turns to. You.'

'Well, why wouldn't she? I'm her father, after all.'

'Yeh?' Simon fixed him with shining green eyes that simmered with resentment. Alcohol was releasing a flood of pent up emotion he'd kept to himself for years. 'Well, that's what you think.'

Enzo stared at him. 'What's that supposed to mean?'

'Nothing.' Simon avoided his eye now, refocusing on his glass.

'That wasn't nothing, Sy. If you've got something to say, you'd better say it.' All the same, he wasn't sure that he wanted to hear it.

Simon's breathing had become erratic. He looked up again, holding on to his glass to stop his hands from trembling. 'She's not your kid,' he said through clenched teeth.

Enzo's world stood still. His whole body tingled with shock. 'What do you mean?'

'She's mine.'

'That's a lie!'

'No, it's not.'

Hurt and anger and disbelief welled up through Enzo's confusion. 'You're a liar!'

'You remember how it used to be, when we were in the band? It was always you, me, and Linda. I always had a thing for her. You know that. But it was you she wanted. It's always you they want. That's why I left, went to study law in London. You guys were going to get married as soon as you graduated, then I don't know what happened. You suddenly split up. I never knew why. It only lasted three weeks, but I wasn't to know that. I came back up from London like a shot. Linda was in a state. I got her on the rebound. And I thought, this is it. Then suddenly you guys are an item again, and the wedding's back on.' The secret he'd held on to for all these years was out, like pus, and Simon's release in finally lancing the boil was patent. 'I never knew I'd made her pregnant. Not till you left, ran off to France and left the two of them to their fate. And there's me back in Glasgow again trying to pick up the pieces.' He drew a deep breath. 'That's when she got drunk and it all came out.'

Enzo was numb. 'You bastard!'

'Hey!' Simon raised his hands in self-defence. 'I didn't do anything wrong. Neither did Linda. When I slept with her, you guys had split up. Then, when she realised she was pregnant, and I was the father, you were getting married. So she kept it to herself. None of it came out until after you'd gone.' He poured more wine into his glass. 'Think how hard it's been for me all this time. Knowing I was Kirsty's dad and couldn't tell her. And now, seeing you two together, like I don't even exist any more.'

He took a mouthful of wine and leaned across the table. 'But you can't tell her, Magpie. You can't ever tell her.'

Enzo sat in stunned silence. He remembered carrying her up the stairs when she was only five, singing to her as he went. He remembered standing outside Simon's apartment less than two hours before, her head resting on his chest. He remembered threatening to do Raffin harm if he ever hurt her.

None of that had changed. She was still his little girl. He still loved her. He looked at Simon, and felt angry and betrayed, and knew that he could never think of his friend the same way again. If anything had been destroyed by the revelation, it was the friendship of a lifetime. He pushed his glass towards him. 'You'd better fill that up.'

◇◇◇

She had only settled in her bed for a minute, when she remembered that she hadn't taken her pill. With a curse under her breath, she had got up to go to the bathroom, and only just opened the door when she heard her father say, *Well, why wouldn't she? I'm her father, after all.* And Simon's response. *Yeh? Well, that's what you think.*

Now she stood with her back pressed against the bedroom door, their whole confrontation echoing in her head. Ending with Simon's insistence, *You can't tell her, Magpie. You can't ever tell her.*

Too late, she thought. And she felt nothing beneath her feet. No floor, no earth, no world, as she dropped soundlessly into the abyss.

Chapter Thirty-Five

The Essex plains were thick with early morning mist, and the flight was delayed by more than half-an-hour. Enzo and Kirsty sat in the concourse looking out through tall windows at the grey expanse of dull, wet, southeast England fading off into an uncertain distance.

They had hardly spoken on the train ride out from London, each lost in thoughts that couldn't be voiced. There was an awkwardness between them that neither knew quite how to dispel. Enzo bought a newspaper, and buried his face in it while they waited. But he wasn't reading. And when finally Kirsty's flight was announced, he folded it up and left it on the seat beside him.

They walked together to the gate, and stopped short of it, not knowing how to say goodbye. How to be natural with each other. He put down his overnight bag and wrapped his arms around her. At first she was reluctant to respond, and when she did he tightened his hold on her.

In the end it was Kirsty who drew away, and they stood looking at each other. 'Are you alright?' he asked. She was so pale.

She nodded. 'Just tired. Didn't really sleep well.' She glanced towards the departures board. 'They still haven't announced your flight.'

He shrugged. 'The fog's put everything back.'

'How will you get there from Barcelona?'

'I'll rent a car. It's probably only about an hour-and-a-half by road.'

'I'd better go.' She reached up and brushed his cheek with her lips. 'See you when you get back.'

'Yeh.' And he watched her go through the gate with a breaking heart.

◇◇◇

The flight passed in a haze of uncertainty. If she had slept at all during the night she hadn't been aware of it. Her head ached, as did her throat, and her eyes felt raw from the tears that had soaked into her pillow. It occurred to her, thinking about the little boy who had been abducted all those years ago in Spain, that there must have been a moment when he discovered that he was someone else. A stranger who had lived a lie all of his life.

Just as she wondered, now, who *she* was, who *she* had been.

And yet on the surface, nothing had changed. Not a single moment of her life had passed any differently. A childhood filled with the love and certainty of a father whom she had thought would always be there. And then all the years without him, resenting him, even hating him. The constant presence of Uncle Sy. Someone she'd been fond of, but who could never have replaced her dad. Her *real* dad. And now it turned out that he *was* her real dad. So what difference did it make? It was all just genetics, blood, and family. How did that change her relationship with Enzo? But somehow it did.

The thought brought fresh tears to her eyes, and she turned her head towards the window to avoid the stares of a man across the aisle who'd been eyeing her lasciviously since they boarded the plane. She let her head rest against the cool glass and couldn't wait until she saw Roger at Clermont Ferrand. Someone to confide in. A shoulder to cry on. Strong arms to hold her. Her only grasp left on a world disintegrating around her.

◇◇◇

She was disappointed when it was Anna who met her in the arrivals hall. The older woman kissed her on both cheeks.

'Where's Roger?'

Anna hesitated. 'He had to go back to Paris.' She peered at Kirsty. 'You look terrible.'

'Thank you. You look pretty good yourself.'

Anna smiled. 'I'm sorry. You just looked like maybe you'd been crying.'

'I didn't sleep very well, that's all.'

They walked outside to the car park, and bright winter sunlight angled down from the mountains to the sprawling, flat basin of land that cradled the city of Clermont Ferrand high up on the Massif Central. It was colder here than in London, but a welcome change from the grey misery of a damp southern English November.

They took the A75 *autoroute* south before leaving it at Massiac and heading west on the N122, up into the mountains of the Cantal. Kirsty sat staring from the window, but barely registered the changing landscape, the dramatic swoop of fir-lined hills crowned by jagged peaks of snow-covered rock. The road turned and twisted through mountain valleys that never saw the winter sunshine, before emerging suddenly into patches of dazzling sunlight squinting down between the peaks.

Anna contained her curiosity until they were nearly home, climbing steadily through the trees towards the ski resort of Le Lioran. Another few kilometres and they would begin their descent into the tiny valley that cradled the village of Miramont. Finally she glanced across the car at her silent passenger. 'What's wrong, Kirsty?'

Kirsty awoke as if from a dream. 'What?'

'You haven't said a word all the way from Clermont.'

'Sorry. I was just thinking about what happened in London.'

'What did happen?'

'It wasn't the killer's DNA in the database. It was his twin brother's, a brother who was abducted in Spain when he was just a child. Everyone thought he was dead.'

'Is that why Enzo didn't come back with you?'

Kirsty nodded. 'He's gone to Spain.'

She turned to look at Anna. 'We saw him, you know. The killer. He was stalking us in London. But we managed to lose him.' She was lost in thought for a moment. 'It was really scary.'

'That's not why you've been crying, though.'

Kirsty's head snapped round. 'Who says I've been crying?'

'Kirsty, I've seen enough red-rimmed eyes looking back at me from the mirror to know when someone's been shedding tears.'

Kirsty held her gaze for a moment, before turning away, and Anna flicked her indicator and braked suddenly, pulling them round into an unexpected left-hand turn. Kirsty saw the welcome sign to Le Lioran, and the road dipped down into a sprawling car park. Pine covered slopes rose all around the nearly deserted ski resort. Alpine cabins, an ugly apartment block, a hotel, a tiny shopping mall, stores filled with ski equipment and souvenirs. Chair lifts were threaded up between the trees, but the chairs hung silent and empty, swinging in the cold wind that sheered off the mountains. There were hardly any cars in the parking.

'The season hasn't started yet,' Anna said. 'And the summer tourists are long gone. Looks like we've got the place pretty much to ourselves.' She pulled up her car and switched off the engine. She turned towards Kirsty. 'So are you going to tell me, or are you going to bottle it up forever?'

Kirsty shook her head. 'There's nothing to tell.' But she wasn't sure she could keep it to herself for very much longer.

'Trust me, Kirsty. I have an instinct for these things.'

Kirsty was fighting now to contain her tears, staring straight ahead of her at nothing. 'How would you feel if you suddenly found out that your dad wasn't really your dad?'

Whatever Anna might have been expecting, it wasn't this. She sat silently for a few moments absorbing the revelation. 'Does *he* know that?'

'He found out at the same time as I did. We were staying with his oldest friend. My sort of surrogate dad. The one who was always around when Enzo wasn't. He was drunk. Jealous, I think. And there was some kind of tension between them.

Then it all came out. I'd gone to bed. I wasn't supposed to hear, but I did.'

'So he doesn't know that you know.' Kirsty shook her head. 'Are you going to tell him?'

Kirsty stared at her hands. 'I don't know. I don't think so. I don't know what to do.'

'And how do you feel about it?'

'How do you think I feel about it?'

'No, I mean, how do you feel about Enzo? Does it change anything?'

Kirsty flashed her a tear-stained look. 'It changes everything.'

'How?'

Kirsty became shrill. 'I don't know. I can't explain it. It just does.'

Anna put a hand over hers. 'I'm sorry. I guess you're pretty confused right now. I didn't read the warning signs very well: *Private. Keep Out.* Right?' Kirsty took her hand and squeezed it tightly. Anna waited until the grip on her hand relaxed, before reclaiming it to open the car door. 'Come on, there's something here you should see.'

As she slammed the door shut and rounded the car, her breath billowed around her head, caught in the sunlight that streamed across the frozen car park. Kirsty sat for a moment, before getting out of the passenger side. 'What is there to see in a place like this?'

Anna took her hand. 'I'll show you.'

There was no snow here in the resort, or on any of the lower slopes. But the peaks above them glistened white against a diamond blue sky. The *bar-brasserie* was empty. In the covered shopping strip, only a handful of desultory figures wandered amongst the stands of cards and mugs and ski jackets. Shop signs swayed in the wind. *École de Ski Les Yétis, Spar Alimentation, Salon de Thé.* A bored-looking receptionist doodled behind the counter in the empty lobby of the drum-shaped hotel above the mall.

They climbed steps into the large terminal building of the Téléphérique, and in the deserted ticket hall Anna bought them a couple of return tickets on the cablecar that would take them to the peak of the Plomb du Cantal, the highest mountain in the range. Summer and winter there would have been long queues standing patiently on the concrete concourse upstairs. But in this dead time between seasons there wasn't another soul, and a frozen-looking employee punched their tickets and waved them through to the landing stage.

From here they had a view of the twin cables stretched between stanchions, rising steeply through the grassy gap between the trees towards the snowline. Their cablecar stood in its dock. The other had just left the landing stage at the peak, a distant speck descending through a blaze of white.

They crossed the docking area, with its red-painted barriers, and walked through open doors into the empty cablecar. It had sliding doors at each corner, and panoramic windows at either end. A notice warned that the car was limited to eighty passengers maximum. But it seemed that today there would only be two. Anna leaned back against the blue rail and folded her arms. She said, 'I grew up here in the Cantal. This is where I learned to ski.'

Kirsty said, 'I've never skied.'

Anna looked at her in disbelief. 'And you come from Scotland?'

'I grew up in Glasgow. There weren't many ski slopes in Byres Road.'

'You have to try it. It's wonderful.' Her face glowed from some kind of inner passion. 'Exhilarating. Once you lose your fear, there's nothing quite like it.'

'I'm not sure I'd ever lose the fear. I'm not good at balance. I can't even put on roller skates without falling down.'

The man who had taken their tickets emerged from the terminal, stamping his feet and clapping his hands. He entered the cablecar through the far door, opened a wall panel to access the controls and pressed a button to shut the doors. He nodded towards Anna and Kirsty. '*Mesdames.*'

He pressed another button and the cablecar jerked, the whine of an electric motor engaging the wheels on the cable above, and they bumped their way out of the dock to begin rising away from the terminal. Rows of empty wooden picnic tables set on the apron around the hotel rapidly became tiny, like furniture in a doll's house, and green pasture opened up all around the resort, reaching up to the treeline and the snowy peaks beyond.

There was a sense of floating, almost flying, dipping suddenly at the first support pylon, then rising ever more steeply. The world began to spread itself out below them, the horizon dropping away on all sides to a ragged, snowy fringe on the skyline, patchwork sunlight on green and white. The other cablecar, making its descent, passed them on their right, hanging from the upward curve of the arm that hooked around the cable, only a few hardy souls aboard it.

And then they passed the snowline, black rock breaking in ragged patches through the still scant covering. Anna and Kirsty moved from the back of the car to the front as they approached the terminal building on the peak, a square structure of wood and steel and concrete built out on struts to allow the cablecars to dock. They stepped out on to a grilled platform, the mountain falling away disconcertingly beneath their feet. Then up steps onto solid concrete, huge yellow wheels set in the roof overhead to haul the cables.

The cablecar operator lit a cigarette and watched as they passed through open doors into a concrete hall, water lying in icy patches on an uneven floor. A sign advertised Stella Artois, but the cafeteria was shut. They passed through a short corridor, then out through swing doors into the icy blast. The snow lay thick, beneath a towering radio mast, and a well trodden trail led up the final three hundred metres to the summit. There were just a few other hardy souls up here on the roof of the world, in fleeces and boots, examining a representational mountain map with its trails and ski slopes, before heading on up to the peak itself.

Kirsty drew her coat more tightly around herself and felt the icy edge of the wind burn her cheeks. 'Why did you bring me up here?'

'You'll see. Come on.' Anna held her hand and led her past a line of fenceposts sunk in the snow, over a rise that took them above the cablecar terminal. The world sheered away beneath them. 'Look,' she said. 'Just look at it, Kirsty.' And Kirsty looked, turning slowly through nearly three hundred and sixty degrees. France shimmered away in every direction to a horizon lost in unfocused distance. 'You can see for, literally, hundreds of kilometres. It's glorious. Can't you feel it? That sense of…' she searched for the right word. '…insignificance. You, or I, just one tiny little speck on the edge of infinity. I used to come up here any time life was getting on top of me. Every time I started to obsess about myself and my problems. And I always found a kind of equilibrium. That sense of balance that comes with perspective. With remembering that whatever troubles you have, they are nothing in the grand scheme of things. Nothing compared to this.'

Whether it was the lack of oxygen six thousand feet up, or the pure, bracing quality of the wind in her face, Kirsty found herself almost intoxicated by the sense of insignificance that Anna spoke of, like staring drunkenly at a star-crusted sky on a summer's night and realising that it had no beginning and no end. She breathed deeply, and felt some of the burden of uncertainty slip away. But she could find no words to describe her feelings, and her only response was to turn to Anna, a reluctant smile breaking across her face, and silently nod her understanding.

Anna said, 'If it were me, I wouldn't want any secrets from the people I loved. Secrets are poison, Kirsty. You need to let them out.'

'I'm scared.'

'Of what?'

'That it'll change things.'

'It already has. You said it had changed everything.'

But Kirsty was still confused by a surfeit of conflicting emotions. 'I don't know what to think, or what to say.'

'If you loved him before, then you love him still. He hasn't changed, and neither have you. You can't alter the past, but you *can* make the future.' She turned away, then, staring out across the vast central plateau of her native land, and Kirsty saw the hint of a tear in the corner of her eye.

'What is it?' She took her arm.

But Anna blinked away the tear, and smiled to cover it. 'I never knew my own father that well. I was always too busy. Always thought there would be a tomorrow. Some time when we would sit down and talk and get to know each other, finally. Then he upped and died on me, and there *were* no tomorrows, no going back.'

Kirsty looked at her. 'When was that?'

'Ten years ago.'

And a strange stab of apprehension spiked through Kirsty's pain.

Chapter Thirty-Six

Although the sun was low in its winter sky, there was a good deal of warmth left in it. The display in Enzo's hire car had shown twenty degrees celsius. Parking in the Plaça Frederic Rahola was no problem at this time of year. La Plaja Grana, beyond the statue of Salvador Dali, was deserted. Only a couple of tables on the seafront café were occupied. He walked around past the Casino and the Entina tapas bar and into a tiny cobbled square where leaves clung stubbornly to the trees that would shade it in summer. He checked the map he had acquired in the tourist office then looked up to see a narrow slated street climbing steeply up through an archway into the old town.

He shrugged aside the ghost of last night's revelation about Kirsty and Simon. It had haunted him all through the flight and the drive north from Barcelona. But now he sensed that he was only a touch away from Rickie Bright. Bright would know that, and like an animal cornered, become even more dangerous. Enzo needed all his concentration.

Many of the street names and shop fronts here owed their origins to a strange Catalonian language that hovered somewhere between Spanish and French. The streets were paved with slabs of slate, laid end on, an uneven surface cambered for drainage, and so narrow that they never saw the sun, except in high summer.

A gaggle of schoolkids passed him on the steep climb, satchels slung across shoulders, spirits high at the end of the school day.

A man on a ladder was painting a wrought-iron balcony. Ahead of him, an old lady wearing a headscarf, fresh from her siesta, sat on the doorstep of her house, hands folded on a pink apron. She watched him pass with a dull curiosity.

Through a maze of tiny, intersecting passageways, Enzo found himself, finally, on the street that ran straight up to the church. The house he was looking for, he knew, was immediately below it at No. 9. On his right, below a gnarled bougainvillea vine, he passed a small restaurant called El Gato Azul. There was a painting of a blue cat on the panel beside the door. On the wall opposite was a menu spattered with paw prints. A little further up, on the other side of the street, was a double door the colour of dried blood. Next to it, the number 9.

Enzo looked up at the white washed three-storey house. All its shutters were tightly closed, and his heart sank with the thought that he might have come all this way only to find that she wasn't at home. There was a bell-push above the letter box at the side of the door. He pressed it, and heard a bell ringing distantly, somewhere in the depths of the house. After a moment, he heard slow footsteps beyond the door, the rattle of a lock, and one half of the doors swung open to reveal a small, dark-haired woman of indeterminate age. She was dressed all in black, except for a white pinafore. Her skin was olive dark, and her face deeply lined. This was not, he knew, the woman he sought. She looked at Enzo half-obscured by the dark interior of the hall, and he felt the house breathe its cold, damp air in his face.

'I'm looking for Señora Bright.'

The dark-haired woman shook her head. Enzo tried again in French, but still she didn't seem to understand, and his grasp of Spanish was limited.

'*Donde esta Señora Bright?*'

She raised a single finger, bidding him to wait, and she turned away to be swallowed by the dark. He waited for what seemed like forever, until she returned to hand him a scrap of paper. On it she had scrawled the word, *iglesia*. It was close enough to *église*, the French word for church, for him to understand. He pointed up the street.

'Up there?'

She nodded and closed the door abruptly in his face. He shifted his satchel from one shoulder to the other, the weight of his laptop computer starting to make the muscle ache, and climbed the last few metres into the tiny square in front of the church. A panel on the wall read, *Església de Santa Maria*. A cat sitting on the step watched him with wary eyes. *Església*, Enzo figured, must be the Catalan for *church*. He had read in the archive, downloaded from the internet, that Señora Bright prayed for her lost son here every morning. Perhaps she was also in the habit of saying an evening prayer for Rickie.

Inside it was cool and dark, and he wandered the length of the nave looking for a face amongst the handful at prayer that he would recognise from the newspaper photographs. It wasn't until he had discounted them all, that he noticed the small side chapel behind net drapes. A solitary figure knelt at its altar, candles burning on either side. He brushed the drapes apart and walked down the aisle between the pews. The squeak of his rubber shoes on the polished tiles echoed high up into the roof. He stopped beside the lady in black. 'Señora Bright?'

And when she turned to look up at him, he saw that it was her. He saw, too, a strange look in her eyes. Of both fear and hope. And he suddenly felt like a harbinger of doom, bearing news from the Gods. Good news and bad. 'Yes,' she said, and got stiffly to her feet.

'I think I might have news of your son.' The words she had waited thirty-six years to hear.

◇◇◇

As he walked with her down the steep incline to the house, the sun was setting beyond the red-tile roofs, the sky a blaze of red beyond the hills. The bay below, as still as glass, was the colour of copper.

She opened a door at the side of the house, almost obscured by ivy and bougainvillea, and he followed her into a small, walled garden shaded by tall trees. Grass and flowers grew between the paving stones, and water tumbled across a tiny rock garden into a pool half-hidden beneath fleshy lily leaves. She flicked a switch beside French windows leading to the house, and hidden lamps cast soft light around the garden. They sat in chairs around a white-painted, wrought-iron table, and Señora Bright lifted a small bell and shook it vigorously.

'Tea, Mister Macleod?'

'Thank you .'

'I only have Earl Grey.'

'That's fine.'

The maid who had opened the door to Enzo just fifteen minutes earlier emerged from the dark of the house and Señora Bright spoke to her rapidly in Spanish. The maid gave a tiny bow and disappeared again inside.

The old lady sat and looked at Enzo thoughtfully, almost as if she were putting off the moment. She folded her hands on the table in front of her and examined them for several seconds. Then she looked up again, courage summoned, ready to hear the worst. 'So, tell me.'

'I'd like to hear your story first, Señora.'

'Angela,' she said. 'Only the Spanish call me Señora.' She sighed. 'Are you determined to torture me, Mister Macleod? I'm sure you must have read all about it in the newspaper archives.'

'I'd prefer to hear it from you.'

She breathed her exasperation into the night, worn down by the years, and endless disappointments. 'We were a little later than usual that night. We'd met another couple from Essex and Rod had ordered a second bottle of wine. Oh, how we laughed together. When all the time someone was upstairs stealing our son.' She looked very directly at Enzo. 'Have you any idea how destructive guilt can be? It eats away at you, Mister Macleod, from the inside out, until there's nothing left but the most hollow of shells. Just what you see before you.'

'You had employed the hotel babysitting service.'

'Oh, yes. Promised to check in every fifteen minutes. Some young girl distracted by the kitchen apprentice. Our son lost to teenage hormones. They were both sacked, of course, but that didn't bring Rickie back. When we got up to the room Billy and Lucy were fast asleep, like nothing had happened. But my baby was gone.'

'Did you have any thoughts, then or now, who might have taken him?'

'At the time I was almost sure I knew who'd done it. I told the police, but I think they thought I was imagining it.' She shrugged. 'It's funny how certainty diminishes with time. Now, I can barely even recall the moment. Just my telling of it.'

'What moment?'

'The previous day, I'd taken Rickie down to the pool. It was hot, about midday, and most people had gone for something to eat, or found patches of shade to lie and sleep in. But Rickie had been fractious all morning. Hot, almost feverish, and I thought I would take him into the pool to cool him down. When we came out of the water I took him into the shade of the umbrella to dry him off, and there was a woman sitting at the next table. Rickie was still in a bad mood, trying to push away from the towel, whining and fighting me at every turn. And she was just watching, with this sort of smile on her face, looking adoringly at Rickie. I told her he was hungry. You know, just an excuse for the way he was behaving. And she got all defensive on his behalf. Everyone gets grumpy when they're hungry, she said. God, I can still hear her!'

'What nationality?'

'Oh, she was English. No doubt about that. Bit posh. Sort of Home Counties.'

'Age?'

'Thirty, early thirties. I don't know. Difficult to tell. She had a good figure, but wasn't showing it off. She had a kind of old-fashioned one-piece swimsuit. Her hair was sort of frizzy, pulled back in an untidy knot. She wasn't very pretty.'

'And what made you think it might have been her?'

Angela Bright shook her head. 'I have no idea. Just something about her. Something in her eyes. Something like hunger. Or jealousy. I don't know. The way she looked at Rickie. She never once met my eye.'

'You hadn't seen her around before?'

'No. Not that I was aware of. And then when the police began their investigation, there wasn't anyone staying at the hotel who even looked like her. They definitely thought she was some figment of my imagination. But women have an instinct, Mister Macleod. That woman coveted my child. I didn't realise it at the time, but when I thought about it later…' She broke off, almost choking on her words. 'Too late. Too damned late!'

The maid returned with a silver tray laden with cups, a teapot, hot water, and white sugar. She laid it on the table, then retired once more to the house. Angela Bright poured. She had recovered her composure.

'Sugar, Mister Macleod?'

'No, thank you.' Enzo poured in a little milk and took a sip. He hadn't tasted Earl Grey for years, and for a moment it took him back to another place, another life. Perhaps that's why Angela Bright persisted with the habit. A reminder of who she had once been, in her previous life as wife and mother of three, happier days when her family was still intact. He looked at her thoughtfully. 'The newspaper reports said there was blood all over the hotel room.'

'They exaggerated. There was a little blood. Smears on the floor, some spots on Rickie's panda. It seemed so vivid then. Spatters of red on white fur. All gone brown now, like faded rust.'

'You still have it?' Enzo felt his pulse quicken.

'Of course. In the end I persuaded the police to let me have it back. It's the only thing of Rickie's I still have. The only part of him that still belongs to me.'

'May I see it?'

For the first time she seemed reluctant to co-operate. 'Why? Who are you, Mister Macleod?'

'I used to be a forensic scientist, Angela. Thirty-six years ago, the only thing anyone could have told from the blood they found in Rickie's hotel room was the blood type. Now, we can tell a whole lot more about a person. Their genetic code, for example. Their DNA. It's unlikely that whoever took your son will be found in any DNA database. It all happened too long ago for that. But we can at least tell the sex of Rickie's abductor.'

'From thirty-six-year-old spots of blood on a cuddly toy?' She seemed incredulous.

'With luck, yes. Then we'd know for certain whether it was a man, or maybe your woman at the pool, who took him.'

Angela Bright rang again for the maid, and issued a curt instruction. Then turned back to Enzo. 'You told me you had news of my son.'

Enzo hesitated, uncertain of how much to tell her. 'I've been trying to track down a missing person,' he said. He chose his words carefully. 'In the course of my investigation, I discovered two identical samples of DNA, each of which came from a different person. Which is impossible.' Again he hesitated. From here there would be no going back. 'Except in the case of identical twins.'

Even in the gathering darkness, Enzo could see that her face had drained of colour. She was not a stupid woman. 'And one of them was Billy's?'

'Your son, William, yes.'

'Which means that Rickie is still alive.'

'It meant he was still alive in 1992. It was from then that we recovered his DNA. I also believe that six years earlier he broke into William's flat in London and stole his passport, and his identity.'

Enzo watched closely for her reaction. But it almost seemed as if she were no longer there. Her eyes were glazed and distant. Then, in a tiny voice that whispered into the night, she said, 'I knew it.' And she dragged herself back to the present, finding focus again on Enzo. 'It was twelve, fourteen years after he'd been taken, sometime in the mideighties. I was sure it was him. As sure as I've been of anything in my life.'

'You saw him?'

'In a minimarket in town. He was wearing a baseball cap and sunglasses. For a moment I thought it was Billy. But Billy had gone back to England. He was just standing there, staring at me. And when I saw him, he turned and ran out of the store. I went after him, but by the time I got into the street he was gone.' Her eyes lifted slowly towards a darkening sky studded with stars. 'I've replayed that moment so many times. You've no idea. So often that in the end I began to doubt it had ever happened.' She looked back at Enzo. 'Until now.'

The door from the house opened, and the maid emerged, clutching a toy panda, the same size as a child's teddy bear. It was tousled, and dirty, and threadbare in places. She gave it to the lady of the house, and Angela Bright pressed it to her chest as if it might have been her lost boy. Enzo held out his hand. 'Can I see?'

Reluctantly she handed it to him, and he very quickly found the spots of dried blood, still caked amongst the clumps of wool. Some of it had flaked off and it's colour was faded, but there was enough left to obtain a decent sample. Enough to run any number of tests.

He looked up, hardly daring to ask. 'May I take this? Please. I promise I'll return it.'

She stared at him, eyes stripped suddenly of all emotion, lacking any sense of self-deception. 'A forensic scientist recovering samples of my son's DNA.' She paused, her expression hardening. 'What has he done, Mister Macleod? What has my son become?'

Enzo drew a deep breath. There was no longer any way to avoid the truth. 'I think your son is a murderer, Angela.'

Chapter Thirty-Seven

All light had been leeched from the sky by the night, except for the stars that pricked its blackness. The moon had not yet risen, and the back streets of Cadaqués were almost impenetrably dark. Out of season, its restaurants were closed and its holiday lets empty. Those few residents remaining were locked up tight behind closed shutters, watching television until late, when it would be time to eat.

Enzo made his way carefully down the steeply sloping cobbled street, clutching Rickie Bright's toy panda in a plastic bag, and carrying with him the memory of a mother's despair. Thirty-six years of hope, both fulfilled and dashed in the same dreadful moment. He could only imagine how Angela Bright would deal with the truth about her son. In his presence she had been brave, polite. Courteous but cold. God only knew what demons awaited her now that she was left alone to face the night.

Somewhere on the street above him, he heard the sound of footsteps descending through the deserted town. Soft, stealthy footfalls in the dark. The temperature had fallen, but although the evening had not yet turned cold, Enzo felt a shiver of disquiet. He stopped to listen, wondering if perhaps he had imagined it. But no, there they were again. Someone was following him, just out of view beyond the curve of the street.

He turned to his left and hurried down the narrowest of alleyways. There was almost no light at all here, and he had to feel his way along the wall, tripping and almost falling over a short flight of steps leading up to a door that was shut firmly against the night. After a short distance, the alley split into three. One leg of it climbed the hill to his left. One carried straight on. The other descended towards the shore. He could see, beyond the roofs, the first glimmer of moonlight reflected on the still water of the bay. Behind him, he heard the footsteps still following. Faster now, determined not to lose him.

He wondered if Rickie Bright had somehow managed to follow him. Or whether he had simply anticipated his next move. Either way, it would be clear to him beyond doubt, that Enzo knew now who he was. Or, at the very least, who he had been. No point, any longer, in trying to short-circuit an investigation. Only one course would remain open to a desperate man.

Enzo took the turn to his right, leading down towards the bay, and started to run. He could hear the following footsteps increasing in pace, trying to match his. Over his shoulder he caught the merest glimpse of a dark shadow emerging from the labyrinth above, and he squeezed left through a narrow alley, running its length, and then turning right again, descending so steeply that his own momentum was quickly robbing him of control over his legs. The street curved away to his right. Through gaps in the houses he could see streetlights along the waterfront. And almost at the same time, he heard music rising up through the night. An accordion and violins, a Spanish guitar. There were whoops and hollers and the sound of laughter. People. Safety.

At the foot of the hill, the street turned sharply right. Beyond the low wall that bounded its curve, splinters of light forked up into the dark through a weave of rush matting stretched tightly over a wooden frame, a flimsy roof to contain the music and merriment in an open square below. Slithering and sliding on the dew-wet cobbles, Enzo realised he wasn't going to be able to stop. He raised a foot to brace himself against the wall at the bottom of the hill and pitched up on top of it, arms windmilling as he tried to retain his balance.

He spun around to face back the way he had come, and as he tipped backwards into space, he saw the dark figure of his pursuer turn into the street above. For the briefest of moments he had a sensation of floating, before his full weight landed on the rush matting below. It dipped violently beneath him, breaking his fall, and he thought for half a second that it was going to support him. But then he heard it rip, a harsh tearing sound all along one edge, and it tipped him out of its cradle into a confusion of music and light and bodies.

He landed heavily on a makeshift wooden dancefloor, a softer landing than the cobbles beneath it. Still it knocked all the wind from his lungs. The music stopped very suddenly, and his ears were filled with the sounds of women screaming. Through lights that seemed to be shining directly in his eyes, he saw figures retreating around him like displaced water. Musicians on a small stage were frozen in suspended animation, staring at him in disbelief. Enzo raised a hand to shade his eyes from the light and saw men in dark suits, a young woman all in white. He saw tables set out in the square. People with glasses in their hands, cigars in their mouths. Everyone standing now. He had just dropped in unannounced, and uninvited, on some unsuspecting couple's wedding night.

A short, stocky man, with black hair oiled back over a balding pate, stooped to help him to his feet. He looked up at the hole in the rush matting above, and a hush descended on the gathering. He dropped his eyes again to look at Enzo and fired off a salvo in Spanish.

Enzo was still trying to catch his breath. 'I'm sorry, I don't speak Spanish. English or French.' He bent to pick up the panda in its bag.

'Okay, Eenglish,' the man said. 'You no invited to thees wedding, señor.'

'I know. I'm sorry. But someone's trying to kill me.' As soon as the words left his mouth he realised how ridiculous they sounded.

The man translated for the assembly, and there were some stifled sniggers. 'Why someone try keel you in peaceful place like Cadaquès, señor?'

'He's a murderer.' Enzo compounded the madness. 'He's been following me. If you'd just call the police...'

'Señor, in Cadaquès, I am police. Who is thees *asesino*?'

But before Enzo could answer, they all heard the footsteps running down the stone staircase from the street above, and the guests fell silent. Everyone turned, as the figure of Angela Bright's maid ran into the circle of light, and stopped suddenly, breathing hard, blinking in the glare, startled and perplexed.

Enzo stared at her in astonishment. She was holding his satchel.

'Is thees your keeler, señor?' Again he translated for the others, and now they roared with laughter. Enzo flushed with embarrassment, and the maid held up his satchel. She had no idea what the joke was, but smiled anyway.

Enzo said, 'I must have left my bag at Señora Bright's house.' He almost snatched it from her. 'Why didn't you just call after me?'

His translator interpreted for the crowd, eliciting another roar, and some applause. 'Señor. She could not. Maria Cristina Sanchez Pradell ees *muda*. Mute. She has not spoken seengle word her whole life.' He allowed himself a broad grin. 'You have very veeveed imagination. Señora Sanchez never harm anyone.'

The bride stepped forward, her veil drawn back from a beautifully slender latin face, large black eyes viewing him with amusement. She spoke rapidly and the small man looked towards her bride-groom for confirmation. The young man nodded, and the Cadaquès policeman turned back to Enzo.

'She say not often tall, dark stranger fall eento wedding. Maybe lucky. How about you stay for drink and dance?'

Enzo looked around the assembled faces watching for his reaction, and for the first time he saw a funny side to it all, a release of tension after his chase through the dark streets of the town believing that Rickie Bright was right behind him. He said,

'If you put a glass in my hand, I'll be delighted to drink a toast to the happy couple.' He looked at the gorgeous young woman smiling at him on her wedding night, and thought how lucky was the young man at her side. They had the whole of the rest of their lives together. His time with Pascale had been so short. But he forced a smile. 'As long as I get to dance with the bride.'

PART FOUR

Chapter Thirty-Eight

Enzo sat nursing a glass of red wine in the window of the Café Bonaparte. He watched the faces streaming past in the Place St. Germain de Prés outside. Pale faces on a grey November afternoon breathing dragonfire into polluted winter air. And he wondered if someone out there was watching him. If Bright had any idea where he was, and if so, what he might be planning to do about it.

Raffin was late, as usual. Just as he had been when they'd met here for the first time more than two years ago. Enzo had flown directly to Paris from Barcelona, and been there for two days, calling in favours, before taking the decision to call Anna. Which was when he'd learned that Raffin had left the Auvergne several days earlier to return to the capital. He immediately called him at his apartment to arrange a rendezvous.

'Do you want another of these?'

Enzo looked up to find Raffin unravelling a blood-red scarf from around his neck. His long camel coat hung open, its collar turned up. Beneath it he wore a beige crewneck sweater over black jeans. His brown leather boots were polished to a shine. He was pointing at Enzo's glass.

'No thanks.'

Raffin shrugged, and as he sat signalled a waiter to order a small, black coffee. 'So…what news?'

'How much do you know?'

'Only what Kirsty told me on the phone.' Just the mention of her name was enough to evoke the depression that had dogged Enzo since the night at Simon's apartment. 'About the Bright twins, and Rickie Bright stalking you through the London underground. How did you get on in Spain?'

Enzo told him about his meeting with Señora Bright, her suspicions about the woman by the pool, the blood-stained toy panda.

'Can you do anything with the blood?'

'I've got someone working on it right now. We should have a result later this afternoon.'

Raffin rubbed his hands cheerfully. 'It's turning into quite a story, Enzo.' Whatever enmity there was between the two men, whatever words might have passed between them, Raffin seemed to have banished to some other compartment of his life. The journalist in him smelled a scoop. Enzo had already solved two of the seven murders he had written about in his book. Both of them had generated copy and controversy. Now it looked like they were on the verge of cracking a third.

'Why did you come back to Paris, Roger?'

Roger flicked him a glance, and Enzo detected a note of caution in it. 'I was going insane cooped up in that bloody house. Besides, I have a living to earn. I don't have some university paying my wages while I go around playing Sherlock Holmes.'

'Weren't you worried?'

'About what?'

'That Bright might come after you?'

Raffin laughed. 'No. It's you he's after, Enzo, not me. I'm probably in more danger when I'm with you than when I'm not.' He took a sip of his coffee. 'You said you had a meeting set up for this afternoon. Is that about the blood work?'

'No, it's about the cassette I sent to my voice expert here in Paris. The recording of the conversation between Bright and Lambert the day before the murder.'

Raffin cocked an eyebrow. 'What about it?'

'I don't know yet. That's what we're going to find out.'

◇◇◇

Pierre Gazaigne was project leader of a study in the analysis of spoken French sponsored by the Université Paris-Sud 11, and the Université Pierre et Marie Curie. The project was based in a small suite of offices and sound labs on the top floor of a converted nineteenth century apartment block in the Rue de Lyon in the twelfth *arrondissement*.

Enzo and Raffin walked south from the *métro* stop at the Place de la Bastille. They found the building three hundred metres down, on the west side of the street, and squeezed into a tiny elevator that took them to the sixth floor. They stepped out into a gloomy hallway filled with cigarette smoke and the grey faces of half a dozen nicotine addicts puffing morosely on their cigarettes.

One of them coughed, phlegm rattling in his throat. 'Are you looking for someone?'

'Professor Gazaigne.'

The smoker flicked his head towards the glass door. 'Go on in. You'll find him in the lab on the right at the far end of the corridor.'

Gazaigne was sitting at an enormous console with a bewildering array of sliders and faders beneath a bank of computer screens. Sound graphs flickered in various colours, and a loud screeching noise issued from huge speakers on either side. He turned as the door opened and flicked a switch. The graphs flatlined, and the screeching stopped. He was an elderly shambles of a man in a grubby white labcoat, white hair scraped back over a flat head. He had a pencil stuck behind one ear, half-moon glasses perched on the end of his nose, and a twinkle in dark, brown eyes.

'*Ah, c'est l'Ecossais!*' He jumped to his feet and thrust a large hand at Enzo. 'You look older every time I see you.'

'That's because you only see me about once every ten years.'

'That would explain it.'

'This is my colleague, Roger Raffin, a journalist.'

Gazaigne crushed Raffin's hand '*Enchanté, monsieur.* Pull up a chair.' He waved a hand towards the console. 'A few years ago there would have been banks of reel-to-reel machines in here. Nagra, Sony, Revox, Teac. Now it's all digital. State of the art electronics. Random access. But, you know, it takes a lot to beat good old-fashioned tape running at 76.2 centimetres per second. The treble response you got off those old recorders was unbeatable. Sadly, the people with the purse strings believe the PR of the manufacturers, so now we've gone digital. Like it or not. And we've lost a lot in the process. Progress at any cost, I say, even if it's backwards.'

He looked at the two faces looking back at him and burst out laughing. 'But you don't want to hear some old fart going on about things not being what they were in the good old days. You want to know what I found on your crappy little cassette.'

'What did you find, Pierre?' Enzo said.

'Some shit quality sound, I'll tell you that.'

'And what else?'

'Well, you were right about the *shibboleth*, Enzo. *Portsmoose.* Dead giveaway. You see, I can't even say it. But this guy pronounced it like a native. Very interesting. Because he isn't. He comes from the south of France. More specifically, and almost certainly, the Roussillon.'

'How can you tell?'

'Number of factors. I thought it was interesting the way he used *tu* and the other *vous.* As you suggested, a very pointed way of establishing a pecking order. The *tu,* however, tells us more. Not that it's much in evidence. But if you listen carefully, the pronunciation is telling. He says the *tu* almost like *ti.* Listen…' He swivelled away to tap at a keyboard and pull up a menu on one of his screens. He ran a cursor down a list of files, and selected one. He double clicked and a graph immediately began spiking on an adjoining monitor as Bright's voice boomed out from the speakers. *J'ai pensé que tu te demanderais pourquoi je n'avais pas appelé.* 'Do you hear? *I thought you would wonder why*

I hadn't called. The *tu* next to the *te* seems to emphasise it. He definitely leans towards pronouncing it as *ti*.'

It was too subtle for Enzo, but Raffin nodded. 'I hear it,' he said. 'Now that you've pointed it out, but I can't say I'd have noticed.'

'*Ti as* or *ti es* for *tu as* or *tu es*, is originally derived from a working-class Marseilles accent, but has gained a certain *caché* among the young over the last couple of decades. Particularly in the South where the accent is broadly similar anyway.'

'But you said this guy was from the Roussillon?'

'That's right.'

'How can you be so sure of that?'

'Vocabulary.' The old man grinned. 'You live in the Midi-Pyrénées, Enzo. If you went into a *boulangerie* you'd probably ask for a *chocolatine*, while the rest of France would ask for a *pain au chocolat*—and they'd know where you came from. But the Midi-Pyrénées is a big area with lots of different dialects, so they wouldn't know exactly where. The Roussillon, on the other hand, is a smaller area, formerly known as Northern Catalonia, and corresponding almost exactly to the present-day *département* of the Pyrénées-Orientales. And that's where it gets interesting.'

He turned back to the computer and selected another file and hit the return key. Bright's voice boomed out again. *Ecoute-moi. Il faut que nous parlions.* And Gazaigne turned to Enzo. 'Tell me what you think he said.'

'He said, *listen, we need to talk.*'

'Specifically *listen to me? Ecoute-moi?*'

'Yes.'

But the old professor shook his head. 'Sounds like it, doesn't it? I wasn't sure at first. But I've listened to it a dozen times, slowed it down, run it backwards, you name it. There's a lot of noise on the tape, and I had to try and filter that out. So listen again.'

This time he selected another file, and Bright's voice sounded sharper, clearer, and slowed down perhaps fifteen to twenty percent.

'What do you think now?

Raffin said, 'It sounds like *écoute-noi*. But that doesn't make sense.'

'It does if you come from the Roussillon. There's a lot of Catalan still spoken down there. After all, historically, it's not that long since it was still a part of Catalonia. A lot of Catalan words have come into common French usage there, particularly slang words.' Gazaigne turned to Enzo. 'Just like in Scotland. You use a lot of Gaelic words without realising what they are. Even French words, absorbed into the language when the French and Scots were allies against the English. You talk about a *bonny lassie*. But actually, *bonny* derives directly from the French word *bonne,* meaning good. Except that you've made it mean pretty.'

He hit the return key and played the line again. *Écoute-noi.* Enzo heard it this time, quite distinctly.

'*Noi* is the Catalan word for *friend,* or *pal.* Equivalent of the French word *mec* or *gars.* So your killer was actually saying, *listen friend,* or *listen pal,* which was a lot more threatening, even if his victim didn't understand it.' He grinned again. 'Not a huge amount to go on, and I'm not a gambling man. But if you asked me to put money on it, I'd say your man comes from the Roussillon.'

Enzo gazed thoughtfully off into some middle distance. The Roussillon was at the western end of the French Mediterranean, forming the border with Spain at the southeast extreme of the Pyrenean mountain range. Not much more than an hour's drive from Cadaquès. Whoever had taken little Rickie Bright hadn't taken him very far.

◇◇◇

'What do you think?' Raffin turned up his collar and swept the trailing end of his scarf back over his shoulder as they stepped out into the Rue de Lyon.

The roar of rush hour traffic was almost deafening. Enzo had to raise his voice. 'I think that there are an awful lot of people in the Roussillon.'

'So where do we begin?'

'With an Englishwoman who arrived in the Pyrénées-Oriental with a twenty-month-old son in July 1972. There may have been a father, but more likely than not, she'd have been on her own.'

'How can you be sure it was an Englishwoman?'

'I can't. But the woman Angela Bright met poolside at the hotel was English. Posh, with a Home Counties accent, she said. And I can't escape the fact that Rickie Bright pronounced Portsmouth like a native. If he grew up in the Roussillon, then that's how he'd speak his French. But if his mother was English, and spoke only English to him in the house, then he'd speak it as an Englishman would. Just as Sophie speaks English with my Scottish accent, even although she's never been to Scotland.' He looked at Raffin. 'So Rickie Bright would be able to pass himself off as French or English.'

Chapter Thirty-Nine

Paris, November 1986

Fontenay-sous-Bois was only three stops out from the Gare de Lyons on the RER red Line A. Richard barely saw the grey Paris suburbs that smeared past the rain-streaked windows of the train. It was all just a blur, like every one of the eighteen years of his life to date. Only the future lay in sharp, clear focus. A decision taken. A determination to carry it out. All he had in the world was contained now in the suitcase he had stolen from his brother. The suitcase he had lived out of for the last six weeks. A procession of cheap hotels in Pigalle, spending his brother's money, eking it out while he made his plans.

Now he had butterflies colliding in his stomach. This was no short-term commitment. There would be no turning back, no second chance. This was who he was going to be. A man of his own making. A future determined by no one but himself. But, still, it scared him.

It was drizzling when he got off on to the station platform at Fontenay, pushing through huddled crowds to the street outside. It was raw cold here, and he pulled up the collar of his jacket, feeling the chill of it creeping into his bones. He walked the length of the Rue Clos d'Orléans before turning north into the Route de Stalingrad. At Rue Vauban he turned right, and took only a few minutes more to reach the deep stone arch built into the wall of the fort. It was dry in the tunnel, and beyond it he could see another, and the red blaize parade ground beyond that. Below the legend, *Fort de Nogent*, carved in stone around the arch were the letters that spelled his destiny. *Légion Etrangère*.

A soldier on guard duty stopped him at the entrance. 'What's your business?'

Richard straightened his shoulders and took courage from his own voice. He spoke boldly in English. 'I am an Englishman. My name is William Bright, and I have come to join the Legion.'

Chapter Forty

The café on the Avenue de l'Opéra was full to bursting. Condensation fogged the windows, and waiters squeezed between crowded tables balancing drinks on trays above their heads. It was a popular haunt for students, the breath-filled screech of Raphaël's *Caravane*, surpassed only by the demented conversation of young people fresh from a day's study.

Maude had kept them seats in an alcove, well-worn leather bench seats on either side of a beer-stained table. It afforded them at least a little privacy.

'Darling, you're late.' She kissed Enzo twice on each cheek when he slid in beside her, and then with pouting lips planted a wet kiss on his mouth. 'But I forgive you. For you've brought such a pretty young man to see me.' She turned come-to-bed eyes towards Raffin across the table, and he blushed to the roots of his hair.

Maude laughed uproariously, delighted by her small, mischievous pleasures. She was somewhere in her late sixties. She wore a voluminous cape, and her long silver hair was piled untidily on top of her head. There was too much rouge on her cheeks and too much red on her lips. But you could see that she had once been a very attractive woman. A smouldering sexuality still lurked somewhere not far beneath the surface.

Enzo took pleasure in Raffin's discomfort. 'Maude and I go back a long way,' he said. 'She taught me the meaning of the word *allumeuse*.'

Raffin seemed puzzled. 'Prick teaser?'

'That's me, darling. As Enzo said, we go back a long way. But we never went quite far enough, where I'm concerned.' She raised an eyebrow and gave Raffin an appraising look. 'You'd do, though.' And she turned to Enzo. 'Is he free?'

'He's dating my daughter.'

'Ah. The young. Yes.' She turned her focus back on Raffin. 'They might look good on your arm in a restaurant, or going to the theatre. But I'll give you a better time in bed, darling.' She grinned. 'I'll order a bottle, shall I?' She waved her hand in the air and somehow caught the attention of a waiter. 'A bottle of Pouilly Fuisse, and three glasses.' She smiled sweetly at Enzo. 'And, of course, you'll be paying.'

'Of course. Do you have the results?'

'*Bien sûr, mon cher.*' The array of silver and gold bracelets dangling from her wrists rattled as she delved into an enormous sack of a bag on the seat beside her. She pulled out a large, beige envelope which she slapped on the table, long red fingernails polished and gleaming. 'Everything you always wanted to know about blood but were afraid to ask.'

'Were you able to recover DNA?'

'Yes, of course. Not very interesting though. There's so much more you can learn about a person from their blood.'

'So what other tests did you run?'

'Blood type, of course. I did a complete cell count. And a blood chemistry profile. Fascinating results.'

'Like what?'

'Well, for a start, the person who spilled blood on the little boy's panda is a hemophiliac.'

Enzo was unaccountably disappointed.

'You don't seem very pleased.'

'I'd rather hoped that it was going to be a woman, Maude.'

She patted him on the arm. 'Now don't go jumping to conclusions, Enzo. Contrary to popular opinion not all hemophiliacs are men. I know that woman are normally just carriers. But if a female carrier marries a male sufferer, then any children will be sufferers, too. Male *or* female.'

'So it *is* a woman?'

'Yes.'

Raffin leaned his elbows on the table. 'How can you tell?'

Maude puckered her lips and blew air through them, as if she were dealing with an idiot. 'Because the sex marker in her DNA was female, dear.'

Enzo took a moment to digest this. 'So she probably never had a child then, Maude.'

'Unlikely. The risk of bleeding would make it ve-ery dangerous. In fact, women with bleeding disorders are fortunate just to make it through puberty.' She turned doe eyes on Enzo. 'Just having sex could be fatal. Which would be a terrible affliction, don't you think?'

'Absolutely.'

'But what a way to go!' She winked at Raffin then turned back to Enzo. 'Tell me, darling. Does this woman live in France?'

'Almost certainly.'

'Then you should be able to find her. Hemophiliacs are always well known to their local health authorities. They have to be. Their lives depend on it.'

◇◇◇

It was dark by the time Enzo and Raffin got off the *métro* at Odéon and walked the short distance up the Rue de Tournon to Raffin's apartment. The gold-domed Sénat building at the top of the street was floodlit, painted in light against a bruised black sky. Intermittent spots of rain blew down the street on the edge of a blustery wind. Green canvas screening flapped against rattling tubular scaffolding erected by stone-cleaners on the building opposite the apartment.

Raffin punched in his code, and pushed open one half of the heavy green doors to let them into the gloomy passageway that led to the courtyard beyond. Cobbles glistened wet in the rain from the lights of windows rising up all around, and the old chestnut tree above the garage, stripped bare of leaves, creaked and groaned in the wind. As there always seemed to be when Enzo visited Raffin, someone in one of the other apartments was playing a piano. Tonight the piano player was practising scales. Monotonous, repetitive, and hesitant. A child perhaps.

Both Enzo and Raffin were grateful to escape into the dry warmth of the stairwell, and they climbed up through bright yellow electric light to the first floor. 'I'm going to open a bottle of Gevrey-Chambertin,' Raffin said. 'To celebrate.'

'We haven't got him yet,' Enzo warned.

But Raffin just grinned. 'We can't be far away now. How many female English hemophiliacs can there be in a single *département?*'

'Finding the woman who abducted Rickie Bright, won't necessarily lead us to him.'

'Oh, for God's sake, Enzo, stop being such a pessimist! He's just a breath away. I can feel it.' He unlocked his door and pushed it open for Enzo to go in ahead of him. The apartment was in darkness, but the doors to the *séjour*, and Raffin's study beyond, stood open, and the light of the floodlit building opposite reached through the window in a long rectangle across the floor towards them. It was in that light that Enzo saw the folded white sheet of paper lying on the floor where it had been slipped under the door.

As he stooped to pick it up he heard the glass in the window shatter, a sound like someone being punched, and Raffin grunted. In his startled confusion, Enzo looked up to see Raffin stagger back into the landing, slamming into the door of the tiny elevator, before tipping forward to fall heavily on his face in the doorway. Enzo stood up, bewildered, still slow to understand what had happened. The wooden architrave two inches to the right of his head split open. A large splinter of wood speared his cheek. And suddenly he realised they were being shot at.

He dropped like a stone, pressing himself into the floor beside Raffin before daring to look up. He felt the rush of wind blowing through the broken window. There was someone up in the scaffolding on the building opposite. A figure obscured by the flapping green canvas.

Enzo became aware that his hands were sticky wet, and he had the iron smell of blood in his nostrils. In a moment of panic he thought he had been hit. Before realisation dawned that it was Raffin's blood. He wasn't thinking clearly at all. But he knew he needed to. He rolled onto his side and turned the journalist on to his back. Raffin's beige crewneck had turned scarlet, the colour of his scarf. Enzo heard the sound of blood gurgling in his chest and throat. His eyes were open wide, filled with the panic of a rabbit caught in headlights. His mouth opened, but there were no words.

The light in the stairwell went out, its sixty seconds expired. Was it really only a minute ago that they had punched the switch at the foot of the stairs? Enzo got to his knees and scrambled out on to the landing. He grabbed Raffin's legs and pulled him fully out of the apartment, then got to his feet and propped him against the wall, safely out of the line of fire. Raffin coughed and spattered blood all over him. The light was dying in his eyes.

'Jesus Christ, man, hold on!' Enzo reached up to hit the light switch, and with bloody, fumbling fingers, dialled the emergency number on his cellphone. When the operator responded it took a great effort of will to stay calm. He gave her their address, then heard his own voice rising in pitch. 'There's been a man shot. Critical. We need an ambulance fast!'

By the time he looked back at Raffin, his eyes were closed. And somewhere, in the building above them, the pianist was still practising scales.

Chapter Forty-One

Enzo had no idea how much time had passed. He was still in shock. Raffin's blood had dried rust brown on his hands and clothes. He sat on a dining chair, leaning forward on his knees, head bowed, staring blindly at the pattern on the floor.

His eyes hurt and his head was pounding. The lights erected in the apartment by the police photographer were blinding. Forensics officers were everywhere, dusting for prints, collecting every tiny piece of evidence, bullets and hair and blood. He overheard someone expound the theory that the apartment might have been broken into ahead of the shooting.

The street outside had been sealed off, and yet more officers swarmed over the scaffolding on the building opposite, searching for any traces that might have been left by the shooter.

After Raffin was taken away, a medic had checked Enzo, cleaning the wound on his cheek, disinfecting it and taping it over with a wad of cotton. Then he had given the go-ahead for Enzo to be questioned by the investigating officer.

It had been a long and confused interview. Enzo still wasn't thinking clearly. But the officer knew who he was. The publicity surrounding his resolution of two of the unsolved cases in Raffin's book had earned him a certain notoriety with the French police. He was regarded by them with a mixture of suspicion, awe, and downright dislike. When it became clear that Enzo and Raffin had been working on the Lambert case, he'd heard one of the other plain-clothed officers saying, 'Get Martinot on the phone. See if we can't get him over here.'

He'd been aware for some time now of a low murmur of voices coming from the entrance hall, then looked up as he heard his name. 'Monsieur Macleod.' A familiar voice, speaking softly, an empathy in it that had been lacking in the others. 'I never expected to be out at another crime scene.' Jean-Marie Martinot was wearing his dark blue overcoat with the food stains, and Enzo noticed that his socks still didn't match. His trademark wide-brimmed felt hat was pushed back a little on his head, and he brought in with him the reek of fresh tobacco smoke. He reached out to shake Enzo's hand, but Enzo just opened his to show him Raffin's blood and shrugged an apology. Sometime soon, perhaps, they might let him go and shower and change his clothes. Though he doubted that any amount of showering could wash away the horror of Raffin's shooting. 'I guess it was you he was after.'

'I should think so.'

'So how did he miss? After all, we both figured he was a pro.'

Enzo nodded towards the slip of paper lying on the table. It had his bloody fingerprints on it, but he had not even thought to look at it. 'Someone must have pushed that under the door. I bent to pick it up just as the shot was fired. Pure goddamn fluke that Raffin got hit and not me. He must have known he missed me first time, so the second shot was probably fired in haste.' And Enzo remembered Raffin's almost prophetic words from earlier in the day. *It's you he's after, Enzo, not me. I'm probably in more danger when I'm with you than when I'm not.* 'Do we know how he's doing?'

Martinot looked grim. 'Not well, monsieur. One of his lungs collapsed, and he lost a lot of blood.'

'I know, I have most of it on me.'

The retired *commissaire* regarded him thoughtfully. 'So why's our man trying to kill you now? Do you know who he is?'

'I know who he was.' And Enzo told him about the trip to London, his meeting with the twin brother, the abduction from

Cadaqués in the early seventies. 'The fact that he has an identical twin means we know exactly what he looks like. If we can get a picture of William Bright, then it'll pass for a picture of him. You can distribute it to police forces across France, put it out on the media. We also know he's missing his right earlobe. So that should help.'

Enzo's presence of mind was returning, and along with it a reticence about telling Martinot too much. He didn't trust the police to put all the information he had to best use. And so he kept the revelations about Bright's upbringing in the Roussillon, and his hemophiliac abductress, to himself. After all, none of that was going to help Raffin now. That was in the lap of the gods.

Martinot sighed. 'I admire your skills, Monsieur Macleod. But, you know, you really should leave this kind of thing to the professionals.'

Enzo looked up at him. 'The only reason I'm involved is because the professionals failed first time around.' And he immediately regretted his words. Martinot, in his day, had done what he could. He'd been a good cop, with a good heart. He just hadn't had the technology at his disposal.

The old man's face darkened. 'You'd better get yourself cleaned up,' he said. 'It's going to be a long night.' And with that he turned and went back out into the hall.

Enzo sat for a moment, shock and depression crushing down on him, a relentless weight. Then he reached for the slip of folded paper on the table. The note that had saved his life. He opened it up with trembling fingers. It was from Raffin's maid, to say that she wouldn't be able to come tomorrow.

Chapter Forty-Two

Aubagne, South of France, 1986

William Bright's diary
December 5

We arrived by train this morning from Paris. Fifteen of us. EVs, they call us. *Engagés Volontaires.* This is the home of the *1er Régiment étranger*, the headquarters of the Foreign Legion. It's a lot warmer in the South. More like I'm used to. We're still a long way from the sea, but I like the sharp colour of the Provençal sun on the hills and that clear blue of the sky. It reminds me of home.

They took everything I had. My clothes, everything, and put them in plastic bags and made an inventory. They said that if I fail selection, they will be returned to me. If I go on to take *La Déclaration,* I will never see them again.

They gave us all track suits, and that marks us out as newcomers. Someone said we'd be up at five every morning, and that they'd have us loading trucks and cleaning the toilets and stuff like that. And that they'd be watching us to check for bad attitude.

Mostly we are English. But there is also a Jap, and a French Canadian called Jacques—at least, he said that's what his name was—and a guy from New Zealand. There are lots of nationalities here, but the common language of the new guys is English.

The first officer who spoke to us said we would be paired with a French-speaker for the first week. When I said I spoke French, he laughed and asked me to say something. I reeled off the words of the *Marseillaise*, and it was all I could do not to laugh when I saw his jaw drop. I told him I spent all my childhood holidays in the south of France, and he said he would pair one of the other newcomers with me. I got the Jap.

The corporal said that over the next three weeks we would be tested for physical and psychological health, security, intelligence, and physical fitness. Next week, he said, those of us who were still here would be issued with a set of combats, and given a green flash to wear on the shoulders. If we survived to the third week, we would wear red flashes on the epaulettes. But not to hold our breaths, because most of us would never get that far. If we did, then we would sign the oath, a commitment to put our lives in the hands of the Legion for the next five years. And we would be sent to Castelnaudary for basic training. I can't wait.

My first one-to-one interview was in the afternoon, with the major. He looked at my passport and said they would be checking that I had no criminal record. I figured my brother would turn up clean. Then he put my passport in a drawer and said that's the last I'd be seeing of it—unless I didn't pass muster.

From now on William Bright no longer exists. From now on I have a French name and a French identity. I am Yves Labrousse. I've always liked the name Yves. The English think it's a girl's name because it sounds like Eve. But it's a good French name.

The major said after three years, if I wanted French nationality I could have it.

He didn't know I was French already. But now they've given me a gift. I'm someone else altogether. Not even who they thought I was. If I can stick this out, I'll be Yves Labrousse for the rest of my days. A man with no past. And a future only I'll decide.

◇◇◇

December 26

It was hot when they dropped us off in Aubagne today, in the Rue de la République. It didn't feel at all like Christmas. We were all wearing red flashes on our combat fatigues. The corporal told us we had five minutes to write and post letters or cards. It was the last time we could write to anyone outside of the Legion, he said. It was the last time we would be allowed out on our own.

I followed the others into the Maison de la Presse, but I don't really know why. I had no one to write to, no one to share any last thoughts with before my life would change forever. Only a handful of the guys I arrived with in Aubagne three weeks ago have lasted the pace. Jacques, the French Canadian, who's now Philippe, the Jap—it seems strange calling him Henri—and a few others. The New Zealander and several of the English were sent packing days ago.

I watched Philippe scribbling on the back of a postcard and wondered what he was writing. What do you say to someone when it's for the last time? It was on a pure impulse that I lifted a card from

the rack—a sunset view of red light washing over
the foothills of the Alpes Maritime. I turned it over
and picked up a pen from the counter, and wrote
her name, and the address I've known all my life.
It's funny, but I've never really thought about what
she might be thinking, how she felt when she went
to my room and found I'd gone. Is she any happier,
or is she mourning for me just like my real mother
did for all those years?

After I'd written the address, I had no idea what
to say.

Philippe punched me on the shoulder. 'Come
on, pal. We'll get shit if we're late!'

I still didn't have a clue what to say to her, and
I almost tore up the card.

'Come on!' he was shouting at me from the door.
'The truck's waiting.'

And so I scribbled very quickly, and very simply,
Au revoir. And signed it, Yves. I licked the stamp
and thumped it with the heel of my hand and ran
the ten metres down the street to the post box.

It wasn't until I was climbing into the back of
the truck that I wondered what on earth she would
make of it.

I can see her face, picture her confusion. And
the thought makes me laugh. Good riddance. I'm
off to a new life, off to learn how to use a gun, how
to fight. How to kill.

PART FIVE

Chapter Forty-Three

There was an embarrassed silence in the room. No one knew quite where to look. Sophie's instinct was to leap to her father's defence, but she saw the warning look in Bertrand's eye and held her peace. Their stay in this big, rambling "safe" house, hidden away in what others might have viewed as an idyllic mountain valley, was turning into a nightmare. Endless days of boredom and frustration, lives on hold while the world passed them by. It had become like a prison. And now this.

Nicole, too, was tempted to speak up for her mentor, but she knew better than to interfere in another family's conflict. And so it was with difficulty that she kept her own counsel, and sat staring at her hands, pink-faced with embarrassment.

Anna, across the hall in the kitchen, could hear every word, but carried on with the preparations for lunch as if nothing was happening.

'You're unbelievable, you know that? Unbe-fucking-lievable!' Kirsty's face was pink too, but with anger verging on tears. She was still in shock. The shock of learning that Roger had been shot, and then anger that Enzo hadn't even phoned. That it had happened forty-eight hours ago and she'd known nothing about it.

She'd called Roger several times in the last few days, and couldn't understand why he never answered, either his home number or his cellphone. Now she knew.

'If I hadn't been here to stop you, you'd have gone running off the Paris without even stopping to think.' Enzo tried to reason with her.

'Damned right I would.'

'And put yourself straight into the firing line.'

Kirsty shook her head vigorously. 'No. Not as long as I kept well clear of you. You're the one who's caused all this. You're the Jonah. You ought to have a fucking health warning stamped on your forehead. Stay away! Anyone who gets too close is in danger of being blown up or shot!' A look flicked at Bertrand. 'Or having their world burned to the ground.'

As she turned away, Enzo grabbed her arm. 'Where are you going?'

'Where do you think? I'm going to Paris.'

'No, you're not.'

And so now they were in a state of stand-off.

'You can't tell me what to do.'

'I can stop you being an idiot. Going to Paris will not make a blind bit of difference to whether Roger recovers or not.'

'So what are you going to do? Ground me? Lock me in my room?'

'If I have to.'

'Oh, fuck off. I'm not five any more. There's nothing you can do to stop me.'

'So how are you going to get there? Walk?'

'Bertrand'll give me a lift to the station at Aurillac.'

Bertrand flushed deeply.

'No, he won't. Because he knows I'm right. And because he's not going to do anything that would put you at risk.' Enzo looked at Bertrand. A look that required no words. Bertrand's nod was almost imperceptible. 'And neither will Anna.'

Kirsty stared at him, eyes wide and glazed with tears. 'You've no right...' She was starting to lose control. 'You can't tell me what to do.'

'Yes, I can.'

'No, you can't!'

'I'm your father.'

Anna appeared in the doorway, the movement registering in Kirsty's peripheral vision, and she turned her head quickly to catch Anna's look, the tiny shake of her head. She turned back to meet her father's eye. She wanted to shout, no you're not! You're not my father, you've never been my father! The words were right there in her mouth, balanced precariously on the tip of her tongue. But something stopped her, some instinct that made her swallow them before they could escape. Instead she said, 'You never liked Roger, did you? You never wanted me to be with him.'

Kirsty's dam finally burst, a flood of tears sweeping her out of the room and up the stairs. They could hear her sobbing all the way up to the landing, and then the door of her room slamming shut.

In the silence she left behind, Enzo could hear the slow tick, tick of the grandfather clock in the hall. Motes of dust hung in suspended animation in the sunlight. Outside, the sound of children in the playground of the village school came to them across a frosted field. A normal, happy world, that seemed to exist in another universe entirely.

◇◇◇

Enzo found Nicole in the computer room. It was half an hour after Kirsty's outburst. Sophie and Bertrand had gone out. For a walk, they said. Anything, Enzo figured, to escape the awful atmosphere in the house. Anna had returned to the kitchen, and Enzo had found himself alone, reliving his conflict with Kirsty.

He felt a sudden surge of anger towards Rickie Bright. All of this was his fault. None of them would be here if it wasn't for Bright. The man had set out to deconstruct Enzo's life, to stop his investigation, but he could never have known just how successful he would be. In many ways, Enzo no longer cared why Bright had murdered Lambert. He just wanted to get him. To make him pay. To peel away all the layers of his deception, to reveal him to the world for the callous, cold-blooded killer he was. A destroyer of lives. A purveyor of pure, undiluted evil.

Nicole was embarrassed to meet his eye. She had retired to the safety of the computer room immediately after Sophie and Bertrand went out, seeking solace in the ether where she controlled the world with her fingertips.

'I've got some more faces for you to look at,' she said.

'Faces?' For a moment he had no idea what she was talking about.

'Your phony doctor.'

'Oh. Yes.' He wasn't sure how much that mattered any more.

'I came across a really good website. An *annuaire* called the *Bellefaye Directory*. It's a listing of all the writers, technicians, directors, and actors working in the French film and television industry.'

She ran nimble fingers over her keyboard and brought the *Bellefaye Directory* up on screen.

'It's really great if you're a producer or director wanting to cast someone with very specific looks.' A row of different coloured boxes along the top of the screen allowed you to choose from among *Actors, Agents, Technicians, Companies, Film Schools.* Nicole clicked on *Actors.* More boxes appeared. *Gender, Type, Language, Age, Height, Weight, Eyes, Hair.* 'It's easy, you just select each of these criteria in turn and define what they should be.' She clicked on *Gender* and selected *Male.* Then *Type,* and chose *European* from a selection of nine ranging from African, through Nordic and Asiatic, to Indian. She looked up at Enzo, I just entered your description of him in each category. Hair and eye colour, height, weight. And it came up with a list of fifty-six actors matching those criteria.'

She slid her mouse across its mat and pulled up a page saved in *Bookmarks.* It was the list produced by the *Bellefaye Directory.* She scrolled down it.

'As you can see, they don't all have photographs. But twenty-one of them did. I pulled them all out and copied them into a single folder for you to look at.'

She brought up the folder, selected the jpegs and opened them up in a full-screen slideshow. Images of men in early middle-age, with short, dark, greying hair, mixed one into the other, all smiling for the camera. What felt like an endless sequence of unfamiliar faces. Enzo stared at the screen, almost without seeing. He was still replaying the fight with Kirsty. And he was finding it hard to rid his mind of the image of Raffin lying in his bed in intensive care, tubes and wires trailing from his broken body to machines that beeped and flashed, delivering blood and fluid to replace the litres he had lost. His face had been unnaturally pale. Unreal. Like a death mask laid over living features. And Enzo hadn't needed Kirsty to tell him that he was to blame.

Suddenly he became aware that a man he knew was looking back at him from the monitor. 'Stop!' Nicole paused the slideshow, and Enzo found himself staring at the face of the man who had told him he was dying. How could he ever forget what he had taken for the sympathetic sincerity in those cold blue eyes? Only now they were smiling, full of warmth, hoping to persuade some producer or director to cast him in a starring role. And maybe he deserved to be. The role he had played for Enzo had been brilliantly convincing. 'Who is he?'

Nicole toggled back to the *Bellefaye* list and clicked on the name Philippe Ransou. Up came his CV. She scanned it. 'French-Canadian. Also speaks English. Seems to get a lot of work. But mostly small roles in action movies and TV dramas. Military types, or thugs. Sometimes does his own stunts. No one seems to have cast him as a doctor, though.'

'Until Bright. I wonder how he chose him.'

'Is it him?'

'Yes.'

She beamed with pleasure. 'I told you I'd find him. What do you want me to do with the information?'

'Print out a couple of copies of his photograph and CV, his agent. Everything you've got. We'll send them to the chief of police in Cahors, and to Monsieur Martinot in Paris.' One way or another, Enzo was determined that Philippe Ransou would pay now for the pain he'd caused. 'But before that, there's something else I need you to do, Nicole.' He had to force himself to focus.

'Anything.'

'I want you to try to get hold of a list of all hemophiliacs living in the Roussillon.'

He saw her surprise. The question forming behind her eyes. But all she said was, 'That's the *département* of the Pyrénées-Oriental, isn't it?' Enzo nodded. 'So Perpignan'll be the administrative capital.'

'Probably.'

'Okay. Hemophiliacs.' She paused. 'Is there anything in particular I should be looking for?'

Enzo drew a deep breath. 'Yes. A woman.'

Chapter Forty-Four

The afternoons were getting shorter as November wore on. The sun was low in the sky now, shadows lengthening almost as you looked. There wasn't much warmth left in the air, the heat of the day, such as it was, rising into the big, wide, empty sky above. A sky that paled to yellow in the west, and then orange and finally red, as the earth turned on its axis. The ghost of a full moon was already visible in it.

Kirsty had not come down for lunch, and the five of them had eaten in uneasy silence. Afterwards, Nicole had retired to the computer room, and Bertrand and Sophie sat down to compose the latest response to an ever increasing traffic of forwarded correspondence with the insurance company over compensation for the gym.

Enzo and Anna walked through the village wrapped in coats and scarves, their breath condensing in the final, cold light of the day. She had wanted to know how much he had found out, and it helped him clarify his own thoughts to go through it all for her, step by step.

'It's the strangest tale. A kid, just twenty months old, abducted from a holiday hotel on the Costa Brava nearly forty years ago. A kid who grew up to be a killer. Stolen by an Englishwoman and brought up, probably somewhere in the Roussillon, just a couple of hours away from where he was snatched. All the time unaware that just a short drive to the south his mother had refused to leave the scene of his abduction. Determined to stay there in case he should ever return.'

He looked at Anna and saw the warmth in her dark eyes, transported by his words to another time, another place.

'At some point, sometime in his teens, he must have discovered the truth. Found out who he really was. By the time he was eighteen, he'd tracked down his real family, and found that he had an identical twin brother living in London. He stole his money, his clothes, and his identity, and embarked on a new life as his own twin.'

'You think he's still masquerading as his brother?'

'I doubt it. He probably only used that as a stepping stone to another persona. But at least we know now what he looks like, and it's a good starting point for our search.'

'So how likely do you think it is that you'll catch him?'

'Oh, I'll get him.' There was steel in Enzo's voice. 'If he doesn't kill me first. I also know where to look for the woman who abducted him. It may be that I'll find something there, some clue that'll take me another step closer.' He drifted off into speculative thought before coming abruptly back to the present. 'And we found the actor he employed to masquerade as my doctor in Cahors. Another loose end. Another thread that could to lead us to him. I'm closing in on him, Anna. Almost got him on the end of my line. And when I have, one way or another, I'm going to reel him right in.'

She slipped her arm through his and gave it a small squeeze. 'You told me last time you were here that you thought he was some kind of professional.'

'That's right.'

'So…what did you say his real name was…?'

'Bright. Rickie, or Richard Bright.'

'So Bright didn't kill Lambert for personal reasons.'

'I don't think so. I think he was probably hired to do it.'

'And are you any nearer to figuring out who it was who hired him, or why?'

Enzo shook his head. 'Not at all. I figure the only way we're ever going to know that is by getting Bright into custody and persuading him to tell us.'

They walked past the row of trees in front of the church, brittle, frosted leaves crunching underfoot. The granite stone of the village houses sparkled in the dying sunlight all along one side of the street, and the streetlights flickered and shed ineffectual electric light into the gathering gloom on the other.

Anna said, 'You mustn't take what Kirsty says too seriously.'

Which brought Enzo's mind back from that other place it had wandered to again. 'She always seems to want to hurt me,' he said. 'To lash out and do damage.'

'Sometimes when we're hurting, the only people we can take it out on are the ones we love.'

'She spent her whole life blaming me for all the hurt in it. I thought she'd got over that.' He wanted to tell her about the night at Simon's. To share it with someone, to offload the burden. But he was afraid that to give it voice would make it somehow more real. And he still didn't want to believe it. He had no way of knowing that Anna already knew, that his own daughter had told her. And so they were two people divided by a common knowledge they couldn't share.

'You can't underestimate how vulnerable she is right now, Enzo. She barely escaped with her life in Strasbourg. Her best friend was killed. She thought her father was dying, and then he was arrested for murder. And now her lover's been shot, and she doesn't know if he's going to survive.' There was more, but like Enzo she wasn't going to go there. 'You're at the centre of it all. So who else is she going to blame?'

Enzo stopped and took her face in his hands. He gazed into the dark eyes she turned on him, and kissed her softly on the lips. 'I don't know what I'd have done without you, Anna. I really don't.'

She kissed him back. 'You and me both.'

'Just promise me...If I have to leave again, you won't let her go to Paris.'

She smiled. 'I won't let her do that, Enzo. I promise.' And then her face darkened, as if a cloud had passed over it. 'You know why he left?'

'Who?'

'Roger. Why he *really* left?'

Enzo tensed. 'He said he needed to get back to work.'

'He made a pass at me. Damned near raped me. If I hadn't been as fit as I am he might have succeeded.'

'Jesus! Does Kirsty…?'

'No, of course not. I made it clear to him that if he didn't pack his bags and get out, then I would tell her. And that the only reason I wouldn't was to protect her, not him.'

Enzo felt a wave of fatigue wash over him. He wasn't sure how much more of this he could take. It just seemed to be one thing after another. 'She mustn't know, Anna. You mustn't ever tell her. If Raffin survives, then I'll deal with him myself.'

◇◇◇

It was dark by the time they got back to the house. Light from the kitchen spilled out into the unlit hall. Sophie and Bertrand were watching television in the *séjour*. Some girl singing badly, and a voice-over which Enzo recognised as belonging to the host of *Star Academy*. There was still no sign of Kirsty. The door to the computer room stood ajar, and a crack of light zig-zagged its way up the first few steps of the spiral staircase. Nicole's voice called out of the darkness. 'Is that you, Monsieur Macleod?'

'Yes, Nicole.'

'I've got some information for you.'

When he went into the computer room she turned and beamed at him, clearly pleased with herself. Anna leaned against the door jamb and listened.

'What did you find?'

'Well, it's not easy getting access to confidential medical information online, Monsieur Macleod. So I telephoned the Hôpital St. Jean, the *centre hospitalier* in Perpignan, and told them I was a researcher at the Ministry of Health in Paris. I said

I needed access to the register of hemophiliacs living in their *département*.'

'And they believed you?'

'Why wouldn't they? I mean, why would anyone else want that kind of information?' She grinned. 'Anyway, I did a little research before I made the call. You know, there are only about three-and-a-half thousand hemophiliacs in the whole of France. Which means that, statistically, in an area like the Pyrénées-Oriental, with a population base of less than half a million, there are only likely to be around twenty-three.'

'It's a rare disease, Nicole. Where's this leading us?' Enzo was struggling to contain his impatience.

'Well, statistically again, they're all likely to be men.' She paused dramatically. 'So guess what?' But she didn't wait for them to guess. 'There were actually twenty-two on their list.' She lifted a sheet of paper from the printer and handed it to Enzo. 'And contrary to statistical expectation, one of them is a woman.'

Enzo looked at the printout held in trembling fingers. He remembered Raffin's words in Paris. *He's just a breath away. I can feel it.* And for the first time he felt it, too. That Rickie Bright was just around the corner. Very possibly biding his time, simply waiting for Enzo to appear.

He barely heard Nicole's triumphant *coup de grace*. 'Her name is Elizabeth Archangel. She lives in an old fishing port on the Mediterranean, not far from the Spanish border. It's called Collioure.' The tiniest pause for emphasis. 'And she's English.'

Chapter Forty-Five

Enzo parked in the Place du 8 Mai 1945, in the shadow of the Château Royal. In the tourist season, he knew, it would be virtually impossible to find parking here, but *hors saison* the town was almost deserted, a creeping air of neglect in the cool haze of misty morning air that dropped down from the foothills of the Pyrénées. Shops and galleries and restaurants had closed up for the winter. Pavements, stripped bare of colourful summer displays of goods and art, seemed sad and empty. The plane trees all along the Avenue Camille Pelletan had shed their leaves along the quayside, where only a month before people would have sat dining at tables in the soft, Mediterranean autumn. Now these same tables and chairs were stacked up and covered over until next Spring.

There were a few vehicles parked in the gully below. A dangerous place to leave your car during summer storms, when heavy rainfall would bring run-off from the hills coursing through its dry stone bed to sweep out into the bay. But today there was no hint of rain in the chill-edged breeze that blew off the sea.

Enzo made a mental note of the sign in the window of the Café Sola on the far side of the Rue de la République—*Accès Wifi*, wireless internet access—and walked along the Quai de l'Amirauté, past the *boulodrome*, to the little bridge that spanned the gully. He stopped on the bridge and watched as soldiers under the command of the Centre National d'Entraînement

Commando, were put through their paces by barking officers. Young men burdened by full kit, with close-cropped hair and lean, determined faces, pushed rubber dinghies out into the bay. The same routine, though he wasn't to know it, that the young Rickie Bright had watched daily on his walk home from school thirty years earlier.

He got a street map from the tourist office opposite the Police Municipale in the Place du 18 Juin, and walked through an arch in the old town wall to the Boulevard du Boramar. From here there was a view across the shingle beach and the bay to the diving school opposite, where boats rose and fell on the gentle pewter swell, tethered and covered over for the winter.

At the south end of the boulevard was the Eglise Notre Dame des Anges, with its golden domed bell tower. At the north end was the quay made famous by André Derain's painting of garishly coloured fishing boats with canted masts and rolled up sails. A couple of them still remained, a reminder for tourists of what life had been like here in Derain's day, nearly a century before. Collioure was a town rich in art and history. A refuge for Spanish and French artists fleeing war and persecution. A place where penniless painters had paid for food and lodgings with paintings alone. Desperate men who really had lived by their art. And innkeepers who had profited handsomely from their future fame.

He turned south and then north into the old fishing port which climbed the hill towards the fort. The Rue Bellevue, on its south side, was bounded by the remains of an ancient fortified wall. Enzo stopped to peer through a crumbling arrow slit down to the grey seawater breaking green and white over the black rocks below. Three-storey pink, and cream, and peach-painted former fishermen's dwellings, dominated the north side of the street as it rose steeply to the top of the hill, where a row of stone cottages was built along the edge of the cliff. Red-leafed vines twisted around rusted iron trellises that in summer would provide a shady respite from the southern sun. A fleshy-leafed cactus looked tired and careworn. A cobbled passageway led to a flight of steps beside an arched gate, and Enzo climbed them to a small parking area that served the clifftop cottages.

Below him, the little brick-arched gateway led to a private garden full of flowering winter shrubs, a stone fish perched precariously on its wall. Off to his left, an area of coloured paving, filled with trees and terracotta potted plants, led to the first door in the row. An old wrought-iron sewing table and folding chair sat on a tiny, shaded terrace. Blue shutters were closed over square windows. There was an old, rusted ship's bell attached to the wall beside the door, and Enzo pulled its rope. The sharp, resonant ring of metal on metal vibrated in the cool air, and after several moments, Enzo heard a lock turning in the door.

It opened into a long, narrow hallway, and beyond it Enzo could see into a sitting room with large windows looking out over the Mediterranean. A small lady with short cut white hair peered at him from the gloom. A lady in her late sixties or early seventies. Her skin was remarkably unlined, but her age was betrayed by the brown blemishes on the pale skin of her face and hands. She wore a knitted cardigan over a white blouse and a checkered tweed skirt and had a short, pink, silk scarf tied at her neck.

Enzo said nothing, and she looked at him for a long time with blue eyes so pale they were almost colourless. And then realisation washed over her, and she wilted visibly, eyes clouding suddenly as if by ripened cataracts.

'You know, don't you?' Her voice was a whisper barely audible above the sigh of the sea thirty feet below. Enzo nodded and she said, 'I've been expecting you for nearly forty years.'

◇◇◇

She served them tea in bone china cups, pouring from a long-spouted teapot in the sitting room with the sea view. It was a small room, in which all her furniture seemed large. A walnut buffet against one wall, a Welsh dresser against another, and a big, soft, old sofa with two matching armchairs, hand-embroidered antimacassars on the arms. Every wall and shelf space was covered by framed photographs. A record of a life, a young boy in all his stages from toddler to teenager. A record that seemed to stop abruptly in midteens. In most of them he appeared to be scowling, but there was one that stood out from all the others, his face transformed by a radiant smile, blond curls tumbling across a wide forehead. He wasn't smiling at the camera, but at something to camera left. An unusually happy moment caught in an unhappy life.

Elizabeth Archangel followed his eyeline. 'Yes, it does stand out, doesn't it? He was not a boy prone to smiling, or to expressing any kind of emotion. I often felt, during all those years, that he somehow knew, that he had always known, and resented me for it. But, of course, he couldn't have. Sugar?'

She held out the bowl, but Enzo shook his head. 'No thank you.'

'Of course, it wasn't me he was smiling at. He would never have smiled like that for me. It was Domi. His dog. Normally I wouldn't have had animals in the house. Too big a risk of scratches or bites. But there wasn't anything I wouldn't have done for Richard, even if he never did appreciate it.'

And Enzo realised that she had kept the boy's name. His real mother had called him Rickie. The woman who had stolen him preferred the more formal Richard. So he had grown up as Richard Archangel.

'Of course, it was me he blamed when we had to have the dog put down. Even though I wasn't the cause of it. It had been alright at first, but he somehow developed an allergy to the animal. So bad my doctor felt it could be life-threatening. I had no choice.' She paused, lost in sad recollection. 'He never forgave me.'

Enzo looked again at all the pictures, and felt nothing but a simmering hatred for this child who, even then, must have borne the seeds of destruction in his soul. He had to force himself to remain objective. He turned to the old lady. 'Why did you steal him?' It seemed odd to speak of *stealing* another human being.

She closed her eyes and her head trembled a little. 'Be careful what you wish for, lest it comes true. That's what they say, isn't it?' She opened her eyes again. 'I had a difficult childhood,

Mister Macleod. I couldn't take part in any of the games the other children played. I was wrapped in cotton wool and kept safe from the world. There can't be anything much worse that watching life slip by your window and never be able to participate in it.

'My parents were paranoid. That it was their fault never seemed to occur to them. My mother always claimed she didn't know she was a carrier, but I'm certain now she knew and wanted a child anyway.' She added quickly, 'Not that I blame her. I didn't understand then. But when I became a woman, I knew what it was to want a child of your own. And when you know you can't have something, you want it more than anything in the world.'

She sipped her tea and gazed out over water reflecting a leaden sky. The wind was rising, banishing the mist, and raising little white crests on the ruffled surface of the sea. 'I don't have the worst form of hemophilia, Mister Macleod. My blood was always possessed of at least a few clotting agents. And with obsessive parental care, I made it through childhood almost without incident. But they couldn't protect me from puberty. That's when the real nightmare began. With menstruation. There were times it simply wouldn't stop. I had repeated transfusions, and then they put me on drugs, hormones, to try to control it. They kept me alive just long enough for the introduction of the birth control pill in 1960. I was one of the very first to take it, prescribed and paid for by the good old British health service. Estrogen and progestin to make my body think it was permanently pregnant, to make it stop producing eggs, and to hold my endometrium together so I wouldn't bleed. The irony being, of course, that I could never get pregnant in reality. Not without facing almost certain death.'

'So you stole someone else's child.'

'Oh, no, Mister Macleod. I wasn't that desperate. Not yet. And I did something much worse before I resorted to that.'

Enzo frowned. What could be worse? 'I don't understand.'

'I fell in love. Met a man who stole my heart, and all my reason and married me. Not that any of it was his fault. He knew, right from the start, that we couldn't have children. He knew that making love to me would be a tentative and dangerous thing. That he would have to take the utmost care never to make me bleed. And he never did. I've never known anyone so gentle and caring. It was always me who wanted to throw caution to the wind. I had a passion in me, don't you see? I needed to live, after all those years of deprivation, even if it meant I would die in the process. Which is why, in the end, I stopped taking the pill.'

She exhaled deeply.

'Of course, I didn't tell him. He had no idea why I was making such sexual demands of him night after night. Not that he objected. But I knew, that if I could get pregnant in reality, then I would survive stopping the pill. The only question then, was whether I would survive giving birth.'

'And did you? I mean, get pregnant?'

'To Reginald's absolute horror, yes. He couldn't believe I had put myself at such risk. He had always accepted that we would never have children. But I couldn't. And I was prepared to die trying. He just couldn't comprehend that.'

Enzo looked at the little old lady sitting in the armchair across the coffee table, and realised that she must have been driven in a way that he, just like her husband, would never comprehend. What instinctual urge could possibly motivate you to want children more than life? He found himself drawn into the horror of the Archangels' lives, empathising with the distraught husband who had unwittingly made her pregnant, and who lacked any real understanding of his wife's obsession. 'So what happened?'

She sighed heavily, draining the last of her tea, and placing the cup carefully in its saucer. 'You may remember a plane crash near Manchester in March, 1968. No doubt you were just a teenager then, so maybe not. It was a flight from London to Glasgow. A hundred and thirty-three people died. My Reginald was one of them. I was three months pregnant, and the love of my life was gone. Somehow, then, it was all the more important that I go through with it. That I have my baby. It was all I had left of him.'

She was becoming agitated now, wringing her hands in her lap, unfocused, almost unaware of the presence of the big Scotsman sitting opposite. 'The doctors did everything they could to prepare me for the birth. But it is almost impossible to avoid even the smallest tear. And I very nearly bled to death. It was touch and go over several days and many transfusions. The bleeding was internal, you see. Very difficult to stop. But they did, and within a week I was holding my own baby boy in my arms, the only surviving part of his father.' Her face darkened. 'But that's where all resemblance between father and son ended. He owed too much of himself to his mother. I'd given him my curse. A fifty-fifty chance. But for him the coin had landed the wrong way up.'

Her focus returned, along with a certain calm, and she looked at Enzo as if she were surprised to see him. 'More tea?'

'No, thank you.' He laid his cup and saucer in the tray. 'What happened to your son, Mrs. Archangel.'

'Why, he died, of course. Just eighteen months old. I had taken such care, Mister Macleod, to protect him against any possibility of injury. Worse than my own parents with me. I never let him out of my sight. I was planning, when it came time, to educate him at home.' She shook her head. 'Perhaps, in some perverse sort of way, it was better for him. What sort of life might he have had, isolated from the world in the bubble I would have built for him?'

She turned towards the window, biting on her lower lip. 'I was with him when it happened. Saw him go down, and couldn't do a thing about it. The exuberance of a toddler learning to walk, the lack of coordination. Clumsy feet. We were in the kitchen. A stone floor. Very unyielding. He tripped and pitched forward. Landed right on his face. I almost heard his nose burst. And then there was the blood. And I panicked. Oh, God, how I panicked. Because I knew, you see. I just knew. I phoned the ambulance straight away, but it was never going to get there on time. I did everything I could, but the bleeding just wouldn't stop. Such a tiny body. Just a little person. Not that much blood to start with. He was dead within minutes.'

She lifted the teapot. 'Are you sure I can't help you to more tea?'

Enzo shook his head, and she poured another cup for herself, concentrating on the minute processes. The single sugar cube, stirred till dissolved. The splash of milk. The swirl of the spoon. The cup brought slowly to the lips for the tiniest of sips. Then she lifted her eyes again to the sea, that seemingly endless, ever-changing expanse of water that she must have gazed upon during untold solitary hours.

'And so I was alone. My baby and my lover both dead. My whole world in ruins around me. I felt truly cursed, Mister Macleod. You can have no idea. I would never be with another man. No one could ever replace my Reginald. But I could give nurture to a child. Bring some meaning to a life that had lost all purpose. Although I knew that even if there had been someone to make me pregnant, I would never have survived another birth.'

She took several small sips of tea before replacing the cup in its saucer. 'You know, everywhere I looked, all around me, women had children. Women who didn't deserve to have children, or even want them. Women who got pregnant at the drop of a hat. A night of fun, a moment's carelessness.' She looked at Enzo, an appeal for understanding. 'And I could never adopt. Not back then. A single woman. A hemophiliac. It was so unfair.'

'And you thought it was fair to steal someone else's child?'

'Oh, I chose very carefully, Mister Macleod, I can assure you. It wasn't a spur of the moment thing. I took several months to prepare. Reginald had left me well provided for in his will. I sold the house in England and came to France. I had no living relatives, so I had no ties, no one to know my history.

'I found this house here in Collioure. I bought and furnished it. When, finally, I moved in, I would be the grieving English widow, escaping tragedy in England, bringing her young son with her to start a new life. I'd had Richard put on my passport, you see. I still had his birth certificate. The people at the passport authority had no way of knowing he was dead.'

A sudden understanding dawned on Enzo. 'Richard. Your own son was called Richard?'

'Oh, yes. Actually, that was what clinched it for me in Cadaqués. I had already selected the boy before I discovered that his name was Richard. It was too great a coincidence. I thought that it was fate. That it was meant to be. Although now I realise that, if anything, it was meant to be a punishment, not a blessing.'

Her smile was wistful and distant, full of pain not pleasure at the process of recollection. 'I was staying at another hotel, just around the bay. I'd been there for a couple of weeks, and I would spend my days sitting around the pools of other hotels, watching families and their children. Sometimes following them. Sometimes striking up conversations. No one ever saw me as a threat, you see. A young woman on her own, a ring still on her wedding finger. If anyone asked, I told them the truth. My husband had been killed in a plane crash, and I was escaping the horror of it all for a few short weeks.

'That's when I first saw Richard. At the poolside with his family. And then later, on the beach. I even took a photograph of them and got a studio in town to develop it for me. He was such a beautiful boy. Fair, like my own Richard. But what made it so perfect, do you see, there were two of them. Identical. Whatever the pain of losing one child might be, his mother would always have the compensation of the other. And there was another sibling, too. An older sister.'

'And that made it alright?' Enzo couldn't keep the disapproval from his voice.

She responded as if pricked by a pin, stung to self-justification. 'She already had three children, and could have had more if she wanted. She was a Catholic, so she probably would.'

'So you took him.'

'Yes. I could give him so much more. And my attention would be undivided, not spread thin across a whole family. I spent several days devising a way of doing it. But in the end it was almost too easy. They made it that way for me. Leaving their children alone in the hotel room each night while they ate and drank and laughed with their friends in the restaurant. And that stupid girl who was supposed to check on them, too busy flirting with a boy from the kitchen. A rendezvous each night out by the bins. Adolescent groping. Disgusting. Taking Richard should have been so very simple.'

'And it wasn't?'

'It was a disaster. As I lifted him from the cot, he was still half asleep, and his little hand came up to hang around my neck. As it did, the sharp corner of a fingernail tore the skin of my cheek and I started to bleed. Such a stupid, silly little thing. But I couldn't stop it, do you see? When I bleed, I bleed. I'd been going to take his little panda as a comforter, but in the end I had to let it go. It was all I could do to carry Richard and try to staunch the blood at the same time. I nearly abandoned the whole thing. I was out in the corridor, in two minds about putting him back, when I heard someone coming up in the lift. So I ran. The die was cast. There was no going back.'

She lifted her teacup again, but the tea was tepid now, and she pulled a face and laid it down again. 'It took just two hours to get him back here. But we'd crossed a border, and in those days the media was not as all-pervasive as it is now. There was virtually no coverage of the abduction in the French press. I knew the police would search the immediate vicinity, Cadaqués and its environs. And they'd probably search far and wide. Throughout Spain, and no doubt in the UK. But two hours up the coast, in France? I was fairly certain that no one would ever think of looking for us here.'

She smiled a strange little smile, full of bitterness and irony. 'And so we were free to begin our dream life together. Except that the dream turned into a nightmare, and I only had him for sixteen years. Sixteen long, difficult years.'

'What went wrong?'

'Oh, nothing went wrong. It was just Richard. How he was. How, I suppose, he would have been, no matter what. A difficult, disobedient, sulky, sullen, solitary boy. Maybe he missed having a father figure, a role model like Reginald. He certainly didn't want me. He recoiled from my touch, hated it when I kissed him, wouldn't hold my hand. You can have no idea how distressing that was for a mother. How, in the end, I grew to dislike him so much, I think perhaps I started to hate him. When he went, it was both a heartbreak and a relief.'

Enzo noticed how easily she referred to herself as his mother, as if almost from the start she had believed it to be true. Some enormous capacity for self-deception. He doubted if she had even followed the story in the British press. British newspapers would have been available here, even then. But she wouldn't have wanted to read about how she had devastated a family, ruined a mother's life. That would have made the self-deception so much harder to maintain. 'So what made him leave?'

'I came home one day to find him in a state of extreme agitation. I had left him studying for his *baccalauréat*. He wasn't particularly gifted academically, but he could have done better. He lacked concentration, motivation. Which is, I suppose, why he abandoned his studies that day and went exploring in the attic. That's how he found all my old papers. The photographs I had taken in Cadaqués, birth certificates, marriage certificate. Reginald's death certificate.' She paused. 'My Richard's death certificate. Which, as far as he was concerned, was his own.'

Enzo could only imagine what kind of shock it must have been to stumble across your own death certificate. 'What did he say?'

'He demanded answers I couldn't give him. I wasn't prepared, you see. There was no convincing way I could lie to him. So I simply stonewalled. Accused him of prying, of meddling in things he didn't understand, of jumping to all the wrong conclusions. He said in that case I should explain it to him so he *would* understand. But I refused to discuss it any further and sent him to his room.' Her face lapsed into a set of weary resignation. 'I didn't dare try to speak to him again that night. And when I went to rouse him in the morning he was gone. Taken hardly anything with him. Just a few items of clothing. The window was open, so I assume he'd jumped down to the garden.'

'And you didn't report him missing to the police?'

'How could I? Any kind of investigation would only have uncovered the truth, especially if they'd found him. No, Mister Macleod, he was gone and I just had to accept it. Alone again, like it seems I was always destined to be. I told his school he'd gone back to England, and that was an end to it.' She looked at Enzo with sad, pale eyes. 'I suppose you'll be reporting me to the authorities.'

'You committed a crime, Mrs. Archangel. A long time ago, perhaps, but you still have a debt to repay, particularly to his mother. She's still there, you know. In Cadaqués. All these years later, waiting for her son to return.'

He saw the old lady draw in her lips to contain her emotion. These were things she had never wanted to hear, never dared to imagine. 'And Richard? What's become of him?'

His voice was empty, emotionless. 'He murders people for a living, Mrs. Archangel. He's a professional killer.'

The shock that flitted across her face was, for a moment extraordinarily vivid, a reflection of an inner emotional turmoil. Horror, fear, revulsion. And then it passed, to be replaced by a kind of acceptance, a silent acknowledgement that she had raised a monster, and that maybe she had known it all along.

'It's possible that he might be using the name of William Bright.'

Her eyes lifted sharply. 'His family name.'

'William is his brother.'

'So he found them, then?'

'So it seems.'

'And do they…do they know?'

'They do now.'

She closed her eyes. The lie that she had lived nearly all of her adult life was over. God only knew what the future would hold. When she opened then again, they were filled with tears. Of self pity.

'Did you ever hear from him, after he left?'

She shook her head. 'Never.' Then some distant memory forced a revision. 'Well, once. Just once. I'm certain it was him, though he didn't say so.'

'I don't understand.'

'Wait.' She eased herself stiffly out of the armchair and crossed to the Welsh dresser. She rummaged in a drawer for several minutes, shuffling through a folder of papers, before turning with a postcard in her hand. Enzo could see that it was a vividly coloured sunset scene, red light on blue hills. 'This came a few months after he'd gone.' She lifted reading glasses and peered at the card. 'Dated December 26th, 1986.' She raised one hand in a small gesture of exasperation. 'All it says is *Au revoir*. But it's his handwriting. I'd have known it anywhere.' She peered at it again. 'Strangest thing, though.'

'What is?'

'He signed it, *Yves*.' She looked up. 'Why would he do that?'

'Maybe, Mrs. Archangel, by December 26th, 1986, that was his name.' He held out his hand for the card and she gave it to him. And he saw quite clearly from its postmark that it had been sent from a place called Aubagne.

Chapter Forty-Six

Yves watched from the Rue St. Sébastien as Macleod left the house. The tall, ponytailed Scotsman crossed the small car park and disappeared down the steps to the Rue du Mirador. But Yves lingered. He knew there was no danger of losing him, and so he was prepared to allow himself the luxury of a little bittersweet nostalgia.

He stepped out from the shadow of the trees and walked slowly across the tarmac to the house where he had grown up. Nothing much had changed. Everything had grown. The shutters had been repainted. At the top of the steps, he looked down at the little arched gateway through which he had made his escape all those years ago. He could see his bedroom window, and felt a pang of something unfamiliar. It might have been regret. The sea beyond was as it always had been. Like him. Moody, changeable. He listened to it breathing, the sound of his childhood. He smelled its salty fragrance. Breathed it in.

There was a new sign at the entrance to the cottages. *Rue Sans Issue*. Dead end. It had always been a dead end street, where he had lived a dead end life. On the wall next to it was a framed print of a painting someone had done of the cottages. Bright Mediterranean colours, sunlight lying in patches across the hills on the headland beyond.

For several minutes he simply stood listening. He was surprised to discover that he was afraid. Afraid he might see her, meet her, hear her voice. The woman who had stolen his life. But the house was silent. No voices, no footfall in the hall. He moved on to the *terrasse* and saw the wrought iron sewing table where she used to make him sit and read his schoolbooks. The fold-up chair he had sat in so often. The metalwork was painted blue to match the shutters. In his day it had all been green.

She was there, somewhere just on the other side of the door. He knew she was at home. He had seen Macleod going in, and he had been there for more than an hour. No doubt he knew even more now about the young Richard Archangel, his history in both Cadaqués and Collioure. Yves had failed completely to stop him. He should have been dead by now. Only a fluke in Paris had saved his life. And here he was, still digging up the past, pawing through the shit.

Yves tried to control his breathing, to calm himself. Anger was not the answer. Success in killing the Scotsman would depend on cool calculation. And kill him he would. Of that he was certain.

From somewhere inside the house came the sound of breaking glass. He tensed and listened intently. But heard nothing more. He was breathing rapidly again, his heart punching against his ribs like a boxer in training. Stab, jab-jab, stab, jab. Gloved fists pounding the punchbag.

He had no idea what moved him to do it. Some morbid fascination, a strange sense of returning to the safety of the womb, no matter how unhappy his time there had been. He reached for the handle and opened the door, pushing it gently into the darkness of the hall. All his senses were assailed by a smell that summersaulted him back through time, momentarily robbing him of his composure. He reached out to touch the wall and steady himself. He felt like a ghost haunting his own past, and expected any moment to see himself emerge from his bedroom, to climb down the stairs to the sea-facing terrace where he had spent so much of his time reading, thinking, dreaming, crying.

There was not a sound. The living room seemed empty. Then, as he stepped into the room, he was shocked to see his image on every surface, on every wall. Like a place of worship, an altar where she prayed for the boy he had once been. Or, perhaps, the boy she had wanted him to be. He moved to the window and peered down on to the terrace. No one there. Then to his bedroom door. He hesitated for a moment, a sense of dread building inside him. Did he really want to open this door to his past? He pushed the handle down and let the door swing open, and found himself transported back through twenty-two years. All his posters were still on the wall, faded now, and curling around the edges. His guitar was leaned up in the corner. One of its strings had broken. The bed was made. The same bedspread that had covered it the night he left.

It was almost more than he could bear, and he pulled the door quickly closed again.

Where was she? She couldn't have gone out. Unless she had somehow managed to slip through the arched gate into the lane below without him seeing her.

The tiniest sound caught his attention. At first he was unable to identify it. Then there it was again. A drip. The sound of water on water. It was coming from the bathroom. He moved with the silent steps of the ghost that he was, down the hall to the bathroom door. It was not quite shut. With a hand that he could not hold steady, he pushed it open.

She was lying naked in the bath. A strange, shrunken, white-haired old lady. Almost floating. Her arms at her sides, palms face up, blood issuing in bright red pulses from the dark gashes in her wrists. He glanced down and saw the bloody pieces of broken mirror on the floor.

She was still alive. Her eyes wide open, watching him with that same pale blue intent. For just a second he saw some fleeting emotion flare like the flame of a match before dying again as the phosphor burned out. He stood in the doorway and watched as slowly the eyes glazed over and the light went out. He knew she was dead when her heart stopped pumping blood into the water.

Chapter Forty-Seven

From his seat in the window of the Café Sola, Enzo could see across the street to the market square, and the repair truck from the garage parked next to his car. The mechanic, in his blue overalls, was pumping the handle of a pneumatic jack to lift up the far corner of the vehicle. Enzo had found that the trunk contained only an emergency spare, so there had been no point in changing the punctured wheel himself. The garage had sent a mechanic to come and remove the wheel. Now he had returned with a new tyre.

Enzo refocused on his laptop, and heard it ringing as he waited for Nicole to respond. His own image from its built-in webcam looked back at him from an open window on the desktop. Then the ringing stopped, and his head shrunk to a postage stamp in the top corner, to be superseded by Nicole's smiling face.

'Monsieur Macleod. Where are you?'

'Still in Collioure.'

'Did you talk to her?'

'I did.'

'And?'

'I'll tell you all about it later, Nicole. Right now, there's something I need you to do for me.'

'Of course.'

It was something he could have done himself. But he had other reasons for making the iChat call. 'How's Kirsty doing?'

Nicole shrugged. If she was embarrassed, she was masking it well. 'Okay. At least she's talking to us all again. Apparently Roger's off the critical list, so it looks like he's going to pull through.'

Enzo found himself entertaining uncharitably mixed feelings. But all he said was, 'Good.' Then, 'Nicole, I need you to find out anything and everything you can for me about a place called Aubagne. Have you heard of it?'

She shook her head. 'Do you know where it is?'

'No idea.'

'Okay. Let me have a look on the net. I'll call you back.'

As he disconnected, the café door opened and the blue over-alled mechanic came in. He sat in the seat opposite. 'All done, Monsieur Macleod.' And with scarred, oily fingers, broken nails delineated in black, he wrote out an invoice and tore off the top copy 'One hundred and twenty euros.'

Enzo wrote him a cheque which the mechanic took and examined briefly before standing up. He hesitated, scratching his head through a thatch of thick, wiry hair. 'It wasn't no accident, monsieur.'

Enzo frowned. 'What do you mean?'

'Your puncture. Someone put a blade through the wall of the tyre.'

Enzo felt his face tingle as if he had been slapped, and fear stabbed him suddenly in the chest like the blade which had pierced his tyre. All he could do was nod.

The mechanic gave him a peculiar look, then folded the cheque and slipped it in his pocket. '*Bonne journée, monsieur.*' And he was gone. For the second time, Raffin's words rang in Enzo's recollection. *He's just a breath away. I can feel it.* He looked up through the window and let his eyes wander across the square opposite, searching for a familiar face amongst the residents of Collioure going about their daily business. But he saw no one he recognised. The huge stone edifice of the Château Royal rose dark against the grey sky, and in the bay beyond, a sail boat was banked steeply in the wind, tacking out past the harbour wall. He was startled by the ringing of his computer.

Nicole's face reappeared. 'Aubagne is in Provence,' she said. 'Somewhere between Aix and Marseilles. In the *département* of Bouches-du-Rhone. It's not very big. About forty thousand people. Nothing much to distinguish it. The only thing it's really known for is being the home of the Foreign Legion.'

'Jesus,' Enzo said, as the full impact of what she had just told him sank in. 'He must have joined the Legion.'

'Do you think? Hang on...' He could hear her tapping away at her keyboard. Then she was silent for more than a minute, and he could see her scanning something onscreen. 'Well, that would make sense, Monsieur Macleod. Apparently joining the *Légion étrangère*, is a well-travelled route for foreigners wanting to change their identities. Frenchmen aren't allowed to join. If they do they have to take on the persona of someone foreign, like French Canadian or French Swiss. Then everyone's given a new identity as soon as they've enlisted.'

But Enzo knew that Bright had already acquired a custom-made foreign persona. That of his brother, William. An Englishman.

More tapping on Nicole's keyboard. 'It seems they have to sign up for a minimum of five years, but they're allowed to take French citizenship after three.'

Enzo sat back in his seat as full realisation washed over him. 'Bright had effectively laundered his identity. Stolen his brother's, then traded it in for a new one in the French Foreign Legion. Five years later, at the age of just twenty-three, he would have rejoined the real world as someone else altogether, with no ties to the past. Fit, experienced, and trained to kill.

'Thanks, Nicole. I'll get back to you.' He disconnected, and felt fear and excitement welling in his chest. Rickie Bright's carefully managed trail of obfuscation was rapidly unravelling. Enzo already knew the Christian name of his new identity. *Yves.* All he needed now was the surname.

He went into his wallet and found a slightly dog-eared business card. He straightened its corners between thumb and forefinger and looked at it with a renewed sense of betrayal. Perhaps now Simon could do something useful for his old friend.

He slipped the card into his pocket, and brought Google up on his computer screen. He searched for, and found, *Mappy*, the online French route planner, and plumbed in Collioure and Aubagne. The map and directions it presented were straightforward enough. It was *autoroute* nearly all the way, east across the southern fringes of France. A drive of less than four hours. He checked his watch. If he left now he could be there by late afternoon.

He closed down his computer and shut the lid, dropping a few coins by his empty coffee cup. As he got up he glanced through the window. Rickie Bright was standing in front of the Hôtel Frégate across the street, watching him.

Chapter Forty-Eight

By the time he had packed his computer into its bag and stepped out on to the street, Bright was gone. Enzo stood for several minutes with the blood pounding in his head, looking up and down the Rue de la République and across the square. The traffic filed past, belching its bile into the cool November air, but there was no sign of Bright. Enzo had taken his eyes off him for a only moment, but in that time he had somehow contrived to disappear.

His legs were like jelly as he crossed the road and placed his computer in the trunk of his car, all the while glancing around him, afraid that at any moment Bright was going to lunge at him from some unsuspected place of concealment. But nothing. No Bright. No attack. Just the old Mediterranean fishing port of Collioure going about its unhurried, out-of-season business.

Enzo sat in his car and gripped the steering wheel, made tense by a mixture of fear, anger and uncertainty. For a brief few seconds, he considered abandoning his plan to drive to Aubagne. But he had no other options open to him. What else could he do? He had embarked on a course and had no choice but to see it through.

He drove out of the square and up through the town, past the anchovy processing factory, and on to the road that wound up the hill to the dual carriageway that would take him to Perpignan. In his rearview mirror, he saw the town disappearing below, the sea levelling out towards a hazy, distant horizon. There were several vehicles on the road behind him. A solitary driver with dark hair, a car containing a family of four. He couldn't see the others, and almost drove into the car in front as it slowed to take the exit to Argelès sur Mer.

It took nearly half-an-hour to get to Perpignan, and he spotted what he was looking for in a strip mall on the outskirts. He pulled into the parking lot and stood watching the other cars that turned in after him. Still no sign of Bright. He waited for several minutes before deciding that if the killer was anywhere around he wasn't going to show himself. Which made the thought that he was still out there, unseen, all the more unnerving.

He went into the Halle aux Vêtements and selected an extra large, dark blue suit from a long line of hangers, and then an XXL white shirt. Enzo's big frame would require the largest size in a range of clothes designed for the slighter built Mediterranean man. Finally, he chose a tie. He couldn't remember the last time he had worn one. He paid for it all at the cash desk and asked if he could change in the store. He emerged from the shop with his old clothes in a plastic bag, and caught sight of himself reflected in a window. Someone he nearly didn't recognise. A stranger in a suit, stiff and uncomfortable. Only the ponytail marked him out as less than the conventional figure he wished to present. And the scuffed white training shoes. They wouldn't do at all.

He went into the Halle aux Chaussures next door and bought a pair of unyielding, black leather shoes. His feet felt constrained by them, constricted, and during the short walk to his car they had already started to chafe. In the driver's seat he loosened his hair, and then pulled it back as tightly as he could to minimise the effect of the ponytail. In the end he decided that he had probably done enough to pass muster as a lawyer, even if he did look like one more used to chasing ambulances.

He drove out of the car park into the stream of traffic heading north on the ring road to the A9 *autoroute*, and glanced in his rearview mirror.

The car immediately on his tail was a black Renault Scenic. Rickie Bright sat at the wheel, his cold blue eyes obscured behind a pair of Ray-ban sunglasses.

◇◇◇

Bright remained within a few cars of him all the way to Aubagne. It was the most stressful three-and-a-half hours Enzo had ever endured. He checked continually in his side and rearview mirrors. Bright was always there, no more than a car or two away, keeping Enzo constantly in his sights.

There must have come a point on their journey when Bright realised where it was that Enzo was going. And he must have known then, beyond doubt, that the Scotsman was on the point of putting the final piece of the jigsaw puzzle in place.

As they drove into Aubagne, the sun was starting to sink behind them in a sky streaked with pink cloud. Enzo followed the road out to the southern suburb where the Foreign Legion occupied a sprawling plot of land behind high walls and fences. Large signs read *Terrain Militaire,* and *Défense d'entrer.*

Bright pulled up on the sidewalk, fifty metres back, as Enzo turned into the main entrance. The gatehouse was a long, low building with shallow sloping red roofs. A pink stone wall was emblazoned with the name of the regiment. Beyond the barrier stretched a vast parade ground. At its centre was a globe mounted on a marble plinth above the legend, *Honneur et Fidélité.* It was guarded by four bronze Legionnaires. White barracks and administration blocks rose up the hillside on the south side, tall trees casting long shadows over manicured lawns.

A sentry stepped out to stop him at the barrier. Enzo handed him Simon's business card. He had to work hard to keep the tremor out of his voice. 'I'm a lawyer from the London law firm of Gold, Smith, and Jackson. We telephoned last week. I represent the estate of the late William Bright, an Englishman whom we believe spent a number of years in the service of the French Foreign Legion during the nineteen eighties. We're trying to trace next of kin, and I'm here to see if the Legion can provide us with that information from its records.'

The soldier looked at him as if he had two heads, then did what all foot soldiers do when presented with an insoluble problem. Passed it on up the chain of command.

'One moment, sir.'

He disappeared inside the gatehouse, and Enzo could see him speaking animatedly on the telephone, glancing frequently at the card Enzo had given him. Finally, he hung up and emerged into the fading sunlight. He leaned down to Enzo's open window and pointed.

'If you turn around and go back out, turn left and left again, and then follow the road round to the museum. You'll see it behind the fence on your left. Park there and wait inside. Someone will come and get you.'

As he turned out of the entrance, he saw Bright's car bump down off the sidewalk further along the street, and then trail him at a discreet distance. He turned left and followed the sentry's instructions, cruising slowly along a tree-lined country road to the museum, which was housed in a two-storey white and brownstone building on the far side of the parade ground.

The car park was empty. Enzo pulled into the slot nearest the museum. He climbed out of his car as Bright turned his Renault into the lot behind him and drew up at the far side of it. He left his engine idling, and watched Enzo from behind his dark glasses. No attempt at concealment now. Enzo looked back at him across the tarmac. Only twenty metres separated them. The hunter and his prey. The palm trees, the pink sunlight on blue hills, warm air filled with the fragrant scent of Mediterranean flowers in winter bloom. None of it seemed quite real. It could hardly have been less threatening. But all of it served somehow only to heighten the sense of menace that hung incongruously in the air between them. Enzo felt sick.

He turned and walked by the mementos of the Legion's military past carefully placed among the trees. A tank, an armoured jeep, a cannon, a machine gun. Carved blocks, like tombstones, were set in the grass, a commemoration of battles fought and lives lost. *Ile de Mayotte. Indochine. Algérie. Maroc.*

Inside, military mannequins in glass cases stood guard over a celebrated history. Rifles lined the walls, flags and emblems, display cases filled with medals and memorabilia. A red *képi*, a pair of white gloves, a belt, a letter written to a long forgotten lover but never sent. Enzo peered into the darkness of the room where they kept the wooden hand of Capitaine Jean Danjou, one of the most decorated officers in the history of the Legion. With only a few hundred troops at his disposal, he had taken on the might of the Mexican army in 1862, and fallen in battle. Only two of his soldiers survived the fight, and were spared to accompany his body back to France.

'Monsieur Gold?' Enzo turned, and a young soldier in khaki emerged from a brightly lit bureau. 'Follow me, please.'

They went down a corridor and out through a door at the back of the building. As they climbed the steps towards the long, white administration block at the top of the hill, Enzo glanced back and saw that Bright was still waiting for him in the car park.

◇◇◇

'Who was it you spoke to on the phone?' Captain Mérit examined him with uncomfortably intelligent eyes from the other side of his desk.

'I didn't. It was a legal secretary in the office. She was simply told that if we wished information of that sort we would have to present ourselves in person.'

'Our records are confidential, Monsieur Gold.'

'I understand that Captain. I have no wish to see them. Only to obtain the names of next of kin, if any.' He reached into his bag for a notebook. 'The young man is dead, after all, so we won't be compromising his right to anonymity.' He started flipping through his notebook. 'From my records, I see that William Bright joined the Legion in December, 1986, at the age of eighteen. You provided him with a new identity. Yves…Yves…' Enzo flipped through more pages, as if had momentarily forgotten the surname and was searching for it.

Captain Mérit conveniently filled the gap. 'Labrousse.' Enzo could hardly believe his luck. He would have been happy to leave there and then. But he was obliged to continue with the deception for at least a little longer. Mérit opened the folder on the desk in front of him and lifted up the top file. Enzo could see that there was a photograph attached to it. 'Applied for and was given French citizenship in 1989. Was honourably discharged at the end of 1991. Saw active service in Chad in 1987, and the Gulf War in 1990, where he was wounded and lost half of his right ear.' He riffled through the other sheets of paper attached to the file and cursed. 'Merde! It seems his application form and background checks are not in this file.' He closed the folder. 'If you'll excuse me for a moment.' He got up and left the room.

Enzo sat listening to the silence. It was almost dark outside now, the last red glow fading on the western horizon. He twisted his head to read the label on the front of the folder on Mérit's desk. *Recruitment Intake, December, 1986.* On an impulse, he turned it towards him and somehow managed to spill its entire contents over the floor. 'Jesus!' In a panic he scrambled to retrieve it all and stuff everything back in the folder. As long as Mérit didn't look inside again, he wouldn't notice that it was all now in a different order. Enzo was about to close it and put it back where he had found it, when his eye was caught by the photograph clipped to the file which was now on top. He caught his breath, and found himself looking at the face of the man who had condemned him to death. Philippe Ransou. French-Canadian. Real name Jacques Of. So Bright, or was it Labrousse, had not chosen Ransou at random to play the good doctor. They had joined the Legion in the same month. Had probably trained together, been comrades in arms together. Someone he could trust without question.

He heard footsteps outside the door and quickly closed and replaced the folder. Mérit came back in holding a sheet of paper. 'I've copied this for you. He only listed three names under next of kin.' And he proceeded to reel them off. 'Parents Rod and Angela. Sister Lucy.' He handed Enzo the photocopy. 'And I'm afraid there's really not much more that I can tell you.'

And Enzo thought that, actually, there was nothing more he needed to know.

Chapter Forty-Nine

The car park was floodlit, white buildings on the hill stark against a black sky. He had only ever spent three weeks here, but it felt to him like he was back on home ground. Day had departed with the final setting of the sun, and Yves' sunglasses now sat on the dash. His face was stinging from shock and anger. If he had looked at himself in his rearview mirror he would have seen how his skin had darkened. He slipped his cellphone back in his pocket. He had wanted to finish it here. Tonight. Back in the place where, in many ways, it had all started. He could not understand the instruction to wait. But like the good soldier he was, he always followed orders.

He saw Macleod, accompanied by a legionnaire, coming back down the steps and into the museum. A few moments later the Scot emerged on his own to walk through the trees to the parking lot. He stopped by his car and glanced across the asphalt towards Yves. He looked weary. Yves had no idea why he had bought himself a suit, but it seemed oddly out of character. Their eyes met, and Yves saw the indecision, before suddenly Macleod began walking towards him.

Yves was startled. Perhaps the Scotsman felt safe here in the full glare of the floodlights, several hundred armed soldiers working, eating, sleeping in the garrison behind him. Not that it would have mattered to Yves. A single shot and he'd have been gone. Soldiers would have run out to find a man dead by his car, lying in a pool of his own blood. And if they'd seen Yves at all, it would have been the merest glimpse of a dark car vanishing into the night.

He leaned forward to start the engine. Still Macleod was striding purposefully towards him. He slipped the car into gear, revved the motor and accelerated hard from a standing start, to the accompaniment of squealing tyres. His Ray-bans flew off the dashboard. Macleod stopped, frozen like an old stag caught in the headlights. How easy it would be simply to run him down. To spin him through the air, then reverse over the body just to be sure. He could see fear, and the certainty of death in Macleod's eyes, before he pulled the wheel hard to his right. He missed him by centimetres, leaving tracks of rubber on the tarmac, then accelerated out through the gate and off into the darkness.

◇◇◇

Enzo stood breathing hard, the revving of Yves car fading into the night. He knew just how close he had come to dying right there and then in the car park of the *Légion étrangère*. It had been madness. Trying to beard the lion in his own den. Enzo was not sure what had possessed him. Why had he ever thought he might be safe anywhere from a man like Yves Labrousse? A professional killer desperate to keep his identity to himself. And yet he had just given the man every opportunity to kill him, and he hadn't taken it. Why not? Was he toying with Enzo? Playing some kind of game? Procrastinating for pleasure? Somehow Enzo doubted it. This man was a professional. He killed for money, not pleasure. And he was desperate to stop Enzo in his tracks. So why hadn't he?

Enzo walked slowly back to his car and slipped into the driver's seat. He was shaking from head to foot, trembling as if from the cold. But the night was warm, almost balmy. The worst thing was the unpredictability of it all. Not knowing. Not understanding. He would have to find a hotel room now, and he saw a long, sleepless night ahead of him.

Chapter Fifty

Kirsty sat staring at herself in the mirror. The soft glow of the bedside lamp barely reached across the room to the dressing table. She looked terrible. Perhaps it was just the light, or the lack of it. But her eyes were lost in dark smudges, her cheeks seemed hollow. Her hair had somehow lost its lustre, and she had drawn it back to tie in a loose ponytail, just like her father. Except that he wasn't her father. No matter what had happened, the thought still haunted her.

She rose suddenly from the dressing table, cursing herself. How many times was she going to replay it? Like the words of a song you can't get out of your head, it just kept going round and round and round.

She left the room, and the old floorboards on the upstairs landing creaked beneath her feet. As she wound her way down the spiral stairs, she heard the murmur of the television from the *séjour*. Voices, laughter. It seemed like such a long time since she had laughed. The laughter subsided as she walked into the room. Sophie and Bertrand and Nicole looked almost guilty. Nicole said, 'How's Roger?'

'Out of intensive care. They say it'll take time, but they expect him to make a full recovery.'

'So cheer up, for God's sake!' That Sophie had lost patience with her was clear. And she probably harboured resentment towards her for the way she had treated Enzo. He was her father, after all. Her real father. And Kirsty knew that she loved him unconditionally.

It seemed that everyone loved Enzo, including her. But she was the only one who didn't know how to express it.

'You've been moping around for days. You're not the only one affected by this, you know. We're all in it together.'

'I think, perhaps, that Kirsty's had more to deal with than the rest of you.' Everyone turned at the sound of Anna's voice as she emerged from the computer room. She gave Kirsty's arm a tiny squeeze, a silent acknowledgement of a secret shared, an implicit understanding. 'I'll get dinner on.' And she headed on through to the kitchen.

'I'll give you a hand.' Nicole leapt up from her armchair and hurried through after her. If there was going to be a scene, she didn't want to be any part of it.

But Kirsty had no intention of staying around to trade accusations with Sophie. 'I'm going to get some air.' She lifted her coat and scarf from the coatstand on the way out. But once she had closed the door behind her, she had no desire to go walking off into the night on her own. So instead she stayed on the *terrasse* at the front of the house, leaning on the wrought-iron railing, and gazing out across the frosted field to the floodlit church and school. She lowered her head to rest on her clasped hands, and closed her eyes.

There was nothing she could do to change the past, to alter the events that had so transformed her life. But as Anna had said, she could still play a major role in shaping its future. She still had that power within her gift. Anna was right. There was no future in secrecy. If there was love between people there should be no secrets. She thought about her mother, and the truth she had kept from Enzo all those years. And Simon, and how he had shared in that secret with Linda. An ugly, deceitful secret that, in the end, could only ever destroy them. He might be her blood father, but in truth she didn't think she really liked him very much.

She stood up straight, pressing her hands into the cold metal rail. She breathed deeply and made a decision. She couldn't continue to live the lie with Enzo. She had to come clean and tell him that she knew.

Chapter Fifty-One

The hotel was in a commercial park on the east side of Aubagne, a vast, sprawling suburban shopping mall ringed by hills on the edge of town. By the time Enzo had eaten and driven out there, it was completely deserted. Acres of empty parking lots shimmered under yellow street lamps. The hills cut dark shapes against a starry sky, and the air was filled with the smell of pine from the Mediterranean *pins parasols* that lined the streets.

He drove past fast food restaurants closed up for the night, brooding, boxy, corrugated stores with flashing neon and dimly lit windows. A motor mall, rows of shiny cars gleaming under floodlights. Citröen, Renault, Peugeot, Mercedes. There was not a living soul in evidence, not another vehicle on the streets.

He saw a sign for the Palais des Congrès, and his mind drifted back to Strasbourg, where the nightmare had begun. But Aubagne could hardly be further removed from the sleet and snow of a frigid Alsace, and it was simply a reminder of how far he had come in only a few days, and of how much everything on which he had built his life had shifted seismically beneath his feet.

He had found the man who murdered Pierre Lambert in Paris all those years ago. But the killer was still free, and still intent, it seemed, on despatching Enzo to the same fate. The only thing Enzo didn't know was where and when. Yves Labrousse, aka Richard Bright, aka Richard Archangel had spurned the opportunity just a few hours earlier, but Enzo was certain that it wasn't the last he would see of him.

He turned right at the end of a long, straight avenue, and saw a sign for the Etap hotel where he had booked a room by telephone earlier in the evening. The car park, behind a high wire fence and locked gate, was nearly full. Moths battered about under tall lamps that washed it with light. Enzo drew up at the gate and got out of his car. An empty street ran past the hotel into a smudged, dark distance. Lights glowed in the hotel entrance, but there was no one at reception. They had told him on the phone that it was self check-in. They had taken his credit card number and all he had to do was slip his card into the machine at the door. It would issue him with a code, giving him access to the parking, the hotel, and his room. The charge would be lifted automatically.

He stopped at the door and turned to look back the way he had come, straining for the sound of a motor, watching for the flicker of a car's headlamps. But there was nothing, except for the endless croaking of frogs in some nearby pond.

He turned back to the self check-in machine as the door opened and a dark figure emerged suddenly and unexpectedly, silhouetted against the backdrop of light in reception. Enzo stepped back, an exclamation escaping involuntarily from his lips. The figure raised a hand, and a sudden flame illuminated his face. He puffed smoke into the night. 'Sorry mate. Didn't mean to startle you.' He wandered off across the paving stones towards the deserted terrace of a café opposite, still sucking on his cigarette.

Enzo waited until he had his breathing under control, before slipping his credit card into the slot and being issued with his six-digit code. He tapped it into the pad beside the gate, then drove his car into the parking lot. He retrieved his laptop from the trunk, and let himself into the hotel, walking the length of a long, featureless corridor until he found his room right at the very end.

It was a small, basic room with a toilet barely big enough to turn around in. A metal table was pushed into one corner opposite an unyielding double bed. But it didn't matter. He had no intention of sleeping.

He took the room's only chair and inserted the back of it under the door handle so that it angled to the floor and jammed it shut. He made sure the window was securely locked and drew the curtain. The room was in complete darkness now. He fumbled for the TV remote on the bedside table and turned on the television, immediately muting it. The screen provided him with just enough flickering light to see by.

For a long time he sat on the edge of the bed trying hard to relax, to let the tension of a traumatic day seep slowly from every straining muscle. And as his breathing slowed and his body unwound he was almost felled by a sudden wave of fatigue, and he immediately tensed again. He mustn't let himself sleep. If Yves Labrousse was going to come for him tonight, then he wanted to be ready.

He opened up his computer bag and removed his laptop. It took around sixty seconds for it to load its system and log into the hotel's wi-fi. He typed in his cellphone number and service provider, hit the return key and ten seconds later received a text on his cellphone with the password for the wi-fi. Now he was connected to the internet, and almost immediately his computer issued an alert to tell him he had mail. He clicked on his mailer, and with an unexpected jolt saw that there was an e-mail from Kirsty.

He hesitated for a long time before finally finding the courage to open it.

Dad…

The very word made winged creatures flutter in his chest

…I call you that, even though I know you aren't…

Now they were everywhere, in his chest, his stomach, his head. Panicking wings beating in frenetic flight.

…I can't speak about it in an e-mail. But I overheard you that night at Uncle Simon's. I know he's my blood father. And I have to talk to you. I can't carry the secret around any longer. But not here. Somewhere we won't be interrupted. Somewhere private. There's a place that Anna took me to at Le Lioran. You know, the ski resort. It's not far from here. I know it'll take you most of the day to drive

back tomorrow. So meet me at nine. Where the cablecars dock. There's a stairway at the side of the téléphérique *building.*

He could almost feel her pause.

I love you.

Chapter Fifty-Two

Kirsty sat looking at the desktop on her screen. The computer room was in semidarkness, glowing in the light of all the monitors that Nicole had left running. She had just wakened her own laptop from sleep and knew immediately that someone had been using it.

She felt anger spike out of nowhere. Her computer was private. A place where she kept her life, her secrets. For someone else to use it without permission made her feel violated. She pushed back her chair and strode through to the *séjour*. 'Were you using my computer, Nicole?'

The eight o'clock evening news had just started, and three faces turned towards her from the television.

'No.' Nicole was indignant. 'Why would I use your computer?'

'I don't know, but someone did.'

Sophie said, 'How do you know?'

'Because the *Finder* was missing from the desktop. I *never* close the *Finder*.'

Bertrand shrugged. 'Maybe it was Anna. She was in the computer room last night.'

Kirsty glanced across the hall towards the kitchen. 'Where is she?' Usually, at this time of night, she would be preparing dinner. But the kitchen was empty.

'She went out somewhere this afternoon,' Sophie said. 'I didn't hear her come back.' She looked towards the others for confirmation.

Bertrand said, 'I was out getting wood ten minutes ago, and the car's not there.'

Kirsty glanced at the clock on the mantel. 'She's late.'

And Nicole said, 'I suppose we'd better think about fixing something to eat ourselves, then.' As she got out of her seat, they heard the crunch of gravel in the drive, and the lights of a car raked past the windows. 'That'll be her now.'

She went out into the hall to switch on the outside light, and opened the door. A car was idling at the foot of the steps, but it wasn't Anna's. A middle-aged couple stood with their car doors open staring hesitantly up at the house. They seemed alarmed when Nicole stepped out on to the *terrasse*. And there was something both frightened and aggressive in the man's tone. He spoke in English. 'Who the hell are you?'

Nicole was taken aback, and as the others filed out from the house behind her, it was Kirsty who responded. 'Who are *you*?'

The woman's voice was shrill as she turned to her husband across the roof of the car. 'John, let's just go and get the police now.'

But he was determined to stand his ground. 'This is our house,' he said, his voice filled with indignation. 'We own it.'

Sophie's face broke into a smile of relief. 'Well, that's alright then. We're friends of Anna's.'

'Jo-ohn,' the woman wailed.

Still he wasn't giving up. 'Anna who?'

Sophie and Kirsty, Bertrand and Nicole looked at him in astonishment. Kirsty said, 'Anna Cattiaux. The former Olympic skier.'

The man glanced at his wife. Some unspoken communication passed between them and she immediately got back into the passenger seat and slammed the door shut. He turned his face up towards the *terrasse* again. 'I'm going for the police. If you're still here when we get back, you can explain yourselves to them.'

He got hurriedly behind the wheel and slipped the car into reverse. They saw him twist in his seat as he reversed at speed back along the drive.

Nicole turned towards the others, bewilderment all over her face. 'What was all that about?'

But Kirsty's mind was racing, cogs and counters in her brain clicking backwards and forwards searching for a combination that would unlock understanding. 'Shit!' she said suddenly. 'We don't know anything about Anna, except what she's told us. And I never really thought about it before. But some of that just doesn't add up.'

'What do you mean?' Nicole was becoming alarmed.

'She told my dad that she was in Strasbourg to see her parents. Plural. But she told me her father was dead. She also told me she'd been in Strasbourg for the funeral of a friend.'

'That's funny,' Sophie said. 'We were just talking about that the other day. Well, not exactly *that*. But she told me she'd never had kids, and Bertrand said she'd told him her son was killed in a road accident. We figured one or other of us must have misunderstood.'

Nicole said, 'Well, there's one easy way to find out the truth.' She pushed past them into the house and hurried through to the computer room. The others followed and gathered around the back of her chair as she brought up the Google homepage on her laptop and typed in *"Anna Cattiaux" skier*. There were more than sixty thousand hits. At the top of the first page of ten was the entry in French Wikipedia. Nicole clicked to open it. 'There. Anna Cattiaux. French champion skier. Represented her country at two winter Olympics, narrowly missing out on the medals both times.' She stopped, and her hand froze on the mouse. 'Oh, my God!'

'What?' Bertrand leaned over to try to read what she was looking at.

Nicole's voice was hushed. 'Anna Cattiaux died in a freak skiing accident twelve years ago.'

There was a long silence as they absorbed this.

'So who is she? I mean Anna, or whatever her name is.' It was Sophie who voiced their common thought.

Kirsty said, 'Nicole, put the name into Google Images.'

Nicole's fingers rattled across the keyboard, and up came a screenful of images. A pretty, blond-haired girl, sometimes in ski gear, sometimes in jeans, occasionally in a cocktail dress at a function or dinner. Always smiling. And nothing like the Anna who had shared in their lives for the last ten days.

'Jesus!' Kirsty whispered. All the things she had confided in her, secrets shared, stories told. She felt tricked and cheated, and a single word kept bouncing around inside her head. Why? Why? Why the deception, why the lies? And what was it all about? Who was she, and where was she now? Then a thought returned to her. 'So if it wasn't any of you, it *must* have been Anna who was using my computer.'

Nicole said, 'Well, let's have a look and see. People always leave a trail.' She turned her seat towards Kirsty's laptop and hit the space bar to wipe off the screensaver. 'May I?'

'Go ahead.'

Nicole went to the *Apple* menu and scrolled down to *Recent Items*. Up came a long list of the applications and documents which had been most recently used. 'Anything you see that you haven't been using recently? Or any unfamiliar documents?'

Kirsty scanned the screen. Nothing stood out from the list of documents, and she raised her eyes to the applications. She saw her diary and calendar software. Word processing, her internet browser, her iTunes collection of music and videos.' Suddenly her heart was beating more rapidly. 'My mailer. I haven't sent an e-mail since before the bombing in Strasbourg.'

Nicole opened up the mailer. 'Your inbox is a mess,' she said. 'Don't you file stuff?'

Kirsty ran down the long list of e-mails which had been received and read but remained in her inbox. 'I always mean to. I just never seem to get around to it.' There were several unread mails which must have been received during the last week to ten days, but never picked up from the server until whoever it was had used the computer and opened up her mailer. 'Why would she want to look at my e-mails?'

Bertrand said, 'Maybe it wasn't *your* e-mails she was interested in. Look in the *Sent* box.'

Nicole clicked on the *Sent* folder, and up came a fresh screen, empty except for a single e-mail. Under *Date Sent* it said *Yesterday*. Kirsty said, 'I never sent an e-mail yesterday!' She ran her eye along the line. 'Oh, God, it's addressed to Dad! He'll think I've sent it. What does it say?' Nicole opened it up.

Only the hum of the computers broke the silence in the room as they crowded round to read it. Kirsty's face burned, almost as if from a fever, and she felt sick to her stomach, hollowed out, betrayed.

Sophie's head swung round to look at her, a strange light in her eyes. 'Is that true? Uncle Sy's really your papa?'

Kirsty nodded, unable to prevent the tears that welled in her eyes from spilling silently down her face. 'I told her about it. There was no one else. Roger had gone, and I needed to share it with someone. And I was going to tell Dad I knew, I really was.'

'Only she beat you to it,' Bertrand said.

'You can't call him papa anymore.' There was a hint of resentment in Sophie's voice. Since Kirsty had come on the scene she'd had to share him with her. But not any longer.

Kirsty wiped the tears from her face. 'Yes I can. Because that's what he is. The biology doesn't matter. He's my dad, and he always will be.'

Suddenly Nicole said, 'What time is it?'

Bertrand checked his watch. 'Half past eight.'

'Call him! Call his cellphone.'

Bertrand flipped open his cellphone and selected Enzo from its memory. He listened intently as it rang several times before a message told him that the number he was calling was not online. He left a message anyway, more in hope than expectation that Enzo would pick it up in the next thirty minutes.

Sophie was starting to panic. 'Oh, my God, can we get to Le Lioran in half an hour? He thinks he's meeting Kirsty at nine. But it's some kind of a trap. It has to be.'

Chapter Fifty-Three

Sleet spattered softly on his windscreen, caught in his headlights like stars at warp speed, driven on the edge of an icy wind that gusted off the mountains. The temperature had dropped by more than twenty degrees during his six-and-a-half hour drive from the south. But it was warm in the cocoon of his car, and his eyes were heavy after a night with little sleep.

He had managed to stay awake until after 5 am, before slipping off to float through shallow seas awash with vivid dreams that carried him into the dawn, and the first light cracking around the curtains. He had wakened with a start shortly after eight and checked his route north on Mappy. With stops, it would take him more than six hours to get to Le Lioran, but he wasn't due to meet Kirsty until nine, and so he had not checked out of the hotel until noon, waiting until the last possible moment before venturing back out into a world where somewhere, he knew, Yves Labrousse was waiting for him.

But there had been no sign of the killer, or his black Renault Scenic, and Enzo had found a restaurant near the Palais des Congrès. He had eaten there in silence, alone with the thoughts that had disturbed him through all his waking hours and the dreams that followed.

That Kirsty had overheard his exchange with Simon in London had shaken him to the core. But it had, at least, explained her mood at Stansted Airport when they'd said their strained goodbyes. He had no idea how to feel about it now, but all his instincts told him it was better out in the open than festering in the dark where there was every chance it could turn toxic. He knew it would never change how he felt about Kirsty. What he didn't know was how it had changed the way she felt about him. The one thing he held on to was the way she had signed off her e-mail. *I love you.* Three small words that, in the circumstances, seemed to him to say so much more. It was that thought which had sustained him throughout the long drive.

Now, as he turned into the tiny ski resort at the base of the Plomb du Cantal, all his fears and doubts returned. And the confidence he had so carefully constructed during nearly five hundred kilometres travelled, evaporated in a moment.

The resort car park was spread over three levels, but there were only a handful of cars beneath its sodium lamps, sleet slashing through haloes of pale yellow light. A mere handful of lit windows pricked the dark squares and triangles of apartment blocks and chalets, and through glass doors Enzo saw that the dimly lit foyer of the hotel was empty. In just a few days the resort would be transformed as the season opened on the first weekend of December. By then, what was falling as sleet down here, would have covered the upper slopes in thick ski-able snow. The hotel and most of the apartments would be full, the car park jammed with winter holidaymakers. But for now it was like a ghost town.

Although he had watched the outside temperature drop on the digital display in his hire car, he was unprepared for the blast of ice cold wind that cut through him as he opened the car door. The wind chill factor was dragging the temperature down well below zero. He took his jacket from the back seat and buttoned it against the driving sleet, turning up his collar and thrusting hands deep into his pockets. He put his head down and ploughed off into the night, cleaving his way through the sleet, up a grilled metal stairway to the next level.

The *téléphérique* building was huddled in the dark on the edge of the resort, and he thought what a crazy place this was to meet. Why not in the bar of the hotel? They would almost certainly have had the place to themselves.

Pine trees rising up on all sides pressed around him as he followed the tarmac round the side of the building, to where five flights of red-painted metal staircase doubled back and forth up to the docking area where the two cablecars sat snugly side by side.

Enzo climbed the lower steps and leapt over the barrier at the first landing. The staircase rattled and shook beneath him, clattering above the noise of the wind. His face was wet and stinging with the cold. His hands and feet had already lost all their warmth. His jacket was soaked through, and he could feel the chill seeping into his bones. This was madness.

He hurried up the remaining stairs to the E-shaped concrete docking platform and saw that the nearer of the two cablecars stood with its lights on and its doors open. He looked around for Kirsty but there was no sign of her. He called her name, and the wind seemed to whip it from his mouth and throw it away into the dark. It brought no response. He checked his watch. It was just after nine, and for the first time he wondered how she might have got here. Perhaps Anna had loaned her the car. If he had thought, he would have checked for it in the car park.

He called again. 'Kirsty!' And followed the spine of the E past the second cablecar. There was no one here. He retraced his steps and looked inside the nearer one. Empty. He stepped inside, a brief respite from the wind outside, and saw that the door to the control panel on the opposite wall was lying open. Beneath a square of illuminated buttons, a telephone receiver hung from a cradle, and a sheet of white paper taped to its handle was flapping in the draft. Enzo crossed the car and pulled the sheet free. There were two words written on it. *Call me.* He didn't recognise the handwriting, but the letters had been printed, and so he couldn't say if it was Kirsty's or not.

He held the piece of paper in his hand, staring at it blindly. Something was wrong. Why would Kirsty want to meet him in a place like this? Why would she leave him such a cryptic note taped to a telephone receiver in an empty cablecar? And yet there was no doubt in his mind that it was Kirsty who had written to him. Who else could possibly have known the awful secret which had been aired that night at Simon's flat in London?

He lifted the telephone and put it to his ear, listening intently. It clicked several times and then began to ring. He waited, almost rigid with tension. On the third ring, someone lifted the receiver at the other end. Silence. Filled only by ambient sound. But there was someone there. Enzo was certain he could hear breathing. He said, 'Hello?' And immediately the doors slid shut.

He dropped the receiver and in two quick strides crossed the cablecar to try to stop the nearest door from closing. But he was too late, and he spun around to stand in the middle of the floor, breathing hard, looking about him in a panic, like a wild animal trapped in a cage.

The car jerked, and he grabbed for the handrail as it scraped and bumped its way out of its dock, before swinging free into the night. Enzo had a strange, awful sense of floating away in the dark. From its lit interior, everything beyond the windows of the cablecar seemed black. But he could see the lights of the car park, dropping away steeply below him. He felt the cablecar shudder, battered by the wind. The sleet melted and ran down the windows like tears.

He knew now that he had been tricked. And trapped. If Kirsty had written that e-mail she had been forced to do it. By someone who somehow knew their secret. But who? There was no way he could make sense of it. And he didn't dare imagine in what circumstance she might have been made to do it.

But it had to have something to do with Labrousse and the murder of Pierre Lambert.

The car dipped suddenly in the dark as it passed the first support pylon, and rose yet more steeply. Enzo began to panic. There was absolutely nothing he could do. He went back to the control panel and pressed every button. Nothing happened. Somehow the cablecar's independent controls had been disabled and it was being manipulated remotely. He felt quickly in all his pockets, before remembering that he'd let the battery in his cellphone run flat, and left it charging in the car. He couldn't even call for help. He was trapped in this damned box, being winched up a mountainside in the dark to meet God knew what fate at the top.

His breathing was coming in short, sharp bursts, and he moved to the far window, pressing his back against it and grasping the handrail, preparing to meet head on whatever might be waiting for him up there.

The sleet had turned now to snow, coating the windows at the front, as they rose higher into the night. The car dipped again. The second pylon. Enzo glanced out of the side window, and saw village lights twinkling through the snow in a valley far, far below, somewhere away to the west. Light from the windows of the cablecar reflected darkly on the mountainside as they slid up through cut rock. Ahead Enzo saw the dark shape of the mountain-top terminal loom suddenly out of the night, and then the snow ceased as the cablecar bumped and rattled into the shelter of its dock. It jerked to a standstill and the doors slid open.

Enzo stood stock still. He could hear the wind howling through the cavernous concrete space around him. Cables and corrugated sheeting rattled and flapped and vibrated, the noise of it echoing all about him. The only light came from the cablecar. He could see a metal staircase leading up to an overhead access gallery for maintenance high up in the roof, where the cables turned around huge yellow wheels.

More steps climbed up to a metal platform, and a vast sliding door that opened on to a dark concourse. *Sortie* signs pointed towards a cafeteria and doors to the outside. He could see no one, nor detect any movement among the shadows.

He stood for a long time without moving. His instinct was to stay in the light, to remain within the protective shell of the cablecar. But he knew that any sense of safety here was illusory. He was in the full glare of the very light that comforted him, clearly visible to whoever was out there. The dark would be a better friend.

Almost on an impulse, he ran out of the door, clattering over the metal grille beneath his feet, the mountain falling away below him, and made a dash for the shadows. All the time he braced himself for the bullets or the blows that he was sure would come his way. He scrambled up the stairs, through the open door, and plunged into the darkness of the adjoining concourse. He found a wall and hunkered down against it, fingers pressed into the floor to keep him balanced. It was more fear than exertion that robbed him of his breath. He could hear it rasping above the roar of the wind that squeezed and whined through every space and crack.

It took several minutes for his eyes to adjust to the tiny amount of light that bled through from the now distant cablecar. It was reflected faintly in pools of water gathered on the concrete floor. The corrugated roof above his head thundered like a drum in the wind, and he saw, beyond a sign for Stella Artois, the passage that led out to the mountain. He had no idea why, but all his instincts pushed him in that direction. Out of here, out into the night, escape from this concrete prison into which he'd been lured.

'What do you want with me?' he bellowed at the top of his voice, all his fear and anger fuelling a vocal outburst of pure frustration. But only the wind replied, and he got to his feet and ran for the doors, punching the release bar and plunging through them out into the night.

The wind struck him a physical blow, snow swirling around him like the spirits of demented dervishes. A light came on, triggered by a movement sensor, flooding a snow-covered rise that led off towards the peak. He saw a radio mast disappearing into the white-streaked darkness, and realised what folly this was. He wouldn't survive ten minutes out here.

He turned and stopped dead. A figure stood in the doorway, blocking his return. A tall figure in a dark parka with the hood up. One hand rose to pull back the hood, and Enzo saw that it was Yves Labrousse. The younger man smiled. 'She said you'd come,' he shouted above the wind, and Enzo wondered what he meant. Was he talking about Kirsty?

'What have you done with her?'

Labrousse looked faintly bemused. 'I haven't done anything with her.' He raised his right hand and pointed a gun directly at Enzo's chest. 'You have been such a pain in the ass. You have no idea.'

'I know everything about you,' Enzo shouted at him. 'Your whole history. Your abduction from Cadaqués. Stealing your brother's identity. Joining the Légion Étrangère. And I know about Philippe Ransou and how you met.'

'And all that knowledge will die with you. But just a little sooner than Ransou predicted.'

'No.' Enzo shook his head vigorously. 'You're rumbled, Labrousse. Or Archangel. Or Bright. Or whatever it is you call yourself. Do you think I'd come here without passing on what I know? Do you think I didn't know you'd be coming after me? I spent last night writing up the whole damned story, and this morning I uploaded it to my blog. It's all out there on the internet. Whatever you do to me now can't change that.'

Labrousse glared at him, hate and anger burning in blue eyes. 'You fucker!' He took a step towards Enzo and his foot skidded from under him. Loose gravel beneath wet snow. He stumbled and almost fell. Enzo turned and ran just as the light on the terminal building was suddenly extinguished. The mountain top was plunged into blackness.

Enzo felt the snow in his face, his feet slipping and slithering as he ran blindly into the night. He heard Labrousse shouting his name, a voice whipped away on the edge of the wind. The incline grew steeper as he climbed. He felt his legs becoming leaden, the sound of his own voice gasping, almost roaring, as he tried to gulp in more air. But everything was against him. The weather, the lack of oxygen, his age, and he felt himself wading as if through treacle, or like a man fighting in slow motion against the blast of a hurricane.

Until, finally, his legs folded beneath him and he dropped to his knees, utterly exhausted. He fell forward into the snow and rolled over on to his back, and saw the shadow of his pursuer loom over him. Labrousse was gasping, too, fitter and stronger than Enzo, but still disabled by six thousand feet of oxygen deprivation. 'I never knew a man harder to kill,' he said. He raised his gun and fired three times.

Enzo braced himself for the bullets and grunted in pain as the dead weight of Labrousse fell on top of him. He felt the warmth of the other man's blood oozing through his clothes, compounding his confusion. He struggled to push Labrousse to one side, but couldn't move him.

Then suddenly the weight was lifted, and Labrousse rolled off and into the dark. Another figure leaned over him, and he felt a warm hand on his face. The snow seemed to have stopped.

'Are you hit?'

This was a dream. It had to be. He was certain it was Anna who had spoken. 'No. I don't think so.' He tried to catch his breath. 'Anna?'

'Poor Enzo.' She ran the back of her hand lightly across his cheek. 'You really don't deserve this.'

'What are you doing here, Anna?' He forced himself up on to one elbow, and in that moment the sky parted and the light of the moon washed silver across the white peaks of the Cantal all around them. He saw the gun in her hand. 'You shot him?' He knew for certain now that he was either dead or dreaming.

She said, 'The scenario where two people shoot one another is never very believable. But if you shot Labrousse and then somehow lost your way and slipped and fell, you'd die of exposure long before the night was out and anyone found you. That would work. I'm pretty sure they'd go for that.'

'Who? What are you talking about?'

She sighed and sat down in the snow beside him. 'The people who employed Labrousse to kill Lambert never did trust him to shut you up. They were scared that anything that led to him would lead ultimately to them. So I was their back-up. If you got too close to Lambert I was to take him out. And you.'

Enzo looked at her in disbelief. 'You're going to kill me?'

She looked at him and smiled sadly. 'Oh, Enzo. I don't want to. I really don't. You and me…well, in another life we could have, you know, been good together. But if I don't kill you, they'll kill me. Because I could lead you to them, and they don't like loose ends. You're too Goddamned smart for your own good. And mine.'

She got to her feet and pointed her gun at him. 'Come on, get up.'

Enzo got stiffly, painfully, to his feet. 'Are you going to shoot me?'

'No, I couldn't do that to you, Enzo. I'm going to leave you to fall asleep here on the mountain. Only, you'll never wake up, and you won't feel a thing. Turn around.'

'I don't understand…'

'Just turn around.'

He did as she asked and she hesitated for only a moment before felling him a with blow from the butt end of her pistol. He dropped to his knees and fell face-first into the snow. She turned him over and dragged him by his feet ten metres to a line of wooden fencing that ran along the edge of a steep drop. She kicked away the cross slats and stooped to press her gun carefully into Enzo's right hand. She looked at him for a moment before bending over to kiss him lightly on the forehead. 'I'm sorry, Enzo,' she whispered. She stood up and pushed him with her foot through the gap she'd made in the fence. He slid over into darkness.

Chapter Fifty-Four

Bertrand clutched the tyre-iron from his van in gloved hands. It was the nearest thing to a weapon he could find. Kirsty had been here before, and so the others followed her as she pointed her flashlight into the sleet ahead of them. Clattering up grilled metal stairs from the car park and slithering across the concourse, past the tourist office, towards the brooding dark of the *téléphérique* building. The sleet in their faces was nearly blinding as they ran around the side of it to the red staircase that climbed up into the night.

The landing stage was deserted, and only one cablecar was in its dock. It stood in darkness, its doors locked. 'There's no one here!' Kirsty shouted above the wind.

Nicole bellowed, 'Look!' She pointed, and they all peered up through the storm of sleet to a distant light on the mountain top. Which was suddenly gone.

'They're up there. They must be up there!' Sophie's voice wailed among the metal struts and beams overhead. She ran along the dock. 'Can't we get this thing to go?' With icy fingers she tried to pry open the nearest of the cablecar's doors.

Bertrand said, 'Hang on.' He crossed to examine a large metal box bolted to the outside wall of the *téléphérique* building. Thick cables exited from the bottom end of it, trunking fixed to the wall every few centimetres until it disappeared into the concrete of the floor. A stout steel clasp on its door was fixed with a heavy padlock. He started hacking at it with his tyre-iron.

"What are you doing?' Sophie shouted.

'Looks like this could be the power box. If I can get it open we might be able to start the cablecar. Kirsty, bring the flashlight over here.'

By it's light they saw that the metal of the door was peppered now with small dents around the lock. But Bertrand was making little impression on it. He stopped and examined it for a moment, then slotted the straight end of the iron through the hoop of the padlock, and braced himself with his foot against the wall. He pulled with both hands, arm and shoulder muscles straining, veins standing out on his forehead. Years of pumping iron finding practical use beyond mere aesthetics. The metal of the box groaned loudly as the door buckled inwards. But still the padlock held.

Bertrand stopped to take fresh breath and gather himself, then got himself back into position and pulled again, yelling finally with the sheer effort of it, as the whole front of the box ripped free of its fixings. He almost fell as it gave. Inside was a large power switch, and when he threw it, the control panel below it lit up, and the whole landing stage was flooded with light. He punched the button marked *Portes* and the doors of the cablecar slid open. Fluorescent lights flickered inside it then filled it with luminous bright light.

'Shit,' he said. 'Someone's going to have to stay here to operate the thing.'

But Kirsty shook her head. 'No. The operator rides up with it. There are controls inside.'

They all bundled in, and Bertrand found the control panel beside the far door. He closed the doors and hit the green start button. They heard the whine of a distant motor, and the cablecar jerked forward, scraping its way out of the dock before swinging clear and rising steeply towards the first pylon.

Only now did young imaginations start working overtime. None of them had the least idea what, or who, they might find at the top. And they stood avoiding each other's eyes, afraid almost to acknowledge the sudden fear that moved amongst them like a fifth presence. Their silence was laden with anxiety. Bertrand tightened his grip on the tyre-iron.

They reached the dipping point at the first pylon, then rose rapidly again into a darkness almost obscured by snow.

It was Sophie who broke the silence. 'Look, there's a light.' She pressed her face against the window at the front of the car, peering up towards the peak. A faint glow was threading it's way through the snow and the dark towards them, descending at speed. Kirsty shielded her eyes from the interior light and strained to see.

'It's the other cablecar. It's coming down.'

'Shit,' Bertrand muttered, and he examined the control panel. But there didn't seem to be any way to stop the car in midascent. They all rushed to the side window, shadowing the glass to see out as the other cablecar approached. When the two converged, they almost seemed to pick up speed. The light of the other car arced out through the driving snow, and in the few seconds it took to pass, they saw Anna looking back at them, her face pale, angry, intense. Her lips moved in a curse they could read, and then she was gone, dipping away below them into the dark.

Silence returned to the ascending car. None of them knew what to say. Fear was replaced now by apprehension verging on dread.

Bertrand turned to Kirsty. 'How much longer does this take?'

'Just another few minutes.'

But it seemed like an eternity before the cablecar was sucked into the darkness of its concrete berth and shuddered to a halt. Bertrand took the flashlight from Kirsty. 'Stay close behind me. We don't want to get separated up here.' And he stepped out on to the grilled walkway and shone the flashlight around the cavernous arrivals hall. The wind was so much stronger at the peak and the noise of it reverberated around the stark planes and angles of the concrete construction. The beam of the flashlight pierced its emptiness, pausing for a moment on the open door of a wall-mounted control panel like the one Bertrand had broken into down below.

There appeared to be nobody here, and cautiously Bertrand moved forward, tyre-iron held ready. The girls followed him up the steps and through to the concourse that led to the cafeteria. Here, too, there was no sign of life. Just the mournful holler of the wind. Bertrand lowered the beam of the flashlight and they all saw the trail of wet footprints across the concrete. There was something almost reassuring about them. Something that said people had been here, but were gone. Bertrand broke into a run, following them to the exit doors.

The blast of snow in the wind took their breath away. And as soon as Bertrand stepped through the doors, the motion sensor triggered the exterior light. Immediately he saw the tracks in the snow, footprints not yet covered over. He kept the beam focused on them, and followed their trail up the incline towards the peak. They hadn't gone far before the lights behind them went out, and it felt suddenly very dark and exposed up here.

Sophie grabbed his arm and pointed beyond the ring of light. 'There's something on the track up ahead.' Bertrand raised the beam and they saw the dark shape of a man lying in the snow, the scarlet glow of fresh blood glistening on virgin white.

Kirsty ran past them and knelt by the body, and as Bertrand brought the light up close, she found herself looking at the face of the man who had picked her off the floor of the convention centre in Strasbourg. The man with the missing earlobe. His eyes were open, staring emptily into eternity. She almost cried out in relief. Sophie's voice rose above the wind. 'Where's Papa?'

'What's that?' Nicole grabbed the flashlight from Bertrand. Something or someone had been dragged away through the snow. Blood was smeared among the tracks. 'Oh, God.' She started running. The others chased after her, an awful inevitability somehow in what they expected to find at the end of it.

The trail stopped abruptly by the broken fence, and Nicole leaned past it and shone the flashlight into darkness. Snow sliced through its beam as it scanned the slope beneath them, before picking out a huddled shape lying at the foot of a fifteen foot drop.

Bertrand snatched the flashlight back and plunged over the edge, slithering down the slope to the body below. As he reached it and turned it over, the girls came sliding down after him, and they saw blood all over Enzo's chest.

'Oh, my God, she's shot him!' Sophie was nearly hysterical.

But Bertrand was feeling the pulse in his neck. 'He's still alive.' And he tore away Enzo's bloody shirt. 'It's not his blood. There's no wound.'

Kirsty stripped off her coat and quickly wrapped it around him. She leaned over and kissed his forehead, just as Anna had done ten minutes before. 'We've got to get help,' she said.

But Bertrand was already punching the emergency number into his cellphone.

Perhaps it was her warm breath on his face, or the familiar scent of her perfume. But Enzo opened his eyes and saw her bent over him, and from somewhere found a smile that made her cry. 'Hold on, Dad,' she said. 'Hold on.' And he took her hand and held it. Blood or not, she was still his little girl.

◇◇◇

Anna strode across the car park in a fury and slammed the door of her car shut behind her. She sat gripping the wheel, teeth clenched, glaring at the sleet on the windscreen. For the rest of the descent, after she had passed them in the cablecar, she had been trying to figure out how they had known. What it was that had led them here.

And then it had come to her. Her own stupid fault. She hadn't erased the e-mail after she sent it. She had meant to. But the sound of voices in the *séjour* had prompted her to close down the mailer prematurely. They must have found it, God knows how. They would find Enzo, she was sure, and the only way to be certain of putting an end to this, finally, would be to kill them all.

But she couldn't wait for them to come back down. All of the kids, she knew, had cellphones. They were probably phoning for help right now. She banged the steering wheel with the heel of her hand and cursed her carelessness. Now she was the loose end. The only thing left for her to do was to run. And run. And hide. Looking over her shoulder for the rest of her life.

'Damn you!' she shouted at the night. And she slipped her key into the ignition.

◇◇◇

They saw the explosion from the peak. A huge plume of fiery orange light that shot up into the night sky, before subsiding again almost as quickly. The sound of it came seconds later, like thunder following lighting.

Chapter Fifty-Five

From his hospital room he had a view out across the rooftops of southwest Cahors to the wooded blue hills that rose steeply on the far side of the river.

During the long transfer by ambulance, depression had settled on him like a winter fog. And now even the sunshine outside couldn't lift it. He had found a killer, but not those who had hired him. He was no closer now than he had been before to knowing who had wanted Lambert dead or why. He had failed.

And even although she had tried to kill him, he mourned for Anna. He knew that wasn't her name, but he couldn't think of her as anything else. Poor Anna. There had, somehow, been something immeasurably sad about her. Who knew what truth there had been in anything she had told them? But that her life had been blighted in some way by tragedy seemed to him beyond doubt.

The only chink of light in his darkness had been the visits from Kirsty and Sophie. He had worked hard to put on a brave face for them. Strangely, the two seemed closer than they had before. Like real sisters. Blood sisters. Not even half sisters. And between Kirsty and Enzo there was a bond stronger now than blood. Unspoken, but shared nonetheless. The bond they had forged during those first seven years of her life, more durable than all the torment that had followed. Greater even than Simon's revelations. Simon had never been her father and never could be.

Bertrand expected to have his gym functioning again in its temporary home of the Maison de la Jeunesse within two weeks.

The insurance cheque might take a little longer, but Enzo had told him he was in no hurry for it.

Raffin had been moved from hospital in Paris to a recuperation unit in the suburbs, and was continuing to make a good recovery. But there was, Enzo knew, still unfinished business between them.

He turned his head from the window as the door opened, and Commissaire Hélène Taillard stood in the doorway clutching a dark green folder. Her uniform jacket was buttoned tightly against the swell of her bosoms, and carefully contrived licks of hair hung down from either side of the blue hat pinned to the coiffure piled up beneath it. She smiled at him. 'You just can't keep out of trouble, Enzo, can you?'

He forced a smile. 'You always did look sexy in that uniform, Hélène.'

She crossed the room and sat on the edge of his bed, smiling at him fondly. 'I always thought I looked good out of it, too.'

'What, you mean…naked?'

She tilted her head and gave him a look. 'You know what I mean.'

He grinned, but her smile faded.

'We arrested Philippe Ransou in Paris. As soon as you're able, they'll want you to identify him. He's already been picked out by the manager of the *agence immobilière* as the man who took the lease on the building in the Rue des Trois Baudus. He's admitting everything, except any involvement in the murders.' She forced a rueful smile. 'But at least it gives you your alibi. You're no longer in the frame for the murder of Audeline Pommereau.'

Enzo remembered poor Audeline with a stab of guilt, and grief. He knew that in the coming days and weeks her death was something he would dwell upon, feel responsible for.

The *commissaire* opened her folder and glanced inside it. 'Amazingly the *police scientifique* in the Cantal recovered DNA from the burned out car at Le Lioran. Unfortunately, it wasn't in any database we have access to, so we're none the wiser about the true identity of the woman who called herself Anna Cattiaux.'

She closed the folder and looked thoughtfully at Enzo. 'These people really didn't want you to find them, did they? And they don't seem to care who they have to kill to stop you. And that includes you.' She paused, and her sigh was filled with concern. 'You know there's every chance they're still going to try?'

Enzo nodded grimly. 'I guess it all began with the attempt on my life at the *château* in Gaillac last year. That must have been Bright.'

But the chief of police was slowly shaking her head. 'I'm afraid it wasn't, Enzo. We ran a DNA check with the blood sample recovered from the *château*. It wasn't Bright who tried to kill you in Gaillac. So you can probably assume it wasn't even related to the Lambert case.' She drew a long breath. 'Which means it's likely that there are still two unrelated sets of people out there who want you dead.'

Enzo glanced from the window to see the sunlight turning pink across the hills, the sky beyond them shading to a dusky blue. Then he turned back to the *commissaire* and contrived a pale smile. 'I'm glad you dropped by to cheer me up.'

To receive a free catalog of Poisoned Pen Press titles, please contact us in one of the following ways:

Phone: 1-800-421-3976
Facsimile: 1-480-949-1707
Email: info@poisonedpenpress.com
Website: www.poisonedpenpress.com

Poisoned Pen Press
6962 E. First Ave. Ste. 103
Scottsdale, AZ 85251